# NEON NIGHTMARES

**Neon Nightmares by Isaac Nightingale**

Cover design by Liam Blaney

Edited by Tali Wilson

First published 2024 by Scary Paper

First edition

ISBN: 978-1-7395255-2-1

# NEON NIGHTMARES

Isaac Nightingale

SCARY
PAPER

# Author's Note

Just like the first book, this one has a soundtrack!
Just like the first book, the soundtrack is bangin', if I say so myself (and I do).
If you want that extra cinematic experience, whack it on and turn up the volume.

Each chapter has a prompt that looks like this:

## [Track]

If you want to listen to the song that inspired the chapter, just scan the code pictured below, or go to the website:
beacons.ai/bmoviebloodbath
Scroll 'till you find the section and choose the soundtrack in whichever app you prefer, then follow the order from the top.
(You may need to pause/turn off auto-play so the next song doesn't play too soon.)

Or if you didn't bother listening to the first book's soundtrack, ignore this entirely. It's not like I can jump out of the page and fight you over it.
Not yet, anyway.

# October 29ᵗʰ, 1980. Again

The eighties hit me like a truck. It brought big hair, bright lights and a killer soundtrack. For the most part I was in my goddamn element. But on this particular night: I was certainly fucking not.

I know, I know, I've told you this before: weird vagina monster in a truck stop bathroom. But I never told you how it ended, did I?

Strap in.

So there I was standing at the urinal in a truckstop bathroom at three in the morning. I had just undone my zipper and commenced my business when another patron entered. In this specific cesspool the urinal was what I call a 'piss shelf'. It's basically a long metal trough. What it lacks in privacy it makes up for in splashback. This one was a good eight feet long, bear that in mind, okay? Now, I'd had a long night. I'd done a lot of driving, and it had left me real tired and a little cranky. But what made my night even worse was having a stranger walk into the bathroom as I took a piss, and join me at the piss shelf no more than nine inches to the right of where I stood.

That's not even the worst part.

What really ruined my night was that this man— this heathen—made direct eye contact as he dropped his pants right down around his ankles to join me in taking a slash; his bare ass shining like the moon in the dingy twilight of the bathroom's one flickering lightbulb. He maintained eye contact for five long seconds before breaking and looking directly at my junk. After way more than a glimpse, he nodded to himself and placed his hands on his hips, leaving nothing but fate to control his stream. There was something seriously wrong with this guy. The fact that he had two missing fingers didn't help his look, either.

I finished my business with a shake and zipped up. I took a step back and caught the weirdo watching me move. Any other day I'd have handed out some strong words for every single thing he'd done since walking through the bathroom door, but I just wanted to get to a nice motel and get some rest.

## [Track 1]

After a few steps towards the exit I took one last look over my shoulder to confirm his pants were around his ankles, just in case I'd imagined it in my tiredness. And there they were, fully dropped, ass out, no shame.

I muttered to myself, "Some people just have no goddamn mann—oh Jesus Christ what the fuck."

He was making eye contact again, but so much worse this time. He stood there, hands on hips, pissing into the urinal, with his head twisted a full one-eighty degrees to face me.

"Dammit dude," I said, too tired for this kind of creepy bullshit. "You best twist that face of yours back the right way around before I blow your teeth through that wall." I pulled out my revolver and waved it in his general direction, didn't even bother aiming until I'd turned to face him head-on.

He kept on lookin' but I guessed he must have finished his piss on the account of a faint zipping noise coming from the region of his pants. We stood in a standoff: him staring at me with his head on backwards and me wishing he'd quit it so we could just forget the whole thing so I could leave the damn bathroom without pebble-dashing the walls with his brains. I moved to take another step back towards the exit. He took a step backwards—or forwards depending on how you look at it—towards me.

"I really can't be bothered with this shit tonight. Look, man, I've been driving around looking for a goddamn serial killer for three days now. I'm just about on my last nerve and I really want to get some shut-eye. Can I just leave? What are you anyway? A murnock? Tentaclari? No? Come on then, what?"

"Fuurgluh," was his response. His body snapped around to face me, quick as a blink. All was normal again. Right up until his bottom lip split down the middle and just kept on going, down the middle of his neck. With a sharp grunt the freak tore his shirt open to reveal the entire top half of his body splitting and opening up. I stood and watched, fully intrigued, as his flesh unzipped itself and spread apart to reveal thousands of long fangs inside the cavity of his upper body.

"No thanks. Not today," I told him, shaking my head. I took a few steps backwards and raised my gun as he came flapping towards me. The teeth looked seriously fucking sharp. I gave the trigger a squeeze before Freaky could get too close and give me a full body French kiss. My bullet hit a home run. The shot blew Freaky's head apart, splattering the majority of it against the wall behind him. He stumbled backwards. Half of his head remained and his left eye spun around in the socket as if trying to see where the other eye had rolled off to. The fucker didn't go down. In fact, he took another step towards me. A clean shot to the head usually does the trick, but not this time. I emptied the chamber, spraying a generous amount of gore around the bathroom. And yet he kept coming right towards me. I lowered my gun thinking this is it. This is how I die: eaten by a big toothy vagina monster.

Fuck.

I raised my other gun. Shot after shot, the toothy motherfucker stumbled and flapped around but didn't hit the deck. I had one bullet left. I seriously couldn't be bothered to deal with this thing. If he wouldn't stop coming at least I slowed him down by blowing holes in him. I took aim with my last shot and put a slug through his left knee. It blew the leg apart at the joint making Freaky splat down on the piss-soaked floor. He flapped about for a moment then finally lay still.

A quick boot to some part of his flesh confirmed Freaky's demise. He lay folded over on himself like a humanoid omelette. With a quick spin of the Sisters I kicked the door open and finally made my exit as I tucked the girls away nice and snug.

Tex looked up at me from the back seat of my car as I popped the door and threw myself down beside him.

"Your turn to drive," I said, handing him the keys.

"I thought you fell down the shitter."

"Nah just made a new friend. I ain't seen anything like this one before. Didn't you hear the shots?"

"Sure I heard. So what was he like?"

"Kinda like a half-human half-tooth-filled-meat-curtain-from-Hell."

"He sounds a real catch," Tex said, with a hint of sarcasm.

I gave him an eyeballing. "I just had some fleshy Iron Maiden stare at my merch and try to suck on my face. Why so nonchalant about it?"

He let out a chuckle. "He's been following us since this morning. I wanted to see if you'd notice. And if you didn't, I wanted to see how you'd handle him trying to getcha."

I heaved a sigh. "Picked a great time for a lesson, didn't you? So what the fuck was it?"

"They're called phlogluts. They'll see a bit of you they fancy and, uh, assimilate you? Absorb? Whatever. They suck you up and make whatever they wanted from you their own. Disgusting, aren't they? This one was clearly after your eyes. They are a pretty colour."

11

"It was missing a couple of fingers. I thought it was sneaking a peek at the goods. I guess it must have been after my hands the whole time."

"I guess so. Or your johnson. Oh, and I counted twelve shots. Could have downed it in one, you know?"

"Left knee?"

"Always the left knee. It's where their brains are."

I closed my eyes and slumped back into the seat. "Tex?"

"Yeah?"

"You can be a real asshole at times, ya'know that?"

"All part of my charm, son."

# Pause. Rewind. Play.

Okay, let's pause for a moment and address the burning question that's clearly on everyone's minds: what the fuck happened to Rapey and Roids? Yes, those two fuckers, the pair of vampires who murdered Suzie. Well, let's pick up from where we left off a little over three months ago...

## [Track 2]

Tex lowered his eyes to the floor and sighed. "So I guess this is it? This is the grand finale?"

"Just one more thing, for now," I said before holstering Sofia and flipping Rapey so he was face down in the dirt, whimpering, with his ass in the air.

"One more thing?" Tex said, raising an inquisitive eyebrow.

I nodded toward the bag on the ground. It had something green and spiky poking out of it.

"Is that what I think it is?"

"Yes, yes it is. Tex?"

"Yeah?"

"Pass the cactus."

Tex heaved a sigh and kicked the bag over to me. What happened next needs no explanation, but let's just say, what goes up, doesn't always come back down. That cactus hooked itself in real cosy and decided to stay for good.

But I was far from finished. A cactus up the asshole was foreplay, and death just wouldn't cut it for these two. Sure, I had originally planned on giving them a taste of their own medicine then removing them from existence, but I couldn't bring myself to do it. I couldn't kill them.

"Help me chain them both up again and get them in the car, would you, Tex?"

"Sure, as long as that's all you want me to do."

"Don't worry. The horrors that'll happen to these two are going to be by my hand and mine alone."

"What did you do?" I hear you ask.

For the first month or so I rented out a small warehouse on the far side of town, and there my guests stayed. I visited daily, using them as living punching bags and science experiments. It took a while, but there's only a certain number of times you can push needles into eyeballs, take hammers to the tenderest of areas and perform live dissections before the thrill of it wears off. By the gods, I made them suffer.

Roids, the dumb fuck that he is, ended up buried alive in a thick, metal, silver crucifix-lined coffin deep in the woods. Right where we first met, actually. He's in constant agony with no escape. Lucky him. On calm, quiet nights I could just about hear his muffled screams from below.

And Rapey? He's in a metal box full of silver crucifixes at the bottom of Blackwater Lake. Of course, he got special treatment. Before I put him in the box, I made sure to give him plenty of open wounds. You see, his coffin has holes in it just big enough to let in water and a few fish. Not only can he not move without causing himself incredible pain due to the crucifixes he also has the constant state of drowning to deal with. And if that wasn't enough, those open wounds make sure he's being eaten alive by the lake's fish. I hear having them eat you from the inside out isn't pleasant at all. I've pulled him to the surface a few times just to check on him. Turns out, if you leave a sucker in water too long they eventually bloat and split apart like a regular old corpse, but with the added benefit of living through it all, slowly regenerating, and going through it all again. Safe to say, things went downhill for Rapey and Roids since the night I got my hands on them. Knowing they were both endlessly suffering, and would continue to until I decided to give them the mercy of death, that really put a smile on my face.

Now that you're all caught up let's get back to the future...

# Babyface

After taking a nice break in a motel a few miles down from the truck stop we were on the road again driving to the last location on our list. By this point we had been driving around for almost four goddamn days on the hunt for a serial killer. Thankfully, Tex sat behind the wheel so I could kick back for a while. We'd had a tipoff from Gabriel about this guy which was a first-time thing for me. The jobs are usually strictly supernatural in nature: deal with a demonic possession, kill some vampires, clear someone's basement of ankle biting fairies, that kind of shit. But, as Tex put it, every now and again a plain ol' human will do something so shitty Gabe will get us to deal with it.

This particular psychopath went by the name of Babyface Benjamin, and from what Tex was in the process of telling me, he sounded like a total shitbag.

"He's a real twisted fucker. It's no wonder Gabriel's picked up on this one."

"More so than any other serial killer?"

"Oh yeah, know why he's called Babyface? Go on, take a guess."

"I'm gonna assume it's not because he has such youthful good looks?"

"Nope."

"C'mon then what's his deal?"

Tex took his eyes off the road to make eye contact for emphasis. "Babies, Night. The sonofabitch abducts and murders babies."

I'd had the feeling that'd be the case but hoped it wasn't. "Shit, that's dark even by our standards."

"Son, that's not even the worst of it. He's called BabyFACE. He fucking wears their face skin on his own face. Night, he skins babies. Babies damn it. Makes me sick."

"Fantastic, so we're looking for a bargain-brand Leatherface then?"

"Texas Chainsaw sounds pleasant compared to this guy."

"Well let's hope we find him. Our list of possible locations has run dry," I said as I scribbled over the previous locations on the map.

"We've saved the creepiest possible place 'till last. He's got to be here."

Tex wasn't wrong. The last location on the list happened to be an old, abandoned fairground, sitting on the outskirts of New Orleans. A spooky place in the spooky capital of the world looking for some real spooky fucker. The last location had been in the middle of some Alabama backwoods. Obviously, we didn't find Babyface Ben, but we did find a whole group of assholes that may well have been relatives; a whole village of sister-mothers, uncle-brothers and all manner of hicks. They weren't so welcoming, but we refrained from pulling our guns on them on account of them not really doing anything wrong, you know, aside from potential inbreeding.

After an ass-pounding of a drive Tex brought the car to a stop on the side of the road right in the middle of—you guessed it—butt-fuck nowhere somewhere near New Orleans. I hadn't been paying attention. The road was long and gloomy with tall trees and swampland surrounding both sides as far as the eye could see. The sun loomed over the treetops, setting slowly.

"It's in the middle of the forest, isn't it?" I asked.

"Sure is."

"Why do I always end up fighting freaks in forests?"

"Night, I've got centuries' of occult knowledge right here." He tapped his forehead. "But that's one question I don't have the answer to."

I let out a heavy sigh. "Let's get this over with, shall we?"

"Let's indeed."

I popped the door and stepped out into the humid air. An earthy smell of trees and dirt filled my nostrils. A good stretch felt necessary to get the blood flowing and regain feeling in my ass which I then used to nudge the door shut. Didn't feel a thing. Tex joined me a moment later wielding an aluminium baseball bat.

"You think we'll need that?" I asked, eyeballing it.

"Well, are you taking the Sisters?"

"Nah, don't reckon I'll need them."

"In that case, you might need this," he said, shoving the bat in my direction.

"And what are you going to be doing while I hit a home run with Babyface's skull?"

"I might hit the candy stall. See if there's any treats left over. C'mon."

With that, he set off down a beaten path into the trees. The plan seemed somewhat unfair to me. I get the serial killer while Tex finds some sugary delights, great. Walking down what was clearly a shortcut to the fairground seemed counter-productive, considering there had to be an actual entrance to the damn place. Going for the element of surprise seemed pointless but I didn't argue against it.

Five minutes into our walk the twinkling of lights shone through the trees. A little further along we broke out through the treeline. A chain-link fence stood between the trees and the fairground, but our path took us directly to a human-sized hole in it. The fairground was overgrown and falling to bits, but certain sections were still lit up with what lights were left unbroken. A big roller coaster sat at the far end. Bits of track were hanging off and threatening to squish anyone who dared walk beneath them. Rows of amusements and games stretched down the centre and an assortment of rides sat dotted along the left and right. Out of all the lit-up sections, the haunted house shone the brightest. It had glowing green skeletons, bright red devils, the lot.

I nodded in its direction. "I wonder where Babyface could be hiding."

"I don't know. A serial killer hiding in the haunted house sounds far too cliché, don't you think?"

"That's exactly why I think he'll be in there. Bad guys love clichés."

"That's where you can start looking then. I'll be hunting for some candy. Scream if you need me," he said with a smile before slapping me on the back and wandering off towards the stalls.

I held up the baseball bat and took a practice swing. "Looks like it's just you and me, sugar."

The humidity was making my T-shirt stick to my back causing some minor irritation. The cool sanctuary of the haunted house looked quite attractive so I made my way towards it swinging the bat down near my feet as I walked. The ghost house looked incredibly tacky from the outside, but knowing that Babyface could be in there, I expected to see some real fucking horror lurking within.

I whistled a cheerful tune as I approached trying to keep the mood light before squaring up to a baby murdering maniac. Some cheesy atmospheric music greeted me as I stepped up to the house. The entrance door read "Abandon hope all ye who enter here!" in paint styled to look like dripping blood. I took a moment to listen for any signs of movement on the other side. The Hot Sauce raged through my body, as my heart rate increased, heightening my senses. A slight shuffling noise inside told me this house had a tenant.

I used the bat to push the door open prompting a voice to boom out of some hidden speakers, yelling, "Face your fear! MUAHAHAHAHA!" sending my element of surprise straight down the shitter. The sound of something scraping and clattering echoed through the entire damn place. Someone had been alerted for sure. The first room had been set up to look like a torture chamber complete with life-sized rubber humans with their guts hanging out and screams echoing around. At least I assumed they were rubber. They could well have been some of Babyface's actual victims, but from what Tex had told me the sick bastard liked 'em young.

Whoever built the room had put a lot of effort into making the displays as accurate as possible. One dummy lay on a table with a caged rat burrowing into its stomach and feasting on its guts. Another had a wooden stake rammed up its ass, coming out the mouth, and looked way too happy about it. I moved around the dummies and took a step towards the door leading into the next room. I put out my free hand to push it open and froze in place.

## [Track 3]

I could hear footsteps. The sound of heavy feet pounding the floor, charging in my direction on the other side of the door. It burst open a moment later as I jumped back to distance myself. Within the space of a heartbeat the door had been torn off its hinges and replaced by an absolute monster of a human. This fucker stood at an easy seven foot tall, and almost as wide. True to his name he had what looked to be the faces of several babies stitched together and draped over his own face. This guy had stepped straight out of a horror movie, no doubt about it. What wasn't mentioned was the fact that his entire ensemble looked to be made of human skin, not just his mask. To give him credit he had clearly put a lot of work in and had mastered his craft. In another life he may well have been a respected tailor, but certainly not in this one. The only thing he hadn't crafted himself was a nice set of baby leather shoes. He stood in the doorway dressed to the nines in corpse, but completely barefoot and rocking the worst set of toenails I'd ever witnessed.

Big ol' Babyface Ben let out a shrill scream and came lumbering towards me with his arms outstretched. I didn't feel like a hug so I swung the bat and hit him hard in the ribs. He stopped, squeaked and then came at me again this time swinging fists. I backed up so his meat shovels couldn't smack me into the next decade. He moved forward grunting and swinging harder by the second.

"Can't catch me huh, Big Ben? Maybe you'd move a bit faster if you trimmed those damn toenails."

He responded by letting out a wail and tearing the nearest rubber corpse from its display before hurling it in my direction.

I stepped aside and let it sail past my shoulder. "C'mon Benny Boy, I expected better."

My comment was met with flailing arms before he turned and ran back through the door he'd come through. I propped an elbow on the guy enjoying the butt-stake. "Did I hurt his feelings?"

The next room turned out to be a dark corridor filled with doors and old-style paintings with eyes that followed wherever you went. I made my way down it to the sounds of recorded screams against an eerie, warbling ambient noise. I gave the handle a try on the first door. It shook but didn't seem to be usable. The second door rattled as I moved closer, but I could hear the mechanism behind it. I knew this wasn't the door I wanted. I passed by and listened for noises behind the third door. I heard winding, the tightening of a spring. I brought the bat up and edged closer. With a scream and a flash of light the door swung open and a skeleton with glowing red eyes burst out in front of me. The jaw wiggled as it laughed for a moment before tucking itself away. The door swung shut revealing the last door now bathed in green light with mist coming out from underneath it. I pushed my way through. It slammed shut behind me, leaving me in complete darkness. The ambient warbling died down to be replaced by the stereotypical spooky carnival tune.

I held the bat out in front of me, using it to feel my way in the dark. A swing to either side gave me a clink. A push forward gave nothing but air. I took a step forward. A lightbulb flickered to life overhead followed by another, and another until it revealed the small corridor leading me to a hall of mirrors.

"Fuckin' great," I sighed.

A low whine came from the opposite side of the room. I kept my bat out in front so I didn't walk face-first into a pane of glass. The noise shifted to the left. I tried to follow but the bat bumped against glass. After a few taps and bumps I found my route and followed passing by countless mirrored images of myself. The bat hit glass up

23

ahead a moment later. The sound of Ben's whining floated from somewhere off in the distance. I waved about with my left hand and hit nothing so I turned the corner and came eye to eye with Babyface Ben. Seeing him so close startled me. I pulled back, and swung the bat at his head with all my might. The swing hit him square between the eyes, shattering his head into a thousand pieces. The rest of his body followed suit and crashed to the floor.

"Shit!"

I stepped over the shards of glass and through the hole I'd made. Thousands of Isaac Nightingales stepped into view with the towering shape of Babyface standing right behind them. I spun on my heel and swung the bat, hitting nothing. Ben had disappeared.

"You know what, I don't wanna play along anymore," I said to all my reflections.

"Wuuuuurrhhuuuuu," was the response, somewhere to my right.

I tightened my grip on the bat and started swinging, smashing my own head into pieces again and again. Smash, step forward. Smash, step forward, smash, step until the hole opened up and revealed a door covered in bloody handprints. This one looked authentic, like a maintenance door, not part of the attraction. Smelled authentic too. Couldn't mistake the smell of blood. Shuffling sounds floated out from behind the door. I took a moment to prepare for the possibility of a booby-trap or ambush, then kicked the door open while bringing the bat up to take a swing. All the effort turned out to be worthless. The door swung open and revealed nothing but some plain old steps down to the basement.

I could hear Ben whining at something while shuffling around, panicked. I made my way down the stairs. The smell of rot and chemicals grew stronger with each step. By the last step I almost retched. Ben stood in the far left corner hunched over a bloodstained workbench. All kinds of tools lined the walls; hammers, hacksaws, scalpels,  you name it. I edged closer with my bat at the ready as pipes hissed overhead.

"Hey big fella, wha'cha workin' on?"

Babyface Ben spun around to reveal his handiwork: a pair of clawed gauntlets strapped to each hand. Four claws on each made of sharpened bones.

"Gruh," he grunted.

He looked like a bull about to charge. I readied myself, and sure enough he came barrelling over faster than I expected. His fists swung in all directions. No technique to his fighting whatsoever; just flail and hope for the best. I dodged to the right and swung the bat at the base of his spine. It hit hard but he didn't seem too bothered by it. Dumb and numb.

He came charging again, same as before. I dodged and gave him a crack to the back of the head. He stumbled for a moment and steadied himself on the workbench.

"Night? That you making a racket down there boy?" Tex called down the stairs.

"Yeah, I've got the big bastard."

Tex's boots appeared as he plodded down the stairs. "Hot dang, that smell is from another dimension," he said as he reached the bottom, "and you weren't joking when you said 'big' huh?"

I turned back to look at Babyface. He stood motionless in the corner. His heart pounding in his chest.

"I don't think he understands what's going on. His heart's going apeshit right now. He seems scared."

"You understand what we're saying, big guy?"

Ben nodded and let out a strained wheeze. I stepped aside so Tex could speak to him.

"Can't you talk?"

"Huuurrh," Ben replied, shaking his head from side to side.

Tex crept forward. "Why not?"

Ben lifted a hand to his face, grasped his ghastly mask and peeled it off to reveal a mangled face beneath. A mess of twisted scars made up what remained of the bottom half of his face with nothing but a messy hole for a mouth.

We both stood for a moment taking in the sight.

"Something really messed you up huh?"

Ben nodded.

"Know why we're here?"

He shook his head.

Tex sighed and turned to me as he lowered his voice, "Bad enough being sent to deal with a baby killer; he doesn't even understand what he's doing."

"Pretty fucking sure he does. He pulled a clever trick with the mirrors."

"Woulda made it easier if he wasn't mentally challenged, you know."

"I mean sure, but he's wearing the skin of countless babies I can't say I'm gonna feel bad for doing him in."

"Let's just get it over with. Go grab that chain over there."

I spotted the chain hanging in the corner and sighed. "Sure."

Tex raised his fists and said, "C'mon then big fella, put up your dukes."

Ben hesitated for a moment before barrelling forward, swinging hard.

I pulled the chain down, wrapped some around my fist and let the rest drag across the floor. Tex ducked and weaved occasionally taking a jab at whatever bit of Ben he could reach. Ben flung fists in a fit of rage completely oblivious to anything but the human-shaped bug he wanted to squash.

Tex dodged a swing to the head, nodded at the length of the chain by my feet and held out a hand. I gathered up the end and threw it over Ben's left shoulder. Tex caught it, pulled it tight and darted around Ben to meet me. I ducked under his bit of chain as we crossed each other, and did the same again in front of Ben before meeting at his back. Before he could process what had happened we had him on a tight leash. Tex handed his side of the chain to me, glanced at the pipes above us and then got right back to handing out jabs to keep the big fella distracted.

I swung the ends up over the pipes, caught them and gave a hard tug. Ben stumbled backwards, losing his balance and almost going down. I pulled harder, tightening the chains, as Tex came over to join me.

Ben found his footing and turned to take a swing at us. I put all of my weight on the chains and brought Ben up onto his tiptoes. Tex grabbed the chain above my hands and followed suit putting a few inches between the floor and Ben's nasty toenails.

"Fuck, he's heavy isn't he," Tex said.

"What, did you think it'd be like hanging a wind chime?"

"Very funny. Just don't let—aaahh, fuck," Tex trailed off.

Warm blood rained down on our faces. Ben—the big dummy—had tried to grab at the chain around his neck and managed to stab himself in the jugular with one of his bone claws. Blood pumped out in spurts as Ben's writhing grew weaker until he fell limp.

Tex let go of the chains to wipe the blood from his face. "Keep him up there, I'll be a moment," he said.

"Sure, no problem, we can hang around all night."

Tex dragged Ben's workbench over and took the loose ends of the chain, wrapping them around it before pulling out some large nails and a hammer and nailing the chain in place.

"You can let go, that should hold."

I slowly loosened my grip. Ben dropped an inch or so, but the chains held.

"I guess we're gonna leave him like this?"

"Yup, looks to me like he couldn't live with the guilt of his crimes any longer. We'll give the police a tip-off at the next payphone. Ben's found and some families finally get some closure."

"Shame we couldn't have got him before… this," I gestured at his suit.

"I know, but at least we've put an end to it. Now, c'mon, it's a long ass drive home and it's almost Halloween."

# The Night We Came Home

We arrived back at Tex's place on the evening of the twenty-ninth. We could have been back sooner, but I insisted we stop off a few times to get some last-minute Halloween shopping in. I had talked Tex into decorating his house and getting a boatload of candy for the local kids back before we set off looking for Babyface. The house had been attracting a lot of attention in the run-up to Halloween so I reckoned more candy would be necessary for the swarms of trick-or-treaters I was expecting.

Gabriel greeted me with a loud, "CUNT!" as I stepped through the door.

"Yeah good to see you too, Dickbeak," I said, pulling a handful of seeds out of my pocket. He flew over and perched on my forearm eating from my palm.

"Fucking bird," Tex grumbled as he shut the door behind him, "I take care of it every damn day, for longer than I remember, and it's never been that friendly with me."

"He says nice things about you, at least."

"I'd be more inclined to believe you if you told me he'd started shitting gold."

Gabriel cawed at Tex's remark.

"I know, grumpy isn't he?"

"You would be too if you had to deal with his bull for this long. Grab me a beer, would you?" Tex said, kicking off his boots and sitting down on the sofa.

"Sure thing."

I put Gabriel on his perch on my way to the kitchen before dropping bags filled with candy and a couple of costumes down on the floor. The fridge had been pre-filled with snacks and beers for our triumphant return. I grabbed some jerky and a couple of bottles of Tex's favourite beer: Chateau Lova. The unmistakable sound of a VHS being inserted into a player drew me from the kitchen.

"Thought we could watch a bit of horror before we call it a night?" Tex said.

I passed him his beer. "We pretty much live in a horror movie, and you still insist on watching them?"

"We could watch Grease instead?"

"Play the damn movie."

* * *

## [Track 4]

"The Jack-o-lanterns are lit. Expect hordes of kids any minute," Tex yelled from the hallway.

"Thanks, I'll be out in a moment."

It had just ticked over to 6:30pm when I applied the finishing touches on the makeup for my costume. Tex was already dressed, kicking back and watching TV. I

31

strolled out of my room and put myself between him and his show.

"Wha'dya think?"

"I always knew you'd turn to the dark side."

"Psshh, regular suckers wish they looked this good."

Dracula was my costume of choice and I looked great if I say so myself. Tex, on the other hand, did not. He had bought himself a werewolf costume, but wore it for a total of five minutes before complaining the mask was difficult to breathe in and promptly ditching it. He'd decided to put in the maximum effort and had cut two holes in a bedsheet for that extra spooky ghost look. He'd secured the sheet in place by wearing his reading glasses over it and his cowboy hat on top. Horrifying.

"You think we've got enough candy?" he said.

"Maybe enough for every kid in town if they come by five times each."

"Jesus Christ..."

"Nope, it's me, Dracula! Muhahaha!"

Tex rolled his eyes. "Whatever. This was your idea. You can answer the door most of the night."

"Suits me just fine." And it really did. Halloween has been my favourite holiday ever since I was a kid. That love had stayed strong even after all the horrors I'd witnessed and shit I'd been through. Hell, I had dressed as the very thing I hated most. Sort of a 'fuck you' to the real vampires.

The first knock hit the door just before 7pm as dusk set in. I swung the door open and yelled, "Whooo deeesturbs Count Dracyoooola?"

A young girl dressed as a witch—complete with green face paint—jumped back towards her mother and squealed, "Ahhh! It's me, Lily!"

"Lily? Boot I know ov Lily. She lives down zee street. Yooou are a vitch! Have yooou eaten her?"

"It's me, Mister Nightingale, I promise," she said, taking her hat off to show her bright ginger hair.

"I doo not know zis Mister Nightingale. I am Dracyoola! But you are a very scary vitch. Take lots ov candy and doo not curse me," I said, bringing the bowl out from behind the door.

"You're silly," she said, taking a handful, "thank you Mister Night."

I slowly backed behind the door making sure it creaked as I closed it. "Yooou are velcome. Gooodbyeeeee."

Witchy Lily skipped down the path as her mom smiled and waved goodbye.

Tex appeared behind me. "Gonna keep up that cheesy accent all night?"

"Only if it's annoying you," I said before flashing him the plastic fangs.

The door hadn't even shut before another knock came. I flung it back open to greet the next ghoul.

"Whooo deeesturbs Dracyoooola?" I repeated.

The kid in front of me wore a dirty orange jumpsuit and a sack over his head with buttons for eyes.

33

His sack of candy sat on the ground next to him. He didn't seem to care for my theatrics.

I looked around for the kid's parents. "Whoo stands before meee?" Nobody seemed to be taking any notice of him. I dropped the accent, "Aren't your parents with you?"

The kid shook his head.

"Are you lost? Do you need me to call somebody?" Another shake.

I held out the candy dish. "Okay, well stay safe, and come back if you need me to call your parents. Yeah?"

He nodded in response before taking a fistful of candy and dropping it in the sack.

"Stay safe, kid," I said as he turned to leave.

He didn't respond, just turned and walked down the path dragging the sack of candy across the ground behind him.

I turned to see Tex watching over my shoulder. "What's that kid dressed as?" he asked.

I shrugged. "Nothing I've ever seen before. I'm kinda concerned for him though."

"Ahh he'll be fine, it's a safe area. Look, here comes a miniature you."

I took my eyes off the lonely kid and saw little Johnny from across the road bounding towards us.

"Another Dracula! How can this beee?" I yelled.

"Hi Night, hi Tex," he yelled back, running up the path, "there's lots of us. I saw three other Draculas already."

"Three? Well, you're the scariest Dracula I've ever seen."

"Don't say that," Tex mumbled, "you might piss off the real Drac."

"Shaddap, haunted laundry."

Tex grumbled and headed back to the sofa.

"Am I really the scariest?"

"You sure are, here, grab a load of candy."

He grabbed a bunch and said, "Thank you Night, see you later, and bye Tex."

"See you, Johnny," Tex yelled from the sofa.

He skipped off in the direction of his house. I set the bowl on the doorstep by one of the Jack-o-lanterns and stuck a note on it saying: "Back in 10. Help Yourself." I closed the door and made my way to sit on the sofa. Tex handed me a cold beer as I sat, keeping his eyes fixed on the TV's ads.

"What we watching?"

"News."

"Anything interesting happening in the world?"

"Waiting to hear a story on New York City. There's apparently been a fair few murders."

"Business as usual for the Big Apple then, eh?"

"Not entirely. These murders are different. All the victims are criminals: rapists, murderers, that sort of thing."

"They've got a vigilante on their hands then?"

"Seems so, they're interviewing a witness in a moment. Set your peepers and let's watch."

The news jingle rang out and cut to a heavily moustachioed anchor with a hefty perm. The anchor announced: "And now we have an eyewitness to describe the events to us. Over to you Sam."

The screen cut to a man in a purple suit with slicked back hair sitting next to a silhouette of another person. "Thanks Hank," the suited man said. "Here we have our eyewitness. For safety reasons the witness will remain anonymous."

The silhouette nodded.

"So, tell us, what exactly did you see on that fateful evening?"

"It was terrible, Sam," the silhouette said, "I had just stepped into the back alley to take out the trash and I was choked by a strange mist."

"How was the mist strange?"

"It had colours. Not like a normal mist, it was thick like smoke but brightly coloured."

"And then what?"

"And then I saw them: two men beating the living daylights out of another man. They were savages. They kicked him over and over. I was frozen stiff with fright. I couldn't move."

"What happened next?"

Music built in the background as the silhouette took its time answering. They'd clearly been told to pause for effect. Build the tension.

"One of the men took out a gun and shot the guy in the head. Shot him dead."

"But that's not all is it?"

"No, they turned around to leave and saw me standing there."

"What did they do?"

"They just... disappeared."

"Disappeared?"

"It was like they exploded. They just went... POOF! In a big burst of smoke, and they were gone, the mist too."

"There you have it ladies and gentlemen. An eyewitness report on New York City's murderous magicians. Are they anti-heroes? Avenging spectres from beyond the grave? Or are they just common criminals? Back to you, Hank."

Tex took a big gulp of beer and turned to look at me. "So, what the fuck do we think? Reckon they were telling the truth?"

"If you'd asked me ten years ago I'd say they were cuckoo. Now, I'll believe just about anything."

"I'm not so sure. Not something I've ever heard of."

I shrugged and set my beer down on the floor before making my way to the kitchen to fill another bowl with candy.

"Trick or treat," Gabriel said as I passed by.

"Hello to you too."

"Trick or treat," he repeated. "Trick or treat. Trick or treat. Trick or treat."

"Uhh, Tex? Is this a call?"

"Oh shit could be." He jumped up and made his way over.

I left them to it and filled the bowl. Sure enough, Tex and Gabriel were babbling away at each other as I headed for the front door.

The bowl I'd left out was almost empty. I tipped the remaining candy into the new bowl and wandered down the path to stand in the street. Kids and adults alike passed by in all manner of costumes: vampires, werewolves, witches, skeletons, all the classics. A few scarecrows here and there, some devils, a couple dressed as a priest and a nun. I took in the sights, offering the bowl to anybody and everybody that came near me.

After about ten minutes of handing out treats Tex opened the door and floated out in his spooky sheet.

"What's up, Casper?" I asked. I didn't even need to see his face; I could tell by his eyes that he had a big shit-eating grin under that sheet.

Tex waved his arms in the air and put on a bad ghost voice, "Guess whoooo we're goooing tooo fiiiiind?"

# Neon Nightmares

"Ever been to the Big Dirty, Night?"

"Don't you mean Big Apple? And no, never been."

"Nope, you'll see why I call it Big Dirty when we get there. Place is a goddamn jungle. Los Angeles may be Vamp Capital but if you want downright filth, you go to New York City."

"Sounds like I'm in for a good time."

"Oh trust me boy, you're gonna see some shit, and you'll love it."

We'd barely scraped a couple of day's downtime before Gabriel called and sent us on another long ass drive. I always loved a good drive, but goddamn I'd had my fill of it since that night I met Tex and butchered a bar full of suckers. From then on we'd been driving all over the damn country. I'd recommended something that would take us a little less time and effort, you know, like a fucking flight. But no, Tex insisted on driving.

Dusk settled in as New York City's skyline came into view, all sky-scraping silhouettes against an amber backdrop. It sure was a pretty sight, I'll say that much. You never forget your first time seeing that skyline. According to Gabriel, we needed to head straight to the core of the Big Apple. Tex pulled up on West Forty Third Street and killed the engine. He popped his door and stepped out, I followed. The paintwork on the Impala gleamed under all the lights; I had to take a moment to appreciate her.

"This way," he said, setting off at a leisurely pace. "Gabriel said to head to Vidstar Video on Times Square; it's only a five-minute walk from here."

"Don't tell me that fucking pigeon sent us all this way to pick up some damn videotapes."

"He said it's a good place to start looking, you know how selective he is with details. Something there should give us a lead on the Killer Killers. We may as well take a look at the selection while we're there though; it's the biggest Vidstar in the country."

"The Killer Killers, that's what you're calling them?"

"Better than Magical Misty Murderer Murdering Men, isn't it?"

"I think I prefer that one."

"You're a fucking idiot."

## [Track 5]

The unmistakable glow of Vidstar's neon lights burnt my retinas as we turned the corner of Forty Seventh and landed right in the middle of Times Square. The entire area itself was bright, but goddamn, Vidstar was brighter. The whole place assaulted the senses as we stepped through the doors. The neon lights attacked my eyes, the special video store smell attacked my nostrils, and the sound of trailers repeating on wall-mounted TVs attacked my ears. I fucking loved it.

Tex made his way right over to the horror section, leaving me to scout the place for clues on the guys we were looking for. According to him, they could turn out to be friends or foes, so I had to be careful. Through all the collective supernatural shit we'd faced, neither of us had come face to face with wraith-like entities.

The counter was manned by a pair of guys in bright neon Letterman jackets, one green and the other purple, both wearing sunglasses. They matched the store's colour scheme pretty damn well. I made my way over to catch their attention.

"Hey there fellas," I said.

"Sup bro!" Green said enthusiastically.

"Let me guess, horror fan with a preference for horror-comedy," said Purple.

His insightfulness blindsided me a little. "Erm… uh… yeah. How'd you know?"

"Superpowers. Check out Attack of The Killer Tomatoes in the horror section, it's a scream."

Green added, "Or if you wanna catch something on the big screen, Motel Hell is playing at the Ziggy."

"The Ziggy?"

"The Ziegfeld, my guy, over on West Fifty Fourth, it's killer."

"Thanks", I said, "speaking of things that are killer, I'm looking for a couple who've been in the news lately. My friend over there calls them the Killer Killers. I prefer the Magical Misty Murderer Murdering Men. Heard of them?"

41

Purple shot me a displeased look, "You mean the Neon Vigilantes."

"Is that what they're called?"

Purple opened his mouth to speak again when Green cut in, "Nah dude, I thought we're the Neon Nightmares."

I raised an eyebrow.

"Dude," Purple muttered, "shudthefuckup."

"I uh... they, that's what THEY are called, so I hear," Green said, smiling at me.

I sighed. "It's you guys, isn't it?"

They both shifted nervously, shaking their heads. Tex slapped a hand down on my shoulder and dropped a stack of tapes down on the desk.

"Evening fellas, what's occurring? I'd like to buy these."

"I was just asking these gentlemen if they've heard anything about the so-called Neon Vigilantes."

"Neon Nightmares," Green chimed in.

Purple picked up the tapes and tried to change the subject. "Halloween, Jaws 2, Superman: The Movie and American Graffiti. Awesome selection bro. Sure you wanna buy? It's gonna cost a helluva lot more than renting."

"I'm sure," Tex said, fanning out a fistful of hundreds, "and my friend Ben Franklin here sure would be pleased to hear any information you might have on the Neon Nightmare Vigilantes."

"It's them, Tex," I said.

"What?"

"Yeah, what?" Purple said.

"Yeah, yeah what?" Green added.

I nodded at the two neon dipshits, "They're the guys."

"No way it's that easy," Tex said.

"They're called the Neon Vigilantes th—"

"Nightmares, bro!" Green snapped.

I started again, "They're called the Neon Nitwits; they're wearing fucking neon-coloured jackets and work in a goddamn neon-soaked palace."

Purple piped up, "We *own* a neon-soaked palace, my dude," he pointed at himself, "we are the proprietors of this here establishment, and many others across the states."

"You two own the Vidstar Video chain?" Tex asked.

"We sure do," Green replied.

"And you're the guys who've been offing murderers," I said.

"Shhhhhaddap," Purple said as Green nodded. "Look, just take your tapes and go, please."

Tex slapped down his cash. "Not until we have a good ol' chat."

Green looked at Purple and shrugged, "We may as well bro, they ain't dumb and they clearly ain't cops."

"Fine," Purple conceded, "meet us in the alley round back in thirty minutes. We're just waiting on the staff getting here for the late shift."

Thirty minutes passed. We were waiting in the alley around the back of Vidstar just as agreed. Tex was right to call the place the Big Dirty. I'd seen some filthy back alleys, but this was on another level. The smell of piss was so strong I could taste it.

We were both well aware that the two nitwits could have lured us into a trap, but I had no strange rumblings in my guts, and they didn't seem to be a pair who'd think that far ahead, so we took the chance.

I kicked a rotting pumpkin at the opposite wall, splattering seeds and pumpkin guts all around. I'd been keeping my eye on the back door to Vidstar but hadn't seen any sign of the vigilantes. By my watch, they were late. I turned to Tex and tapped my wrist. He shrugged and opened his mouth to speak but paused and frowned at something behind me.

I turned to see the alley filling with a thick, swirling mixture of neon green and purple smoke. I took a step back towards Tex as the Neon... whatevers, stepped out of the fog.

"Wassup bro," they said in unison.

"What's up is exactly what we'd like to know," Tex said. "Who are you? What are you? Why are you doing what you're doing?"

I made a show of brushing my jacket back, giving them an eyeful of the Sisters, just in case they felt like getting rowdy.

"Getting straight to business huh? Well, it's pretty simple really, like the name suggests, we're vigilantes."

"From your worst nightmares," Green cut in.

Purple sighed. "Alright dudes, your opinion, what's a better name: Neon Vigilantes, or Neon Nightmares?"

I shrugged, "Neon Nightmares has a better ring to it."

Tex nodded.

Purple turned to Green, "Guess you win, we're the Nightmares."

Green pumped his fist into the air..

"Anyway, we hunt down bad guys."

Tex stepped forward, "What kind of bad guys?"

"Murderers, rapists, that kind of thing."

"And how'd you go about identifying them?"

"We keep an eye on the news on TV and in the papers, and float around during the night. You drift around Manhattan long enough and you'll find some kind of crime soon enough."

Tex nodded his head and took out a hip flask to take a swig of bourbon.

"Killed any vampires?" I asked.

"Vampires? Fuck no. Are they even, like, real?"

I pulled a couple of fangs out of my pocket and threw them over to them. "They sure are." They caught one each.

"Radical!" Green said.

Tex finished a long pull. "So what are you, wraiths?"

"I guess you could call us that," Purple nodded, "so listen up, here's our superhero backstory." He waved his hand, trailing purple smoke through the air. "We were simple business owners until a couple of months ago; a pair of movie lovin' bros livin' the sweet life doing what we love and raking in fat stacks of dollars. One night when we were shutting up shop, some asshole with a gun burst in and tried to rob us. We built up Vidstar from nothing, with our blood and sweat, no way some punk from the streets was gonna take what we'd earned. So we fought back. And he shot us dead. The sonofabitch murdered us for the sixty dollars we left in the cash register, two candy bars, the latest issue of Thunder Jugs and an old copy of Super Schlong 4: The Space Babes Are Coming."

Green snorted. "Good movie, in all fairness."

"Now bros, don't ask how because we don't know shit about science or the afterlife, but our souls got... lost. They must have flown up out of our bodies and bonded with the gas in the neon lights or something, got real fuckin' confused, and landed back in our bodies all jacked up on gas. So we came back with these rad crazy superpowers. BOOM!" He clapped his hands together, creating a cloud of smoke around them.

Green added, "It got a little awkward after the first couple of days though. We were controlling our bodies, but they were still dead. Started to stink and look like shit. Had to secretly arrange to be buried back home. Luckily we learned how to take physical form before our bodies rotted away. Looking like a pair of zombies wouldn't have been good for business."

"Coulda been a good publicity stunt though," Purple shrugged.

I've gotta say, I found the story quite entertaining. "So, what are the superpowers?"

Green replied, "We can turn into smoke and disappear."

"Like Dracula?" Tex said.

"Like Dracula," Green nodded. "We can't get hurt. Can't be stabbed or shot anymore. Erm, what else… we can get really fuckin' bright and blind people too."

Purple added, "Coolest thing is: we can get inside people. Get into their lungs and tear them up from the inside. Long story short, my dude: We're fuckin' unstoppable."

Tex held out his flask, offering them a swig of the good stuff. "We wouldn't dream of stopping a pair of gents putting in such good work, both in-store and out. You see, we're not so different. You kill your monsters, we kill ours."

"So, what now?" Green shrugged.

"I propose a team up. We're hunting for the biggest baddest vamp there is, and we could use a pair of badass dudes to flex some muscle."

They looked at each other and nodded. Purple said, "You scratch our back, we scratch yours. We're looking for our own supervillain right now. He ain't a vampire, but he's still a menace. Help us take him down and you've got a deal bro."

Tex looked to me for my opinion.

I shrugged. "Why not."

Tex nodded, "You fellas have got yourselves a deal."

"Radical!" they said in unison before fist-bumping each other and disappearing in a bright pink flash.

We stood in silence for a moment, letting things sink in.

"What the fuck do we do now?" I asked. The Neon Nightmares had disappeared, leaving us standing in the alley like a pair of dumpster dwellers.

"Guess we check ourselves into a hotel for the night and come back in the morning. I expected them to fill us in on the what, when, where and why but hey ho."

"Kinda strange, aren't they?"

"Pair of nuts in a sack."

# Murder Nerd

Morning came far too fast. We had rented a damn nice room at the Plaza and went hard and heavy on the room service. Tex lay sprawled out on the sofa in his boxer shorts with a slice of pizza on his chest. A bottle of fancy scotch sat tucked into bed next to me. I got up to take a shower. The scotch followed me in.

I set the temperature as high as it would go and stepped in. Multiple jets of steaming hot water soaked me from all angles. An incredibly high tolerance for pain was one of the perks of the Hot Sauce. Under the bathroom's bright white light I could see the faint orange glow of the Sauce in my wrists. I took a sip of the scotch and sighed as the shower melted away all my stress from the past few days and months. So much had happened in only seven months. Life had been manic. I'd barely taken any time to process things. I'd woken up from an eight-year coma, ended a man's life, killed a nest of Tentaclari, killed a fuck load of vampires, made a bunch of friends, performed an exorcism, tortured the shit out of Rapey and Roids, hunted down a serial killer and met a pair of fucking neon ghosts. Goddamn. It had been wild.

I corked the bottle and set it down before taking a nice long time shampooing my hair. It almost reached my shoulders. I hadn't shaved in a couple of weeks either. Tex was starting to call me Captain Hobo, but I liked the look.

A knock on the door pulled me out of my daydreams.

"Hurry up, boy, Texas is about to get heavy rains."

This meant he needed a piss.

I flicked off the jets, slung a towel around myself and opened the door. Tex strode in without hesitation, the slice of pizza still stuck to his chest. I hurried out in good time to avoid catching an eyeful of his junk as he reached to get his shorts out of the way.

I closed the door behind me and heard him say: "Oh hey, pizza."

I took my time getting dressed, enjoying a nice leisurely morning. I was fully clothed and ejecting Jaws 2 from the VCR when Tex burst out of the bathroom wearing a fluffy white bathrobe.

"I called for breakfast when you were washing your locks, should be here soon," he said.

"Full English?"

"Is there any other kind of breakfast?"

Score. I'd always loved full English breakfasts. Mom was originally from England, so I grew up eating them. The fact that Tex loved them as much as I did was a coincidence I was eternally thankful for. "You know, of all the unbelievable shit I've seen, I'm more amazed that your cholesterol levels haven't killed you."

"I may be about one cheeseburger away from meeting Gabriel in person, but that's a risk I'm willing to take."

After breakfast, we made our way back over to Vidstar in hopes of finding the Neon Nut-jobs. The guy at the counter pointed us in the direction of the office when we asked for the bosses. I gave a light knock on the door and heard a bunch of clattering.

"You may enter," someone said.

Tex gave me some side-eye as he pushed the door open. We entered to the sight of the guys sitting in swivel chairs with their backs to us, both wearing the same jackets from the previous night and still wearing sunglasses. Green let out a small snigger as they spun around at the same time.

"We've been expecting you," Purple said, "please sit."

I pulled the door closed and just about heard Tex's eyes rolling as he took a seat on one of the chairs in front of the desk.

"Yeah, well you didn't really leave us with much information last night, did you?" he said.

I sat and chipped in, "Names would be helpful too, by the way. I'm Night, this is Tex."

Green pointed to himself and said, "Adrian."

Purple whipped off his shades, "Leon."

I immediately understood why he wore them. Instead of regular eyes, he had nothing but purple swirling mist. It reminded me of Mystic Mickey and how he always wore shades to hide his yellow orb peepers.

Tex leaned over to me. "It's always the goddamn eyes, ya'know. Anything supernatural always got fuckin' weird eyes."

I nodded along before saying, "So what's the job, fellas? Who are we looking for and when are we going after them?"

Leon put his shades back on and said, "Well, he calls himself Power Master."

Adrian continued, "But we call him Murder Nerd. Long story short, he's the head honcho of a gang of criminals making a mess of our beautiful city."

"I'm guessing the guys who murdered you are part of this gang?" Tex said.

Leon nodded. "You guess right. We want him and his cronies gone. We couldn't do jack until we got gassed, but now we have great powers. And with great power comes great respon—"

"Yeah, we get it," I cut in, "big superhero spiel aside, how come you need our help? I thought you couldn't get hurt?"

"As far as we know, we can't, but Murder Nerd knows about us. And from what we know of him, he's most likely made some supervillain tech that could take us out. If you guys fight vampires, you'd be pretty safe backup."

"You think he could actually make something that could hurt a pair of... whatever you guys are?"

"Yeah, dude's supposedly a genius, builds all kinds of crazy shit. He could have made, like, a phantom catcher, or wraith wrecker, or a umm..."

"Or a ghost buster," Adrian said.

Leon nodded. "Ghost Buster has a cool ring to it. Whatever, he'll have something to deal with us, I'm sure."

Tex grunted, slumping down in his chair. "Alright, so when do you need us?"

Leon looked at Adrian and said, "Now, really."

Tex raised his eyebrows. "Now?"

Adrian leaned forward. "Got a car, don'cha? Well, we've got directions if you'd be so kind."

I turned to Tex, "We've got nothing else going on. Sooner we get this guy out the way, sooner we can get back to looking for Atrocitas."

"Atrocitas?" Leon asked.

Tex twiddled his thumbs. "It's what the Vamp King calls himself, Dominus Atrocitas."

Both guys snorted.

"And I guess today is as good as any. Throw in a video to cover the cost of gas and you've got a deal."

They both reached a hand across the desk for a shake. Tex shook with Leon; I shook with Adrian. "Deal," they said together.

Leon went on, "Meet us back here at sundown. Tonight, we have our vengeance."

\* \* \*

Tex pulled up in front of the store as the sun tucked itself away behind New York City's skyscrapers. Leon and Adrian made their way out as Tex fiddled with the radio. I stepped out and swung my seat forward. Leon crammed himself into the back without hesitation. Adrian stood glancing at the front seat.

"You're not riding shotgun," I said to him.

He hung his head and mumbled, "No fair," as he squeezed into the back.

I flicked the seat back, made myself comfy and pulled the door closed as Tex eyed the guys in the rearview mirror.

"Where to, fellas?" he asked.

Leon handed him a map and pointed to a cross he'd marked on it. "Tribeca, this area here. It's about a fifteen-minute drive. The goons we made squeal said Murder Nerd's base is here on Harrison Street, nice view of the Hudson."

"I know where Tribeca is, kid," Tex grumbled.

"Rad. Let's go bust some skulls."

Tex nodded, turned up the radio's volume and floored the gas pedal.

We tore down Seventh Avenue with "Heroes" by David Bowie as our soundtrack. Very fitting. Tex slowed to a roll as we turned the corner onto Harrison Street. The buildings all looked the same to me, as did much of New York City. Being from a small town that nobody has ever heard of, big cities all looked the same to me: the hulking buildings, dark alleyways and far too many streets, all a mess of concrete and steel.

Adrian leaned forward and pointed to a big blocky beast on the left. "Pull up by that one bro, that's the place."

"Doesn't look like a supervillain lair," I said.

"They never do in real life, dude. It wouldn't work out well for them if they had big, bright, comic book supervillain signage."

I shrugged. "Good point."

Tex pulled up in front and killed the engine.

I stepped out and reached to pull the seat forward when the guys burst into a cloud of bright smoke and disappeared. I gave Tex a look that said, "These motherfuckers," before turning to find them both standing behind me.

"Couldn't have got in the car that way?" I asked.

Leon shrugged. "Don't wanna do it so often it's not cool, ya'know."

Adrian nodded his agreement.

Tex joined us and said, "So what, are we striding in guns blazing and dicks a-swinging or taking things slow and steady?"

Adrian snorted. "Go hard or go home, my dude."

"I'll leave my trousers in the car then."

"Please don't," I said, "the last thing I wanna see is you prancing around in your undies, or less."

"Suit yourself. Some would pay good money to see such a thing."

"I think I can speak for everyone here when I say our wallets are staying firmly in our pockets."

Leon whipped off his shades. "As long as you kick the shit out of some cronies, you can wear whatever the fuck you please, buddy. Let's do this."

He stepped forward, leading the way through a small loading bay to a roller shutter on the front of the building. He winked at us before disappearing in one of their trademark puffs of smoke. The shutters rolled themselves up a moment later. The sound of panicked voices came from the other side. Adrian took his shades off too, looking like he meant business. He strolled right on into the lair with his arms up, flexing his biceps.

"Who ordered front-row tickets to the gun show?" he asked.

Ten oddly dressed guys crowded around a map-covered table in the middle of the room, with who I assumed to be Murder Nerd at the head of it; a scrawny guy with messy hair and a large pair of glasses. He couldn't have been any older than eighteen. He wore a shiny silver jacket with a large propped up collar and a cape which was trailing to the floor.

"What the fuck is this?" Murder Nerd yelled.

A swirl of purple smoke appeared by Adrian's side. Leon stepped out of it and joined the stroll towards the goon squad.

Leon and Adrian stopped, stood side by side and said, "We're the Neon Nightmares and we're here to take out the trash."

I held back a chuckle as Tex visibly cringed.

"Get them!" Murder Nerd roared.

Tex and I made for cover behind some crates as the goons pulled guns and started poppin'.

"I like their weird uniforms," I said to Tex, "makes me feel like we're in The Warriors."

"It's a good movie, they've definitely taken inspiration. You feel like shooting anyone from here?"

56

A wet bursting sound came from behind our cover.

"Not really. Whenever someone takes cover in movies they get to peek up and take some shots and all the bad guys' bullets seem to miss. I know for a fact if I try, I'll get a bullet right between my eyes, no sequel for me."

Yelling, screams and gunfire echoed around the warehouse as we spoke before the sound of an alarm rang out.

"We've dealt with much worse and came out fine, look at how the car chase with all the suckers from Saltstone turned out," Tex yelled over the noise.

A severed hand hit the floor next to Tex's foot. He shoved it aside with his boot.

"Yeah, but I can't pull a Gatling gun out of my ass like I did back then, can I?"

"I don't know, can you?"

The gunfire died down to what sounded like a couple of people popping off at random. A spray of blood came over the crates and splattered our heads.

The shooting stopped.

"Now's our chance to find out," I said before pointing a gun over the top of the crate and quickly peeking to assess the situation.

Blood and chunks of viscera dripped from the ceiling and walls. The whole place stank of shit and the metallic tang of blood. One goon in glittery green dungarees was waving his gun towards the Heavens, muttering, "Where are they?"

I stood and pointed my piece at him; Tex joined me in standing and pointed his gun at a fella wearing what looked like a leotard. Murder Nerd had disappeared. I whistled to catch their attention. They both froze and dropped their guns.

"Please, we've not hurt anybody, we just get paid to protect the boss," Dungarees said, "fuck, please, call the other guys off."

"Where's Murder Nerd?" Tex asked.

Leon and Adrian materialised beside us, to the horror of Dungarees and his buddy.

"You mean Power Master? He's up there," he said, pointing at a door up on a metal balcony with a set of stairs leading up to it on the right.

"Get outta here," Leon said.

Adrian continued, "And don't let us catch you doing any shady shit again, or you'll end up like these guys," he gestured to the puddles of gore.

The goons nodded and booked it out of the building.

Tex strolled over and picked up their guns.

"Looks like your guy's cornered," I said.

"Time for the dramatic showdown," Leon said, cracking his knuckles.

Adrian began, "How are we gonna do th—"

CRASH!

The door on the balcony burst off its hinges and flew over our heads. Murder Nerd stood where it used to be, holding his fists out in front of him. He wore a pair of hi-tech looking gauntlets with sparks of electricity fizzling and zapping from them.

"Behold my power!" he yelled.

Leon and Adrian's jaws dropped.

"No fucking way," Leon said.

Murder Nerd thrust a fist forward, aiming at them.

Adrian smiled. "That's so fucking coo–aaaaarrggg."

A huge blue laser blast shot from Murder Nerd's right glove and hit Adrian, vaporising half of his head and his entire right shoulder. What was left of his arm fell to the floor. His tongue flopped from the side of his head as he turned to look at Leon before collapsing in a heap.

"Holy fucking shit," I yelled.

Leon watched his buddy slump to the floor with his mouth hanging open, before looking back to the balcony. "Drop the gloves, Murder Nerd!" he yelled.

"My name is Killatron the Power Master," Murder Nerd squealed as a fresh wave of armed goons flowed through the doorway and onto the balcony. He looked back through the doorway into what appeared to be a large office and yelled, "Serj, play that song I like while I eliminate these fools."

Tex and I stood with our guns at the ready, waiting for the goons to raise theirs while Murder Nerd set the soundtrack.

## [Track 6]

Music flowed out through some speakers. Murder Nerd looked horrified. "Not that one you fucking idiot," he yelled through the doorway.

The song came to a stop with a record scratch, and we all stood in awkward silence as Serj searched for the right one. Almost a minute passed before the music came to life again.

## [Track 7]

A big ol' grin spread across Murder Nerd's face as he started bopping his head along to the music. Serj had clearly got the right track this time.

We watched as he did a little dance for a few seconds then gave his goons the signal to get to shootin'. They raised their guns and hailed bullets, but we had the good sense to get out of the way, jumping behind a shipping container to the left of us. Leon burst into smoke and disappeared. The bullet storm rained down for what felt like an eternity before stopping. The sounds of footsteps clattered down the stairs, coming towards us.

The first goon stepped into view and raised his gun towards us before letting out a sudden scream. His chest exploded. Purple smoke poured from the corpse as it fell to the floor, then billowed off out of sight to make friends with some other poor fucker's insides.

Not being one to miss out on any action, I winked at Tex and threw myself from behind the hiding spot. I ducked, weaved and whirled, popping off bullets at miscellaneous henchmen while dodging blasts from Murder Nerd's Power Gloves. He stood alone on the balcony, firing laser blasts in sync with the beat of the music. I had to give him props, the kid could keep up a good rhythm. A beam fizzled past my head as I put a bullet through a goon's. Between the four of us, we were making short work of them. Having a pair of murderous ghosts on the team made for easy pickings.

I shot the knee off of a goon in a pink sequined jacket. He fell forward just as I stepped back and a laser beam zapped between us. The goon fell right through it and ended up bisecting himself.

Murder Nerd stomped a foot in frustration and thrust another fist in my direction. I had been a little too distracted by watching his goon spread apart and fall to the floor. All I saw was a blinding flash of blue before something struck me dead in the chest and knocked me flying off my feet. My head struck the concrete hard and I blacked out for a moment. My vision slowly returned as I came to. I found myself lying on my back, staring up at the ceiling. A blurry figure shambled over to me, getting clearer as it grew closer. I blinked to make sure my mind wasn't playing tricks.

Adrian stood over me, his arm had reattached, and his head was slowly rebuilding itself with a red mist floating around it.

"Hoo urkuur?" he gurgled. His jawbone fixed itself into place under the exposed muscle as it knitted itself together.

I ran a hand over my chest, feeling for the gaping hole.

"What?" I said, pulling myself up and taking a look down. Nothing. Not a damn scratch. My head was bleeding from the fall, though. I looked around and found Tex lying facedown on the floor behind me.

I glanced at the balcony to make sure another blast wasn't coming. Murder Nerd was on his back, writhing and clutching at his throat. Purple smoke swirled around him, flying in and out of his nostrils. All of the goons had been taken care of.

"Tex," I said, pulling myself to my feet and stumbling towards him, "buddy?"

A perfect circle had burnt through the back of his jacket and shirt but only blistered his skin. He groaned and rolled over to face me.

"You okay kid?"

"Yeah, you?"

He stuck a hand out for me to help him to his feet. "Fuckin' dandy."

"How are you breathing right now?"

"Laser must have just scraped me."

I looked to Adrian for answers. He shrugged.

"Tex, you've got a big laser-shaped hole in your clothes."

He waved a hand in dismissal. "Like I say, it grazed me. Leon got Murder Nerd?"

We all turned to check in. Leon had materialised and was in the process of prying the kid's gloves off of him. He pulled them off without much struggle and threw them over the balcony. They landed at our feet.

Enough of Adrian's face had regenerated for him to say, "Fuck him up, broski."

Leon smiled and gave two thumbs up before turning to smoke and disappearing up Murder Nerd's nostrils. He shook violently and let out a shrill squawk before exploding. All manner of gore splattered the walls and spilled down from the balcony.

Tex stood in awe, rubbing his face.

I picked the gloves up from the floor. "What should we do with these?"

"I call shotgun on them," Leon said, popping into existence in front of us.

"Seems fair," I said, "he was your supervillain after all."

"Hell yeah," Leon nodded, taking the gloves and passing one to Adrian.

They each slipped on a glove and fist-bumped with them.

Tex and I turned to walk back to the car as they thrust their fists into the air, blasting huge blue lasers up through the roof and into the sky, adding a couple more lights to the New York City skyline.

# Homecoming

We'd donned a fresh set of clothes, packed our bags and hit the road within a few hours of our encounter with Murder Nerd and the Neon Nightmares. We had done all we came to do, no need to stick around any longer. I'd planned on spending Thanksgiving at home with Mom, and Tex reckoned I needed a break. I wasn't going to argue; driving around the country kicking all kinds of ass does get tiring, so we agreed to get my own ass back to Blackwater and then have a bit of well-earned downtime.

Tex drove through the night, passing through Pennsylvania and Ohio before pulling up at a diner right in the middle of Fort Wayne, Indiana, just over ten hours after leaving New York. The clock ticked over to six thirty in the morning as he killed the engine.

I stretched and let out a groan, trying to regain feeling in my ass.

Tex looked at me and said, "Of all the shit we do, the ass-numbing drives have got to be the hardest, eh?"

"You got that right."

"C'mon, let's get breakfast."

"You don't have to tell me twice."

I popped the door and swung my legs out, giving them a rub to get them going. The air had a chilly bite to it, more so than back in New York, and it'd only get colder the closer I got to home.

Tex held the diner door open as I hobbled inside. We found an empty booth, Tex sat right away. I stood for a while longer, absorbing the smell of bacon and coffee.

A waitress drifted over and asked, "You all good, honey?"

"Long drive, just savouring the ability to stand before sitting down again."

"How about some coffee to get the blood flowing again?"

"Sounds great," I said.

She looked at Tex, "Coffee too?"

He nodded. "And two plates of whatever your breakfast special is please."

"Comin' right up," she said.

I lowered my ass to the seat and said, "So, we gonna talk about last night?"

"What's there to talk about?"

"That laser blast didn't skim you, Tex, it hit you dead on. I saw what happened to Adrian. It should have vaporized you."

Tex let out a heavy sigh. "Okay, fine, it hit me. But can we just leave it for now? I'll explain some other time."

"You better. You're supposed to be showing me everything you know. This isn't the kind of thing to keep secret."

"I did say that, yes, but there's just some shit you're not ready for. I'll tell you in time, you have my word."

The waitress appeared at the booth and set down our coffees. We picked them up and sipped in silence, waiting for breakfast.

* * *

### [Track 8]

I drove the rest of the way home from the diner, mostly in silence with Tex getting some shut-eye. We made good time, taking only a couple more breaks, and hit Blackwater Lake by four in the afternoon. Home.

I pulled up in front of Mom's house, greeted by the sight of my Firebird sitting on the driveway, right where I'd left her. We'd been using Tex's Impala ever since finding Rapey and Roids. I'd been itching to get back into my own car the entire time, itching to see Betsy the Gatling gun again. I came to a stop and slapped Tex's arm to wake him while removing the keys. He let out a grunt and pulled his tattered old cowboy hat off his head.

"This is my stop, old man. Are ya coming in for a while before you fuck off back to Gabriel?"

"Sure thing, I gotta drop a load real bad, if you'd be so kind as to let an old man use your shitter? And any chance I could stay the night? I'm pooped today; don't entirely fancy more driving just yet."

"I'm sure Mom'll allow it. Oh, and if you could keep her distracted, I'll get all our dirty clothes in the wash before she sees the blood stains."

66

"Good idea."

I stepped out of the car and inhaled the cold, clean air. A light layer of snow lay on the ground and the wind had the harsher chill of a Blackwater Lake winter riding on it. Tex made his way to the trunk and helped gather my stuff. He handed me one rucksack while swinging the other over his shoulder. With all accounted for, we made our way up the path.

Mom peeked out the side of a curtain and swung the door open a moment later.

She put her arm out to embrace me. "Isaac, sweetie! Hurry up, get in, it's getting cold out. You too Tex, good to see you again."

Tex nodded. "Good to see you too, ma'am. Mind if I use your, uh, facilities?"

"Not at all go, go, go."

Mom closed the door behind us; Tex dropped his rucksack and darted up the stairs. I picked it up and put both of them down on the sofa, with my ass following close behind. I let out a contented sigh as I sunk into it and kicked off my boots. The feeling of relaxation washed over me. Mom's place calmed me like no other: always clean and tidy, always cosy, the perfect temperature, the constant pleasant smell. It was home. I let out a long sigh, breathing out my stress.

"Pass those boots here," Mom said, bending to grab them, "the pair of you look haggard. I'll make us all some hot chocolate, and I'm making poutine later too. Will Tex want some?"

I stood and followed as she made her way into the kitchen, setting the boots down by the front door as she passed.

"Sounds great, and I doubt he'd refuse."

"Good, is he heading off soon or would he like to stay the night? What about you?"

"I'd say a sleepover is on the cards for tonight if that's alright? And I'm home 'till after Thanksgiving now, I reckon."

"Of course, the spare bed's already made up. And I'd hoped you'd say that. Edward is working away for a little while. A bit of company would be nice. Pass the milk, would you?"

I made my way to the fridge, pulled out a bottle for her and said, "It'll be good to see him again. How've things been?"

"Wonderful, we go dancing twice a week and he takes me on some lovely walks. You should see some of the pictures he takes; he's such a wonderful photographer. Oh, that letter is for you by the way, it came a few weeks ago," she said, pointing to an envelope in the middle of the table.

I picked it up and looked it over. Sure enough, it had my name on it. "For me? That's weird. I don't know anyone who'd write."

"Maybe you've got a secret admirer."

"Let's see," I said, tearing it open.

The letter read:

Night,

I don't know when you'll receive this letter. I know you were planning on doing a lot of travelling, so I don't expect you'll be reading this soon, but I wanted to write anyway. I hope you're well, and I hope you've done what you set out to do and are now at peace with the world.

I've never been much of a writer, so I'll keep this short and get to the point...

I'm a free man, my friend. My time in Blackwater Maximum was cut short, but the story is long. If you'd like to get a drink and catch up sometime, I'll tell you all about it. For the foreseeable future, I'll be staying in town. If you'd like to come buy me a beer, I'm at Jackie's bar on Barker Avenue almost every evening after seven. I hope to see you there at some point. Otherwise, I'm currently living in room four at the Hard-Nap Motel on the edge of town, until I get back on my feet.

I hope to see you soon.

Your friend,

Ali.

"Holy shit," I muttered.

Mom set my hot chocolate down in front of me and whacked me over the head with a spoon. "Oi, language. What is it?"

"Ali, one of my friends from prison, he's been freed and is staying in town. He's the one who looked out for me and David."

"Oh? Does he have any friends or family here?"

"I was his only friend last time we spoke, and no family anywhere."

Mom sipped her chocolate and gestured for me to follow her into the living room. She set Tex's drink down on the coffee table and sat in her big armchair. I took the sofa.

"Are you gonna go find him?"

"Heck yeah, he's a great guy. I thought it'd be years before he got out. I hope he's still around. Says he's at Jackie's most nights, I might head over tomorrow, and see if I can find him."

"Why not go tonight?"

"First night home and you're trying to get rid of me already."

The noise of the toilet flushing interrupted the conversation. Tex came stomping down the stairs a moment later. He joined us in the living room and sat down next to me with a loud sigh.

He eyed the hot chocolate. "Oh, this one for me?"

Mom nodded. "Hope you've been looking after my boy while you're off doing... what is it you're doing again?"

I gave him some hard side-eye, telepathically willing him not to mention the monster hunting. As far as she knew, I went on my own little road trip to explore and collect something for a friend. This wasn't entirely a lie, I did drive to San Felipe to collect the Sisters, and I did spend a little time exploring. I just killed off a whole bunch of monsters and made friends with some in between.

Tex thought for a moment before saying, "Restoration. Old cars and all that, takes us all over the country doesn't it, Night?"

I nodded, letting him do the talking.

"Yeah, lots of old cars are out there sitting in scrapyards and barns. We buy 'em and restore 'em, Night's learning real fast too. It's pretty fortunate that we bumped into each other. I needed an apprentice; he needed a job. We've just been hunting down some cars in New York City, haven't we?"

I nodded again. "Uh, yeah."

"No luck finding anything?"

"Nah, hard to find anything decent in such big cities but we thought why not give it a shot? I figure we've both earned a rest, so I'll head home in the morning, maybe do a bit of work between Thanksgiving and Christmas," he turned to me, "if Night's up for it?"

"Of course."

We spent the rest of the night catching up on life with Tex expertly dodging any of my mom's questions that could have led to her finding out what we actually got up to. After being loaded to the brim with enough food and hot chocolate to last the winter, we called it a night and hit the hay. The thought of a few weeks without having something, or someone, try to murder me sent me drifting into the best sleep I'd had in weeks.

* * *

The smell of bacon and coffee caressed my nostrils as I woke. I threw on a robe and a pair of comfy slippers and made my way downstairs. Tex had already washed, dressed and sat himself down at the kitchen table. He greeted me with a nod and a grunt.

"Mornin' honey," Mom said, "Tex and I were thinking bacon sandwiches for breakfast, you want one?"

"You betcha," I gave her a peck on the cheek before pulling out a chair and sitting in front of steaming coffee. I eyeballed Tex. "Heading off so soon?"

He looked at his watch, "Yeah, it's eight now, I figure if I set off by nine I'll be home by about four tomorrow morning. Sleep till eleven then get a bit of writing done."

"Sounds good. What's the plan for getting back to work?"

"We've earned a bit of downtime. Like I said last night, I might do a few jobs between Thanksgiving and Christmas."

"Sure thing, just give me a call if you need me. What about the, erm, big job we still need to do?"

"Not much we can do until we get more information on the... car's whereabouts." Tex finished his sentence with a wink.

Mom set the sandwiches in front of us and joined us at the table.

"Many thanks, Mrs Nightingale, I appreciate the hospitality."

Mom flapped a hand at him, "It's nothing, I love having guests over. What are your plans for the holidays, Tex?"

"I must admit I don't have any. I usually spend them working, a lonely old goat like me doesn't have much cause to celebrate them."

"In that case, why not come back up here for a while? We can have a big Thanksgiving and Christmas, give yourself a bit of a rest too, huh?"

I nodded along, fond of the idea.

Tex sat and pondered it for a moment. "You know what, I'd love to, thank you for the offer. It'll certainly beat sitting in my workshop. If I remember correctly it's the twenty-seventh this year, so I could drive up to be here in the afternoon of the twenty-sixth?"

"Perfect," Mom said with a smile, "oh, it'll be the first big one in almost ten years."

I sat and ate my sandwich as Mom chatted with Tex. She practically vibrated with excitement at the thought of having a full house for the holidays. I liked the idea myself; it'd be nice to have a small slice of normal life before getting back to the driving and the shooting and the almost being eaten, skinned, melted, absorbed, vaporised, or just plain ol' murdered by man or monster. I slouched back in my chair with the coffee cup resting on my chest, enjoying the sounds of good ol' regular person conversation.

The clock ticked over to nine in a heartbeat. Tex heaved himself out of the chair with a sigh and thanked Mom for breakfast again before gathering what little he'd brought in with him. Mom walked to the door with us and pulled him into a tight hug.

"The twenty-sixth, don't you go forgetting."

"Sure won't, ma'am. I'll see you soon," he said with a nod, holding his hat against his chest.

I walked him the few steps to his car.

"If anything comes up, in the meantime, let me know?"

He popped his door open and sat himself down in the driver's seat. "Sure will, might be quiet 'till after Christmas now though."

"Does evil celebrate Christmas?"

"Actually, yes, in a way. Not quite like we do, most have a kind of Anti-Christmas."

"Sounds a hoot. Anyway, I'll let you get gone. See you soon, Tex."

"Enjoy the rest, sonny, you'll need it," he said, as he twisted the keys and fired up his ride, "see you in a couple of weeks."

I stepped back as he pulled the door closed and brought the car to a roll. With one last wave from the window, he gunned the ignition and tore off down the street.

# Resurrection

I stepped off the bus at Barker Avenue just after seven-thirty. Mom had spent a good portion of the day telling me to be careful in as many different ways as she could, according to her Jackie's could be "a bit rough". I pushed the door open expecting to walk into a total dive filled with ruffians on the verge of a brawl. What I got was a dingy but quiet place with a few grizzled-looking bikers and not much else. I scanned the tables for Ali but couldn't see him anywhere, so I approached the bar. The lady behind it gave me a hard stare as I sat myself down on a stool, I couldn't tell whether she was frowning at me, or all the piercings in her eyebrows were weighing them down.

"I know you from somewhere? Ain't seen you in here before, but I know your face," she said.

"You might have seen me in the papers a while back."

She picked up a glass and started polishing it. "You that kid that got locked up for murdering his girl?"

I nodded.

"Yeah, I thought I recognised you. That's some shit luck you've had, kid. What can I get you?"

"Two of your best whiskeys, please."

**[Track 9]**

75

She nodded and set two glasses in front of me before turning to pick up a bottle of whiskey I couldn't pronounce the name of.

I pulled out my wallet and flicked through my bills.

"Put it away, kid," she said as she poured a hefty measure, "first drink's on the house."

"You do that for everyone?"

"Not for everyone, but for anyone that's spent time on the inside for something they didn't do... that deserves a free drink."

"Well, shit, I appreciate it."

"No problem," she said with a slow, heavy wink.

I sat in silence, cradling my drink as I watched her make conversation with other customers. It seemed a friendly enough place to me, nothing rough about it. But then, when you've been in the middle of a vampire bar brawl and watched limbs fly past your face, what normal people would call a rough place is tame in comparison. Sitting in a bar with old battle-hardened bikers was about as scary as playing in a box full of kittens.

About thirty minutes passed before I heard a voice behind me say, "Night?"

I turned to see Ali standing behind me with a huge grin plastered across his face.

"It is you," he said as grabbed a fistful of my jacket and pulled me off the stool into a hug, "you got my letter, eh?"

I slapped him on the back as he broke it off. "Sure did. You've got some explaining to do you sneaky bastard, here, this drink's been waiting for you." I handed him the second glass. "What happened here?" I traced a line down my face from the bridge of my nose to the side of my mouth, reflecting the fresh scar on his.

Ali took the glass and sat by me. "You remember the skinhead, Big G, one of Bill Bingsley's Nazi cronies? He gave me this not long after you were released, caught me off guard in a hallway."

"I hope you repaid in kind."

"Oh, I repaid with interest, dumb fucker is blind now, and has to hold somebody's hand to get around anywhere. He can't even wipe his own ass without help. Other than getting slashed, the prison isn't too bad of a place now. After you killed Uncle Jimmy it all kind of calmed down." He pointed at his scar. "This was Big G's attempt to get rid of me and take over as the next big bad boss. But it didn't work out, and nobody else stepped up to try. Warden Spencer's got it quite easy now. We should invite him out for a drink sometime, I have his number."

I took a sip of my drink and nodded. "That'd be nice, would be nice for all of us to have a drink together outside of that place."

Ali nodded and raised his glass. "Well this one's for David, hopefully he's up there watching us with a drink in his hand, too. To David!"

"To David," I said. It brought back bittersweet memories. David was a good guy; he should have been sitting with us. Uncle Jimmy had paid for what he'd done to him, but it didn't make his loss any less painful.

After a few moments of silence, Ali perked back up. "Anyway, I bet you're wondering about my great escape, huh?"

"You're damn right I am, come on, spill it."

"Well like I said, Spencer's had it easy for a while. Things slowed down and there wasn't really any more work for me to do. You know what he's like, always grateful for the help, so he came up with a plan to get me out. It took a bit of organising but it was pretty easy in the end."

"C'mon get to the good stuff."

"Well, to keep it short, I'm as good as dead."

"Huh?"

"We faked my death. Spencer got Doc in on the whole thing. We staged an accident, Doc declared me dead, and they shipped me out of the prison in a body bag one night. We'd arranged it for when Spencer had left to go home. He just left and parked up down an old dirt road a few miles away, Doc drove me there, and I hopped out of the bag and into Spencer's car. Alejandro Santos is technically buried in East Street Cemetery just down the road."

"Sneaky motherfucker."

"Sneakier than you know," he said. "The guy in my coffin was an inmate too. Poor bastard was three days away from release and died of a stroke. No next of kin, no known friends or anyone to remember him. So I took his identity and he took mine."

"You've got a new name then?"

"Well, if anyone asks, I'm Lemar August."

I stuck out a hand. "Nice to meet you, Lemar."

Ali shook it with a smile and looked past me to the bar lady. "Jackie, two more please."

"That's Jackie, as in Jackie's bar Jackie?"

"Sure is. That lady is a goddamn angel. Spencer set me up with some cash to tide me over till I found work but Jackie here's the one who gave me a job."

"You work here?"

"I'm usually at the door working security."

"You're a bouncer?"

Jackie appeared and started pouring our drinks. "He sure is. I haven't had a damn lick of trouble since I hired him. First night on the job I watched him carry a guy out the door by his throat; now nobody fucks with the big Mexican"

"Nobody fucks with the big Mexican," Ali chuckled.

Jackie corked the bottle and left it on the bar in front of us.

"Sounds like you're getting by nicely."

Ali necked half his glass. "I am. The pay's good and I'm still staying in the Hard-Nap so the rent's cheap."

"Why not get a decent place? I can't imagine the Hard-Nap's the best place to lay your head."

He shrugged. "Better than prison in every way. Besides, I'm not gonna be in town much longer."

"You're leaving?"

"I only ever intended to stay here temporarily. Jackie knows the score and says I'm welcome back any time if I need the work, but I need to go home. I need to go back to San Felipe. It's been too long."

79

"I guess I understand. I've barely been home myself lately. I'm only here 'til after Christmas then back on the road."

"What are you doing for work then?"

"I uh... guess you could say I'm a bounty hunter, I suppose."

"Very nice, my man, you're putting what I taught you to use, huh?"

I laughed. "I sure am."

Ali suddenly downed the rest of his drink and slammed the glass down on the bar. "How could I have forgotten?" he asked.

He'd managed to startle me, and everyone else in the bar.

"Forgotten what?"

"It should have been the first thing I asked... did you manage to find the fuckers you were going to look for?"

"I sure fuckin' did."

"C'mon then, my friend, what did you do to them? I want to hear every gory detail right now."

"Well... I hope you haven't eaten recently."

# Fast Forward

Thanksgiving and Christmas flew by in a flash. It felt as though someone had hit fast forward on the videotape of my life. One second, I was sitting in a bar with Ali, the next, it was Boxing Day. Edward had made it back in time for Christmas, so Mom was the happiest I'd seen her in a long time. We'd had a big Thanksgiving and a bigger Christmas Day. Of course, Mom had invited Ali to both events, so he had the pleasure of meeting her, Edward and Tex, all of whom he got along with like a house on fire. It was a great few weeks. One of the happiest times I'd had in a long time, but there was still a void left by Suzie's absence that no amount of good times could fill. Christmas just didn't feel right without her.

A new arcade had opened in town just after Thanksgiving, right opposite Vidstar Video. After a good amount of hassling, I'd finally talked Tex into coming along to check it out, as well as driving me there. We stepped out of the car and turned the corner to the sight of swarms of people buzzing around town. It had snowed real heavy so most of the roads had been closed, leaving the main street through town pedestrian only. Kids and adults zipped back and forth between shops as snowballs flew through the air.

"Ali said he'd meet us in Vidstar before we head to the arcade, let's see if he's here yet," I said.

Tex nodded while grunting through his scarf.

Ali had arrived before us and stood browsing the action section. I gave him a light punch on the arm as I made my way to his side, taking note of the tapes he'd already picked out: Attack of the Space Babes and Booberella 2: The Long, Hard Quest.

"Interesting choices there, buddy."

Tex snorted.

Ali looked at the tapes in his hands and shrugged. "You know how long I was in prison. I've got many years of not seeing titties to catch up on.

"Can't argue with that logic," Tex said.

"Here," I said, picking up a copy of The Warriors, "you'll enjoy this one."

"Thanks," Ali said. "This'll do me for now I guess." He nodded towards the window looking out at the arcade. "Want to head over there while I sort these? I'll catch up in a moment."

Tex and I nodded at each other.

"Sure thing, gives me a head start on some high scores."

Ali sniggered. "You'll need more than a head start to beat my scores; I got here early and snuck a few games in."

"Sneaky fucker, we'll see about that."

Tex had already shuffled to the door. I followed him out and ducked as a snowball flew towards my head.

"Sorry mister," a kid to my left yelled.

I looked to my right to see he'd hit his friend square in the face. "Good shot," I said, giving him two thumbs up.

"You're quite good with kids, aren't you Night?"
Tex said.

"I guess. Never really thought about it."

"Ever thought about having them?"

We stood outside the arcade; the sounds of the machines floated out into the street. The big neon 'Empire Arcade' sign buzzed above our heads.

"Years ago, I might have. I don't have a hope in hell now. It's not something I bother considering. Suzie is gone, and I just don't seem to have any interest in anybody else."

Tex nodded. "I understand. The lifestyle we've chosen doesn't exactly foster a good work-to-family balance, if I'm honest. Would you give it all up if you could have her back?"

"Give up the monster hunting? Nah, if she were still here, she'd want in on it, especially if she'd had the chance to meet Rapey and Roids again. She always said she wanted to go Sasquatch hunting, find the Loch Ness Monster... maybe see some ghosts. She loved this spooky shit; she'd be having a hell of a time."

"Sounds like you'd make it work, that's good."

I nodded. "Any point in this conversation, Tex?"

He stared for a long moment, mulling something over. "Just curious, is all."

"Yeah, well, you're curious, but I'm cold. How about we go inside and blast some aliens?"

"Sure. Aliens are one thing I've yet to encounter."

"Yeah, don't you fucking jinx it. Knowing my luck, I'll end up abducted with some sci-fi doodad rammed up my ass."

We made our way inside, it was my first time in an arcade and I didn't know what to expect. What I got was a load of kids darting back and forth between machines in a big dingy room, illuminated by nothing but black lights and game screens, lighting up a carpet covered in funky neon shapes. The majority of the people in the arcade had crowded around one guy playing an early release of Pac-Man. I made my way over to the nearest free machine while pulling a few quarters from my pocket.

"Space Invaders, I read about this one the other day," I said.

Ali appeared by my side. "Check out the high score."

"Nice, I'm guessing that's yours?"

"Damn right it is, my friend," he said.

"Mind if I speak to you about something?" Tex said to Ali.

"Not at all, what's up?"

Tex pulled up a stool and sat down behind me.

"Night told me it was you who taught him how to fight while you were both in prison, so I'm assuming you're a man who can handle himself in tough situations?"

"I sure can, and I've got the scars to prove it."

I hammered away on buttons while listening in on their conversation.

"And I'm assuming you know the stories about your old guns, the Sisters?"

"You don't own a pair of weapons like that without knowing their legend."

Tex nodded. "You believe in that kind of stuff then, Ali, the supernatural and all that?"

"Do I believe the spirits of my ancestors are haunting a pair of revolvers? Of course, I do. I've seen some shit, and I've seen what those guns can do. Never missed a shot, have you Night?"

I shook my head. "Not once."

"Neither did I when I owned them." Ali took a glance at the screen and said, "Not bad."

"Hmm… ever seen a vampire?"

I stopped pushing buttons and turned around to face Tex with a 'what the fuck' look.

"Excuse me?" Ali looked at me, then back to Tex.

"A vampire. Have you ever seen one?"

"In movies, sure."

"Night, how's your Roid-head friend doing? Still in his box?"

"Should we be having this conversation, Tex?"

"Sure we should. Let's blow this place and take a ride."

\* \* \*

After a verbal standoff with Tex, he managed to sway me to his way of thinking. It would be good to have another friend privy to what we do, especially one who could lend a hand if we were ever in a pinch.

Tex had driven us out to the woods where I'd buried Roids. The three of us trudged through the snow with shovels thrown over our shoulders. Ali didn't look entirely pleased to be out in the cold, but his curiosity had gotten the better of him. I came to a stop in a small clearing, recognising the markings I'd made on the trees.

"We're here," I said. I drove my shovel into the ground right above where I'd buried Roids.

"Now what?" Ali said.

"We dig."

"I swear to God, if you've got me out here digging up your stash of weird porno I'm taking half."

Tex sniggered and said, "Oh trust me, what you're about to see is a whole lot weirder than weird pornos."

"Let's just get this over with," I said, and the three of us set to digging.

The ground was hard with the cold, but we broke through easily enough. About four feet down the sounds of muffled screaming floated up to greet us. Ali gave me a perplexed look, shook his head, and kept on digging. The screaming grew louder as the hole got deeper until my shovel finally struck something with a loud metallic clang.

I scraped the dirt off the top of the box before pulling out a ring of keys to tackle the locks all the way down one side. It took a minute to get them all, but I got there in the end. I stood on top of the box, looked up at Tex and Ali, put my arms up and said, "Pull me out of here quick and get back even quicker."

Tex smiled. Ali nodded. His eyes were close to bulging from his head. They grabbed an arm each, and hauled me out of the hole.

We all jumped back as the lid of the box flew open and Roids came crawling out, not a scrap of clothing on his back. His screams bounced off of the trees and the smell of decay and burnt pork filled the clearing. Roids' flesh had been charred by the silver lining of the box. His lidless, yellowed eyes darted around as he dragged himself out of the hole. He'd lost a lot of his weight and muscle on account of being starved.

"Ali, meet Roids, one of the fuckers I told you all about, in the extra crispy flesh."

Ali looked like his fight-or-flight instinct was about to kick in. "What the fuck, Night? When you said you put him in the ground, I thought he was dead. How is this man still alive?"

Tex shrugged. "The supernatural, and all that shit."

Roids pulled himself to his knees, his screams died down to mumbles. He set his eyes on me first then looked at Ali, then Tex.

"Oooh, he looks hungry," Tex said.

"Dios mío," Ali said, crossing himself. "Fucking hungry? He looks more than hungry."

I stepped to the side and pulled out one of the Sisters as Tex gave Ali a push towards Roids.

"Dinner," said Tex, pointing to Ali.

Roids looked from Tex to Ali.

"Wait, what?" Ali barely managed to get the words out.

Roids' charred face cracked, the raw flesh splitting apart as his jaw extended and his fangs forced their way out of his gums. The process took little more than five seconds. Happy with his transformation, Roids sprang from the ground and straight towards Ali. His burnt dong flapped as he soared through the air.

Ali reeled back, fear flashed across his face, but only for a moment. The fear immediately made way for a look of anger as he pulled back and swung a fist at Roids' face. His knuckles struck hard, square on the nose.

Roids let out a yelp as he fell to the ground in a heap, clutching his face. Ali made no hesitation with his follow-up and swiftly stomped on Roids' chest before kneeling on it to rain down a heavy storm of fists.

After a minute of beating Roids' face into a messy lump of flesh and broken fangs, Ali stood up, spat on the ground and swung around.

"What the fuck is this?" he roared. It had been a long time since I saw him this pissed.

Tex put up a hand to calm him. "Like I said, supernatural shit. Now you know vampires aren't just in the movies."

Ali marched over and stuck a blood-covered finger in Tex's face. "So you've just tried to fucking feed me to one?"

Tex hesitated for a moment. "Yes and no."

I waved my gun to get Ali's attention. "It wouldn't have had the chance to bite you."

The sight of one of the Sisters seemed to calm him. He lowered his finger and took a deep breath.

"I'll cut the shit," Tex said.

"Please do," Ali snapped.

"I needed to see how you'd react. This is what we do for a living. We're not just regular old bounty hunters. We kill shit like this," Tex pointed to Roids, "and we could do with a few more sets of fists for a fight we've got coming our way sometime soon."

"Basically, we need your help," I said.

"You know there's easier ways to ask for it? If you had just told me, I would have believed you."

Tex sighed. "People say that, but they're never really prepared to see their first vampire. Lot of people don't survive their first encounter. And there's worse shit than vampires out there."

Roids attempted to crawl away while we were distracted, I put my gun away and moved to his side. He turned his mangled face to me and spluttered, "Please, kill me."

I put my boot on his shoulder and shoved him back into the hole, following him in. His flesh sizzled against the silver. "You're not getting off that easy," I said before hopping up and slamming the lid shut. His mumbles turned to screams as I locked up the coffin and pulled myself back out of the hole.

I caught Ali saying, "You've made your point, but I don't see how I can help."

"Let me worry about that for now. If you think you can beat the shit out of more vampires, just give me a call. I've got something that can help you."

"You do?" I asked.

"I do," Tex winked.

Ali walked over to the pit and started shovelling dirt back into it. "I don't understand; how do you both do it? This one was fucked up already, and it was quick. I'm not sure I could take a stronger one."

I threw a pile of dirt into the hole. "You remember Uncle Jimmy?"

"Of course I do. That little pendejo," he spat.

"That Hot Sauce he injected me with never left my system, pretty sure that's what keeps me going. You ever try it back in the day?"

"Fuck, yeah. I found a vial full after you were released and used it once or twice in some of the more difficult situations. Shit made me feel like Superman. That shit's still in your body?"

"Yup, still there. Everything you felt when you tried it, just get my heart rate up and it sets it all off every damn time. That's how I do this. Him though," I nodded at Tex, "he's yet to reveal his secrets."

Tex nodded. "Don't you worry, answers are a-comin' real soon. You're just gonna have to make sure you've got your nuts strapped on when they do."

"After this, mi amigo, I'm ready to believe anything," Ali said.

It took less than ten minutes to refill the hole and stomp the dirt back down into place. We spent the walk to the car in silence, letting Ali have a moment to process what he'd just witnessed. Tex drove him home, looking pleased with himself the entire way. He pulled up in front of Ali's door and we stepped out of the car with him.

"Think about it." Tex said, handing Ali a card with his home number on it. "We'll be back at my place in a couple of days. If you can stop in on your way back to San Felipe, I'd really appreciate it."

Ali took the card and stuck it in his back pocket before opening his door. "Sure thing, does this job pay?"

"It'll certainly pay better than bouncing drunks. Now go take a fucking shower. That vampire blood stinks."

Ali took a whiff of himself and recoiled. "Ooh, you're not wrong. I'll see you guys around, come see me before you leave, and I might have an answer for you. And, erm, thanks for showing me that tonight. Sure does explain a lot of things."

"It does?"

He nodded, leaning against his door frame. "When we first met, I said you had the eyes of a kid who'd seen the Devil. I was right all along."

"Yeah, I remember that. Anyway, go have yourself a beer and chill, you'll soon need it."

"I already do. Goodnight fellas."

"Goodnight," Tex and I said at the same time before getting back into the car.

Tex wound down his window as Ali waved, slowly closing his door. "Hurry up and get that blood off you before the smell attracts any more vamps looking for their injured buddy," Tex yelled.

Ali looked down at himself, his eyes widening. "It doesn't actually attract them, does it?"

Tex shrugged, stomped on the gas, and tore off down the road with a mischievous grin.

# Deus Ex Machina

We didn't have to wait long for Ali's decision. Mom called up the stairs as I was packing my bag, getting ready for the trip to Tex's place, Ali was on the phone. I sprang down the stairs three at a time and grabbed the phone, mouthing "thanks". Mom smiled in response.

"Hey man, what's up?"

"Pick me up on your way, I'm in," was all Ali said before the line went dead. I stared at the phone for a moment before noticing Tex was standing beside me.

"All good?"

I put the phone back on the hook. "Yeah, he's in. He says he wants us to pick him up on our way."

"Excellent, I was hoping he'd come with us right away, makes things easier. I'm all packed, by the way, you ready to go?"

"Almost done, I'll be about ten minutes."

Tex nodded and wandered off to sit with my mom.

I found them sitting drinking tea together when I came back downstairs with my stuff.

"It's a shame you can't stay for the New Year," Mom said, "promise you'll call?"

"I promise," I said with a smile.

Tex downed the last of his tea and sighed. "Looks like it's time to hit the road then. Mrs Nightingale, I can't thank you enough for your hospitality, and please do say goodbye to Edward for me."

Mom flapped a hand at him as she stood. "It's been a pleasure. Just don't be a stranger," she pinched my cheek, "and keep this one out of trouble."

"I'll do my best."

I spent a moment saying my goodbyes as Tex took our stuff to his car. Mine sat on the driveway, where it would stay, safe and sound; for now, at least. Mom gave me one last peck on the cheek as I slung my bag across my shoulder. "Don't forget to call, yahear?"

"I'll call when we get to Tex's place, and let you know we're home safe."

"Good, now go on, get out of here," she said with a smile.

I made my way down the path, popped the car door and threw my bag onto the back seat before turning to say, "See you soon, don't have too much fun without me."

I dropped down into the seat and pulled the door closed.

"Ready?" Tex asked.

"Hit it."

Tex set the car rolling as we waved goodbye.

We saw the curtains rustling as we pulled up outside Ali's room at the Hard-Nap a short while later. I stepped out of the car and pulled the seat forward. Ali came bounding out a moment later, fully packed and ready to go.

"Morning, fellas," he said as he threw his stuff, then himself into the back seat.

I put my seat back down and sat, closing the door.

"You're all sorted here?" Tex asked.

"Yup, I've handed in my keys, spoke to Jackie at the bar and everything I own is in my gym bag here. Let's go, I'm ready to hunt some vamps."

With us all in the car, Tex set off again and said, "Not so fast, sugar. We've got to get you to my place and get you kitted out before setting you loose on some poor sucker," he looked over to me, "and I think I've got some explaining to do when we get home."

I nodded. "You sure fucking do."

While Tex took the first shift driving, I took the time to clear up a few questions Ali had about vampires.

"So, what if you get bitten?" he asked.

"It seems like every bite will turn you into one if the vamp doesn't kill you first. It can take a while depending on the person, and on the damage and blood loss. So, if you're bitten, you might die, or you might turn. It depends."

"So I don't need to drink their blood or anything like that?"

"Nope. Whenever they bite down on something with any pressure, they release venom."

Tex nodded along.

"And if I'm scratched?"

I shook my head. "Nah, you'll be fine. I've been scratched plenty of times, it just hurts like a bitch."

Ali nodded, absorbing the info. "Cool, cool, cool. So do they only live off blood?"

I thought about it for a moment. "Pretty much, yeah."

Tex cut in, "They can get by on regular food for a while, and usually eat it for the fun of it. I mean, good pizza is still good pizza, ya'know? But they still need blood to survive and thrive. Doesn't have to be human though. They can live off of animal blood just fine."

Ali frowned. "So why don't they?"

Tex shrugged. "It's apparently not as good. Not as satisfying. Plus, they're almost all evil fuckers. They enjoy the thrill of killing people."

"Well, shit."

I looked him in the eyes through the rearview mirror. "Honestly, just don't let them bite you and you'll get by just fine."

The drive down to Sonora felt like it went by quite quickly; having an extra person in the car made for a little more conversation, and an extra pair of hands to take a turn at the wheel made it a decent road trip. After a few stops for snacks and a slash, we pulled up in front of Tex's house for nine the next morning.

The warm air of a mild Texas winter was a welcome contrast to the harsh cold back home.

The three of us dragged our way up the path, all ready for a proper nap.

Tex paused as he unlocked the front door and turned to Ali. "Oh yeah, don't mind the bird. He's an asshole, but he's harmless."

I was actually looking forward to seeing Gabriel. His swearing never failed to amuse me.

Tex swung the door open and stepped inside. All was quiet. No sign of Gabriel on his perch, and no frantic flapping at our faces. We piled into the house and dropped our stuff. I walked in and peered over the back of the sofa to the left and found Gabriel nestled into the sofa, surrounded by Tex's socks. He saw me and let out a gentle, "Caw".

"Looks like he's been raiding your sock drawer."

Tex took a peek and rolled his eyes. "Goddamn it, for his sake he best not have shredded them."

Ali leaned over to get a look, too. "Damn, now that's a fucking bird."

"Caw," Gabriel replied.

"He's not usually this quiet after I've been away a while, I'll have a word with him soon," Tex said. "Come on, I'll give you the tour. Night, you're in the room you stayed in last time. Ali, you're getting the one opposite."

I nodded and dropped myself down onto the sofa next to Gabriel while Tex gave Ali a walk around the house. I was just about to drift off when they returned. Tex gave me a slap on the shoulder to perk me up.

"I'm gonna grab a couple hours of shut-eye. By the looks of it, you need it too. Meet you back out here in about two hours?"

I yawned and nodded in response. Tex nodded back and wandered off to his bedroom. I followed suit, picking up my bags and heading to my room. Ali followed close behind, branching off into the room opposite mine and giving me a nod before closing the door. I threw my bags down, pulled off my coat, jeans and shirt, and threw myself face-first into the bed. I was out immediately.

I awoke to a knock on the door, followed by Ali's voice floating through. "Hey Sleeping Beauty, Tex has made omelettes."

The promise of food roused me quickly. I threw my jeans and shirt back on and was in the kitchen within seconds. I glanced at the clock, realising I'd slept longer than intended. Tex handed me a plate and followed me into the living room. Gabriel had vacated the sofa in favour of his perch. I took the spot where his nest had been, dropping down next to Ali. Tex took the armchair in the corner by the perch. We sat and ate in silence, watching some morning cartoons. Ali gathered our plates and took them to the kitchen when we were all finished. Tex waited for him to return before standing and shooing my feet off the rug in the middle of the floor.

"So, have you both got your nuts strapped on?"

"Always, mi hombre," Ali said with a grin.

Tex whipped the rug from the floor, revealing a trap door hidden underneath. "It's time to blow your minds." He flung the rug onto the armchair and started tugging at a chain around his neck. I'd never noticed him wearing it before now. At the end of the chain was a ridiculously large key.

"How the fuck have you been hiding that under your shirt without me noticing?"

He shrugged and said, "I don't always wear it, but it's hard to see if you don't know to look for it," before taking the key from around his neck and plunging it into a hole in the trapdoor. A loud booming noise came from beneath the house, followed by the sound of gears grinding and metal clanking. Ali and I glanced at each other, confused.

When the noises faded away, Tex hauled the door up and gestured for us to follow him down. I let Ali go ahead and followed close behind. Looking down into the hole, I could see nothing. Ali descended into an impossibly thick darkness and disappeared. I followed, holding my breath as I stepped down into oblivion. My head crossed the threshold and the room lit up. I stepped off the bottom step and looked up, seeing nothing but darkness where Tex's living room used to be.

"What the fuck." I muttered to myself.

"Strange, isn't it?" Tex said.

I turned to find him standing a few feet behind me, with Ali standing open-mouthed at his side.

"What the fuck is that?" I asked, pointing upwards. "And what the fuck is this?"

"That is hard to explain. This," he gestured around him, "is what I call the armoury."

I stepped forward to soak in the sights. All manner of strange objects littered the room: behind displays, on pedestals and stands, and mounted on the walls. I made my way over to a pedestal holding a beautiful, ancient-looking book; it was leather bound with intricate, decorative writing on the cover in a language I didn't recognise. I pointed at it and looked at Tex.

He grinned. "Remember when I told you I had the true texts, the real unaltered texts our Bible is based off of?"

"I thought you were shitting me."

"It turns out almost everything I say is true, most just can't bring themselves to believe it."

"Dios mío," Ali crossed himself, "and these?" he pointed at a pair of ornate wooden stakes with sharp silver tips and red splotches on the shafts.

"They're the Crucis Stakes, made from the cross Christ was crucified on." He picked them up and admired them before handing one to each of us. "They're infused with his blood, and tipped with the silver Judas earned for his betrayal."

I shifted the stake in my hand, looking at the blood stains on the wood. "So I'm touching the actual blood of Christ right now?"

"You are."

"Holy shit."

Ali chimed in, "Holy blood, actually. But my thoughts exactly."

"You did say you'd show me things that'd tear my mind a new one."

Tex smiled. "And I always deliver on my promises."

I set the stake back on its display and stepped back to admire the rest of the artefacts. All manner of weapons had been mounted to the left-hand wall, some fairly simple, some entirely confusing. I browsed the pedestals in front of the weapons: A pretty glass bottle filled with a shimmering silver liquid, an intricate puzzle box under a glass dome, an antique gold signet ring with a skull and the words 'Memento Mori' etched into it, and another ridiculously large key with the words 'Clavis Inferni' on it.

"What's the deal with your big keys?"

Tex came over, leaving Ali staring at a fleshy-looking mask that seemed to be watching us.

"Well, they unlock things."

"No shit. Like what?"

"This one," he pointed to the key around his neck, "opens this room, and only this room."

"And this one?" I asked, pointing at the one on the pedestal.

"Hell."

"What?"

"Hell."

"Fuuuuck off."

"See, you're struggling to believe, just like I said."

Ali appeared by my side, looking thoroughly creeped out by the mask he'd been looking at. "Hell as in, actual Hell, the opposite of Heaven? That key takes you there?"

Tex nodded. "Yup, it's called the Neatherkey."

"Remind me not to touch it."

"Touching it won't do anything," he picked it up, "see, you need to find a keyhole that fits. You can't use it otherwise, same with the key to this place."

Ali backed up and started looking around again, "I'm still not touching it."

I raised an eyebrow. "So if I were to find a keyhole to fit, it'd take me directly to Hell?"

Tex nodded. "Yup. They work as long as they fit."

"How many of these keys are there? Is there one to go to Heaven?"

"There's a few that I know of, and yes, but that one stays in Heaven." He set the Neatherkey back down.

"Where do the others go?"

"Well, of the ones I know, there's one out there somewhere that'll take you to the place on earth you want the most, and another that'll only take you to the men's bathroom in a bar in LA, but won't get you back. I don't fully understand them myself. Some seem to have a purpose, and some seem totally fuckin' useless."

"Weird."

"Very, but it is what it is."

I shrugged and made my way to the back of the room to look at a cabinet full of glowing balls about the size of baseballs that began to scream as I got closer to them. I decided not to ask about them and made a beeline for Ali, to join him in admiring what looked to be a jewel of the collection. In the right-hand corner, Ali stood admiring a shining white suit of armour, with a fancy matching longsword. The entire thing was decorated in intricate gold patterns with the sun blazing across the breastplate.

Tex joined us and piped up, "This, Ali, is what's going to help you smack the shit out of some vampires."

Ali stood staring, speechless.

Tex continued, "I call this, the Plot Armour."

"Plot Armour?" I snorted.

"Anyone who wears it is immortal. Impervious to any kind of damage as long as it's on. The armour and sword belonged to Lucifer."

Ali gave Tex some hard side-eye. "The Devil?"

Tex shrugged. "Well, kinda. It's complicated. But this is from when he was an angel, the 'Light-Bringer', and such."

"How come I don't get the immortality armour?" I said, feeling slightly miffed.

"Night, you have the Hot Sauce. If anyone needs this, it's Ali. You're a fucking superhuman. And you've witnessed me walk off a direct hit from a death beam."

I frowned at him. "Which you still need to explain."

"And I will in a minute, but Ali, doesn't have what we have," he looked at Ali, "no offence, pal, I'm sure you can fuck up your fair share of scum with your bare hands."

"Sure can," Ali said.

Tex turned back to me. "But he can't move as quick, or heal as fast as you can. I saw you take a bullet to the leg, and it had healed the next day. Ali takes a bullet and he's out of the game for months, or worse."

I nodded. "So Ali gets the Plot Armour, that makes sense."

"Good, I knew you wouldn't be a bitch about it," he said, slapping me on the back, "now come on let's head back upstairs."

I nudged Ali to tear his eyes away from the armour and follow us out. Once we were all back in the living room Tex dropped the hatch door and locked it up. I lay the rug back in place for him. Ali and I sat ourselves down on the sofa, taking a moment to think about the things we'd just seen. Tex disappeared then came back a moment later with three beers.

"I know it's only the afternoon, but I reckon these are necessary," he said, handing us a beer each.

We all sat back and took a swig.

He cleared his throat before speaking again, "And now, to get to the explaining thing. I'm gonna keep it short and sweet so keep your ears switched on, I'll give you the long version another time, okay? Okay. So, a long time ago, I made a deal with a certain somebody. The deal was: I serve as their supernatural bounty hunter for a period of time, dedicate my life to it, and find others to join the cause, and worthy candidates to take over the work when I'm done." He nodded at me. "In return, I'd gain a fast-track pass to Heaven when I finally depart this earthly plain, as well as immortality during the time I serve. Partially so I can carry on honing my skills and dispatching evil, and partially so I can't just shoot my way out of the deal if I ever decided I'd had enough. That's how I survived that death beam to the chest. That's not to say it didn't hurt like a motherfucker, 'cos I tell ya, it sure did."

I shook my head. "Would have been nice to know you've been immortal this entire time instead of having to worry the old man's gonna get shot in the damn head or break a fuckin' hip or something."

"I know, I apologise, but all that information would have been a lot to dump on you. It's just... I'm getting tired. Someday, that deal is gonna be offered to you. I needed to know you could handle yourself, and the burden of it. I've been doing the work for a long time, kid, longer than you'd expect. It's not a decision to be taken lightly."

I swigged my beer, looking to Ali for his opinion. He shrugged at me and stayed quiet.

Tex continued, "I'd have liked to have told you sooner, but I had to be sure."

Gabriel perked up, just in time to stop any argument over the matter. We all looked at him, startled by his sudden vigorous squawking.

"I better get that," Tex said, hauling his ass out of the armchair. He extended his arm. Gabriel hopped on to it and Tex walked him to the kitchen as he started yammering away.

Ali looked at me, confused. "What's that all about?"

"The bird's a celestial telephone; it's how Tex gets his information."

"Who's he talking to?"

"Gabriel, the archangel."

Ali's eyes widened. "From Heaven? Can I speak to him?"

"From Heaven, and I guess you probably could but you'd need to be able to speak their language."

"But he's an angel; surely angels know how to speak all languages?"

I was about to sip my beer, but paused. "Huh, didn't think of that. Would be so much easier if he just spoke English, then we'd be able to listen in and know what's going on."

Ali tapped his temple. "Something to enquire about soon, I think."

Tex strolled back into the room and placed Gabriel back on his perch. He hopped onto it and squawked, "Fucker."

Tex sat back down and grabbed his beer, giving us both a good eyeballing.

"I hope you ladies brought your big dicks with you," he said, "Gabriel's found us a hell of a job. Huge vamp nest out in the middle of the desert, not far from Vegas, all holed up in a Rest in Peace motel."

I nudged Ali. "I burned one of those down a while ago, and it was full of tentaclari."

"I don't know what a testiculary is, but cool."

Tex cut back in, "As I was saying, there's a big nest of them, including a potential lead to the big bad King Bitch himself. This is big, fellas, real big. In fact, I'm gonna call in backup for this one, can't hoard all the fun for ourselves."

"Who ya gonna call?"

Tex took a sip of his beer and smiled. "The Neon Nightmares."

# Almighty Tussle

The Neon Nightmares hit the doorstep about an hour after Tex hung up the phone. Ali wanted to know all about them and how they got from New York to Texas so fast. Something about being able to travel on the wind in their gassy neon forms, but I was far too interested in what was on TV. We'd spent the morning browsing what could've been another dimension filled with all manner of weird shit, and now the pair of fancy ghosts had appeared at the door. I just wanted to watch cartoons.

Both Neon Nightmares sat crammed onto the sofa between Ali and me, while Tex sat comfortably in his armchair giving them the rundown on the plan. They seemed enthusiastic, and ready to get to the murderin'. According to Tex, a whole nest of suckers with potential leads to Dominus Atrocitas had taken up residence in a Rest in Peace just outside of Vegas. We'd take a trip, rock up, throw down, and then walk away triumphant, one step closer to the big baddie himself. Maybe hit up a titty bar or two since we'd be in the neighbourhood. All tomorrow though, he wanted the day to rest up. So, while Ali and the Nightmares went for a walk to the nearest bar to get to know each other, Tex glued himself to his armchair with a book, and I sat and watched my damn cartoons.

* * *

Morning came and we were psyched and ready to party. But the hype wore off about eight hours into the drive. Ali shuffled and grumbled in the back seat. The entire suit of Plot Armour sat next to him and kept on falling onto him while he tried to sleep. Tex drove hard and fast. We tore down countless highways, tailed by a pair of green and purple clouds. The sun had set, the night air grew cold, and as we approached the location of the Rest in Peace, the anticipation hung in the air like electricity. Nothing like a sixteen-hour drive to get you eager for some physical activity.

"Five more minutes and we should be right on top of it," Tex said.

I turned in my seat and gave Ali a nudge. He woke with a snort.

"We're about to fight a fuck-tonne of suckers, how the hell can you sleep so much?"

He opened one eye and said, "I'll be immortal once I've got that armour on, what do I gotta be worried about?"

"Fair enough, we're almost there. Hope you've brought the lube to squeeze into that thing."

Tex looked at Ali and the armour in the rearview mirror. "It'll fit," he said.

We came over the crest of a hill, bringing the Vegas lights into view, way off on the horizon. A small pool of light sat tucked into the darkness of the desert on the right-hand side of the highway, the Rest in Peace, no doubt about it.

Tex nudged me and pointed. "There's a gas station up ahead. We'll stop there for twenty. I'll fill the tank, you grab us some snacks, and Ali, get yourself into that there armour. Don't wanna get dressed outside the motel in case we get made and swarmed before you've suited up." He looked out his side window. "You guys hear that?"

A cloud of purple mist appeared near the window and a disembodied hand popped out of the cloud, giving Tex the thumbs up. He nodded and eased off on the gas before turning in and pulling to a stop in front of a pump. I flung the door open and stepped out, taking a long draw of the fresh air as my joints cracked with happiness. Adrian and Leon, the Neon Nightmares, materialised beside me.

"I'm hungry for some jerky," Tex said.

I nodded and made my way into the store. The bell above the door went crazy as I walked in, with the Nightmares close behind. They split off in different directions to scour the store. I made a beeline for the soda and picked out some ice-cold Cokes. Leon turned the corner with an armful of snacks.

"Grab whatever, dude, I'm buying," he said.

I gave him a nod. Wasn't gonna argue. I met the Nightmares at the cashier with the stuff: jerky for Tex, chips for Ali and a big fancy-looking candy bar called 'Funky Cracker' for me.

"Sweet choice, bro, ever tried that before?" Adrian said, eyeing the candy bar as I placed the stuff on the counter.

I shook my head.

"Shit's got lil' pop rocks in the chocolate; it's like a disco in your head."

"Cool."

The cashier gave us all funny looks as she rang up the goods. I blamed the Nightmares. I looked quite inconspicuous in my black jacket and jeans, whereas those guys were the literal personification of big, screaming, neon lights, with their brightly coloured Letterman jackets and sunglasses at night. I grabbed a bunch of the stuff as Leon handed over a fifty and told the cashier to keep the change. I expected her to crack a smile for receiving such a decent tip, but she just narrowed her eyes at him and kept quiet.

I bumped my way out of the door and threw a can of Cola over to Tex. He caught it with one hand as he finished pumping the gas. Ali stood behind the car, trying to pull himself into the legs of the armour. I set his can on the roof of the car and dropped the snacks into the passenger seat. The Nightmares stood placing an assortment of food on the hood of the car, arranging them like a buffet and bickering over what looked best where.

"Could ya gimme a hand?" Ali said as he pulled the breastplate out of the back seat.

"Sure," I said and took hold of the piece, helping him strap it into place.

I had Ali strapped in and ready to go by the time Tex got back from taking a piss, browsing the store and paying for the gas.

"How do I look?" he asked.

"Impressive."

"Like you're ready to kick some serious dick," Tex said, cracking open his soda.

Leon and Adrian chuckled and nodded.

Tex gestured for us to gather around the trunk. "It just needs its final touch," he said.

We gathered and waited to see what he was about to show us. He clicked the lock open but held the trunk shut to build anticipation. When he was sure we couldn't handle it anymore, he threw the trunk open, revealing the hilt of a glorious longsword that matched the armour, poking out from under a blanket.

Adrian mumbled, "Damn," through a mouthful of chips.

Leon whistled.

Ali reached out to touch it, but Tex batted his hand away.

"Not yet," he said, "once we're outside the motel, you can whip it out and we'll send you in spinning." He slammed the trunk shut.

The hype fizzled back into life. We shovelled snacks into our faces and guzzled sodas as fast as we could, all eager for some action. I wiped my mouth with my sleeve as I crushed my soda can and threw it into a nearby trash can. Ali clinked his way into the back seat with a bit of a struggle. Tex popped the driver's side door and nodded at Leon and Adrian. They nodded back and burst into clouds of colour.

We pulled up outside the motel ten minutes later. Tex made sure to park at the far end of the parking lot, out of the way of any potential carnage. I stepped out and popped my door and pulled the seat forward to give Ali a hand out of the back. By the time I had hauled him out, Tex was at the trunk with Leon and Adrian at his sides. Ali and I joined them. I picked up the Sisters and strapped them in place. Tex pulled the longsword out from under the blanket and handed it to Ali. It looked like a faint light shone from the blade, but I put it down to my eyes playing tricks on me. Ali gave it a swing; it sang as it sliced through the air.

"Bitchin'," Adrian said.

Tex strapped on his holsters, gunned up and gestured for me to pick something from the goodies on display. I'd brought my favourite jacket with me, the one with all the hidden pockets, so I could afford to take a good amount of firepower. I picked out a nice sawn-off shotgun and slid it into my extra-large inside pocket, along with a bunch of shells.

"Take another, son," Tex said, "we're in for an almighty tussle."

I filled my pockets to the brim with all manner of tricks and treats while the Nightmares slipped on the Power Gloves they'd taken from Murder Nerd.

Tex pulled the trunk shut and took a glance at the group. Happy that everyone was prepared for one hell of a showdown, he set off walking to the reception, taking the lead. Ali swung Lucifer's sword over his shoulder and walked with a good amount of swagger.

Leon whipped his shades off, exposing the swirling mist he called eyes. He looked in my direction and smiled as he put his hand on my shoulder and said, "Let's go fuck some Draculas in the ass."

# Rest in Peace, Everybody

Tex pushed the door open and strolled up to the desk. The receptionist was a young fella with shoulder-length hair that didn't look well acquainted with shampoo. He sat behind the desk with his eyes closed and mouth open. Tex cleared his throat, startling the kid. He looked shocked to see five people suddenly in front of him. He glanced at Ali, standing in his suit of armour with a sword slung over his shoulder, then to Tex, who was standing smiling at him.

"Would you fellas like a room?" he asked.

Tex shook his head and squinted at the kid's name tag. "I hear you've got pests... Chad. We're the exterminators. Just point us in the right direction and we'll get to work."

Chad stiffened and almost fell off his stool. "I, uh... Nah there's no problems here bro."

Tex leaned in closer. "You sure, son? It ain't just any ol' vermin we're lookin' for, they're about my size, likely to be lots of 'em. Strange things, too. You witnessed anything like that, Chad? Anything weird?"

Chad looked around the room before leaning in closer. "Look man, they said they'd kill me if I said anything. There's loads of them, a whole bunch checked in a few days ago, all real creepy like. There's been a bunch of hookers coming over, and I haven't seen any leave. It's really giving me the shits, man."

Tex nodded. "Know what they are, don'cha?"

Chad shook his head, starting to visibly sweat.

Ali cut in, "Say it. You know what's staying here."

"Nuh-uh."

I joined in. "Say it, Chad. Vaaam…"

The colour drained from his face. "Oh God," he said, shaking. He ducked his head down and whispered, "Vampires?"

"Bingo, bro!" Adrian yelled.

Chad jumped with fright and stammered, "I don't wanna die, man. I'm just trying to do my job. Please, don't hurt me."

Tex put a hand on Chad's shoulder to reassure him. "It's not you we're here to hurt. It's them. Now, where are they?"

"They've got an entire block, man, rooms fifty to one hundred."

"Is anyone else staying here, anyone normal?"

"Only rooms two and four, man, I've been telling anyone else we're full but those rooms have been filled since before the… uh… weirdos showed up."

Tex gave Chad's shoulder a shake. "You did good, kid, may have saved a few lives by doing that. Now, I'm not gonna stand here and lie to you, son, that entire block has about thirty minutes of life left before it's most likely turned to rubble. Now what I need you to do is go tell those good folks in rooms two and four to stay in their rooms, then you lock yourself up in here and get under that desk, we clear?"

Chad nodded so hard he could have concussed himself.

Tex continued. "Good. And when this is all over, there must have been a gas leak or something. Lucky all those rooms on that block turned out to be empty, isn't it? You catch my meaning, son?"

Chad nodded even harder, "Yes sir. I didn't see nothing."

Tex patted his cheek. "Good man, now skedaddle."

Chad jumped off his stool, ran around the desk and out the door, heading towards rooms two and four.

I took the lead, pushing the door open and heading back out into the parking lot. "Looks like fifty to one hundred's this way," I said, gesturing for everyone to follow. "So, how are we doing this?"

Ali answered, "I guess just take a room each, clear it out and move on."

Tex nodded. "Likely the best way to go about it, but I doubt we'll get far before they all come swarming out. My bet is we start with a room each and just meet them all out in the parking lot once we have their attention."

Everyone nodded their agreement.

It was a short stroll up to the block, nice and out of the way, tucked away in a corner. Room fifty greeted us first, with room one hundred at the far end of the block, upstairs and right at the end. Light flickered out from the windows of a few rooms, but most sat in darkness.

"I'll take fifty," I said.

"Fifty-one's mine," Ali said.

Tex shrugged. "Fifty-two, I guess."

Adrian and Leon looked at each other. "You want three or four?" Leon asked.

"I'll take three, bro."

I took the Sisters out of their holsters and took my place in front of number fifty. I looked down the line of doors as everyone else got in position, ready to go. We took a moment to glance at each other until Tex gave the nod.

"Don't forget what you've got, kid," he said.

"And what's that?"

"Chainsaws for fuckin' arms."

I rapped on the door with the butt of one of the Sisters and waited for it to swing open. Grumbling and shuffling noises came through the door before it creaked open, revealing a tall fella with skin like rich chocolate, wearing nothing but his tighty-whities and a cascade of chip crumbs stuck to his chest.

I glanced to my left and saw everyone watching, waiting for the violence to start.

"Fuck you want?" he asked.

"Hello, friend, do you have a moment to talk about our Lord and Saviour Jes—"

"Get the fuck outta here," he snarled, about to close the door.

I jammed my foot in the door and said, "Well that's just fucking impolite. Now I said, do you have a moment to talk about our Lord and Saviour, Jesus Motherfucking Christ, you messy dickhead."

He flung the door open and came out, pointing a finger in my face. "Now listen here you little punk bitch I don't wanna hear anything about..." he caught sight of the guys lined up in front of the door. "What the fuck is this?"

## [Track 13]

"Salvation."

He turned back to face me and looked right down the business end of my big stinking revolver. For a second, I saw shock in his eyes before they flooded inky black and sunk back into the sockets. He snarled and bared a mouthful of fangs at me.

On your marks. Get set.

"Make your peace with Jesus now, you'll be seeing him momentarily," I said before pulling the trigger.

Go!

The sucker's face made a swift exit through the back of his head, leaving nothing but a ragged stump of a neck with blood flowing down his chest, washing away the crumbs and staining his nice undies.

With the gunshot still ringing through the entire block, the guys made their move. Ali and Tex gave their doors a large serving of boot, sending them cracking open, while Leon and Adrian blasted their way in with their Power Gloves.

A loud squeal came from my room, one of pure despair. I poked my head around the doorframe to see where it had come from. I caught sight of a second sucker, bigger, blacker and balls-out nude, dripping wet with a towel around his ankles.

He spotted me, looked down at my handful of gun, and roared, "You!"

"Me," I confirmed.

He swapped into his creepy face and came barrelling at me with his dong slapping against his thighs. I considered taking aim at it but thought I'd be merciful and blow the head off his shoulders, not off his shaft. I popped one off, splattering his thoughts all over the ceiling. A quick sweep of the room confirmed they were the only ones in there, so I made my exit and checked in on Ali.

I walked in on the sight of him cleaving a sucker in half. Two more lay on the floor, already decomposing. He followed his swing and twirled to face me, ready to take on another. He smiled when he realised it was me, but said nothing. I turned to check Tex's room and found him in the doorway.

"Come see this," he said.

We followed him out and spotted the Nightmares blasting huge blue laser beams from their Power Gloves, cutting through suckers, walls and doors. The commotion had gained some attention. Doors were beginning to open, and suckers started pouring out. As Tex had predicted, it looked like we'd be partying in the parking lot. Door after door swung open until almost all of them had multiple suckers charging out. My guess was at least sixty, maybe eighty, or even a hundred, against five. Good odds in our favour. We backed out into the parking lot as

119

the flood came towards us. All manner of vampires flew from their rooms. Neither gender or race mattered. We'd slaughter them all indiscriminately.

I heard Adrian laughing as he thrust his fist and swept a beam across a wave of vamps, killing at least twenty of them in one stroke.

"We need to get us a pair of those," I said to Tex.

"Nah, kinda takes the thrill out of the fight," he said as he pumped his shogun and blew a hole through a sucker's chest, covering a few of her buddies in chunks of titty flesh.

I could see his point. There was something satisfying about shooting a sucker square in the face one at a time, but that's easy to say when you're immortal. When you've got nothing to protect you but good aim and a large set of testicles, a Power Glove sure would come in handy.

Ali seemed to be having the time of his life too, swinging his sword with reckless abandon, taking off limbs and lopping off heads as if he were trimming some bushes. Leon seemed to share Tex's sentiments. He was using his glove sparingly, vaporising one or two vamps at a time, while Adrian opted to decimate dozens at once.

I heard a sucker yell, "Fall back and protect one hundred. Don't let them near the Lord!"

This caught my interest. Tex clearly heard it too. He caught my eye and pointed at the room. I nodded, putting two bullets into a sucker that had been bearing down on me while I admired the carnage. He fell to the floor in a heap, decomposing as he fell.

About thirty suckers had retreated and headed up the stairs to get in between us and room one hundred. Tex and I made our way to the stairs, flanked by the Nightmares. I watched as Leon burst into mist. The purple cloud he left behind flew up the nostrils of the closest sucker. She frantically scratched at her chest and throat for a moment before exploding in a rain of blood and gristle. Adrian popped off laser beams with a little more precision as we approached the stairs and left Ali in the parking lot to clean up the suckers around him. They were surrounding him, but he didn't care. A set of pearly whites beamed from his blood-soaked face as he bellowed with laughter, windmilling the sword around.

"You can all eat a doughnut off my dick," he yelled.

I tucked the Sisters away, all cosy, and pulled out my sawn-off for a little more crowd control. Tex reloaded his as we took the first of the stairs. A sucker came lunging down, trying to get the drop on us from above. I let him get within arm's reach before sticking the barrels of my shotgun right up into his taint and pulling the trigger. He exploded ass first, the buckshot tearing through the lower half of his body, covering Tex, the Nightmares and me in all manner of smelly, questionable matter. Something small and round bounced off my head and fell to the ground. I chose not to believe it was a testicle. What remained of the sucker sailed over our heads and landed face-first on the concrete behind us. The blast had split him in half but hadn't killed him. He pulled himself up onto his elbows and tried to army-crawl away. Adrian finished the job with a crushing stomp to the back of the head.

"Dude, gross," Leon said, "you've got brains all over your sneakers."

Adrian shrugged. "Night's probably just covered us in shit, bro, I swear I saw some corn fly past me. The sneaks will wash up fine."

The rest of the suckers had fully backed up to block the path from the top of the stairs to room one hundred. They sure as fuck had something interesting in there, and I wanted to shoot it. One had mentioned some 'Lord', and I was damn sure she didn't mean Jesus. I rounded the corner and got to the top of the stairs first. The balcony was only wide enough for two of us to squeeze down shoulder to shoulder. The suckers were packed in tight, twenty-eight of them left, all crammed beside each other, one behind the other right up to the door they were trying to protect. They all kept an eye on me, but none of them attempted to come forward and fight.

Tex appeared to my right, and the Nightmares came up behind us.

"Should we cheat and wipe the lot out with the Power Gloves?" Leon asked.

I replaced the missing shell in my shotgun, flicked the barrel back into place, and said, "Now where's the fun in that?"

Tex smiled and said, "Now what are we gonna do fellas?" loud enough for all the suckers to hear.

The Nightmares replied in unison, "We're gonna fuck some Draculas in the ass."

The suckers at the head of the queue were not too pleased by this statement. Two of them lunged at the same time. Tex wasted no time in taking out the one on the right, sticking his shotgun into the sucker's neck and blowing it out of existence. His head and body went in different directions. I aimed a little too high for my sucker and blew off the top half of his skull. The mouth still gnashed at me as he fell into a twitching heap.

I beat Tex to the next two and bust my other shell off right between them, taking off half of each of their faces. Tex jumped as they fell and gave them a double footed skull stomping just for good measure. He stayed crouched as he landed and pulled my jacket to get me down, letting the Nightmares squeeze out a laser blast each.

The beams cut through six suckers, completely vaporising their heads. Ten down, eighteen to go. I looked down to check on Ali and saw him down on one knee, breathing heavily. The entire suit of armour had been stained red. A gigantic pool of blood filled with dismembered corpses circled him, not a single sucker left alive.

Four suckers came at us at once, clambering over their dead buddies and clawing at each other to be the first to tear into us. I put my shotgun away and whipped the Sisters back out. Tex had put his away too, and had pulled out a hatchet instead.

I blew the knees out of my first sucker. She fell forward with a screech and raked her claws down my legs, from thigh to shin, shredding my jeans and cutting through skin. I gritted my teeth through the pain and stepped over her as she hit the floor, leaving the Nightmares to rearrange her face. Tex stepped to his sucker and swung the hatchet hard, right down the middle of his head. It split in two with a squelchy crack. The vamp's tongue lolled to the side as his eyeballs rolled in different directions, trying to see where either side of his head was going. I took my second sucker out with a shot to the heart while Adrian reached over my shoulder and blew a gaping hole through the chest of the other sucker who'd managed to land a few punches on Tex's face.

"Thanks," Tex said, pulling the hatchet out of his friend's head and kicking him to the floor.

The rest of the suckers backed up, packing themselves tighter to the end of the balcony and closer to the door.

"Our turn?" Leon asked.

"Sure," I said, letting him squeeze in front of me.

Tex stepped aside to let Adrian in front, too.

They both grinned and fist-bumped each other.

"Mind if we just finish them off?" Adrian asked.

Tex looked at me. I shrugged.

"Sure, but whoever's behind that door's ours, before you go and melt their face off."

"Deal," Leon said, turning back to face the suckers.

They took a step forward and stopped, both standing like John Wayne about to shout "DRAW!"

They both began thrusting their hips, slowly at first, then building up speed.

"Who's ready for a butt-fucking? Huh? Who wants it?" Leon said, thrusting at the suckers harder and harder.

Adrian thrusted just as hard. "Are ya ready, punks?"

They stepped forward, still pumping their junk at the crowd. The vamps backed up. I couldn't tell whether they were just trying to protect the door or if they were genuinely scared of the Nightmares' slowly approaching wangs.

"Oh God, here it comes," Leon yelled.

"Hooooo damn," Adrian followed, both of them now thrusting so hard each pump threw them closer to the suckers.

"Here we go, bro," Leon said, looking at Adrian.

A few of the suckers at the back had started trying to scramble over the railings to jump off the balcony.

The Nightmares both gave one last strong hump before leaning back and pumping their fists forward from their crotches, sending two massive laser beams tearing through the crowd of suckers. A spray of blood filled the air as limbs, heads and chunks of flesh flew in all directions.

We gave the carnage a moment to settle before stepping forward.

"A bit theatrical, aren't you?" Tex said.

Leon chuckled. "You have your fun, and we have ours. Door's all yours."

And ours it was. I stepped forward and crashed the heel of my boot into it. It smashed to the floor as I stepped inside. Two sights hit me at once. One was a gnarled old vampire, hunched over in the corner, the other was a young woman bound and gagged in chains behind him, wearing nothing but an old potato sack and the dirt on her skin. I aimed both Sisters at the old ball-sack-looking sucker as Tex and the Nightmares entered the room.

"Is this Atrocitas?"

"Not a chance," Tex said, "no way we'd get to him so easily."

"I dunno, he had a pretty heavy set of bodyguards."

Tex ignored me and stepped towards Old Crusty. "Where's Atrocitas?" he demanded.

The old vampire didn't look like anything resembling a human. Might have done at one point, but the years had betrayed him. He croaked out a laugh, hunching over even more. One extra-long fang jutted out from under his top lip.

"You fools," he croaked, "he'll slaughter you all for this. Your days are numbered. You're nothing but dead flesh. Meat for the King. You—"

BLAM!

A deafening shot filled the room. Tex had put a bullet right between Crusty's eyes.

The old sucker fell to the floor in a crumpled heap.

"Useless. Fucking useless," Tex said, turning to the door to walk away, "all that effort to be yelled at by some old goat."

I opened my mouth to reply when Crusty sprang from the floor and pounced on Tex's back quicker than I'd seen any vamp move before. The old fucker wrapped his arms over Tex's shoulders and plunged his dirty yellow claws into Tex's chest. Blood bloomed over his shirt.

"Oh shit, he's an iscarion."

I raised the Sisters and took aim as the sucker opened his mouth to tear a chunk from Tex's neck, but a hand reached over the top of Crusty's head and pulled him backward off of Tex by the nostrils. The woman from the floor had broken free of her chains. She pulled him back by the nose with one hand and grabbed his lower jaw with the other.

Tex turned to join me and the Nightmares watch in awe as the woman in the potato sack pulled Crusty's head in two different directions, ripping it apart without breaking a fucking sweat.

I dropped the Sisters and my jaw.

She looked at us with fury in her eyes.

"You bunch of arseholes," she said, "you've just cost me my shot at killing their fucking king."

127

# Potato Girl Kicks Ass

Shocked didn't even cover it. I was fucking astounded. The last thing I expected to see in a room guarded by over a hundred vamps was a young woman wearing a potato sack, ripping the head off of an iscarion sucker. It's hard enough to do to a regular vamp, but iscarions are extra tough. Even with my Hot Sauce in overdrive, it took the two of us to rip an Iscarion's head off back when I first met Tex. This girl was something else.

"I... uh... thank you," Tex said, rubbing his neck.

"You okay," I asked him, looking at his chest.

"Peachy, you?" he said, eyeing my legs.

I nodded.

"Damn girl," Adrian said, gawking at her.

She wiped the blood from her hands onto her sack, looking at us all standing around open-mouthed like a bunch of simpletons. Crusty began to decompose. She stepped back so his corpse juice didn't touch her bare feet.

"Do you have any fucking idea how long I've been carted about by these bastards? How long I've waited to do that to their boss?" she pointed at Crusty's torn up head. "Months, fucking months in chains, being fed scraps, and taking beatings from these vile creatures. They were taking me right to their leader, and you've fucked it, absolutely fucked it." She had a strong English accent. I found her cursing quite entertaining.

"We didn't know, sorry."

She raised a finger and opened her mouth to reply when Leon cut in.

"What the fuck are you?" he asked.

She looked offended. "What the fuck am I? What the fuck are you? A pair of neon clowns, an old cowboy, and I don't know what you're dressed as," she said, gesturing at my jacket.

"The length helps me carry more guns," I said, feeling a little self-conscious.

The clinking of Ali's armour came through the doorway before he did. He appeared at the threshold saying, "That was fucking fantastic, but which one of you shit my pants?"

Potato Girl took one look at him and put her hand on her head with an exasperated sigh. "And you've got a knight. Of course you have a fucking knight."

"Who's the potato girl?" Ali asked, looking around at us.

"Ginn," she snapped, "my name is Ginn, not fucking Potato Girl."

"Ginn," Tex said, "my name's Tex. This here's Night, those two are Leon and Adrian, and the guy with the armour is Ali. We were sent here to deal with the vampire nest."

"Well you've dealt with it, now you can all bugger off," she said, rubbing her cheek and smearing some dirt across it. She sat down on the edge of the bed and slumped over.

Tex turned to the guys and waved a hand to shoo them out of the room. They took the hint and cleared out, leaving the three of us to talk.

"Why did they have you chained up here? What are you to their boss?" I asked.

"Not now. It's a weird story," Ginn said.

"Weird? We've just slaughtered a hundred vampires with an armoured Mexican and two laser-blasting ghosts. Weird is what we do."

She raised her head from her hands. "Let's just say I'm valuable to their king and leave it at that for now please, I'm too hungry and pissed off to talk about it right now. Do either of you have any food? I'm honestly starved."

Tex and I took a moment to have a conversation with nothing but facial expressions before he nodded, decision made.

"Ma'am, we can help you," he said, "we have food, clothes, and we're after the same thing. I've been killing vampires for a long time. Their king, Domi—"

"Dominus Atrocitas, I know. Sounds like an edgy teenager gave himself a shitty nickname."

I nudged Tex. "That's what I said."

He gave me a look before continuing, "Atrocitas, yes. I'm trying to find him myself, we both are, Night and I. We could help each other, having a common purpose an' all. Come back with us, we'll get you cleaned up and fed, get acquainted and work together. Wha'dya say?"

"All I had to do was wait it out, and I'd have had him. They were taking me directly to him. Goddamn it," she sat up and slapped her thighs, "well I guess it's not too bad. He'll be after you soon anyway; if I stick around he'll reveal himself eventually."

"Come again?"

She pointed at Crusty. "For one, I've just killed one of his oldest friends. Secondly, you've just wiped out over a hundred vampires in one go. That'll get his attention. And finally, if I do help you, he'll have all the more reason to try and capture me again."

"How can you be so sure?" I asked.

"I'm quite valuable to him. And his friend there was quite chatty, loved to tell me all the things the boss would do to me if I ever escaped. And I have, and now he's dead, so I've made it pretty fucking personal."

"Well that's certainly something to think about," Tex said before extending a hand to Ginn, "but right now I think our main priority is getting you fed and clothed. That old sack doesn't look comfortable in the slightest."

She eyed his hand warily for a moment before taking it and standing.

"You're not wrong, it chafes like a bastard."

We made our way out of the room and down the stairs. Ali and the Nightmares stood by the car, chatting about the recent conquest. They spotted us coming and drifted into silence, waiting to hear what the next steps were. Tex popped the driver's side door and pulled the seat forward for Ginn to get in. She sat down and wiggled to get comfortable before turning to watch us out of the back window. Tex came around and nodded at the Nightmares while pointing at the wrecked set of rooms.

The entire block had doors, windows and chunks of wall missing.

"Destroy it," he said.

"Right on, bro," Leon said.

Adrian pumped his bare fist in the air while punching his gloved one toward the block. Leon followed suit, both blasting streams of lasers from their gloves, cutting through the building and reducing the whole block to rubble in seconds.

Chad the receptionist appeared to our left, with both hands on his head, watching the carnage.

"Man, what the fuck am I gonna tell my boss?" he said.

Tex didn't take his eyes off the rubble. "Gas leak son, this was nothing but a gas leak. What's left of those bodies will be gone in a few minutes."

The Nightmares finished their work and high-fived each other before turning to us.

"It's been tight," Leon said, "we wouldn't mind doing stuff like this more often. If you need us, just yodel into the sky from the top of the highest hill."

"Or, you know, just call," Adrian said.

They both whipped out their shades and put them on before throwing up peace signs and bursting into colourful clouds of mist with a bright flash. The sound of a voice saying "Deuces," echoed through the mist as it dissipated.

* * *

We all breathed a sigh of relief as we stepped out of the car and stretched our bones. Ginn slept the entire trip. By the looks of it, it was the first taste of comfort she'd had in a long time. Being a true gentleman, Ali was the first to offer his room to Ginn. Tex offered him an old camp bed in place of the couch, so we decided he'd bunk with me in my room. It'd be like the good ol' times in prison.

Ginn took a moment to gather her bearings before following us into Tex's place. She took her time stepping through the doorway, getting a good measure of the place before taking the chance on being locked in an unfamiliar place with three strange men. Not that she needed to be cautious. If watching her rip an iscarion apart was anything to go by, she could fuck up the three of us without much trouble.

Ali clinked by, carrying his armour to the bathroom for a clean-up, ready to be put back into the armoury void once it'd had all the blood hosed off it. I picked up the TV remote to put on a little background noise while everyone settled.

Tex came from his room carrying some clothes and a couple of towels for Ginn.

"Here, the bathroom's just down the hall, just tell Ali to wait. These look like they should fit you," he said. "We'll let you get cleaned up."

"A house of three men and you own women's clothes?" Ginn questioned, taking them.

"My late wife's, it's all I have for now but we can do a little shopping tomorrow. Get you something a little more… modern."

"Oh, I'm sorry. Thank you, though."

"My pleasure, ma'am. Wha'dya like to eat? I'll rustle something up while you're getting cleaned up."

"I'll honestly eat anything; I'm not fussy at all."

"Great, I'll whip something up."

"Thanks," Ginn said with a smile before heading to the bathroom.

Tex made a move right for the kitchen and rinsed the dried blood from his hands. I followed him in and took my turn to wash my hands as he started rummaging through the fridge. The rest of me would have to wait.

I sat myself down at the table, glancing at Tex's bloody shirt, then down at my equally bloody legs, thankful I could heal fast 'cos the deep gashes the vampire had left me with were stinging something awful. "What are we gonna do?"

"Well, I'm thinking about burgers and hot dogs. They won't take long, get that poor girl fed good and proper."

I rolled my eyes at his back. "About the girl I mean. You saw what she did to that iscarion. You think we can trust her? She could be a spy or something; bait, maybe."

Tex swung around with a handful of packaged burger patties and a jar of hotdogs and nudged the fridge door shut with his butt. "I don't see why we shouldn't trust her. Sure, there's something about her she's gonna have to explain but she says she wants the same thing we do, and I have a good feeling about her. We may as well work together. With her strength, we'd be fools not to."

"Let's just remember to stay on her good side."

Ali pulled up a chair and sat down. "We discussing the chica?"

I nodded. "Just figuring if we can trust her."

"She seems friendly enough," Ali shrugged, "and if she was gonna kill us she could have done so in the car."

Tex slapped the burgers down into the frying pan and gave it a shake. "We'll do a little shopping tomorrow then give her a test, see what she's capable of."

I raised an eyebrow, intrigued. "A test, you say. Wha'cha got in mind?"

Ali chipped in, "Gonna set a vampire on her like you did with me?"

Tex shook his head. "We know she can handle vampires. I've got something else planned. It'll be something new for you too, Night."

"As long as it's not a ventripede, we're good."

"No, not a ventripede, but it'll be a challenge, nonetheless. Give me a hand prepping this, if you would, please."

Ali and I got up off our asses and helped prep and plate up the food. Ginn walked in as we added the finishing touches, towelling off her hair. She scrubbed up well. Now that she'd cleansed her hair and skin of dirt and put some actual clothes on, she looked entirely different. What had looked like dark brown hair turned out to be a deep, rich red. Wet strands stuck to her face, accentuating her sharp features and jawline.

135

"What happened to the potato girl?" Ali quipped. "It's like seeing a grubby little caterpillar turn into a beautiful butterfly."

A smile crept onto her lips. "Keep it in your pants, hombre, you're barking up the wrong tree."

Ali held up his hands. "Don't mean anything by it, just saying you look like a whole different person."

She pulled out a chair and sat at the table. "Yeah, well, the potato sack wasn't the most flattering option."

Tex set a plate down in front of her as Ali and I joined her with our own plates, with a burger and hotdog each.

"If you get a little nostalgic for your old clothes, I have an old onion bag that might fit you."

Ginn snorted. "Funny bunch, aren't you? So what, do we need to say grace?"

Tex shook his head. "God doesn't buy the food, nor does he kick the ass. Only thing you thank is yourself for surviving, now dig in."

The words had barely left Tex's lips before Ginn inhaled the burger and got to work on the hotdog. The lady could eat. She'd fit right in.

"I heard you mention shopping?" Ginn said with her mouth full.

Tex nodded. "Got a couple of plans if you're up for it. I'm thinking of shopping first; get you a fresh wardrobe and some damn shoes."

"Eh, I've gotten used to not wearing shoes to tell you the truth."

Ali and I sat and crammed food in our mouths, listening to Tex's ideas.

"We'll get some anyway. Then after shopping, if you're actually gonna stick around and help us, we'll need to see what you can do, a test, of sorts. So, I've got something planned for you, something a little different to vampires."

Ginn nodded. "And if I pass this test of yours?"

"If you pass, we'll do some even better shopping, I'll take you to see Spaghetti-o Jones."

I stopped chewing and looked at Tex, but Ginn beat me to the question.

"Who the fuck is Spaghetti-o Jones?"

# Who the Fuck Is Spaghetti-o Jones?

Ali slurped his slushie so loud it startled me awake. I'd steamed up the car window and drooled down my chin. Ginn had called shotgun, so Ali and I were stuck in the back seat, and the man took up a lot of space. I'd been tempted to stay behind, but fear of missing out got the better of me. Plus, I had to see Spaghetti-o Jones for myself. Our shopping trip lasted a couple of hours. Out of all the outfits Tex had bought for Ginn, she decided to wear the most impractical. Knowing Tex had some kind of test planned for her, she decided to face it in hi-top sneakers, a crop top and some of the shortest silver short shorts I'd ever laid eyes on. Totally impractical for a fight, but hey she rocked the look.

She'd kicked her sneakers off and put her feet up on the dash, flashing her odd socks. "How long 'till we get there?" she asked.

"About twenty more minutes," Tex said.

"And what are we doing, exactly?"

"You're gonna show us your moves, then maybe we'll go see Spaghetti-o."

"Yeah, but, any specifics? Do you want me to fight some eldritch horror? Show you how to iron a shirt? What?"

Tex looked down at his shirt and grumbled, "Shirt's fine."

I chimed in, "You may as well abandon all hope of getting any specifics. Tex likes playing his cards close to his chest."

Ali nodded along then stopped and shrugged when he caught Tex giving him the stink eye in the rearview mirror.

Ginn huffed out a sigh and twiddled her thumbs. I understood her frustration. Tex's weird resistance to explaining anything and then giving you a big info dump at a random time used to piss me off like nothing else. I'd gotten used to it. Ali didn't seem to care, he didn't ask many questions. He just seemed happy to go with the flow and see what happened next.

"So what's your deal?" Ali asked.

Ginn twisted to look at him. "My deal?"

"Yeah. Night can do what he does because he's jacked up on Uncle Jimmy's Hot Sauce. You're what, a skinny-ass twenty-year-old ex-captive and you can rip vampires apart. You've got a deal. Why are you so valuable to them?"

Ginn gave Ali a hard stare. "I'm twenty-five. And what the fuck is Uncle Jimmy's Hot Sauce?"

"Doesn't answer his question, and I think we're all itching to know what your deal is. You tell us about yourself then maybe we'll tell you about the Hot Sauce." Tex said.

She stayed silent for a moment. "I was bitten."

"You're one of them?" Ali asked, sitting up straight.

"No. That's why they took me. I got attacked by a group one night, bitten. I think the one that did it wanted to change me, make me his concubine, maybe? I don't know. But one minute I'm walking home from the shops, the next I'm chained to a basement radiator wearing that fucking potato sack. They tried to turn me a few times, but it didn't work. I didn't turn into one of them, but I did change. I took all of the pros and none of the cons. Speed, strength, resilience, but no need for blood. Most importantly, no turning into an ugly fucker the way they all do. The creepy old one I killed even gave it a shot. He said his venom was stronger, purer. Still didn't work. So they kept me in chains, saying they were taking me to their king. They thought my resistance to their venom meant my blood could be some kind of —"

"A cure," Tex said.

"Yeah, a cure. I thought they'd kill me and leave me in a ditch, but the old one said the king would want to do experiments. He wanted me for a fucking lab rat."

"You think they wanted to find a way to cure themselves?" Ali asked.

Tex shook his head. "More likely they'd want to find a way around the resistance. Make sure they can't be stopped. I've never heard of anyone being immune to vampirism. You said Atrocitas will try to find you?"

Ginn nodded.

"And now we know why you're so valuable to him. If we can find a way to make a cure before he can find a way to beat it, we can wipe all his vampire vermin off the face of the planet."

"That's why I went along with it. I let them chain me, beat me and starve me all to get a pop at the leader, to take him out. Then you guys showed up."

"Good thing we did, too," Tex said. "Impressive as your abilities are, you'd have stood no chance. Atrocitas is the strongest of them all and will be well protected. Nobody can take him out alone, and in doing so you'd have lost everyone else the chance at finding a cure. You could be the key to saving countless lives."

Ginn shuffled her feet on the dash. "Yeah, I guess I didn't think of that."

"Only problem is, if you're valuable, that puts us in the firing line when he finds out where you are."

"You mean if?"

"No, when. He'll have eyes and ears everywhere. It's only a matter of time."

"Night, remind me to thank Gabriel for the info," Tex said.

Ginn gave Tex a puzzled look. "You need to thank your bird?"

"I'll tell you all about it later."

We'd been driving out into the middle of nowhere for a while. What started as a turn-off from the highway had turned into a drive down a sketchy dirt track. The car bounced along the uneven surface, throwing us in all directions. From what I could see, we were out in the middle of the desert. Way out in front, a large hill sat to the right, and the beginnings of a forest were to the left. And behind us, nothing but dust.

Tex veered off to the right, heading towards the hill. As we drove closer, what looked like the opening of a cavern came into view on the side of it. When we reached the foot of the hill, Tex brought the car to a stop and put the handbrake on.

"Here we are," he said.

"You've brought us to see a cave?" Ginn said.

Tex smiled and popped his door as the car's engine fell silent, stepping out into the sun. Ali pushed the seat forward and climbed out. Ginn stayed put, eyeing the hole in the hill. I followed Ali out his side and had a nice stretch.

Ginn pushed her door open, getting out without her shoes on.

"Gonna need to wear your sneakers, trust me," Tex said.

Ginn rolled her eyes and picked up her shoes before closing the door. Tex walked to the back of the car and opened the trunk as she pulled them on with a look of displeasure. Various weapons lay scattered around the trunk. Tex picked out a saw and handed it to Ginn.

"What? I don't get one of the guns?"

Tex shut the trunk. "Lady, you ripped the head off an iscarion vamp with your bare hands. I don't think you need firearms."

Ginn shrugged. "They look cool though."

Ali stepped over. "You know what's gonna look cool? A five-foot chica in silver hot pants kicking some ass with nothing but her fists."

"So, what's the test?" I asked.

"Well, Night, you're going in with Ginn while Ali and I relax out here. That there cave," Tex pointed to the cavern in the hill, "is home to a creature called a grimus. Horrifying creatures, you'll see."

Ginn squinted up the hill. "Why do we need to kill it? Way out here on its own, living in a cave. Can't we just leave it be?"

Tex chuckled. "Tell you what, you go into that cave and decide for yourself. I'm sure something in there will change your mind."

"Fine, if it's harmless I'm not hurting it. But if it kills me, I'm haunting your fucking house. C'mon Night, let's go see what's so bad about this thing."

"Yes ma'am," I said, stepping to catch up.

"Bring back its head," Tex yelled after us.

A foul smell greeted us at the entrance to the cave: the smell of death. Ginn turned to see if I was gonna go in first. I was not. She faced the cave and stepped into the shadows. The darkness swallowed us in a few steps. It took a moment for my eyes to adjust. I could just about see where we were going, but not very well. Ginn seemed to be doing just fine. I took a few more steps into the cave, following her.

"Oh fuck, Night watch your st—"

Squelch.

My foot landed in something both crunchy and mushy.

"Oh no no no, shit, no," Ginn said.

"I've stood in a giant turd, haven't I?"

143

I lifted my foot and pulled it back, bringing more rotten stench with it. I could just about make out her silhouette crouching down, looking at what I'd stood in.

"This is horrible, poor kid."

I bent down to see what she was looking at. "Wait, poor wha— oh fucking Jesus shit fuck."

I'd put my foot right through the chest of a dead child. I put a hand over my mouth, stifling a retch.

Ginn dragged the body to the entrance and out into the light. I followed. The kid looked to be a teenager, no older than fifteen, and in the middle of decomposing. I took a look at the pile of mushy organs on my boot and fought off another retch. I'd seen some nasty shit, but this took the entire cake. Thanks to me, he had a foot-sized hole in his chest. What I couldn't explain were his missing legs. Ginn stood by my side, covering her nose and mouth with her arm.

"Did you forget to bring his legs?"

"Couldn't see them anywhere."

"You still think we should let this thing off with a stern warning?"

Ginn shook her head, storming back into the cave. "This thing's as good as dead."

I followed her into the darkness. "Please tell me if there are any more dead kids for me to step on. I don't have vampire night vision like you."

She lowered her voice. "None that I could see. Shut up and hold this." She handed me the saw.

A chittering noise stopped us dead.

"You hear that?"

"Of course I heard it, you bellend. Up there, on the ceiling."

I followed what I could see of her finger up into the darkness and caught a glimpse of a cluster of green eyes glinting in the shadows. "How many of them?"

"Just the one. Back up. Slowly. It's coming towards us."

"What's it look like?"

"Gross. Like a giant spider, but it's... changing."

The eyes flickered out until only two were left. I backed up to the cave entrance, keeping my eyes on the set floating towards me. As we got closer to the light, I could make out more of the creature. The shape changed from the silhouette of a spider to something more slender. We reached the entrance and backed out into the light. I made sure I didn't stand on the dead kid again. The green eyes paused for a moment then flickered out as the grimus approached from the shadows. An upside-down human face floated out at waist height, smiling at us. It took me a moment to realise it was my own face. My face, but wrong.

"What the fuck." I said, moving to pull out the Sisters.

The rest of the thing came into the light. It crab-walked out on its hands and feet, its head tilted up to look at me with my own upside-down face grinning away. The rest of it looked like a naked human, but more formless flesh than anything defined. No nipples, no genitals, just smooth flesh bent over backwards and scuttling towards us.

I had my hands on the Sisters, ready to whip them out and get to shooting, but Ginn pounced on the creature. She wrapped her legs around the middle of it, straddling it like a rodeo horse. It acted like one too, bucking and screeching to get her off. It twisted its head around to get a better look at her, and the face started to change into something resembling her own.

I took a step back and watched as the grimus thrashed and writhed, slamming her into the walls of the cave. After a bit of rodeo, Ginn raised one hand, holding on to the creature's neck with the other. She waited for the right moment then smashed a fist down between its shoulders. The grimus let out a howl as her entire hand tore through the skin, leaving her wrist-deep in its back. She rummaged around for a moment, squeezed her legs tighter, and heaved her hand out of the bloody hole. A fistful of spine came with it, tearing up through the skin until it reached the base of the skull. The grimus stumbled and fell, taking Ginn down with it. She pushed herself out from under it and up from the ground as the creature twitched, blood gushing from its back.

I held the saw out. "You don't even need this, do you?"

Ginn looked down at her bloody hand. "Don't be daft."

I looked at her shoulders, already bruising from being slammed about. "You good? Took a bit of a thrashing there."

"I'm fine," she shrugged.

I turned to walk down the hill as she set herself to yanking the grimus's head off.

"How'd she do?" Tex asked as I approached.

"How'd you think?" I said, turning to point at her.

Ginn came skipping down the hill, swinging the head by a length of spine sticking out of the neck. Tex and Ali looked impressed.

"One big ol' noggin," she said, dropping the head at Tex's feet. "You got any water or wet wipes to get this blood off?"

"Plenty of water and rags in the trunk," Tex said as he bent down to pick up the head. "Creepy fuckers, aren't they?"

I looked at the upside-down face. "You can say that again. It killed a kid too, his body's by the cave's entrance."

"Yeah, they like to do that. They've got a taste for flesh. I'll get Spaghetti-o to call the authorities, have them collect him."

"We gonna go see him then?"

"Sure are, let's go."

Tex started to walk towards the trees opposite the hill, carrying the head in one hand.

"Where you going?"

"To see Spaghetti-o, he lives in a cabin in these here trees, about a ten-minute walk."

I stood looking from Tex, to the trees. Ali and Ginn appeared by my side, her hands washed clean of blood.

"What are we waiting for?" Ginn said. "Let's go to Spaghetti-o's."

# The Cabin in the Woods

Sure enough, after a short stumble through the trees, an old cabin came into view. It looked abandoned, as far as I could see. Moss had grown all over it and the door hung loose on the hinges. The only signs of life were a plume of smoke rising from the chimney and a small generator to the left of the building. Tex walked ahead of us. He put a hand out to tell us to wait behind as he approached the porch.

He stopped just short of it, raised the grimus's severed head and yelled, "Spaghetti-o Jones, I come bearing gifts. I call upon you to appear before us."

Ginn and Ali exchanged confused looks as a gust of wind swept through the trees. The branches groaned and creaked as they swayed. A great roar tore through the forest. It sounded like the wind, but I could have sworn it came from inside the cabin. The winds died down and the door creaked open.

An old dark skinned man appeared from the darkness, his face weathered and worn. He stepped out onto the porch, taking in the sight of Tex with the grimus head held high.

"Your offering pleases me," he said, with an impossibly deep voice before breaking into a smile, "and that's enough with the formalities, come on in." He turned and walked back inside, waving an arm to beckon us.

Tex followed him. We followed Tex.

A burning heat smacked me in the face as I stepped into the cabin. I quickly found the source. In place of a fireplace, Spaghetti-o Jones had pimped out his cabin with a small forge. An anvil sat in front of a blazing furnace and tools were scattered around every surface. Tex dropped the head down on what passed as a coffee table and pulled out a makeshift wooden chair from fuck knows where. Jones appeared behind us with three more.

Tex sighed as he sat, taking his hat off to fan himself. "Spaghetti-o, this is Night, Ginn and Ali."

Jones took turns shaking each of our hands with a smile. "Pleased to meet you all, I'm Spaghetti-o Jones. Or just Spaghetti-o, or simply Jones. Whatever's easiest for yous. Please get comfortable, I know it's hot as hell in here I do apologise. Drinks. Cold drinks? Beer?"

Everyone nodded. I eyed him with a bit of suspicion. I could have sworn he was dark skinned, but in the cabin, his skin looked lighter.

"Yes please, Mister Jones, that would be very kind of you," Ginn said.

I was about to ask why he'd called himself 'Spaghetti-o' when he opened a beaten-up old fridge to the right of the table. I caught a glimpse of the contents. Nothing but beer and tinned spaghetti-os."

"I trust everybody is okay with Chateau Lova?" Jones askes, handing out the beers, popping the caps off with his thumb instead of twisting them.

"You know I am," Tex said, taking a bottle.

Jones nodded and sat on a stool opposite us all. He popped the cap off his beer and took a long pull while he eyed the severed head.

"Thanks for sorting that for me by the way. Damn thing's been a pestilence ever since it moved into that cave. I presume there's a body or five to be collected?"

Tex nodded. "There is. And don't thank me, Ginn and Night did the dirty work."

"But mostly me," Ginn added.

Jones raised his bottle. "Then I am in your debt."

"So, what do you have for us?" Tex asked.

"Straight down to business, eh? I have one request before I show what's on offer."

"Shoot."

Jones turned to me, looking me in the eyes. "May I please see Maria and Sophia?"

What the fuck? "My guns?"

"Yes, please."

I un-holstered the Sisters and laid them down on the table.

"May I?" Jones asked.

I nodded.

Jones set his bottle down and picked up the Sisters with a smile. I made a note of his hands. They looked as worn as his face, but much less tanned than the rest of him. Ali and I exchanged glances, neither of us knowing how the fuck he knew about the guns.

"Hello ladies," Jones said, "it's good to see you again. Yes, it has been a while. Too long."

"You can hear them?" Ali asked.

"I can indeed."

"I thought the whole story behind them was just a legend."

Jones shook his head. "Not just a legend at all, my friend."

"So, my ancestors' souls are actually in the guns?"

"They are. They say they're very proud of you, you've done great things. And you too, Isaac."

I frowned, wondering if Tex had told him my full name already. "What are they saying?"

Jones raised a finger—darker than before—from Sophia's grip and lifted the guns closer to his ears. "They say you've given them a great purpose, and they're having a hell of a time killing vampires and the like with you. They're happy to be part of the posse, they say. Night, Maria says as much as she likes the shoulder holsters, she'd prefer a hip one to be closer to your... oh. Oh Maria, you filthy harlot."

Ginn snorted and prodded my arm. "Your gun fancies yoooou."

Ali's cheeks turned red. "Yeah well don't be getting too fond of that thought; I don't want my friend turning into my new great, great, grandfather or whatever that would count as."

Jones smiled, ignoring Ali, still holding the guns to each ear like a pair of novelty telephones. "Yes. Yes. Oh of course I will, I have no doubt she'll do just fine. Yes. You make sure he does. I will, of course. Good to speak to you too. Sleep well. Goodbye." He set the guns back on the table. "Maria and Sophia give everyone their love."

151

I picked them up and tucked them back into their holsters. "How can you do that?"

Jones flicked his thumb across the tip of his nose and winked. Just as cryptic as Tex. I should have known. Something about him intrigued me, though. My gut told me he wasn't a normal guy, mostly on account of the fact that he seemed to be shifting between skin colours. Talking to the guns confirmed it. But there was something else. Some strange vibe about him I couldn't figure out.

Tex finished off his bottle, slammed it down on the table with a gasp then stood. "Aaahh. Mind if I grab everyone another?"

"Help yourself. Just don't touch my Os."

Tex chuckled and made his way to the fridge. "I wouldn't dare. So, what's on offer Spaghetti-o?"

Jones pushed his chair back and stood, raising a finger into the air. He shuffled to the back of the room and began to rummage around the forge. He picked up an ornate box, similar to the one the Sisters came in, and a long roll of cloth before coming back to the table. Tex joined him, placing a fresh bottle in front of each of us.

Jones set the box down in front of Ali. "For one Alejandro Santos, I give you the Reapers."

Ali eyed the box before slowly opening the lid to reveal a pair of revolvers similar to the Sisters, made of a dark red metal with a matte finish and ornate grips.

"Dios mío, they're beautiful."

"They're the Brothers to the Sisters, you could say. A perfect match in quality and craftsmanship, but unfortunately they come without souls attached."

Ali sat and stared in wonder as Jones placed the roll of cloth in front of Ginn. "And for one, Ginny Tay—"

Ginn gave him a stern look.

"For Ginn," he corrected, "I give you the means to cause destruction like you've never dreamt possible." He whipped the roll of cloth open across the table to reveal what looked like a pair of mechanical swords made of the same crimson metal as Ali's guns. Straps hung from them in various places.

Ginn frowned at them, with a look of confusion on her face. "Thank you, but what are they?"

Jones grinned. "Give me your arm, my dear."

Ginn hesitated for a moment then stretched her arm out.

Jones picked up one of the blades and set about attaching it to Ginn's arm. "What you do is... you strap them to your arms, like so. You take this bit into your palm, like so," he finished strapping it in place and tucked a mechanism into her hand, "and when you're ready, you squeeze."

Jones sprang back and waited for Ginn to take her cue. She looked at the mechanism in her palm for a moment before squeezing. The blade running up the length of her forearm shot out from above her fist. The tip came to a stop an inch in front of Jones's nose.

"Holy shit, that's bloody fantastic," Ginn said, "thank you!"

153

Jones bowed and then turned to me. "And for you, Isaac Nightingale," he paused to rummage around in his pocket before pulling out a closed fist, "I give you the key to your salvation."

I held out my hand. Jones dropped what he was holding into my palm, and I couldn't have been more disappointed.

Tex leaned over to get a look.

"A broken key?"

Jones's gift to me was the top half of a large old key, just a stick of metal with an ornate head and a chain through it. Entirely useless.

Jones nodded. "Wear it around your neck at all times. Put it on now and never take it off, you never know when you'll need it. But you'll need it eventually."

I gave him a good long eyeballing with the key in my hand.

"Better do it," Tex said, "just in case."

I shrugged and slung the chain over my neck, struggling to hide my disappointment.

"What do we owe you for these?" Ali asked.

Jones took a long swig of his beer before pointing to the severed head. "Your debt is already paid. Now I'm afraid I must get back to work. Night, Ginn, Ali, it's been a pleasure to meet you. I hope your gifts will serve you well, and hope we meet again. And Tex, a pleasure doing business. As always."

Tex raised his bottle. "Until next time, old friend."

Jones raised his bottle in response and emptied it with one last drink before slamming it onto the table. It hit the wood with a thunderous crack as the flames of the furnace roared to life, filling the room with a flash of blinding light. It took a moment for my eyes to readjust from the flash, and when they did, Jones was gone.

Ali and Ginn looked around the room, shocked by his sudden disappearance.

I looked straight at Tex and asked, "What the fuck is Spaghetti-o Jones?"

# Scars

Gabriel greeted me in his usual offensive manner as I stepped through the door and into Tex's house. He had no news. No new messages on the flying answering machine. With that in mind, I made a beeline for the telephone to call Mom. It was getting on to about six in the evening and the fact that it was New Year's Eve completely slipped my mind, and if I didn't call for a chat I'd be on the business end of a flip-flop on my next visit.

Ginn came in last and closed the door behind her. She had the swords wrapped up and pinned tight against her chest. She and Ali had big shit-eating grins plastered across their faces. I watched them sit down on the sofa to admire their new toys as I stood with the receiver to my ear.

Mom picked up after a few rings. "Hello?"

"Hi, Mom."

"Sweetie, hey," she said, sounding out of breath.

"Everything okay?"

She wheezed for a moment. "Yes, yes, Ed's just been showing me some new dance moves, we're going out tonight. How are you? When are you coming home?"

"That's good, hope you have a nice time. And I'm okay, I made a new friend recently so there's four of us living here now. And I'll come visit soon, I promise."

"Oh? Living there? Is Texas just going around adopting anyone he makes friends with?"

156

I chuckled. "Pretty much yeah. She's fitting in quite nicely."

"She? A lady, in your boy's club?" Mom sounded surprised.

"Strangely yes."

"What's she like? Is she nice? When do I get to meet her? Is she maybe more than a friend?"

I rolled my eyes at the wall. "Don't get too excited, she's just a friend and that's all. You'd like her though, she's English."

"Ooh, how lovely. Well, if she's part of your little gang she's welcome back home any time, I'll make her my special poutine."

"I'm sure she'd love that."

"Shoot, honey I'm sorry, I've got to run. Talk more soon, okay? Hope you have a good night."

I hesitated for a moment, taken aback by the sudden end to the conversation. I'd expected at least an hour, not little more than a minute. "Oh, okay. Have a good time. Love you."

"Love you too, sweetie. Bye-bye."

"Bye Mom," I said a second before the line went dead. I stood with the phone to my ear for a moment, listening to the empty line before putting it on the hook. I'd been looking forward to a good talk. I felt a twinge of disappointment, but also happiness from knowing Mom was going for a good night out.

I wandered over to the sofa and sat myself down between Ali and Ginn.

Ali leaned over and said, "We're all going for a few drinks in a little while, you down?"

"Where'd you have in mind?"

"The Fire Pit, I've been itching to visit."

Ah, The Fire Pit. The local dive with the motto: 'Booze, Babes and Barbeque,' a fine place to see out the year if I'd ever known one. It lived up to the motto too, I'd been with Tex a couple of times and it was indeed filled with booze, babes and barbeque, and mighty good barbeque at that. The mere mention of it set my stomach rumbling and mouth-watering.

"Fuck yes."

"Good," Ginn cut in, "I've known you lot a grand total of two days, and you've already had me butchering monsters. Somebody owes me a goddamn drink."

A shower and a change of clothes later, and we were on our way. The warm evening air caressed my skin as we left the house; it felt refreshing to be going somewhere in nothing but jeans and a T-shirt. No heavy jacket filled with ammo, no guns strapped to me, and no driving jacked-up cars for hours on end to go kill something, just a nice stroll to a bar with friends, some semblance of normal.

The Fire Pit sat on the eastern edge of town about a fifteen-minute walk from Tex's place, right at the end of a long dusty road. It wasn't hard to miss. If their giant orange neon sign wasn't enough of a beacon, there was also their namesake: a giant fire pit out front, lit every night at dusk. The towering flames drew people like moths to a lamp. I had been before, but it was a first for

Ali and Ginn. Ali looked like a kid on his way to a toy store, Ginn proved a little harder to read. She soaked in the sight with a face set like stone.

The heat of the Pit scorched my face as we passed. I took a deep sniff to inhale the smell of the woodsmoke. A line of well-cared-for motorcycles sat parked to the left; the light of the flames made them gleam. I took a moment to admire them, thinking they looked somewhat familiar. Tex held the door open for us, Ginn's stone expression cracked into a smile as the sound of roaring laughter and loud rock music flowed from inside. Ali strutted through the door as if he was home. Ginn and I followed, taking in the sights as Ali made a beeline for an empty table. The bar sat to the right of the entrance. A small stage sat at the far left, with tables dotted between the two. Most were occupied, mainly by groups of men clad in leather, but a few groups of ladies were dotted around, and one or two tables were taken by families. Two groups caught my eye: one was a bunch of bikers I felt like I recognised, and the other was a trio of ladies sitting at a high table near the bar. One lady of the three had snagged my attention. I caught her checking me out as I walked in, so I returned the favour. Jesus Christ, what a pretty face. Black hair, red lipstick, and eyes so green you'd think she'd sucked out her eyeballs and jammed crystals into the sockets. I looked back to see Tex standing at the bar and gave her a smile as I pulled out a chair and sat down.

Ginn sat to my left and nudged me saying, "You've pulled already dude. Go buy her a drink."

I snorted and wiggled my eyebrows at her, feeling more than a little awkward. I didn't even know where to start. I hadn't really ever tried to chat up a woman. I always had Suzie, so I hadn't honed my chatting-up skills beyond anything more than corny jokes to make her laugh. And while they worked on Suzie, I doubted they'd work on many other women.

"Yeah, maybe later."

Ginn and Ali fell into conversation as I scanned the bar, looking for any signs of potential trouble. When all you've done for a long time is put yourself in danger, it can be hard to switch off the radar. Nothing suspicious caught my eye, just a bar full of regular humans. I let out a sigh and slumped down into my chair. A glass of beer appeared in front of me. I nodded my thanks to Tex and pounced on it to calm my nerves.

Tex sat down with a loud sigh and eyed me to catch my attention. "Overheard a pair of ladies talking about you, boy. One of them has a fancy for you."

I took a couple of big gulps of the beer before tearing the glass from my lips. "The black haired one?"

"I think so," Tex said.

Ginn leaned over the table. "She's been giving him the bedroom eyes since we walked in, she'll have his trousers off by the end of the night."

"How about we stop worrying about what happens to my pants and just fucking drink, eh?" I said, holding up my glass.

"I'll drink to drinking," Ali said, raising his glass. He faced me. "Here's to old friends, new friends, and freedom."

"Cheers," Ginn said.

Glasses clinked together and I threw the rest of my drink down my throat in one go.

"Thirsty?" Tex said.

"Very," I replied, "another?"

Tex looked down at his glass, still full. "I mean, if you're getting a round it'll not go to waste."

I pushed myself up from the table and looked at Ginn and Ali. Ali nodded.

Ginn pushed her chair back. "I'll come with."

I shrugged and turned to make my way to the bar, making brief eye contact with the black haired woman as I walked by. I stood at the bar waiting to be served while trying my best to keep my eyes on the wall of liquor bottles. Ginn stood with her back to the bar, leaning against it and running her eyes over the clientele. I was about to catch the barmaid's attention when she elbowed me in the ribs.

"Be cool, she's coming over," she said out the side of her mouth.

My heart jumped into my throat. A second later, the black-haired lady was standing to my right, leaning on the bar and twirling a lock of hair around her finger.

"What's a girl gotta do to get a drink in here?" she asked. Her voice was soft and musical with a strong southern accent.

My chest tightened. "I uhh, yeah, service is a bit slow, isn't it?"

"Gorgeous guy like you, I woulda thought the barmaid would be right over."

I gave her a nervous chuckle. "Nice of you to say, but I'm not getting lucky."

She smiled and moved closer. "Oh I don't know about that. How's about you and me get to know each other?" The bedroom eyes were in full force.

My mind blanked. "Sorry, I'm, erm... spoken for."

"Oh," she said, the sparkle leaving her eyes, "well she's a lucky girl."

"Thanks," I said, smiling awkwardly. My stomach was in knots. I'd taken a strong liking to her, but I just couldn't talk to her. As much as I wanted her company, every fibre of my soul screamed 'no'.

"Silly me, I've forgotten what drinks I was supposed to get, I better go check. You guys have a good night."

"Yeah, you too."

She hesitated for a second before pushing herself from the bar and making her way back to her friends. She gave them a disappointed shrug as she approached her table.

Ginn had already ordered the drinks when I turned back to her.

"What the fuck was that?"

I pulled out a fifty and handed it to the barmaid. "What?"

"That entire car crash I just witnessed. Why'd you turn her down? To put it like a Texan: I bet she bangs like a shithouse door in a strong wind."

I shrugged.

Ginn rolled her eyes and took the change from the barmaid while I grabbed two of the glasses. She grabbed the other two and followed me back to our table.

Tex and Ali looked at me with eyes full of expectation as I sat down.

"Well, how'd it go?" Ali asked.

Ginn answered for me, "He rejected her. It was brutal."

"It wasn't brutal."

"Night, she could tell you're not spoken for. Poor girl put herself out there and you didn't even have the balls to tell her why you weren't interested."

"Look, it's complicated."

"It's not complicated; you could have just told her the truth instead of being a bitch about it."

Tex and Ali exchanged a look. Tex put his hand out to calm me, but I spoke before he could diffuse things.

## [Track 17]

"What do you want me to do? Huh? Should I go back over there and say, 'Hey sorry I can't talk to you, the trauma of watching the love of my life get fucking butchered when I was a teenager has left me incapable of allowing myself to feel any kind of affection for another woman'?"

Ginn's frown disappeared as her face dropped.

Tex and Ali sat glancing at each other, looking like they couldn't decide whether or not they should say something. The silence stretched on for what felt like hours.

"Oh God, I'm so sorry," Ginn said after a few seconds, "I didn't know. That was incredibly insensitive of me."

The Hot Sauce raged through my heart. I took a breath to calm down.

Ali clapped a hand onto my shoulder and gave it a squeeze. "It's okay buddy."

I shook my head. "Sorry for snapping. It's just a sore subject, but you're right, you didn't know. I've never really spoken about how it makes me feel."

"Trauma can really fuck with a person," Tex said.

I tapped my glass, mulling over what to say. "It's just hard, you know? Like, sure, I still find people attractive, but there's something in here," I tapped my forehead, "something telling me I can't be close to anyone in the way I was with Suzie in case it happens again. And it feels like it would be a betrayal. It makes me feel... hollow."

Ginn put her hand on mine to calm my tapping and gave me a gentle squeeze. "Do you mind if I ask what happened? I realise I don't actually know anything about any of you, other than what I've seen the past couple of days."

I sucked in a lungful of air and felt like my body deflated as I let it out. "We were nineteen. Suzie and I had

164

been together since we were kids. Not like 'together' together, we started off as friends. Best friends. Once the hormones kicked in, we grew closer. I always loved her, though, from day one. It was the summer of seventy-two when it happened; we'd been having a hell of a time. We were on our way back from the carnival and bumped into a couple of guys in the woods. They turned out to be vampires. One of them beat the shit out of me, almost killed me, while the other tried to rape Suzie. She fought him off, though. She always was a fighter. But you know what vampires are like, unless you're jacked to fuck, you don't stand a chance. So he killed her: ripped her throat out right in front of me while his buddy made me watch. I got the blame, was carted off to prison, kicked a rapist's dick off, met this asshole," I nodded towards Ali, "and then got myself injected with a superhuman fighting drug that put me in a coma for eight fucking years. That's the short and sweet of it."

Ginn sat staring, eyes and mouth both wide open.

"That's not all," Ali said, nudging me.

I continued, "Then I was proven innocent and released from prison. That was back in March. It didn't take me long to decide I needed to find the guys who killed Suzie, so I set off looking pretty much immediately. First stop in a Rest in Peace motel, I was nearly eaten by tentaclari. Then, thanks to Ali I found the Sisters. Took them to LA to test 'em out, met a bunch of friendly monsters, learned some new moves then found out Suzie's murderers were on their way back to my town. Stopped off for a drink in a place called Saltstone and met this one in a bar full of suckers," I pointed to Tex, "and here we are."

"You've only been out of a coma for what, nine months?"

I nodded. "Yup."

"So did you find her killers?"

"He sure fuckin' did," Tex said, "but that's a story for another time, trust me."

I sighed. "So yeah, I guess all of that is part of the reason I can't really talk to the ladies. Stick a supernatural horror in front of me and I'm golden. But an attractive woman? Now that's when the fear kicks in. Feels like I'm all thunder and no lightning."

"I'm so sorry. I really put my foot in it, didn't I?"

"It's fine, really. Like you said, you didn't know."

Ginn took a big gulp of her drink and then looked at the other guys. "Does anyone else have a tragic backstory I should know about?"

Both guys raised their hands.

"Quite a set, aren't we?" Ginn said, "Tex, shoot."

Tex dropped his hand. "Much the same as Night, my wife and son were murdered by vampires. I didn't want this life. The work I do, I've been doing a long time. But I wanted a quiet, peaceful life. Used to own a ranch, you see. I abhorred violence. There's a lot we need to explain in time, but my job comes with certain benefits."

"Like immortality," Ali said.

Ginn turned to him, "What?" Then to Tex, "What?"

Tex gave Ali a good amount of stink eye. "Yes, immortality, I'm invulnerable for as long as I serve under

166

contract, but that's not important right now. What I'm saying is I didn't want it. I turned this life away when I was first offered it. If I'd only accepted sooner, I could have stopped what happened to my family. But I didn't, and they died. And I ended up accepting anyway because I had nothing left to lose. I wanted vengeance and a chance to redeem myself. That's all I'll say on the matter right now. But hey, I'm writing my memoirs. You can read all about it when they're finished."

Ginn raised an eyebrow. "Just how long have you been doing this?"

"A lot longer than you'd think."

"I dunno, my friend, you are old as fuck," Ali said with a laugh.

Tex snorted. "Son, I'm older than fuck."

"So, what about you, Ali?" Ginn asked.

Ali opened his mouth to speak when a heavily tattooed arm appeared and set a glass of whiskey down in front of him. More appeared, putting glasses in front of each of us. The arms belonged to four of the bikers I thought looked familiar.

The one standing to my left, a heavy ZZ Top-looking fella clad in full leather, spoke first, "Sorry to interrupt, but we figured we owed you fellas, and lady, a drink."

Tex squinted at them. "What for?"

"We clocked you right away, you saved our asses a while back in Saltstone."

"I knew you looked familiar," I said, "you're the group from the Salty Dog."

ZZ Top nodded. "That's correct, and you and your friend here are the two vampire killers."

"Vampires, among other things," Tex said.

"While we're grateful you saved our asses, we wanted you to know we found another nest of vamps a couple of weeks ago. We lost a few good men, too. Was wondering if you could do what you do? We can pay."

Tex held up a hand. "No payment necessary gentlemen. Where's the nest?"

Ginn looked from Tex to the bikers with a huge grin on her face. "This is so cool, I feel like I'm in a secret badass club," she said to Ali.

He gave her a slow wink. "You are."

ZZ Top continued, "There's a titty bar in San Antonio called the Titty Twirler. Some of the finest pussy you'll ever lay eyes on but—,"

"The finest pussy?" Ginn snorted.

"Apologies miss. What I mean is they're beautiful ladies, all of them, but they're all dirty stinking vampires. They lured us in good, fools that we are. A bunch of the boys went for lap dances and never came back. Something felt off so we hightailed it outta there fast. Found our friend's bodies in a dumpster round back, drained of blood."

Tex raised his glass of whiskey and nodded. "We'll see to it gentlemen, don't you worry."

"Much obliged," ZZ Top said with a nod, "if you won't accept cash, at least let us buy your drinks for the night."

"Deal," Ali said, before Tex could respond.

Tex shrugged. "Sounds fair."

ZZ patted me on the shoulder. "We'll go tell the barmaid to put your drinks on our tab. You guys enjoy your night then, and have a happy New Year."

"You too," I said.

The bikers made their way back over to their table as the opening bars of Queen's 'Another One Bites the Dust' filled the bar. I tapped my foot and drummed on the table in time to the beat.

"Looks like we've got some work to do," Tex said, "set off in the morning?"

I nodded. "Sounds good, does the name of the place sound familiar to anyone else?"

They all shook their heads.

"Hmm, 'Titty Twirler'. They should use something like that in a movie someday."

Tex nodded. "Fun name ain't it, but what kinda movie would use that?"

"Oh well," I said, brushing the thought away, "I'm looking forward to shooting some attractive lady vampires instead of all the ugly dudes we usually get."

Ginn gave me a prod. "And who knows, maybe shooting some sexy suckers will be the therapy you need to get over your fear of girls."

"Maybe," I said, still drumming my fingers on the table, "I just hope this song isn't some kind of foreshadowing."

# Bright Lights, Big Titties

I was the first to get out of bed, so after a quick shit, shower and shave, I whipped up breakfast. We'd had a night of heavy drinking, and hangovers were hitting hard. I was fine, of course. Thanks to the Hot Sauce, it took a lot to get me drunk, and an insane amount to leave me with a hangover. I was right as rain.

Ginn came shuffling into the kitchen wearing a big dressing gown and slippers, rubbing her eyes as she moved. She gave a grunt of acknowledgement before sitting herself down in a seat at the table.

"Good morning to you too."

She gave me a thumbs up. Tex and Ali walked in a second later, both fully dressed but looking rough. I dished out breakfast and we ate in silence aside from the occasional grunt of pleasure over the food. Tex reckoned the Titty Twirler would be like any other titty bar: open from dusk till dawn. It ticked over to midday by the time we finished our breakfast, so we had a nice bit of time to kill before setting off. We could have filled in the time doing something interesting, but for the first time in a while we did absolutely nothing but chill, lounging around like a happy bunch of potatoes.

The clock struck six as the sun crept away, hiding behind the horizon. I collected the Sisters from my room and strapped them in place. The guys had already crammed into Tex's car, all pumped up and ready to test their new toys on a whole load of suckers. Of course, I had called shotgun, so I popped the door and sat down in the king's seat. Tex would argue that the driver's was the king's seat, but since when do kings drive themselves?

For once, we had a short drive, if you could call two and a half hours short. Dusk turned to darkness as we arrived in San Antonio. The bikers had left us with directions drawn on a napkin, as all good directions are. The Titty Twirler sat on the north-east outskirts of the city, conveniently close to a large set of caverns; the perfect place for vampire strippers to kick back after the end of a long shift.

Tex pulled into a spot out front and killed the engine. A few other cars dotted the lot, and a couple of Harleys stood out in front, one red and one black. Both the bikes had a sticker on the tank that I recognised from the back of the bikers' jackets. They must have belonged to their dead buddies. I popped the door and stepped out. The Titty Twirler lit up the night with big, flashing neon signs promising big butts, bare breasts and girls, girls, girls. A gruff-looking bouncer stood beneath it, bathed in the pink glow.

"Christ, this place looks trashy," Ginn said.

I nodded in agreement, watching as Ali helped strap her swords to her arms, killing any hopes of remaining inconspicuous.

Tex closed his door and made his way around to open the trunk. "I'd like to get a measure of the place for a minute when we get inside, so don't go in guns blazing, okay?" he said.

171

"Deal," I said.

Ali nodded, but Ginn seemed to ignore the request.

Tex picked out a few weapons and stuffed them into the inside pockets of his long leather coat. The long leather coats may sound like clichés, but, fuck, when you want to conceal a lot of guns, they're a godsend. I've always attributed our fast friendship to the fact that we were both wearing long leather coats filled with guns the night we met. I did always wonder who could cram the most guns into their coats, though. My bets were on me. Any time I wore the coat, it'd be fully loaded and heavy as fuck. I could probably kill a sucker with the weight of the coat alone.

"Everybody ready?" Tex asked, slamming the trunk shut.

"Let's kick tits," Ginn said.

I chuckled. "Let's kick tits? Is that gonna be your catchphrase?"

"Fucking might be," she said, fastening her hair into a ponytail.

Ali had opted for a pair of hip holsters to hold the Reaper guns. He fastened them into place with a smile.

"You're looking good, murderous, even."

He curled his arms and flexed his big-ass biceps. "They don't call me the Mexican Murder Machine for nothing."

Ginn tilted her head and scrunched up her face. "Does anybody actually call you that though?"

"Yeah, me," Ali said.

Tex took a step forward to lead the way. "When you girls are done flirting, we've got some murderin' to do."

We followed close behind, an oddball-looking group to say the least. Tex and I were decked out in our super cool matching leather coats, and of course, he had his cowboy hat on. Ali wore black shorts and a tight black T-shirt; he'd decided to take his chances and leave the armour behind. And Ginn had decided to come out in a knee-length sparkly silver sequined dress. With no shoes.

"Where's your damn shoes?" I asked.

"Leaving them in the car," she shrugged.

"Why in God's name?"

"I can move better barefoot; you should try it sometime."

"No thanks. You know you're gonna end up stepping in blood, or worse, right?"

"Gonna get everything else covered in blood, so what's it matter?"

I shook my head. "Fair point."

The bouncer moved forward from the door as we stepped up a couple of stairs to the entrance. He held out his hand, instructing us to stop. "I don't think so," he said.

Tex pulled out a fistful of dollars and held them up for the bouncer to see. He was about to respond when something sliced through the air. His eyes flicked between us for a second before the top half of his head slid off and bounced down the steps. The rest of his body took a moment to decide what to do before crumpling into a heap.

"What the fuck, man?" Ali said.

We all turned to look at Ginn. One of her swords stuck out in front of her fist, dripping blood.

"Well, I'm sure he's a vampire, so I figured why waste time?"

Ali stared at the body. "Is he though?"

Ginn shrugged. "Either that or he's shit himself, he stinks already."

"He fucking might have shit himself; you've just cut the poor guy's head in half."

"Tex, am I right?"

Tex let out a sigh. "Watch the corpse. You'll find out in a moment."

All eyes hit the bouncer's body. After a painfully long few seconds, the skin started to bubble and break down, giving off an almighty stench as he decomposed.

"Ha, yes! I knew it," Ginn said, pumping a fist.

Ali hung his head. "Okay, you were right, I apologise."

Tex raised a finger. "Make damn sure you're certain next time you make such a quick decision."

"Yes, fine, okay. You knew though, didn't you?"

"I did, but you didn't. Be careful."

With that, Tex turned to the door and pushed it open. The sounds of pounding pop music drifted out. He turned back to us and said, "Let's spread out, cover more ground, but look out for each other. Any sign of trouble… shoot it."

We nodded and split off in different directions. Tex made his way to the left to go stand near the bar, I made my way straight forward to the stage, Ginn and Ali walked off to the right to grab a table each.

I sat myself down in front of the stage, right by the pole, just as the music changed to rock and the speakers made their announcement: "Next up, heeeeere's Lusty Lizzie!"

Lusty Lizzie strutted out from behind a curtain and took hold of the pole. She wore knee-high black leather boots, a thong, a bra and some heavy black eyeshadow, real biker-chick looking. She swung herself around the pole until her knees touched the floor.

I'd come prepared. I pulled out a stack of ones and made it rain as she crawled towards me on her hands and knees. Sure, I knew she was a vampire and I'd soon be shooting her in the face, but I thought I may as well have some fun while I'm at it. She scooped up some dollars and stuffed them into her bra as she crawled closer. The guy to my right hooted with pleasure and launched a hefty stack of cash at her face. Lusty Lizzie continued scooping as she spun around and backed up to the edge of the stage, ass first. Hooty Man vibrated with excitement, as he pulled out a fifty and waited for her to get close before prodding the note into her ass crack. I took a look around and saw Tex getting a drink. Ali was watching Lizzie, and Ginn sat trying to hide her arms under the table. The smell of blood on her blade was attracting some attention. Lusty Lizzie seemed to be trying her best not to glance in Ginn's direction, but a couple of the other women dotted around were giving her dirty looks.

Tex caught my eye. He raised his glass to his face and pointed a finger at the barman. He had one of the other strippers next to him, whispering into his ear while glancing over to Ginn. I nodded and brought my attention back to Lizzie, who now had a thong overflowing with cash. She hopped up from her knees into a squat before running her hands up her body and behind her back. She unhooked her bra and let it fall, raining dollars onto the stage as she gave the clientele an eyeful. A fella to my left roared and threw a crumpled fistful of ones. The ball of cash bounced off Lizzie's tits and fell to the floor. I was about to give her titties a few dollars more, just for fun, when someone burst through the entrance yelling, "Larry's dead!"

I turned to see a half-naked woman holding the top half of the bouncer's head out in front of her. It was in a bad state of decomposition, but it was definitely Larry. Every vampire eye hit Ginn.

One of the girls ran up to Ginn's table and pointed at her. "You! You did this," she hissed.

Ginn kept her cool and kept her arms hidden under the table.

I stood and gave both guys at my sides a tap on the shoulder and said, "Get out of here now," while flashing a glimpse of the Sisters. They both nodded and made for the door, elbowing past the girl holding what was left of Larry. Tex had done the same; a small group of guys at the bar grabbed their drinks and hurried out.

Lusty Lizzie looked me dead in the eye as her pupils melted, filling her eyes with inky black. I pulled out

Sophia and aimed the business end of the revolver right at the tip of her nose. Ginn watched me pull the gun and took that as a signal. The table in front of her split in half and flew in opposite directions as she brought her blades up through it. She wasted no time, following through with the upwards swing and slicing the face off the stripper who'd accused her of killing Larry. The entire front half of the girl's head flew across the room and landed face-up on another table with a splat. The face looked surprised, to say the least. The girl reached up to feel where it had gone before leaning forward and spilling her brain from the big fresh hole in the front of her skull.

## [Track 18]

A stompin' redneck-sounding song blasted from the speakers as I yelled, "Let's kick tits!"

Chaos erupted.

I pulled the trigger and blew Lusty Lizzie's nose out through the back of her head.

A man who'd refused to leave screamed as one of the girls pounced on him, straddling him in his chair. She rubbed her crotch on him before throwing her head back and pushing her fangs out, ready to take a chunk out of his face. Ginn swung a blade and split her in half, right down the middle. Her intestines spilled out into the guy's lap and showered him with blood before both sides of her corpse fell to the floor.

Tex pulled out his sawn-off shotgun. He relocated the barman's entire face.

Ali had both Reapers out, aiming them at a girl charging at him from the opposite side of the room. She snarled at him with crooked fangs on show. He pulled the triggers and shot her right in the mouth. Her head exploded in a shower of red paste. An eyeball fell to the floor by my foot with a splat before spilling its gloop and deflating.

The man with the intestines in his lap ran out the door screaming, followed by every other regular ol' human. No dinner for the girls tonight. Seven more strippers came charging out from behind the curtain in full vampire mode, titties bouncing, and all in various stages of applying their makeup.

I never thought I'd see a vampire with bright red cheeks and neon blue eyeshadow, but I did, and she flew right at me. I gave her a solid punch to the head and knocked her sideways before someone else's fist bounced off my chin.

Another vamp, in even worse makeup, squared up with her fists raised.

"Did you put your makeup on with a shotgun?"

She roared and threw herself at me, flinging fists.

I sprang back but caught another fist to the jaw, and felt a crack. I spat out a glob of blood and smiled with red-stained teeth. "No? Did Stevie Wonder do it for you then?"

This pissed her off even more. Nothing offends a vampire stripper more than having her makeup skills insulted. She took another swing at my face. Her yellowed claws sailed past my nose, scratching a chunk of skin off the tip. I followed with a concrete shattering uppercut so hard it yanked the sucker's jaw out of place and sent it snapping shut against her face, driving her own fangs through her eyes and deep into her brain.

Nothing like lobotomising a vampire with its own teeth.

Another sucker was trying to creep up behind me. Tex leapt over a table and blew the side of her head off.

"Chainsaws for arms, baby," he yelled.

"Chainsaws for arms," I replied with a smile.

I glanced over to see Ali blasting a hole through two sucker's chests with a single shot from one of his Reapers. Someone had bust his lip and he had a shard of broken glass sticking out of his scalp, but it didn't look like he'd noticed, despite the trickle of blood running down his neck.

The ringing in my ears faded away and I heard the screams of pain mixed with the sound of struggling. Ali and Tex put their guns away, both watching something behind me. I turned to see what they were looking at. Ginn had two suckers skewered on each of her swords, still alive and trying their damnedest to take a bite out of her. The third and final sucker was on her hands and knees, howling in pain with Ginn's foot stuck up her ass, all the way to the ankle.

"What the fuck?" I said, tucking the Sisters away.

Ginn yanked her foot, to no avail. "I kicked her up the arse. A little too hard, apparently; my fucking foot went right up her hole and now it's stuck."

"Bet you wish you'd kept your shoes on now, huh?"

"Shut the fuck up and help, will you."

Tex chuckled and pulled out his shotgun. He aimed it at the sucker stuck on the left blade and shot her square in the chest. An implant went flying as her boobs popped and she fell back off the sword, hitting the deck.

Ginn used the free blade to slice the other sucker's head off. It spun through the air and bounced off the table with the face on it. "Thank you," she said, flicking the mechanism to retract the blades.

I stepped forward and grabbed the sucker on Ginn's foot by the armpits. Ali stepped behind Ginn and wrapped his arms around her waist.

"On three, pull. One, two, three!"

I yanked the sucker forward with all my might as Ginn planted her other foot on the sucker's ass cheek and Ali pulled her backwards. Her foot pulled free of the sucker's asshole with a disgusting sucking sound, followed by a godawful smell. I dropped the sucker onto the floor and took a step back. She didn't even try to fight.

"Just hurry up and fucking kill me," the vamp said, still on her hands and knees.

Ginn retched at the sight of her shit-coated foot but remained unfazed by the blood soaking the rest of her.

"As you wish, ma'am," I said, pulling Maria from her holster. I aimed at the back of her head and squeezed the trigger, splattering pieces of her face all over the floor like a bloody jigsaw puzzle. I twirled the gun around on my finger before tucking her away. "Well, this was fun."

"Sure, if you say so," Ginn said.

"We did good," Tex said, "no innocent people died and we're all fine."

I rubbed my jaw, aching from the punches it had copped, then looked to Ali, who'd just picked the piece of glass from his head.

Ginn had a few cuts and bruises, but that wasn't what was bothering her. "Tell that to my foot."

Tex smiled and reached into his pocket. "Maybe this will cheer you up. Look what I found." He dangled two sets of motorcycle keys in front of her.

"Oh holy fucking shit, dibs on the red one," Ginn said.

Tex winked at her and handed her the keys, then threw the other set to Ali.

"For me?" he asked.

"Figured you could both do with your own set of wheels."

"Fuckin A!" Ali said as he hurried out the door behind Ginn.

I watched them go, smiling.

"Night?" Tex said, coming to walk by my side as we strolled out the door.

"Yeah?"

"You remember when we performed that exorcism and the demon, Sonneillon, mentioned someone called Uncle Luke?"

I frowned. "Erm... vaguely. I mean, we've done a lot in a short space of time. I can't quite remember everything. But yeah, I remember now that you mention it."

"Well, it's time you met him."

# Confession

After we all tended to our wounds, Ginn and Ali took their motorcycles for a spin up to the Fire Pit, leaving Tex and me in the house to have a chat, and do the damn laundry. Once we'd got into some fresh threads, he asked me to sit and wait on the sofa then handed me a cold beer, so I sat and waited for him to join me. He'd been doing his old cryptic routine, leaving out any hint of details. He hadn't said anything more about this Uncle Luke fella other than he wanted me to meet him, so I guessed that's what was happening. I sat waiting for a knock at the door, but it never came.

Tex drifted back through and dropped his ass into his armchair. He looked tired. Tired like I'd never seen before, almost deflated. The wrinkles on his face were more pronounced, the light in his eyes just a little less bright. He leaned forward to speak. "So I figured it's time I told you more about this deal I made."

"About damn time."

Tex nodded. "Thing is, I figured it'll be easier for the man himself to explain it all."

"Man himself?"

Tex drew in a deep breath, sat up straight, then bellowed, "Lucifer."

A bright flash accompanied a godawful, thunderous crack that just about knocked all sense out of me for a few seconds. When I regained my sense of sight and sound, I realised we had company. A tall, dark skinned man stood in the space between us, dressed to the nines in a suit to die for: a deep crimson number that seemed to shimmer. His skin was as black as ink, a void so dark it made it difficult to distinguish his features: all angular and beautiful. I'd never found myself attracted to a man, but this guy was on another level. God-like.

"You summoned me?" the man said, his voice like audible silk.

Tex nodded, wearily. "It's time."

"You're certain?"

"I am."

The man bowed his head before setting his blazing eyes on me and smiling.

Tex introduced us. "Night, this is Lucifer. Lucifer, meet Isaac Nightingale."

I sat stunned, barely able to put a sentence together. "You... you're... are you?"

"I am Lucifer. A pleasure to finally meet you," he said, extending a perfectly manicured hand.

I reached up and shook while mumbling, "The Devil?"

"Not anymore, my friend," Lucifer said, moving to sit beside me on the couch.

I scooted over so he could sit.

"Drink?" Tex asked.

"Please," Lucifer said.

I sat in silence, staring at our guest as Tex fetched him a beer. He returned a moment later and handed Lucifer a bottle, then set another down by my feet.

After giving him an eyeballing for so long it could be considered impolite, I finally blurted, "So you're not, like, Lucifer the Devil kinda Lucifer?"

Lucifer popped the cap off his beer. "I am the Lucifer you're thinking of, but I'm no longer the Devil."

I kept on staring. "What?"

"You see, 'The Devil' is merely a title. Like how you have 'The President'. There's no one Devil in Hell, but an elected individual. I was the first, the original Devil, but I haven't been for a very, very long time. I chose a different career path, so to speak. Astaroth is the current Devil."

I turned to Tex. "Your deal is with the Devil? Or former Devil? Whatever."

"Yes, but it's complicated. Just hear him out, would you?"

I turned to Lucifer and waited for more information.

He crossed his legs and got comfortable. "Your beliefs about me are wildly incorrect. Did I rebel against God? Yes. But I had a good reason. I simply wanted the freedom you humans were given, that's all. Hell was punishment for my transgression, just as it is for anyone else. I chose to make the best out of a bad situation. You see, Hell may be a punishment, but it wasn't always the way it is now. It had order, it was more of a prison for unruly souls, and I was the warden. But being banished from Paradise made some of my brothers bitter, and that bitterness corrupted them, twisted them into the demons they've become."

I took a swig of my beer. "So you're not evil?"

185

"Far from it. This whole monster hunting thing was my idea. I admit I do have an ulterior motive. You see, I'd like to redeem myself and join my brothers in Paradise once more. My redemption comes through the likes of you. But it's mutually beneficial, of course. With each new soul to accept the deal, I get one step closer to going home. And in return for your assistance, you're guaranteed a spot up there yourself when you die; it's a win-win. Not to mention the immortality while you're under contract. In theory, you could live as long as you desire. Centuries. Millennia. It's yours for the taking."

I looked at Tex, all the clues fitting into place: his dress sense, his cowboy-like manner, his tiredness.

As if he read my mind, he spoke, "I took the deal in eighteen-fifty-five. I've been doing this for a hundred and twenty-six years, son. I'm one hundred and eighty-one fuckin' years old. I miss my family. It's time I passed on the gauntlet."

I took a long swig of my drink, absorbing everything. "So, what's the fine print?"

"So, here's the full shebang," Lucifer said, "you agree to serve as a supernatural bounty hunter for a minimum term of twenty-five years. In that time, you'll receive information and instruction through Gabriel. We can't interfere with your free will, so you can do whatever you wish. As long as you're actively reducing the population of monsters and abominations, plus the occasional exceptionally evil human, we won't have any issues. After the twenty-five-year period ends, if you haven't found a successor, the contract continues until you find one and they accept."

"And if I don't want a successor?"

"Like I said, as long as you're doing the work, you can be the one to do it for as long as you wish."

I turned to Tex. "So what happens to you if I take this deal? Will you turn to dust and blow away?"

He shrugged. "I just start ageing as if I'd never accepted it, pick up where I left off and die of natural causes if something doesn't kill me first."

Lucifer added, "Of course, we don't expect you to accept right away. It's entirely your choice. Take your time, think it through."

"Don't take too long, though. My retirement is way overdue," Tex said with a smile.

Lucifer finished off his beer and set the bottle down by his feet. "If you need me, just shout. Hope to see you again soon." He ended his sentence with a wink before another ear-splitting crack and blinding flash filled the room and he was gone.

"How does that all sound?" Tex asked.

I rubbed my eyes and sighed. "Sounds like one hell of a commitment. I'll need a while to think about it, but I guess... what do I have to lose?"

# One Hell of a Deal

We sat in silence for a moment while I absorbed what had just happened.

"It's a lot to take in, I know," Tex said.

"You can say that again. Is he really one of the good guys?"

Tex shrugged. "He's never given me any reason to doubt him. And like he said, he started the whole vampire hunting thing. As I told you a while back, Satan took the 'Devil' title and created vampirism, and Judas was the first one. Well, Lucifer created the first vampire hunters, in a sense, and that earned him a banishment from Hell. So he made his deal with Gabriel to work with humans and try to eradicate vampirism and as much of Hell's influence on Earth as possible."

"Can't he just do it himself?"

"Nope, it's a dumb technicality: the whole 'divine beings can't interfere' thing. He can only do so much, like guide us and offer advice, but anything other than that is out of bounds."

"I guess that's why Gabriel can't just tell you where Atrocitas is hiding?"

Tex shrugged. "That, sure, and the whole loophole of vampirism technically being an angelic gift. The closer the vampire is to the original bloodline, the harder they are to track. And Atrocitas is as close as they get."

"So, this really is a whole thing you've got going on huh? And you're really one hundred and eighty-one?"

"Yup, a whole thing. Have you ever read Dracula?"

I nodded.

"Well, who do you think Van Helsing was based on?"

I sat back in the chair and stretched, groaning. "Don't you fucking dare say it's you."

Tex grinned and nodded.

"But he was Dutch, wasn't he? And a doctor."

"Well, I asked Bram to make a few changes, of course. Didn't want him putting too much of my likeness in the book."

"You knew Bram Stoker?"

"I did. We met through a friend of a friend, in the early eighteen-nineties. Heard he was writing a novel about a vampire and needed some help, so I offered up my services and he based Van Helsing on me as thanks."

I was about to speak when the phone rang.

Tex held up a finger and got up to answer it.

I sighed and stared at the ceiling while Tex took the call. I didn't know what to think. On one hand, being immortal sounded awesome, but on the other, a total curse. Living so long you see all your loved ones die didn't sound like my idea of a good time, but on the plus side, I'd be guaranteed to see them again. Unless they ended up in Hell, then maybe not. The fact that Tex had met Bram Stoker did sweeten the deal, too. It made me curious as to all the possibilities of living an insanely long life. The things you could do and see. It was tempting.

189

Tex hung up and sat back down. "Just had an old friend on the phone, he could do with a little help, says some big-time movie producer in Los Angeles needs to be taken out of the picture."

"Vampire?"

"You'd think so, wouldn't you? But no."

I frowned, "So what then?"

"He's nothing but a plain ol' human. He's supposedly been luring young girls, promising them their big breaks in acting."

I sat forward. "And lemme guess, he's a rapist?"

Tex nodded. "He's a rapist, a child predator, and a murderer all in one fancy suit."

"You can trust this friend's information?"

"With my life," Tex said.

I stood and hiked my jeans up out of my ass crack. "So when do we set off?"

Tex stood too. "I reckon Ginn and Ali are already a few drinks in by now, so I'd say tomorrow morning. In the meantime, I'm gonna go spend some time on my writing. No disturbing me, now. I need to get in the zone."

"Don't worry, I'm gonna go join them at the Fire Pit. I need to drink more drinks than we currently have in the fridge. You have fun," I said, pulling on my jacket.

"Don't forget to tell them we've got a child molester to deal with."

I opened the door and stepped out, saying, "Knowing Ali's love for beating the shit out of them, we might be setting off earlier than planned. Have fun with the stories."

Tex gave a nod and shut the door behind me.

The short walk to the Fire Pit helped clear my head. The deal felt a little too good to be true, but I had no real reason not to take it. The only real drawback was the possibility of losing Tex. Without the protection of his contract, he'd be nothing but a vulnerable old man. Okay, sure, he'd still be a total fucking badass, but even the biggest, best badass can't survive a bullet to the head or an unfortunate bit of dismemberment. I worried about him. Aside from Ali, people didn't tend to have much luck around me. And when you're living such a dangerous lifestyle, there's only a certain amount of time before fate figures out a way to kill you.

The flames of the Fire Pit rose to greet me, dancing to the rhythm of my footsteps. Ginn and Ali's motorcycles were parked out front, looking damn fine, gleaming in the light of the fire. I pushed the doors open and stepped inside. I caught sight of Ali and Ginn by the pool table. Ginn sat sipping an expensive-looking cocktail while Ali played a game with a stranger with a huge beard. He caught sight of me and nodded a greeting. I walked over and took a seat next to Ginn. She smiled and handed me her glass.

"Taste this shit," she said, "it's fantastic. You should get one… or two. I can help drink it."

I took a sip and nodded, she was right, it was delicious; fruity with a hint of mint, "Yeah, it's nice. And real subtle on the hints there. What's Ali having?"

Ginn wobbled in her seat, taking the glass back. "A good time."

191

I rolled my eyes and got back up to head to the bar. Whiskey it is. Service came fast. The barmaid served up two glasses of the good stuff and a cocktail so expensive it may as well have been made of liquid cash. I took a moment to eye her with great suspicion. She was definitely human. Just damn near inhuman when it came to making a drink. I left her a hefty tip and carried the drinks over to the table.

I set the drinks down just in time to catch Ali and his game buddy about to swing fists.

"You're fucking hustling me," the beardy guy said, getting up in Ali's face, "gimme my fuckin' money back."

Ali squared up. "It's called skill, cabrón. Don't be a sore loser. I told you from the start I'd give you an ass whooping."

Beardy stuck a finger into Ali's chest. "I'll show you an ass whooping."

I stood and slid a hand between the two. There'd be no violence this night. Not if I could help it. We had to save our energy for a child predator beat-down.

"Ladies, ladies, ladies, no need for the handbags." I turned to Beardy, "Looks to me like he beat you fair and square. Be a good sport and take it on the chin, eh? Then you can play each other again another time; see if you can double your money."

Beardy backed down, still pissed, but not about to swing. "Next time," he said, pointing at Ali.

Ali nodded. "Next time."

I steered him over to the table and sat him down.

"I was about to shove that cue up his ass and turn him into a popsicle," he said, slurring his words a little. He reached straight past the whiskey and grabbed the fancy cocktail.

Ginn watched him, shrugged and picked up the drink meant for him.

"I know buddy, I know. Save those muscles for another night though, we've got another job to do."

The prospect of potential violence made them both sit up straight and listen.

"Go on…" Ginn said.

I took a sip of my drink to keep them in anticipation for a little longer.

"Turns out some big-time Hollywood movie producer is molesting and murdering young girls. He's not a vampire or anything though, just a real shit bag. That gonna be a problem?"

Ali flexed his biceps. "The Mexican Murder Machine doesn't discriminate," he said.

I looked to Ginn for her answer. "Will killing a human bother you?"

She knocked back a good amount of her drink and smacked the glass down onto the table, spilling some. "Do I object to beating the life out of a murderous nonce? Abso-fucking-lutely not."

I smiled. "Well then, it looks like we're going hunting."

# Come Out to L.A.

Tex and I drove in shifts, as always. Ginn and Ali tailed us on their motorcycles, gunning it all the way to LA. We'd set off on the long drive just after seven in the morning. We made a few stops for snacks and arrived in LA just after eleven that night. Tex pulled up in a parking lot I'd gotten well acquainted with during my last visit to LA. The lot belonged to the Black Cat.

"You know this place?" I asked as Tex killed the engine.

"Sure do. It's an old haunt of mine."

"I used to hang around here too, got a bunch of friends who spend their nights here. Probably in there right now."

Tex squinted at me and smiled as he pushed his door open and turned to step out. I followed suit. My joints popped and cracked as I stood and had a nice stretch. I massaged my numb ass cheeks as Ginn and Ali pulled up alongside the car. The rumble of their engines slowed to a purr then fell silent.

"Thank fuck for that," Ali said, looking towards the bar as he stepped off the bike, "my taint has taken a pounding from that ride, I need a hard drink."

Ginn nodded her agreement, pulling the fabric of her shorts out of her ass crack.

I took a look around the lot and spotted Harriot's car parked close to the entrance. A bunch of monster hunters about to meet a bunch of monsters. We were in for an interesting night.

Tex took the lead, strolling towards the entrance with a good amount of swagger in his step. I followed close behind, hoping to get a read on him when I found the Monster Squad. The welcoming scent of booze and smoke drifted out to greet us as Tex swung the door open. He'd managed no more than five steps before I heard that familiar Scottish roar.

"WAAHEEEEY," Rusty yelled, wheeling his chair out from his table.

But it wasn't me he was cheering for.

"Texas Dickson, you ol' fucker," he called.

Tex reached out to shake Rusty's hand. Rusty shook it vigorously then stopped and looked me dead in the eye.

"Well shite my kecks, if it isn't Isaac Nightingale too! What the fuck are you doing here laddie?"

Tex slapped a hand down on my shoulder. "He's a good friend."

"Aye? He is to us too," Rusty said, gesturing to his table.

Khearo, Morgan and Harriot sat grinning with raised glasses.

My eyes flicked between Tex and the Monster Squad. "You know these guys?" I asked Tex.

Rusty answered, "Know us? He's the one who brought us all together. He's the O.G. Come, sit, we've a lot to talk about it seems."

"Room for two more?" I asked, gesturing to Ginn and Ali.

"More friends, eh? Of course, come on, sit," Rusty said, wheeling himself back to the table.

The guys shuffled around to make space as Tex grabbed some empty seats for us.

Ali and Ginn introduced themselves and took a seat each, both to the right of Harriot. Tex and I took the remaining seats between Ginn and Rusty.

Rusty gave Tex a bit of side-eye and asked, "Do they know?"

"Nope," Tex said, shaking his head.

Rusty cleared his throat. "Right then, before we get sauced off our tits, let's address the elephant in the room. Ginn, Ali, as you're with Tex and Night we can only assume you're in on their shenanigans. Am I right?"

Both Ginn and Ali nodded.

"Well, we call ourselves the Monster Squad. Morgan there's a vampire. And Khearo, Harriot and I are werewolves. We also have a murnock amongst us, but he's not here tonight."

Ginn's eyes widened and Ali's right hand twitched, instinctually moving closer to his hip to grab his gun. His fingers brushed nothing but belt, he'd left his guns in Tex's car.

Rusty continued, "Now don't go jumping over the table to murder us just yet. We're on your side. Long before Tex took off on his lonesome, we were his monster hunting crew."

"Reformed monsters?" Ginn said.

196

"Exactly," Harriot said, smiling at her.

I chipped in, "These guys taught me a lot of my moves. If not for them, my first fistfight with a vampire may have had an entirely different outcome."

"WELL!" Rusty hollered. "That's that out the way, let's drink." He finished his sentence as he wheeled himself away from the table to get some drinks.

Ginn and Ali took the chance to get a little more acquainted with Khearo, Morgan and Harriot. In the few minutes it took Rusty to return with the drinks, they all looked to be getting along quite well. Harriot buzzed with energy over some female company and Khearo's strong beard had made an even stronger impression on Ali.

Rusty parked himself up and set a tray filled with glasses down on the table.

"How did you know?" Ginn asked, as Rusty handed her a fancy cocktail.

He thumbed his nose. "We dogs have impressive sniffers. I can tell you've had one of these recently."

Ali pulled an impressed face and nodded as he took his drink.

Rusty looked to me and then to Tex. "Now, how the fuck do you two know each other?"

"We met in a bar in Saltstone," I said. "A lucky coincidence I guess, the bar was full of suckers. Tex took out a bunch before recruiting me to his mission."

"And what the fuck were you doing in Saltstone so conveniently?" Rusty asked Tex.

"Destiny," Tex said. "Gabriel sent me there. Told me there was a nest of suckers, but also someone I may

197

want to meet was headed in that direction. So off I went to take out the trash and, lo and behold, he turns up." He eyed me from the side. "Tell you the truth, I thought he was just another fool from the road. Expected him to get his face torn off while he was on the shitter. Wasn't until he sent the shithouse door flying off its hinges and I saw two headless suckers on the floor that I realised he was the one Gabriel had been hinting at."

"Well cheers to that fucking bird for bringing the two of you together," Rusty said, raising his glass.

Tex and I raised ours. "To the bird."

We spent some time catching up, swapping stories and drinking into the early hours of the morning before Tex raised the question of why we'd made the drive.

"So, tell us, what's this job you want us to do?"

Rusty slammed his glass down on the table. "Aye, to business," he said. "Harry Westnil is the fucker's name. He's got himself a nice little lair up in Beverly Hills where he diddles wee lasses in his downtime. We want you to sort the cunt out for us."

"Why do you need us to do it?" I cut in.

"You know our reputation around here. We make a few vampires and the occasional slugoracc go missing, nobody bats a fuckin' eye. But if we pop off a big-time movie producer, we're fucked. People know we've been asked to do the job, and they know we want to. So we need your help to do the job, while we sit here and make it very clear we have an alibi."

"Clever," Tex said with a smirk.

"Aye, it is. So, people will suspect us, but we can't be in two places at once, now can we? Whereas you two, the now relatively unknown humans in these parts, can slip in and out of whatever shadow takes your fancy."

"It's a good plan, do you know where this asshole lives?"

"I do indeed lad, pass me a fuckin' napkin, I'll draw you a map."

"What else are napkins good for?" I said, chuckling to myself.

Tex gave me an inquisitive look.

"Just a little inside joke," I said.

"With yourself?"

"Well... yeah. It's just every map I've had these past few months has been scrawled on a napkin."

"Weird."

I shrugged and took a sip of my drink.

"Here," Rusty said, pushing the map across the table, "If our recon is correct, which it is 'cos this cunt's like clockwork, he'll be home tomorrow until about two in the afternoon. Do what you wish with the fucker. Just make sure it hurts a lot... for a long time."

"I could put my foot up his arse," Ginn said, swaying gently with a smile on her face, "like, my whole entire foot. I did it to a stripper the other day. Right up there, to the ankle," she ended with a hiccup.

"Is she serious?" Morgan asked.

"I'm gonna need some context here," Khearo said.

Ali nodded. "It's true. Got it stuck right up a stripper's asshole."

Tex elaborated, "We were taking out a nest of vampire strippers. She kicked one up the ass with her bare foot, and well..."

Rusty burst into a boisterous laugh and then knocked back the remains of his drink. He slammed his glass down and pointed a finger at Ginn. "I like you. Do that to him. Please. But make sure you wear boots. Big ones."

Ginn pulled her leg out from under the table to reveal a big, black biker boot covered in spikes and buckles. "Will this do?"

A big grin spread across Rusty's face. "Aye lass, that'll do nicely."

# Wholesale Beatdown

I woke the next morning with a pillow mint stuck to my face. After leaving the Black Cat, we'd checked into the hotel I'd stayed in on my last visit to LA, just across the street. There'd been no knock on the door and no wake-up call, so I took my time getting out of bed, wearing nothing but the mint.

I glanced around the room, taking the time to have a proper look. It was a good size, and nicely decorated with light walls, oak furniture, a leather sofa and a big TV in the corner. The clock said it was almost ten. I found my jacket lying in a bundle on an antique chest at the foot of my bed, my bag lay in front of it. My pants and shirt were draped across the arm of the sofa with a pizza box sitting on the cushion, tantalising me. I made my way over and flipped the lid. Jackpot: I had about three quarters of it left. I grabbed a slice and made my way to the shower.

About forty minutes later I heard a knock on the door. I hopped up off the sofa and tightened the towel around my waist, so it didn't drop and show the goods. I opened it a crack and peeked out to see Ginn standing in the hall, wearing her trademark short shorts and a bright yellow T-shirt with a pineapple on the front.

"Hey, you dressed?" she asked, before pushing the door open and strolling into the room.

"Thankfully, I'm a little dressed," I said motioning to the towel.

Ginn threw herself down on the bed and looked me up and down. "Not bad."

I pulled a T-shirt out of my bag. "Do you mind?"

"Not at all. We're all ready to go. Tex is gonna go get us some breakfast and meet us at the car, want anything?"

"An egg sandwich would be nice right about now."

"Gotcha," she said, eyeing the mint on the nightstand. She looked as though she was mulling something over as she gave the mint a prod and then picked it up.

"Wouldn't eat that if I were you," I said, just a little too late.

"Why?"

"I peeled it off my face about an hour ago."

She stopped sucking on it for a moment then shrugged. "What's done is done I guess."

I pulled a pair of boxer shorts and a pair of jeans out of the bag while eyeing Ginn. "Something else on your mind?"

She hesitated for a few seconds. "I'm not sure how I feel about this job. Like, I'm fine with killing vampires and stuff, but I've never hurt a normal person before."

"He's far from a normal person."

"Yeah, but you know what I mean? He's gonna be weak and squishy. It seems a bit unfair to send an immortal gunslinger, two superhumans and the Mexican Murder Machine after one guy."

"Ali's title's catching on huh? And, yeah, I get you, you've just gotta remind yourself sometimes monsters are human. A couple of months back, Tex and I hunted down a guy who killed babies and wore their skin. And when I was in prison, I hurt a whole bunch of bad people. Some of them were worse than some of the vampires I've killed."

Ginn nodded. "Fair enough."

"Plus, it's not like you have to deliver the killing blow, so to speak. You don't even have to come if you don't want to."

"And I guess it's gonna be easier to pin it on us if there's four of us marching in there to execute him."

"On top of that, you're not exactly wearing the most incognito of shirts, now if you'd kindly fuck off, I'd like to put some pants on."

* * *

I strolled across the road to the parking lot of the Black Cat and found the guys sitting in the car with all the doors open, Tex in the driver's seat, Ginn in the passenger seat and Ali in the back, all munching away. The smell of their food set my stomach rumbling, even though I'd already had some pizza. I sat myself down next to Ali and nodded my good mornings.

"One egg sandwich," Tex said, handing me a little warm bundle of paper.

"Thanks," I said as I unwrapped it.

He nodded then turned to Ginn. "You sure you wanna come?"

Ginn stuffed the last of her sandwich into her mouth and pulled the passenger door closed before saying a muffled, "Let's fucking do it."

Tex pulled his door closed too, and Ali and I followed suit. Fifteen minutes later, we pulled up outside a luxurious mansion on a quiet street, two houses away from our target.

"Is morning the best time to be doing this?"

"I figure right now most people are at work or out and about. Nice sunny day like this, the only people inside will be the creepy fuckers like this fella," Tex said.

"Let's hope you're right, we've got a fence to hop."

Tex grunted and swung his door open, stepping out. We followed.

"I'm thinking we head down the lane to the side there," he pointed to the left of the house, "use the trash cans to help us over the wall, then we're in through that side window he's conveniently left open for us."

"Good plan, Batman," Ginn said.

Tex gave her a look of disgust. "Darlin', Batman wishes he could be like me."

Ali nodded. "This is true, I think we could all make Batman our bitch."

"How about we stop stroking our dicks and get this over with," I said.

Tex smiled and pulled the brim of his hat down over his eyes before leading the way. We made it into the alley unseen, hopped the wall and snuck through the window without breaking a sweat. The window led us into a large hallway. I made sure to close it behind Ali; I didn't want the screams floating out into the street.

"Split up?" Ali suggested.

"Nah let's stick together, he's more likely to shit himself if he sees the four of us at once," Tex said.

We crept down the hallway, listening for any sounds of movement. We passed by a cabinet filled with awards before hearing someone yelling from behind a door to our left.

"Is that him?" Ginn asked.

"Sure hope so, but only one way to find out," Tex shrugged before booting the door open and charging through. We followed, bursting into the room as fast as we could.

Harry Westnil sat behind a large mahogany desk, holding a phone to his ear with his eyes wide and mouth hanging open.

"Hang up, now," Tex said.

Westnil dropped the receiver into place, eyes darting between us all. "How the fuck did you get in here? What's going on? Who are you?"

Ali stepped forward with a finger raised. "Shush, now, we're angels to some, but demons to others. And we're here to send you straight to Hell." He launched himself across the desk and grabbed Westnil by the throat, dragging him out of his chair.

"Please," Westnil wheezed, "I don't know what you want, I haven't done anything wrong."

"Lies," Ali roared, tossing him to the hardwood floor at our feet.

Westnil clambered to his knees and assumed the prayer position. "I swear, please."

"Bit pathetic, isn't he?" Ginn said.

"An act," Tex said.

"It's not an act, I promise, why are you doing this?"

Tex stepped forward, taking his gun from his holster. "You know why, Harry. Mister Westnil, the big shot movie producer. Big-time child molester."

"What? No."

Tex circled him. "Rapist."

"Nuh-uh," Westnil shook his head, snot bubbling at his nose.

"Murderer."

"You've got the wrong guy, please, just leave me be. You want money? There's a safe in the wall behind the desk, under the picture. Take it all, it's yours."

"We don't want your fucking money, pendejo," Ali spat.

Tex continued circling. "Funny how a lot of young girls who've auditioned at your studio have gone missing, and occasionally turned up dead. Funny how their families suddenly came into money. Lots of money."

"I'm innocent, you've gotta believe me, I had nothing to do with that."

"Keep on lying to me and I'll fold your clothes with you still in them."

I caught Ginn staring at something at the base of a bookcase. "What's up?"

"See those scratches," she said, pointing to the floor, "looks like the bookcase swings open."

206

Tex stopped circling and took a look for himself. "What's behind here?"

The colour drained from Westnil's face. "There's uh... nothing. I had the cases rearranged and it left a scratch."

Tex took a closer look. "Try again. This here's from repeated moving, don't get this many scratches by shuffling a bit of furniture around. Open it; I wanna see what's back there."

"I can't, there's nothing there."

Tex shot back over and pointed his gun at Westnil's forehead. "This is your second chance; I don't give thirds."

I ran my eyes over the bookcase, "I'll bet you have to pull a book to reveal the secret lair, like some shitty Bond villain."

Ginn pointed at one of the books, "Considering he's a dirty nonce, I bet it's this copy of 'Lolita'."

I raised an eyebrow. "What the fuck does nonce mean, anyway? That's twice I've heard you say it."

"It's slang for paedophile."

Tex tugged on the copy of 'Lolita'. The bookcase unlocked with a click. He slid a hand in the gap and pulled it open. It scraped across the wood floor before coming to a stop. Tex stepped inside and muttered something under his breath.

Westnil sprang to his feet and darted for the door, but Ali intercepted him and smashed him against the wall with a hard shoulder barge. He hit the wall face-first, busting his nose. Blood streamed down his face and spattered his shirt as Ali spun him around and kept him pinned.

"Ali, keep him there. Night, Ginn, get in here," Tex said.

Ginn and I exchanged a look before stepping into the secret room. It took a moment for my brain to comprehend what I was seeing. The wall to the right of the entrance was covered in photographs of Westnil, among others, carrying out depraved acts on young girls, some barely even in their teens. Ginn didn't stick around to see any more. She stormed out of the room with a look of rage I'd never seen on a human face before. Westnil started screaming.

While Ginn and Ali worked their magic, Tex and I explored the room. Not like we needed to. The photos alone were incriminating enough. But as well as the photos, there were shelves lined with all manner of painful-looking instruments, many of them phallic. A single armchair sat in the middle of the room, in front of a projector and screen. I didn't want to see what was on the film reels stacked by the chair, so I didn't touch them. Tex stood in the left-hand corner, staring at a glass display case. I stepped over to join him, to see what he was looking at.

"Take a look," he said, flicking a switch to illuminate the display.

The sight punched me hard in the guts. Five small skulls stared back at me through the glass, each with a mini headshot photograph to the right of them.

"Fuck."

Tex nodded. "I've seen these pictures before, on missing person posters. We have all the evidence we need."

Tex left the display light on. The sight of Ginn kicking Westnil in the testicles greeted us as we left the den. He had been forced into a corner, and Ginn was going to town. Her big black biker boots were being put to good use. Ali sat and watched with his feet up on the desk. Ginn caught sight of us and pulled the squealing Westnil into the middle of the room by his hair. Ali got to his feet and joined us, forming a circle to kick the life out of the piece of shit.

After a devastating beating that had Westnil on the edge of consciousness, nothing more than a swollen, bloody pulp of flesh, Tex pulled out his gun and took aim.

Ali put up a hand to stop him. "Wait, wait, wait," he said, "we shouldn't kill him."

"You couldn't give me a good enough reason if you tried," Tex said.

"This is what he deserves, every day. Not death. Death is a kindness we can't grant him. We send him to prison; this is what he'll get, day in, day out."

"No please," Westnil groaned.

Tex shook his head. "It's not guaranteed. He could get off easy."

"I can pull a few strings; make sure he goes to Blackwater. Warden Spencer rules with an iron fist lately. He'll see to it that he suffers. And we make all this shit public," he gestured to the secret room. "If we call the press now, they'll have news vans here way before any police arrive, it'll be worldwide news within the hour."

I nodded. "He's right. For what he's done to all those girls, we can't kill him. That's not justice. It's letting him off easy."

Tex took a moment to ponder the matter then looked at Ali. "Make the call. The press and the police. Shit of this magnitude, we can sit in the car and watch him be dragged out of here and the cops won't even sniff in our direction."

Ali nodded and made his way over to the phone.

Tex put his boot on Westnil's face and pushed his head to the floor. "In the meantime, Ginn, those boots of yours seem friendly with his testicles, don't they?"

# Filth

Not even twenty-four hours had passed before Harry Westnil had his face plastered across the front page of every newspaper in the country. As Ali had predicted, the press got to him before the cops did, so the papers were full of images of Westnil being dragged from his home, beaten and bloody from a visit from a group of mysterious vigilantes who the papers hailed as heroes. Of course, every damn person in the Black Cat had figured it out, so the drinks were free and frequent.

"Not bad, lads and lass, not bad at all," Rusty said as he folded the morning paper and put it down on the table, "I'd have liked to give the fucker a right good kicking myself if only my bloody legs worked."

Tex chuckled. "Don't you worry, Ginn gave him a beating he'll not likely forget, even with the concussion."

Ginn gave the group a wink.

Morgan took a deep breath in through the nose. "I can still smell his blood on your boots. Pity you didn't spill it all. Shouldn't have sent humans to do a monster's job, I say."

Khearo shook his head. "Nah they made the better decision. If he's dead, he's dead. Sure, he'd rot in Hell, but better to let him rot here before he even gets there."

"I agree, let him suffer for as long as possible," Harriot said.

"Anyway," Rusty cut in, "good job either way. Now, on to today's matter. We have a couple of jobs to do if you lot care to help out?"

Tex looked to see if any of us had any objection. We didn't. "I guess we may as well stick around a little while since we're here."

Ginn sat forward, putting her glass of juice down on the table. "Wait, what if Gabriel needs us? He could have a message, and we wouldn't know. And come to think of it, who the fuck feeds him while you're away?"

Tex shrugged. "He's not the only conduit out there, if there's an important message, the angels always find a way to deliver it. And he feeds himself, he knows where his food is and doesn't need help. He's an independent bird. More of a roommate than a pet, and he can leave any time he likes, he's not stuck indoors. So, what are the jobs, Rusty?"

Rusty leaned back in his chair and cracked his knuckles. "Well, Khearo and Morgan are taking a trip underground. There's a scargemooplit living in the sewers. That needs taking care of."

"What the fuck's a scargemooplit?" I said, almost choking on my lemonade.

"Real nasty fucker, don't let the silly name fool you," Khearo said.

Morgan nodded. "Big filthy bitch is what, basically a living pile of shit. They stink worse than anything you've ever smelled and look the part too."

Rusty sighed. "I'd help take care of the fucker, but the wheelchair makes sewer traversal a wee bit difficult.

So, Harriot and I are gonna go sort out a ventripede that's been spotted up in Santa Clarita. I reckon since there's four of you, two could accompany the lads, and two could come with Harriot and me. How's about it?"

We sat exchanging looks for a moment.

Ginn spoke first, "Well I'm just gonna put it out there, I don't know what a ventripede is, but I sure as fuck don't want to deal with a big stinking shit monster."

Tex leaned forward. "I should probably come along if you want to see the ventripede, I've dealt with a few over the years. Very dangerous if you don't know what you're dealing with."

"Fuck," I muttered. I wanted the ventripede. I'd wanted to see one ever since Tex told me about his encounter with the one that almost got the better of him. Shoulda piped up when I had the chance.

"Looks like that leaves us with the stink devil," Ali said, grinning at me.

"Why do you look so happy about that?"

Ali shrugged. "Why not? It's a new experience, and it's all fun to me."

"That's the spirit," Rusty said, "we'll saddle up in a short while and get to work. Night, I know it's not even midday yet, but if you're heading into the sewers, you might want to drink something stronger than lemonade."

After downing a fuck-load of alcohol in an attempt to numb my senses, my group bid farewell and good luck to Rusty's, the lucky fuckers. Khearo and Morgan accompanied Ali and me to the hotel and waited in the lobby while we both threw on a different set of clothes.

213

Not a damn chance I'd be fighting a giant walking turd in my finest.

Ali had beat me. He sat on a large sofa with Khearo and Morgan, showing them his Reaper guns. I strolled over and stood in front of them in my sneakers, sweatpants and an old Rolling Stones t-shirt. Didn't want shit all over my good clothes. Blood is fine, shit is a no-no.

"You ready?" Khearo asked.

"For this? Never."

"You'll love it, princess, trust me," Morgan said. Unlike me, he'd stuck to his guns and committed to going into the sewers in his suit. Always stylish, always looking sharp, even when the suit would face certain doom.

We left the hotel and took a sharp right, following Khearo as he led the way down the street and into an alleyway nearby. Without a moment of hesitation, he hauled the cover off a manhole and threw himself down into the darkness. Morgan followed a second later.

Ali gave me a look that said, "wish me luck," then took the leap into the rotten abyss.

I peered into the hole. The stench wafting out almost made me gag. I turned my face towards the sun and took one last breath of somewhat clear air then stepped off the ledge and into the darkness. I landed on my feet with a splash. Water came up to my knees, and it felt lumpy. My eyes adjusted to the darkness as best they could, but I didn't dare look down to see what was squishing up against my leg.

"It's not far," Morgan said, "the scargemooplit has made a nest in a large chamber a few minutes from here."

214

"Yay," I said. "Remind me, why are we bothering this thing? If it wants to wallow in sewage, can't we just leave it alone?"

Khearo answered, "Well, nah. Aside from causing blockages and damage all over the sewage system, they're a pain in the ass for everybody if they decide to leave."

"How so?" Ali asked.

"They'll eat absolutely anything. People included. And the more they eat, the bigger they get."

I stepped over something that looked like a bloated animal carcass. "Kinda like The Blob?"

"The what?" Morgan asked.

"The Blob, it's a movie from the fifties, it has a weird jello-like alien that gets bigger when it eats people. Steve McQueen's in it."

Morgan gave a blank stare.

"Exactly like The Blob then, yeah," Khearo said.

"Lived for fucking centuries and he's barely seen any damn movies," I muttered to myself.

"I heard that," Morgan said.

"Maybe try seeing some things too, then."

"Shaddap, you two," Khearo cut in, "we're near."

I believed him, too. The stench had doubled, at least. It made breathing difficult. I was about to open my mouth to ask what the plan was when I heard a gurgling noise coming towards us from around the corner, and fast.

"Get back, get back!" Khearo yelled.

We scrambled back a few feet just in time to see a tidal wave of sludge barrel past us and crash into the wall.

"Quick, before it sends another wave," Khearo said before making a run for it, around the corner and into the growing stink.

The rest of us followed, the sludge sucking at our feet, trying to keep us in place. We rounded the corner and found ourselves in the chamber; the nest. Piles of raw sewage, mixed in with trash lay around the chamber. The scargemooplit sat in the middle, on top of a large pile of scrap metal, held together with slime and shit.

"You weren't joking when you said it's a living pile of shit," Ali said.

The scargemooplit looked like nothing more than a giant mountain of turds and trash. Large snot green eyes peered out from a shapeless face. It stood at least ten feet tall, and slime oozed from every inch of it. It opened an empty gaping hole of a mouth and let out a wet, gurgling roar.

"How the fuck do we kill this thing?" I asked, looking at the jagged bits of metal sticking out of it. "Doesn't look like bullets will do the trick."

"You're not gonna like the answer," Morgan said.

We jumped aside, going in opposite directions as the creature reached down from its nest and splashed a wave of sludge in our direction.

"Just fucking spill it so we can get this over with and get out of here."

"You're going inside it."

I shot him a look almost as dirty as the creature. "You fucking what?"

"Gotta let it eat you."

"Nope. No fucking way."

I looked over to Ali. He was shaking his head almost as hard as I was. Another wave came my way, I ran to dodge it.

"It'll catch one of us eventually," Khearo said, "and when it does, that's our chance."

Ali dodged a flying ball of filth.

"Well, why the fuck don't you guys volunteer?"

"We've both done it before," Morgan said, "it's somebody else's turn. Just let it grab you."

I felt like leaving then and there, just turning the fuck around, going back to the hotel and taking a nice hot shower while they dealt with Big Stinky. If I'd known I'd have to be eaten by a shit monster, I'd have taken my chances with the ventripede. At least I'd get to see some titties on a cool monster before I died.

I looked from Morgan to Big Stinky. "And when it eats me, then what?"

He ducked as a blob of shit sailed over his head. "The heart is inside the stomach, just destroy it however you can. But you'll only have about thirty seconds before the stomach starts filling with acid."

"And if it starts filling—"

"It'll fucking melt you," Khearo finished.

Before I could change my mind, I set off running towards the Scargemooplit, splashing through the filth. "If I die, I want you both to know, it's entirely your fault,"

I said as I planted my foot on a pile of trash and launched myself into the air.

Big Stinky swung an arm and caught me by the legs in mid-air. Wet filth wrapped around my shins as it got a good grip before swinging me around like a ragdoll. The chamber turned into a blur. The faces of Morgan, Khearo and Ali whizzed by before the scargemooplit raised me high into the air, threw back its head and plunged me into its stinking wet hole of a mouth.

My world went black, and my head kept spinning. All I could hear was the sucking and slurping as the creature's throat pulled me in, swallowing me whole. I felt something firm wrap around my ankles as I reached the end of the oesophagus, and my head squished through a wet sphincter. I spluttered slime off my lips and opened my eyes as my shoulders pushed through.

I couldn't see shit. Or I guess, that's all I could see. A jittering lump of flesh about the size of my head dangled inches away from my face, with nothing but an empty sack below it, waiting to catch me. I pulled my arms through the sphincter and went to fucking town on the heart, using it as a speed bag as I dangled upside down from what felt like a slime-coated asshole.

The creature's insides gurgled and writhed as I beat the life out of the heart with my bare hands. The sphincter tightened and pushed me through up to the waist, but whatever had my ankles held strong. I placed one hand behind the heart, holding it steady as I put my full force into a set of thunderous punches, again and again until the flesh split, and slime gushed out over my knuckles. I felt the monster swaying, on the verge of collapse. I took the failing heart in both hands as the sphincter squeezed me through to my knees and gave it an almighty tug, severing it from the tubes it dangled from. Slime poured from the tubes. The creature let out a screech that rippled through my entire body before I felt it stumble and collapse.

Whatever had my ankles tugged me back through the sphincter as the monster deflated around me. I slid up through the throat and took a look to see what had a hold of me as I was vomited back into the world. Down between my knees, Ali's face smiled up at me with a– nearly literal–shit-eating grin.

The monster let out a rumbling belch as we fell from its mouth and into the trash nest. I took a look at myself; I was covered in brown slime, sitting in a trash heap in the middle of a sewer with a monster's heart in my hands.

"Good fuckin' job," Khearo said as he slapped me on the back, splattering more slime over the back of my neck.

I looked him in the eyes and tossed the heart at his head. I pointed a finger at him, then at Morgan. "We never fucking speak of this, and I'm not doing it again. Never, you hear me? I draw the line at this shit."

I felt violated. Physically, I was fine. It had been an easy job. A fairly simple monster to kill. Not much effort. But by God, I felt dirty. I needed to bleach my soul and go see a priest.

Morgan held up his hands. "Sure, okay, we hear you. We never speak of it. Right after we tell the other guys all about it, of course."

# Full Time Sucka

I walked into The Black Cat in a real shitty mood. I'd spent the first half of the previous day being eaten by a shit monster, and the other half in the shower trying to get the smell off. Even after leaving the windows open all night, and another morning shower, a faint whiff still clung to my hair. It was nowhere near as pungent as it had been, but the warmth of the afternoon wasn't helping it go away. I considered trying to wash the clothes I'd worn but decided to just throw them down the garbage chute. There was no chance of getting the smell out of them.

I paused at the bar and rummaged in my jacket pocket before pulling out a few business cards and putting them on the countertop. They had been clean and simple when I first got them printed: just pure white with the words 'Isaac Nightingale: Monster Hunter' on the front and 'Find me' on the back. Vague, I know, but when you end up with a heavy reputation, people know who to ask if they have need of your skills. These cards had ended up stained with blood at some point, but they'd do.

A full set of grins greeted me as I made my way over to our usual meeting table. "Not a fucking word from any of you."

Tex held his hands up. "We haven't said anything. You're gonna want to hear what we do have to say though."

I sat myself down in an empty seat with a sigh. "Go on then."

Tex glanced behind my head. "I'll let the man himself explain."

I twisted my head to see Mystic Mickey standing behind me with a smile on his face. He clapped a hand down on my shoulder and gave me a nod as he shuffled by to take the last empty seat.

"Fancy seeing you here, how the fuck ya doin'?"

His voice echoed through my head, "Fantastic, my man, fucking fantastic. Wait 'till you hear the news."

"Come on, then don't leave me hanging."

Ali and Ginn sat looking for an explanation of what was being said. They'd spent the morning getting acquainted before I showed up, but their minds hadn't tuned in to Mickey's telepathic frequency just yet.

"What wears a skin with two thumbs, has the biggest electro-transference tentacles and has two of Dominus Atrocitas' cronies tied up in the old warehouse and ready to squeal?"

I took a moment to absorb the sentence. "Is it you?"

"Booya, motherfucker," Mickey said, giving two thumbs up.

I took a moment to explain what Mickey had said to Ali and Ginn, who just nodded along confirming what they'd heard already.

"You remember the place where you first fought Khearo and Morgan?"

222

"I sure do," I nodded, thinking back to my first full-on fistfight with a vampire and werewolf at the same time, and Khearo's big red undies.

"How'd you fancy beating some information out of some suckas?"

"It'd be my pleasure," I said, leaning back with a smile.

Mickey led the way into the warehouse about an hour later with the whole squad in attendance. It was just as I remembered, cold and damp with nothing inside but a few bits of trash and a makeshift table at the back with a few upturned milk crates scattered around it. The air inside had the damp smell of mildew and mould, a characteristic of a building left to rot.

Mickey had spared no expense in binding the captive vamps. The two of them sat on the edges of one upturned crate. Big enough for them both to sit on, but small enough that the ridge of the crate dug into their asses. He'd wound duct tape around the entire bottom half of their heads and bound them in iron chains with a few hefty padlocks holding them tight. They squirmed and let out muffled yells as we approached. One had grey hair and dark, soulless eyes set in deep wrinkled sockets. The other looked no older than a teenager, just a kid.

We formed a circle, surrounding them.

Morgan took the younger of the two suckers by the head and pulled out a switchblade. "You're gonna squeal for us now," he said. He pushed the blade through the tape where he thought their mouth should be and slashed it from side to side.

223

Blood trickled out through the tape as the hole ripped open.

"Let us go, please," the sucker said.

Khearo stepped forward. "Spill the beans on Atrocitas and we might."

The sucker shook his head and spluttered more blood. "I don't know anything about him, I swear. I didn't even want to be a vampire, they forced me."

"How about you?" Morgan said as he slashed the tape on the older sucker's mouth.

"Untie us you bunch of cunts, or you'll be sorry," he said.

Tex unholstered his gun and let his handful of iron hang by his side. "Friend, I don't think you're in any position to be making threats."

"You'll regret this, mark my fucking words. Dominus will tear you and your little gang of pussies to shreds when he hears about this." He paused and took a long hard look at Morgan. "And you, you should be ashamed of yourself, making friends with dogs, and worse: humans. You're a disgrace."

Morgan set the point of his switchblade on the sucker's forehead and pushed until a droplet of blood trickled out. "Mouthy fucker for someone in such a compromising situation, aren't you?"

Judging from the look on their faces, and their general manner, we'd be getting no information out of the older sucker. The younger one, on the other hand, looked promising. I could smell the fear on him, and thanks to the Hot Sauce, I could hear his heart beating.

224

The bit about not wanting to be a vampire wasn't a lie, and he did indeed seem fresh to the sucking game. He had the potential to sing like a canary so I decided to put the pressure on.

I stepped forward, bringing Sophia out to play. "See this gun kid?"

He eyed the revolver, and his heart rate spiked.

I got a little closer, holding the barrel in front of his face so he could give it a good inspection. "Beautiful, isn't she? She's special too, don'cha know? Haunted by that big guy's ancestor," I nodded in Ali's direction. "Her spirit lives within this gun, guides it. I've never missed a damn shot." I took a step back and turned around, scanning the warehouse for something to shoot.

Ginn caught on to my idea and picked up a fist-sized chunk of wood.

I turned back to the kid to make sure he was watching. The older vamp had kept his mouth shut, watching out of sheer interest. "Ginn, if you'd be so kind as to chuck that block into the air, anywhere I can't see it, please."

Ginn tossed it underhand, high into the air, with a "HUP!"

I closed my eyes, brought the gun up over my head and squeezed the trigger. An ear-splitting bang rang through the warehouse and the block exploded into a thousand shards. Chips rained down, bouncing off everyone's heads.

I tucked Sophia back into her holster. "Well, now that I'm done swinging my dick, whad'ya say, gonna sing us a nice song?"

"Say a word and I'll gut you myself, you little fuck," the older vamp said.

The kid took a look around, taking in the sight of the group with pure dread in his eyes.

"I'm tired of this one's shite," Rusty said, pointing at the older vamp. "Mickey lad, are ya hungry?"

Mickey nodded and stepped towards the pair of suckers, looming over them for a moment before pulling out a key and undoing their chains. The kid stayed put, rooted to the spot. The older sucker shook himself free of the chains, clawed the tape from his face and threw it to the floor with a growl.

"You fucking fool," the sucker said, pointing a dirty claw at Mickey, "I'm gonna tear you all a new asshoo... what the fuck?"

I took my eyes off the sucker, then my hand off my gun as I took note of what had stopped the old fucker in his tracks. A storm of writhing tentacles had burst from Mickey's mouth, flailing around in the air. Mickey took a step forward. The old sucker took a step back.

"What the fuck are yo—ARG!"

The tentacles shot forward and wrapped themselves around the sucker's arms and legs. He yelled and struggled but couldn't break free. The tentacles pulsed and tightened their grips. The free ones writhed in the air, whipping back and forth. Mickey took another step forward as the sucker's feet left the ground. The group stood in awe, and the young sucker sat in horror as the warehouse filled with a crackling sound, followed by the screams of the old sucker. Yellow jolts of electricity sparked and jumped from the tentacles as Mickey's eyes grew brighter behind his sunglasses. The sucker's screams rose to a higher pitch as the electricity arced from his face to the tentacles, before finally petering out with a deflated sigh as his soul left his body.

"Damn," Ali said, speaking for all of us.

Mickey dropped the sucker. He hit the floor with a heavy thud, his eyes already grey and cloudy. The tentacles whipped and writhed back into Mickey's mouth, gone just as fast as they'd appeared.

"Looks like you're next, kid," I said to the remaining vamp.

He shrunk in on himself like a tortoise retreating into its shell. "Oh fuck no, please, I'll tell you anything."

"Where's Atrocitas?" Tex demanded.

The young sucker turned to face him. "Nebraska. There's an old abandoned nuclear bunker out on the plains, past the National Forest, huge but real well hidden. Go up through Colorado and take highway three-eight-five. He has scouts everywhere, though. They'll know you're coming long before you get to the bunker itself."

"How do we find it?"

"Take a left after Chadron Creek, on to Buttermilk Road and drive until you can't no more. You'll get to a dirt track. Follow it north and you'll get there eventually. I promise that's all I know. I've never even met the big guy; I don't know anything else about him."

"And how many suckers are we looking at?"

"I don't know, man, hundreds. That's all I know. Please, just let me go."

Tex held out a hand towards the exit. "Well since you've been so helpful and asked so polite, off you go. Straight to Atrocitas now, tell him we're coming for him."

The kid didn't wait around. He shook out of the chains and darted for the exit. The group watched him go, disappearing out the door.

"Think you guys can track him?"

"Piece of cake, pal. Mickey can keep on his tail," Rusty said.

Tex removed his hat and sat down on the crate. "I reckon he'll lead us right to Atrocitas in time. We're gonna have to prepare, big style. If he's got an army in a goddamn bunker, we're gonna have to be on top form if we want to stand a chance. All of us, together, we have work to do. We can't rush in. We'll stick around LA for a while. Do some monster hunting together, put in the work, get our act real tight. Special forces the shit outta this."

Rusty chimed in, "Aye and with our piggy running back to Papa, you know he's gonna squeal. We're likely to have goons crammed up our asses soon."

Khearo nodded along. "What we need right now is a montage."

The group looked from Tex to Khearo, and then all traded looks between each other, all waiting for something to happen, for some music to magically kick start a badass sequence.

Khearo let out a sigh and shrugged. "No? I kinda hoped it'd somehow happen like it does in the movies."

Tex stood and put his hat back on. "Guess we're doing it the long way."

# B-Movie Bloodbath

Instead of jumping right into a badass montage, we all sat down back at The Black Cat and had words about what to do next. Rusty had a list of outstanding jobs he needed a hand with while we waited for our new vampire buddy to run home and tell Big Daddy Dominus our intentions, so we went through the list, agreeing on who was gonna do what. Since I'd drawn the short straw last time and ended up inside a shit monster, I got to choose first.

"Right lad, whad'ya fancy?" Rusty said, handing me the list.

I scanned it over, trying to pick out what looked to be the easiest job. I'd usually like a challenge or a bit of excitement, but I wasn't in the mood. I wanted something quick and easy, so I could get it over with, order a pizza and kick back in my hotel room.

I read through the list:

Capture the Beverly Hills werewolf.
Find and kill the grimus in the Bronson Caves.
Clear the poltergeist from Mrs Haukman's garage.
Catch the Rialto Ripper.
Exterminate the Santa Monica sandworm.
Re-reinforce the grave so HE doesn't escape.
Refill the Blood Chalice of Oku K'ryzinth.
Squash the flesh-eating gnomes in Derek's basement.

Buy lubricant for my wheels.

"Some fuckin' weird-looking shit on here," I said as I placed the paper down on the table and tapped the Ripper job.

"Rightio, the Rialto Ripper it is," Rusty said, "a fairly straightforward one, I reckon."

Bingo, just what I wanted to hear. "What's the rundown?"

Harriot answered, "Almost every night for the past two weeks now, the Rialto staff have found a corpse when a movie ends. Puncture wounds in the neck. We're thinking it's likely to be a vampire, but must be a real sneaky one. There've been no witnesses so far."

Ali held up a hand and said, "Have the police not been informed on this one? Could be a regular serial killer."

Morgan snorted. "The police? Of course they know about it, but any sign of something supernatural, they just look the other way."

I shrugged. "Looks like I'm gonna catch a movie tonight then, care to join me, Ginn?"

She nodded. "It's a date. We could catch Friday the Thirteenth?"

"Sounds good."

I gave my fist a little pump under the table. Ginn's night vision would make the job a hell of a lot easier.

"Guess I'll take the poltergeist," Tex said.

"I'll join you on that one, easiest access for the chair," Rusty said, rapping his knuckles on his wheelchair.

Harriot took a moment to ponder the list. "I'll refill the chalice; it seems to prefer my blood anyway."

Rusty shoved the list past Mickey and towards Morgan and Khearo. "Mickey gets a pass since he's keeping an eye on our snitch."

Morgan shrugged. "Take the werewolf?" he asked, looking at Khearo.

Khearo stroked his beard for a moment. "Sure, seems to make sense, doesn't it?"

"Grand! We get this lot done today and take tomorrow off to relax. Sound good?" Rusty asked as he snatched the list and crossed off the tasks people had agreed on.

Everybody nodded.

"Right then, Night and Ginn, you may as well chill until sundown, unless you care to help anyone with their tasks in the meantime. Everyone else, let's get to it, shall we?"

As nice as Rusty's offer of more work sounded, much to Ginn's approval, I politely declined. While everyone got up and left to take care of their business, Ginn and I stayed behind and sipped some of LA's finest orange juice.

"So, what would you like to do before the film?" Ginn asked once everyone had left.

I leaned back and slouched into my chair. "Dunno, the city is our oyster. Got anything in mind?"

"We could go back to the hotel and fuck?"

Orange juice erupted from my nostrils. "What?" I coughed.

Ginn howled with laughter and slapped her knee. "I knew that'd get you. Nah, how about the Griffith Observatory? I've always wanted to check it out."

"You fuckin' asshole. Yeah, sure, let's go check it out," I said, trying to wipe the snotty orange juice from my shirt.

\* \* \*

We leaned against the wall of the Griffith Observatory, watching the sun set over the city, turning the downtown skyline into a silhouette against an orange backdrop. Ginn hooked her arm around mine and rested her head on my shoulder.

"It's times like this I forget about all the shit in the world. Little over a week ago I was alone, chained to a radiator in a dirty motel, wearing nothing but a potato sack and surrounded by vampires. Now I'm here, watching a beautiful sunset. And I have friends."

"And more importantly, clothes. If what you wear can pass for clothes, that is."

That earned me a hard prod in the ribs. "Yes, clothes."

I put my cheek on the top of her head. "So, you forgive us for fucking up your plans?"

"As much as I hate to admit it, you guys probably did save me. Say you guys hadn't found me, then what? At best I actually kill Atrocitas myself, and then I get killed by the army that's left. Worst, I fail and he either kills me or keeps me in misery for however long I end up living. Yeah, I forgive you. At least this way, if I'm going to die, I won't die alone."

I snorted. "That's a touching sentiment. You think we're going to die?"

"Now that I know the big baddie has an army in a nuclear bunker, against all nine of us? Oh yeah, we're fucked."

"Well, it's eleven if you count the Neon Nightmares."

Ginn sighed and squeezed my arm a little tighter. "With those two idiots, we're definitely fucked."

We had about an hour until the movie started so we hitched a ride in a cab down to South Broadway. We stepped out of the cab about twenty minutes later. The theatre's marquee shone bright with neon pinks and blues, beckoning us in from the sidewalk. Ginn took my arm again as we made our way to the ticket booth.

"Two for Friday the Thirteenth, please," I said, placing a five-dollar bill on the booth's counter.

The clerk tore off a pair of tickets and handed them to me with my change, without saying a word.

We pushed through the doors and were caressed by the smell of fresh popcorn. Ginn dropped my arm and made a beeline straight to the stand to join the queue. A couple stood in front of us. The guy had his arm over the lady's shoulder, gently stroking her neck with a set of dirty fingernails.

I gave Ginn a nudge and whispered, "Ten bucks says this is our guy."

Ginn mouthed, "You're on."

The guy turned and gave me a good eyeballing as they stepped forward to make their order. My stomach churned as I eyeballed him back, then smiled and pretended to read the offers menu.

A few moments later, they were served and stepping aside to make their way to the screen. I could have sworn the dude took a hard sniff as he made his way past us, but he could have been inhaling that sweet, sweet popcorn scent rather than being a creepy fucker.

Ginn got the popcorn and handed me a bucket as we made our way to the screen.

"Mind if we sit right at the back?" I asked.

"Best seats for a bit of a tonsil tussle, huh?"

"More 'cos we'll get a good view of everyone in there, in case the Ripper shows up."

"Sure, whatever you say," Ginn said, giving an exaggerated wink.

"You'll have no time for a tussle anyway; you'll be doing all the lookin' out while I kick back and enjoy the movie."

She threw a kernel of popcorn at my head. "Hey that's not fair."

I shrugged. "Who has the better night vision?"

"Fuck," Ginn muttered, "you're a superhuman Hot Sauce man with almost every sense enhanced yet you can barely see in the dark. What kind of shit is that?"

"Sucks, but it is what it is. Even Superman has a weakness."

I pushed the screen door open as more bits of popcorn pinged off my head. We took our seats as the trailers started. The first was for 'Evil Dead', followed by 'Halloween II', 'An American Werewolf in London', then 'My Bloody Valentine'. I sat entranced the entire time, oblivious to the murmurs and rustles of the other people. The movie started soon after, and I snuggled down into my seat with the popcorn resting on my stomach.

I tried to keep an eye out for suspicious behaviour while we watched the movie but I didn't see a damn thing out of the ordinary. Granted, all I could really make out were people's silhouettes, but nothing looked off. I hadn't spotted any vampires creeping around, no heads lowered to necks. Ginn confirmed my assessments every now and again with a slight shake of the head.

When the credits rolled, the house lights came on and a few other patrons stood to leave, but most stayed seated to watch the credits. The metallic tang of blood caught in the back of my nose. I locked eyes with the guy from the popcorn queue, a few rows down from us. He had stood to leave, but the woman he'd come with stayed in her seat. He made to move towards the aisle. All appeared to be normal, even though my stomach churned.

Ginn gave me a nudge. "Look at his fingers."

They looked longer than they did when he was in the popcorn queue, and what's worse, they were stained red.

He caught me eyeing them and made a dart for the aisle, knocking the woman as he ran past. Her head lolled over the back of the seat and her dead eyes stared right into mine.

Fuck.

Ginn intercepted him in the aisle. He barged into her, throwing her to the floor. They tumbled down in a heap with him on top of her. He let out a high-pitched screech, scrambled to his knees and straddled Ginn's chest, pinning her arms to her sides. She struggled, trying to break free, but didn't have much luck. I had expected the guy's face to change, go all vampire mode, but it didn't. In the moments it took for me to get from my seat to the aisle, he sat wiggling his fingers at Ginn's face. They pulsated and grew longer. The bloodstained tips swelled, turned purple and split in the middle, letting out a sharp barb of bone with a milk-like liquid dripping from the tip.

Ginn kicked and yelled, "Oh fuck, why do his fingers look like a load of monster dicks?"

She was right, they did.

I yelled, "Hey Dick Fingers," as I flung myself down the aisle and delivered my boot to his jaw.

Dick Fingers (let's call him Dickie) fell off Ginn with a squeal. She scrambled to her feet as he writhed around on the floor, clutching his jaw. His eyes fell on me, and he dropped his hands from his face. His jaw jutted out from the side of his face as if he'd taken a

237

sledgehammer to the chin. Other patrons watched in horror and confusion. Some too scared to move, some wanting to watch somebody kick the shit out of a guy with mutated dongs for fingers.

Dickie shot to his feet and doubled back down the aisle towards a couple who were watching the freak show. He grabbed a hold of the man and plunged his fingers into his neck. His partner let out a blood-curdling scream and tried to make a run for it. She managed three strides before she stopped, and her eyes rolled into the back of her head. The fingers on Dickie's free hand had shot out like a set of long fleshy ropes and broke through the back of her skull. We both stood in shock for a moment and his fingers pulsated, spilling both blood and sticky white goo onto the nice carpet. 'Gotta be a vampire', my ass. I'd never seen anything like this before.

Dickie thrust his pulsating fingers in and out of his victim's bodies, harder and harder before letting out a screech of what sounded like pleasure. Both the man and woman on the ends of his fingers shuddered violently and then burst, exploding into a torrent of gore. The whole mess splattered over everything in a ten-metre radius, Ginn and me included.

Dickie's fingers had grown. A lot. They writhed in the air, whipping back and forth like Mickey's tentacles, spurting pulses of liquid out of the tips. The last of the onlookers wised up and ran out of the theatre screaming.

"Fuck this entire scene," I said as I whipped out both Sisters. A wet mush of flesh fell from the ceiling and landed on my shoulder as I waved the guns in Dickie's direction.

Before I could squeeze the trigger, a guy who appeared to be the manager came storming through the fire exit behind Dickie, yelling, "Now what the fuck is going on in here?"

He barely had a chance to finish his sentence before all of Dickie's fingers shot down his throat and blended his insides to mush. I shielded my eyes with my forearm as Dickie went to town on the fella. I waited for the sound of the poor guy going splat then pulled the trigger.

Dickie let out a godawful howl as the bullets blew through his skull.

"Night!" Ginn yelled.

I dropped my arm and pulled the trigger again, just in time. The barbed fingers stopped less than an inch from my face. They went limp and flopped to the floor as Dickie's legs buckled from underneath him now that half of his head was missing.

"Close call," I said, looking at Ginn, "your swords would have come in handy."

Ginn flicked a chunk of gristle from her boob. "Don't use the words 'come' or 'hand' in my presence for the next month, please. That was some seriously fucked up shit."

I looked around the room, taking in the carnage as the credits came to an end and the music died down. "Sure was. And Tex says I'm the one with chainsaws for arms. He shoulda seen this dude."

239

We stepped closer to the corpse to get a better look at the guy. He looked like a normal dude, aside from the fingers. I made a mental note to find out what the fuck he was, and how to spot such freaks sooner.

"You okay?" I asked.

Ginn gave herself a quick check over. "Bumped my head during the fall, but other than that, I'm good. You?"

I looked down at the blood and guts all over my clothes. "Heavily grossed out, but fine and dandy otherwise. Not a scratch on me."

"What a goddamn mess," Ginn said, looking around and rubbing her head.

I nodded, tucking the guns back into their holsters. "The words 'B-movie bloodbath' come to mind."

# Disco Inferno

The next morning, I awoke to a slow scratching noise on my door. At first, I thought it might have been something creepy trying to get in, like a repeat of the Rest in Peace Motel, but the fact that it was almost midday gave me cause for doubt. I swung myself out of bed, tucked a towel around my waist and eased the door open a smidge to peek out.

"Boo!" Ginn shoved her face through the gap and then like a cat, the rest of her followed.

"Can I help you?"

She sat herself down on the edge of my bed and said, "Yes, actually. I have a bit of a problem."

I sighed as I bid farewell to my day of peace. "What is it?"

"Okay, so, I was taking a walk this morning and some guy took one look at me and ran to a payphone. And like, I recognised him 'cos he paid a visit to the motel when I was being held captive, so I'm pretty sure he was informing some buddies, so, like, I think Atrocitas knows where I am now."

"Well, I guess Atrocitas will already know where we are by now, but if he knows you're with us, that'll complicate things."

"But," she said, holding up a finger, "he had a staff T-shirt on, seems to work at the Razzle Dazzle, so I was thinking, maybe you'd like to go tonight? Pay him a visit?"

I raised an eyebrow. "The Razzle Dazzle? You mean the roller disco place in West Hollywood?"

Ginn swung her legs and bounced on the bed. "Yup! We could invite Harriot; I know she'll want to come."

I pondered for a moment. "Yeah alright then."

Ginn let out a squeak and jumped up from the bed, making for the door. "Excellent, I'll go call her now. It's going to be so fun. I'm going to the mall in an hour or so, wanna come?"

I shook my head. "Nah I'm gonna take some time to chill. Get a bit of alone time, ya'know?"

Ginn took a moment to respond. Her attention had drifted to the fact that I was only wearing a towel. "Sure, sure... alone time, yeah," she said.

I was about to say goodbye so I could go take my morning shower when she grabbed my towel and sprang back, whipping it from around my waist. I didn't even bother trying to cover myself. She'd already clapped eyes on my merchandise.

She threw the towel at my head and stepped back into the hallway, towards her room. "See you later on tonight then," she said.

I gave her a disapproving look.

She hung on to her door before slowly closing it, making sure she got her full effort's worth of looking. I made a move to close my door when she popped back out.

"Oh, and Night?" she said.

"What?"

"Nooooice cock!"

She slammed her door with a laugh.

I closed mine, thinking we might have been better off leaving her with the fucking vampires. I secured the latch and threw myself back down on the bed with a sigh.

No rest for the wicked. No rest at all.

\*\*\*

Later that day, Ginn and I walked down Santa Monica Boulevard with our arms linked as the sun set, bathing the buildings in an orange glow. The lights began to flicker on, and the city's nightlife revealed itself. A couple cruised by in a Pontiac Judge; I admired it as it drove by. The polished paintwork caught the last of the sunlight, accentuating every detail. It was a thing of beauty, and in that moment I decided I needed one. Owning two cars never hurt anybody. My eyes followed the beautiful beast down the road until it rolled past the glowing neon lights of the Razzle Dazzle.

The roller disco stood shining in the dusk, beckoning teens and adults alike. Harriot stood at the bottom of the steps of the boogie palace, with her skates already in hand. She'd opted for short shorts that verged on being dental floss, and a crop top that showed a lot of flesh.

Ginn unhooked from my arm and ran over to give her a hug, yelling, "Daaamn girl, what a fucking smoke-show."

I had to agree, Harriot did indeed look smokin'. I'd always thought she was attractive, but being scantily clad and bathed in a neon glow really worked for her.

"You've got your own skates?" Ginn asked.

"Of course, I'm a roller disco fiend! Never been to this one though, I usually go to the Moonlight Maniac down near Venice Beach."

"Huh, never heard of that one."

Harriot tapped the side of her nose. "It's a well-guarded secret, that one. Shall we go in? Come on Night," she said as she hooked my arm to drag me in.

Ginn hooked the other and they sandwiched me in the middle. No escape. But hey, who'd wanna escape a hot lady sandwich anyway?

Inside was a kaleidoscope of whirling colour and pounding music. I could feel the bass in my chest and the lights dazzling my brain. They'd named the joint well, and it was a great place for vampires to hang out: mostly dark, loud music, confusing lights and frequent screams from people having fun and falling over. I could smell a trap.

Ginn and I made our way over to rent some skates as Harriot found a bench to put hers on. Ginn nudged me in the side and nodded towards the guy behind the desk. I assumed he was the guy who'd spotted her earlier in the day. The way he went stiff and eyeballed her as we stepped forward confirmed it. He was definitely a vamp too. In fact, looking around, all of the fucking staff looked like suckers.

"Erm... size?" he asked, eyes darting between us.

Ginn smiled at him and said, "Five please."

I smiled too. "Ten for me."

He turned to find our skates.

"We've walked into a fucking nest of suckers," I hissed under my breath.

"Yeah, I clocked that too," Ginn whispered back, "what the fuck do we do?"

I shrugged. "What we do best, I guess."

The guy came back over and dropped two pairs of roller skates down in front of us. I handed him the cash and we moseyed over to join Harriot on the bench.

She took one look at our faces and said, "Figured it out huh?"

"You already knew?" Ginn said as she ducked down to pull her skates on.

Harriot chuckled, then nodded. "Oh yeah, I could smell the place from down the road."

I patted the Sisters, strapped to my sides as always. "Good thing I keep the ladies with me."

Harriot leaned back and eyeballed me for a moment. "Ya'know what, I'd like to make a wager."

"A wager?" Ginn cut in, popping back up.

"If Night can go the entire evening without using those guns, I'll give him fifty dollars."

I took a moment to consider the offer. There was no way around it, the evening was gonna end in a fight one way or another. And while I could always go without the Sisters, should I?

"You're on."

"Excellent," Harriot smiled, "you boys are far too reliant on your guns."

Ginn snorted. "Of course they are, they're basically cock extensions."

Harriot howled with laughter.

"Not that his needs any extension," Ginn added, nudging me hard in the ribs.

Harriot stopped laughing and clapped a hand to her cheek. "You've seen it?"

Ginn bumped me with her shoulder and gave me a wink. "He's got a habit of answering the door wearing nothing but loose towels."

"The towel wasn't loose, actually, you fucking snatched it right off me."

Harriot raised an eyebrow and pursed her lips.

"What? Don't look at me, she's a fucking menace."

Harriot stood, still giving me the look as she hooked her arm around Ginn's and they made their way to the dance floor, leaving me to put my skates on alone.

The place was packed with people dressed in funky colours, screaming, whirling around the dance floor and having a great time. It looked fun, but in reality it was nothing but a sucker's buffet. Every last person was on that night's menu and if we didn't act fast, people were going to die. I tightened my laces with a sharp tug, tied them into a nice little bow, and threw myself onto the dance floor to tear it up with my finest grooves.

The joint didn't know what hit it. Harriot and Ginn turned all the heads. And of course they did, they were smokin' for more than one reason. Harriot was a pro. She shredded the floor so hard her skates almost burst into flames. Ginn, on the other hand, was a maniac on the floor, dancing like she'd never danced before. I'd always been a natural on a set of skates, so I joined them, and together we threw the wildest shapes the Razzle Dazzle had ever seen.

It must have been about midnight when the first signs of fuckery started to show. The DJ had been playing a couple of songs with a repetitive, pounding beat and a synced up light show. It was around halfway through the second of such songs when I noticed a bunch of people skating in circles as if they were in a trance. By the end of the song, a couple of the zombified patrons rolled off the dance floor and made their way through a door labelled 'PRIVATE'. Now, at first I figured, hey, maybe they're just going for a mid-boogie quickie in the broom closet, but midway through the third head pounding tune I caught a whiff of blood.

Harriot put on the brakes and whirled to face me. "You smell that?"

I nodded, and pointed at the private door. "Saw a couple go in there earlier. And have you noticed a few people suddenly look a little out of their gourds?"

Ginn screeched to a halt beside us. "They're hypnotizing people!"

"What?" I asked.

She pointed at the DJ. "The music and lights, they're putting some people into a trance," then pointed to a couple who were slowly skating around the floor with their arms by their sides and slack jaws, "I've been watching those two. They were wild until the music changed."

I nodded towards the private door. "Let's see what they're up to."

Harriot and Ginn nodded. We skated off the floor and onto the sticky blue carpet that was splattered with glowing neon-coloured shapes. I set my hand on the door handle and gave the girls the "Ready?" look before throwing the door open and rolling inside.

The suckers had style. The private room was decked out with games machines, sofas, a TV and their own bar. One sucker stood behind the bar pouring drinks, one stood playing a game of pinball, and two lady-suckers sat sprawled out on a pair of comfy looking sofas. Both of them a skater sitting next to them in a daze.

"Hey this is members only!" the sucker behind the bar yelled.

Harriot rolled by to get further into the room. Ginn pulled the door shut behind her and ripped the handle off, shutting us in.

"The fuck, man?" the sucker at the pinball machine said.

I rolled closer and saw tubes poking out of the arms of the dazed patrons. The suckers on the sofas sat sipping blood from the ends of the tubes. I had to give it to them: they had a touch of class. This was the vampire version of fine dining.

I eyed a fire alarm to my right and wasted no time in pulling it. I needed to evacuate the joint before we caused some ruckus.

The vamp at the pinball machine focused on me and swaggered over saying, "Big mistake pal, you don't know what you're fucking wi—OOF!"

Harriot sucker punched him in the side of the head. His face made acquaintance with the carpet. The girl had a mean left hook; the sucker lost his consciousness and his dignity in one punch.

The suckers jumped up from their sofas as the one behind the bar yelled, "Get them!"

The one on the left pounced at Harriot, and the other came at me. I instinctively reached for the Sisters then remembered the wager. No guns this time.

In my hesitation, she got the drop on me and rocked my jaw with a hard right hook. The force of the punch set my head spinning so hard I stumbled backwards and fell on my ass. She rolled forward on her skates and followed up by giving me a hard kicking in the ribs. Really drove in that toe-stopper, too, the fucker.

While she regained her balance, I scrambled backwards and sprang to my feet. The sucker sailed towards me. I broke out the grooves and swerved, circling behind her as she rolled on by. I made to grab her for a good ol' tussle but stopped in my tracks as blood and brains splattered across my face.

Ginn's blood-soaked hand stuck out the back of the sucker's head. It waved "hello" at me, then pulled back and out of the girl's mouth with a wet slurp. She fell to the floor as her skin bubbled and flesh melted off her bones.

"Have I ever told you how awesome and terrifying you are?"

She smiled and shot me the finger guns saying, "Shut up, baby, I know it," before blowing the tip of her finger.

I rolled my eyes as I turned to see Harriot smashing her attacker's head into the pinball machine over and over again. His face had been put through the glass screen and was busy bouncing off the flippers. He put up a bit of a struggle before going limp after the sixth smash, but she kept on smashing. The machine rang out, racking up points and telling her she was doing a great job. When the sucker's face was crumpled in on itself, she dropped him to the floor. The machine flashed and jingled, "HIGH SCORE!"

The three of us turned our attention to the guy behind the bar.

He stood yelling, "Come on, come on," down the phone until someone picked up. "We got a code red. Code fuckin' red, ya hear me? Get the girls on the floor stat!"

Ginn launched herself over the sofas and yanked him over the counter. He sailed through the air and landed in a heap at my feet. Harriot wasted no time and threw a kick so hard the toe-stopper on her roller skate smeared the sucker's nose three inches up his face. He let out a scream as he clutched his ruined schnoz.

I grabbed a handful of his hair and pulled his head up to get him into a headlock pinning his jaw shut. I gave Ginn 'THE LOOK'. She hopped over the sofas and took the sucker by the legs. I nodded, and we pulled. The last time

I'd tried such a move was in the Salty Dog with Tex, and it took a lot of effort, but this time it was like tearing tissue paper. One sharp tug from Ginn and the vampire split at the sides, tearing in half at the waist. An almighty stench slapped my face as the sucker's guts spilled out onto the floor.

I dropped what was left of him and spun on my wheels. "Let's get some blood on the dance floor."

We rolled across the bloodstained carpet back towards the door. The sucker Harriot knocked out still lay on the floor. I rolled past and shouldered the door open as Harriot stomped on his head, popping it like a fat grape.

The Razzle Dazzle had become a ghost town since I'd pulled the fire alarm. The place was empty save for the DJ sitting at his booth still spinning his hypno-tunes. The music came to an abrupt stop with a record scratch as we rolled onto the dance floor. The DJ's voice rang out over the speakers, smooth as velvet, "Alright now boppers, it's time to kick things up a notch and increase the heat, here's a fresh little number that'll really get the blood pumping."

## [Track 25]

The first beats of a pulse-pounding dance tune filled the room as a line of women in tight silver bodysuits rolled out onto the dance floor. All eight of them spun circles around us. I took in the sight of them all: long legs, tight bodies, and generous amounts of

251

cleavage on show. It would have been a damn fine sight to see if they didn't all have black beady eyes, wrinkly snouts and fangs sticking out in all directions.

The girls spun around us, giggling while they circled their prey. I looked from Ginn to Harriot, they were ready, and so was I.

I pushed off on my toe-stoppers and launched into one of the girls with the force of a champion linebacker. She let out a scream as she came off her feet and landed on her back with me on top of her. She wrapped her legs around my waist and pulled me in tight, gnashing at my face. I pinned her arms above her head and crashed my forehead down between her eyes. Her legs loosened up a little, and I delivered another thunder-smooch right to her nose with a squelchy crack. Her legs dropped off at my sides. I hauled myself to my feet as she lay trying to clear the fog from her head. "Maybe this'll help," I said as I delivered a kick under the chin so hard it sent her head spinning over the DJ booth, whirling blood across the floor.

I turned to see why I hadn't already been attacked by another sucker and found Harriot's clothes in shreds on the floor. She was huge, hairy, and in the process of ripping the flesh off one girl's face while two suckers hung from her back. One was already dead at her feet and turning into a green puddle.

Ginn was in the middle of a vamp-girl sandwich, fists flying everywhere, and one sucker was still circling, cheering her friends on.

I rolled over to the DJ booth—which was now abandoned—and pulled a few records off a small pile before giving chase to the girl doing the cheerleading. She skated away as fast as she could, screaming "Fuck off," as I frisbee'd a record at her head. She ducked it and it shattered off the wall in an explosion of black shards.

She wasn't so quick the second time. I launched a seven inch at her head as she turned to see where she was going. The vinyl spun like a saw blade and embedded in the top of her skull, sticking up like a mohawk hairdo. Her legs wobbled as she veered off to the right, swerving towards the barrier wall. She hit it and slumped over before turning and sliding down on her back with a confused look on her face. It had shifted back to human. She was real pretty when she wasn't a monster: big blue eyes and a cute little nose.

"Whassappenin?" she asked, looking up as I stopped in front of her.

"You've got a song stuck in your head," I said.

"Oooh is it a guddwon?"

I tugged the record from her skull and read the label: 'Got a Lot on My Head' by The Cars. "Heh, sure is."

She gave me a bleary-eyed smile before her head drooped forward and blood gushed out of the wound.

I flipped the record over and admired it before flinging it at one of the vamps tussling with Ginn. It hit horizontally and embedded deep in the side of her head, slicing her eyeballs in half. She dropped to the floor as the jelly oozed from her eyes. Ginn gave me two thumbs up.

Blood gushed from a large gash on her forehead, but she just wiped it away and smiled.

The sucker Harriot had been ripping apart was nothing but tattered flesh on the floor. She'd moved on to the other two and was busy repeatedly smashing their faces together, with a head in each big, clawed paw.

I frisbee'd the remaining records into the air and made my way over to one of the corpses on the floor of the private room. I had just got done yanking the short shorts off of her when Ginn appeared by my side. In the clear light of the suite, I could see a lot of bruises forming on her skin, crisscrossed with some deep-looking scratches.

"You good?" I asked. "You're bleeding a lot."

She looked down at her scratched up arms. "It's fine, I'll heal up soon. And it's not all my blood, don't worry."

"Fair enough."

"What the fuck are you doing, anyway?"

I pointed at Harriot, still smashing skulls together even though the suckers were long past dead. "She's gonna need some shorts when she loses the fur suit."

"Hmm, didn't think of that," she said with a nod.

Harriot dropped her toys into a bloody pile and made her way over to us, slowly changing back to human. She covered herself with her hands as the hair fell off her body. "Eyes off the merchandise," she said.

She was covered in a lot of bad scratches too, but nowhere near as bad as Ginn was. Her thick fur proved to be useful in a scrap.

I turned my head away and held out the shorts.

I heard the sound of a zipper a moment later, then, "I think you forgot something."

I turned, saying "What?" and caught sight of Harriot with her arm across her chest.

"Take a guess, smartass."

"Oh!" I sure was glad I was covered in blood 'cos my cheeks were burning red.

Ginn handed her a top and I looked away again as she pulled it on.

"What now?" she asked.

I turned to see her fully dressed, or as dressed as anyone can be in short shorts and a crop top. The top wasn't leaving much to the imagination. The burning in my cheeks grew hotter.

"Torch the place. They'll only come back if we don't."

Ginn shrugged and made her way over to the bar to grab a few bottles of liquor.

"Shame," Harriot said while crouching and ripping the top off one of the dead suckers and tearing it to strips, "I don't really want to contribute to the death of disco."

We kicked off our skates and grabbed our shoes from behind the desk before hauling the vampire's victims onto our shoulders and making our way outside with a few Molotov cocktails, Harriot to my left, Ginn to my right; all of us bruised and bloody.

We set the unconscious victims down on the sidewalk opposite. I pulled out my lighter and set a strip of cloth alight. We clinked bottles together to spread the flame, and said "Cheers," before throwing them through the open doors. Within minutes, the whole place was an inferno, and we watched it burn.

Ginn smiled, flames dancing in her eyes. "Burn baby, burn."

I snorted and rolled my eyes. "Knew some fucker was gonna say it."

"What? Come on, it's the perfect opportunity," she said, pointing at the blazing roller disco.

"She's got a point," Harriot said.

I shrugged. "Guess so," then linked my arms through theirs. "Shall we call it a night ladies? It's been real fun; we should do it again sometime."

Harriot laid her head on my shoulder. "It really has."

I looked down at her and smiled. "And hey guess what?" I bent to whisper in her ear, "You owe me fifty bucks."

# Basement Dweller

A loud knock on the door woke me the next morning. The alarm clock told me it was seven-thirty, an ungodly hour for any visitors. After the bloodbath in the roller disco, Ginn and I decided to get an early night and retire to our respective hotel rooms instead of meeting the others in the Black Cat. I hauled my bare ass out of bed and pulled on a bathrobe to hide my junk in case it was Ginn at the door. I unlocked the door and swung it open to the sight of an unfamiliar man standing in front of me: a short fella with thinning grey hair and a thick moustache to compensate. He looked nervous, his eyes darted back and forth, and he checked over his shoulder before speaking.

"Isaac Nightingale?" he asked, holding up one of my bloodstained business cards.

"Yeah?" I said, following it with a yawn.

The man handed me a scrap of paper with an address on it. "Please come as soon as possible. I've trapped something in my basement, and I don't think the door will hold much longer."

I opened my mouth to ask for more info, but the man turned and scurried off down the corridor.

Ginn's door creaked open, and her head peeked out. She watched the man turn the corner then came out wearing blue silky pyjamas. "What's all that about?" she asked.

"No idea. He said he's trapped something and needs help right away. I guess it must be something a little more dangerous than a pissed-off racoon."

"Huh. Need a hand with it?"

"Nah, I'll take this one myself. Be nice to have a bit of alone time, ya'know. I'll meet everyone at the usual spot later on."

"Fair enough," she said, with a yawn, "catch you later."

She disappeared back into her room, and I followed suit with a good ol' wash in mind.

The heat of the shower got my blood pumping, ready to rumble with whatever awaited me in the stranger's basement. I threw on a comfortable set of blue jeans, a grey T-shirt and my jacket on top to cover the guns strapped to my sides. I locked my door and stepped down the hall to pound a fist on Tex's. It took him almost two minutes to answer the door. His hair stuck out in all directions.

"Mind if I borrow the car? I've just been asked to do a job."

Without a word, Tex leaned to the side and picked the keys up from a unit by the door. He shoved them into my hands and closed the door with a dismissive wave.

"And tell the guys I'll be along later, would you?" I said through the door.

A grunt of acknowledgement floated back through it.

The address took me on a forty-minute drive to the Anaheim area, just south of Disneyland. I pulled up out front and took a good hard gander at the house in case I was walking into a trap. Not that it really mattered, trap or not, I wouldn't be leaving without shooting something. It looked all clear, nothing but another cookie-cutter suburban house. I hopped out of the car and made my way down the path.

The door creaked open as I approached and the man's face peeked out before he threw the door open and waved for me to come in, as quickly as I could. He closed the door behind me and set about locking it with a series of deadbolts, latches and padlocks. When he finished, I brushed my jacket aside so he could cop a good look at the Sisters.

He gave me a hard nod, staring at them. "You're packing. Good. You'll need them for what's down there," he peered down at the floor with wide eyes. "My name's Ron, by the way."

I made myself comfortable on his sofa without being invited. "Nice to meet'cha, Ron. Gonna tell me what I'm getting myself into?"

I took a look around the room. Ron had a lot of pictures of Jesus, and even more crucifixes dotted all over the walls. A shrine to the Virgin Mary stood in the corner with a bunch of candles lighting it up.

He sat in an armchair opposite me and took off his glasses. "I don't know what it is if I'm honest," he said, rubbing his lenses, "I'd dreamt about it for a week straight, then one night I woke up, and lo and behold, it was in the room with me. It looks like a cross between a woman and a snake."

"A snake? You sure it's not half-centipede?"

"No, no, it's definitely a snake-woman. It has a human face, and arms, and…" he held his hands in front of his chest, making squeezing motions.

"Tits?"

"Tits," he nodded.

"So, it looks like Medusa?"

He shook his head. "No snakes for hair, but yes, its bottom half is like a snake."

I took a long look at him, getting the measure of him, wondering how such a weedy-looking little dude managed to wrestle a snake-woman from his bedroom into his basement.

"And you trapped it in the basement? How?"

He shrugged. "It ran, or slithered away, I guess, when I woke up that night. It went down there of its own accord; I just locked it in. I'm not sure why it went down there, but it did. It's been down there for two days now but it only tries to escape at night."

"Well, sounds like now's the perfect time to strike. Show me the basement," I said before clapping my hands onto my knees and standing.

Ron nodded as he got up and made his way past me, waving for me to follow. He walked me down the hallway and stopped in front of a door mid-way between the living room and kitchen. He'd barricaded it with a chair and a few planks nailed across the door. After a few minutes work with a crowbar, the door was free and Ron had his hand on the handle, ready to open it.

"You can definitely take care of this, can't you?" he asked.

"Ron, I kick so much ass my feet permanently smell like farts."

He replied with a weak smile.

I gave him a nod and said, "If I'm not back in five minutes... just wait longer."

I stepped through the door and made my way down the steps and into the darkness. Ron flicked the light on before closing the door. The bulb flickered to life, revealing the basement. It was strangely well fortified, with bars across the small window and a lot of soundproofing around the walls and ceiling. A large lump of something lay curled up in the corner. I drew Sophia from her holster and thumbed back the hammer as I approached. Something felt off, my stomach wasn't doing backflips.

The lump twitched, and a head appeared from the centre of the curl. One bright red eye flicked open and looked right at me for a long moment. I was about to pull the trigger and turn its face to mush when I heard it hiss out a word.

"What?" I asked, holding my gun steady.

"Pleassse," it hissed, "help me."

The creature's head rose, followed by a pair of hands pointed high to the ceiling. The snake-woman unfurled herself and faced me. Her skin was a pale green pattern of smooth scales. True to Ron's word, the top half looked human, and the bottom was all snake.

"What do you mean: 'Help you'?"

"He'sssss trapped me down here," she said.

"And for good reason, were you trying to eat him?"

She shook her head. "We don't eat people, he tellsss liessss. My partner died recently. I just needed ssssome men to carry my children."

I lowered the gun. "What the fuck?" Something about this giant snake-lady felt genuine, like she wasn't actually bullshitting me.

"Only malesss can incubate our young, but they mussst be compatible. If we can't find one of our own, a human will do. It causssess no harm... unlessss..."

I eyed her. "Unless what?"

"Unlessss we do what he made me do."

I looked back up to the door where Ron was no doubt listening in. "And what, exactly, did he make you do?"

"He made me fill him."

I stood staring with a look of disgust plastered on my face.

The snake-lady continued, "We only deposssit a couple of eggsss per human, to causse no harm and for our young to hatch and leave their body with eassse."

"And he's made you..."

"Fill him, yesss."

"I'm gonna need you to elaborate on this whole thing, because what the fuck?"

"I am of an old race, worssshipped by what isss now a sssmall cult of humansss. Thisss man isss a high priessst in their cult. If our partnersss cannot incubate our eggsss, we must give them to human hostsss. It'sss an honour to thossse who worsssship usss. We only have a sssmall time window to transsssfer the eggsss ssso they can sssurvive and hatch. The plan wasss to ssstart with him, then give the ressst to other memberssss vissssiting over the courssse of the night. He lured me into thisss basssement to perform the ritual, then locked me in. When the time window to transsssfer the eggsss had almossst run out, he opened the door and demanded I give them all to him. I had no choice, I wasss out of time."

I tucked Sophia back into her holster. "Surely you could have just overpowered him and left after giving him the eggs?"

"He mussst live until they hatch. I can't risssk harming my children. I might have been able to break the door down, but I need to make sure they hatch."

I heaved a sigh and took a moment to ponder the situation. It wasn't what I'd expected in the slightest, and a part of me wished the snake-lady had turned out to be a murderous monster so I could get to shootin' and get the job done and dusted, nice and quick. But no, she had to turn out friendly.

"Let me sort this."

I turned and stomped my way up the stairs, booting the door when I reached the top. It flung open, splintering off the bottom hinges, and hung ajar.

Ron came scurrying into view. "Is it done? Is it dead?"

I whipped out Sophia and pointed her between his eyes. "Not quite. Get downstairs, now."

263

Ron held his hands up and followed my instruction, tentatively walking down the stairs until he was face to face with his prisoner.

"I think you have some apologising to do to this nice snake-lady. Explain yourself."

"Ssseraphina isss my name," snake-lady said.

"Explain this to me and apologise to Seraphina," I said, pressing the gun into Ron's back.

Ron hung his head in shame. "I thought if I carried all the eggs they'd make me more than a high priest in a cult. And she can't leave me. The children will need both parents."

"The children are ssself reliant once hatched, you damn fool," Seraphina said, "they need no parenting."

Ron raised his hand as if to backhand Seraphina across the face. "Don't you speak to me like that."

I pressed the gun into his back harder. "And don't you raise your fucking hand to her."

Ron looked over his shoulder and pulled a pained face before groaning, "Huuuurrrrggg."

"Dude chill, I didn't press the gun into you that hard."

He doubled over, clutched his stomach and groaned even louder.

Seraphina looked at him, then at me, then back to Ron. "It'sss the children. They're hatching," she said.

"Well that's good timing," I said, holstering Sophia. "You good, Ron? Try to take a breath. I've never delivered any babies before, but I'll try to help if you need me to."

It felt strange offering the weirdo help after seeing how he'd treat Seraphina. It felt even weirder to be offering to help deliver human-snake hybrid babies.

"There'sss nothing you can do for him now, the eggsss were too many," Seraphina said, backing into the corner.

"HHHAAARRRUUUNG," Ron replied, his face bright red.

I stepped forward to put my hand on his shoulder, but he fell to his hands and knees and let out a stream of black vomit, so I stepped aside. Didn't want that on my shoes.

A moment later, a pile of small wriggling creatures spilled from his mouth, out onto the basement floor. For a second, I thought it was over until he let out the loudest scream I'd heard in a while and a torrent of slime and writhing creatures erupted from him. They poured from his mouth, spilled from the legs of his pants and fell out from under his shirt, hundreds of them splatting to the ground.

When Ron was nothing more than a husk, he slowly dropped to his side and let out one last rattling breath as the light left his eyes and the final snake-baby crawled from his mouth.

"Fuck me," I said, before glancing at Seraphina. "Figure of speech. Under no circumstances do I consent to you fucking me."

She pointed at his lifeless body. "That'sss why we only put a couple of eggsss inssside each human. I told him thisss would happen, but he wouldn't lisssten."

265

I crouched down and lifted Ron's shirt to see a gaping hole in his abdomen where the babies had ripped their way out of his body. "Well, I guess he got his wish of having all the kids. Maybe a few more than he expected." I looked at Seraphina, then to the little human-snake babies, all slithering to take shelter in shadows and crevices. "I guess you and your kids are free to go."

She looked up to the open door. "Yesss it ssseemsss ssso. I am in your debt missster...?"

"Isaac Nightingale, or just Night to my friends."

"May I call you a friend?" Seraphina asked, reaching out for a handshake.

I took her hand and shook it; it felt cool and smooth in mine. "You may."

"Thank you, Night. If I can ever repay my debt to you, walk the main trail on Limessstone Canyon with a dead pigeon. The ssscent of a dead pigeon on a human isss a peace offering to my kind. Give the pigeon to whoever findsss you and asssk to sssee me. I will tell my people you are a friend to the naga."

"The naga? That's you?"

"Yesss."

"Cool," I said, feeling like royalty. I'd come to kill a monster and ended up a friend to an entire species.

Seraphina smiled and continued, "I will ssstay here until sssundown then make my way home."

I considered leaving and letting Seraphina wait until nightfall, then remembered she'd be sitting in the basement for about another ten hours, with a stinking corpse to boot, and that didn't sit right with me. I suddenly had a better idea.

"Seraphina, you ever had a ride in a Chevy Impala?"

# Friends in High Places

After a little bit of expert fashion advice, I snuck Seraphina out of Ron's house and into the car. She sat herself down in the passenger seat wearing a lumberjack flannel shirt, baseball cap and a large set of sunglasses. I set a cardboard box filled with her babies down on what I guessed was her lap as I got into the car.

I fired up the engine. "You good?"

She nodded, and I stomped the gas.

I tore down the streets of LA, as fast as legally allowed. So really, it was more of a leisurely cruise down the streets of LA until I pulled up in front of The Black Cat, as close to the entrance as possible. I had no doubt whatsoever that all the guys would be inside. Aside from being the best drinking spot, it also doubled up as HQ. The Monster Squad spent the majority of their time there gathering information about the goings on in Los Angeles, and whatever scraps they could find in relation to Dominus Atrocitas. Not just drinking, like most would assume. Okay maybe a bit of drinking too, but mostly by Rusty.

I made my way to the passenger side to help Seraphina out of the seat. She took my hand and slithered out, leaving her box of children on the seat.

"Are they gonna be okay? Don't baby naga die in hot cars?"

She shook her head. "It takesss a lot more than a bit of heat to kill usss."

I nodded and nudged the door closed as she linked her arm through mine. Now that we were out of the car, her disguise didn't work as well. From the waist up, she looked very incognito. But the giant snake tail instead of legs? Maybe not. Either way, it didn't matter anymore. We pushed through the entrance and into the bar. The eyes of all the regulars hit us, sliding from me, to Seraphina, then down to her tail before going back to their own business without a care.

The gang, minus Mickey, sat at the usual table with maps scattered around, squabbling over where they thought Atrocitas's exact location would be and how best to attack it.

Tex glanced in our direction first and pulled a double-take. His mouth fell open as he reached up and pulled his hat off. "By the gods," he said.

The rest of the gang looked up from the table. Eyes widened, jaws dropped, and Harriot breathed, "Holy fuck."

Tex jumped up and made his way around the table, pressing his hat to his chest. He stopped in front of us and gave Seraphina a deep bow.

She let out a chuckle and bowed in return.

"Good friendsss of yourss?" she asked.

I nodded. "The best."

"Then they are my friendsss also, yesss?"

Tex nodded hard. "Yes."

I could have sworn he was tearing up.

"Please, sit," he said, offering her my usual seat.

Seraphina got herself comfortable and removed her hat and shades while I pulled up an extra chair for myself.

"Girl, you are fucking rocking that shirt," Ginn said as she stuck her hand out.

Seraphina shook it and said "Thanksss," while admiring Ginn's ensemble of a tube top and shiny silver dungarees.

"My name's Ginn, nice to meet you."

The guys took the opportunity to go in a circle, shaking hands and introducing themselves.

"My name is Ssseraphina, it isss a pleasssure to meet you all, friendsss of Night. You can call me Sssera for ssshort."

"Nice to meet you, Sera," Harriot said, "it's good to have another girl at this table instead of another stinking dude.

Morgan chuckled. "Please, when you've got your fur on you could evacuate the bar with your stank."

Harriot shot him a look and raised her index finger in warning.

Tex shut down the bickering with a slap on the table. "So, Night, care to fill us in on your morning?"

"Yeah, what happened to the weird dork from earlier?" Ginn asked.

"He's a little bit on the dead side."

"Dead?"

"Dead."

I proceeded to recap the morning's events from Ron knocking on my door, to the babies spilling from all the holes he had, right up to walking through the bar door.

Sera nodded along, confirming the story.

"So that's about it. Ron turned out to be a bit too weird for his own good, and we've got ourselves a new friend. I said she could hang with us for the day, and I'll drive her home when it gets dark out."

"Well, I'll let you guys get a little more acquainted, I gotta take a slash," I said.

I took my leave and headed to the men's room. My zipper had almost unleashed the goods when the door swung open, and the unmistakable sound of Tex's boots rang across the tiles. He had the good sense to stand a few feet away as he undid his own zipper to join me in taking a piss.

"Any idea what you've just done?" he asked.

I stood staring at the wall in front of me, dong in hand and waiting for the stream. "Whad'ya mean?" I said as the stream began.

"There's a good chance you've just hammered the final nail in Atrocitas's coffin."

I turned my head and made immediate, uncomfortable eye contact.

Tex continued, "The naga are a fiercely proud, loyal race. You've not only saved one of their kind but also protected a naga woman during the birth of her children. You're in. If you ask them, they'll probably fight alongside us."

271

I finished my slash and put myself away. "I don't know, when we were on the way here Sera said they like to keep to themselves and stay hidden."

Tex kept on pissin'. "They do, for the most part. But they've been known to fight for what they consider a just cause. And they're savage fighters when they need to be. Hard to kill too. We could really do with their help."

"I don't know, man, should we really drag an entire species, and a peaceful one at that, into our fight?"

Tex gave a shake and zipped himself back up before joining me at the sinks to wash his hands. "Let's be realistic. Atrocitas has an army. We're nothing but a ragtag band of oddballs with a pair of colourful ghosts to hand. I'm an optimistic guy, Night, but even I don't fancy our chances. This could be our deus ex machina, our way to win."

"I guess it does no harm to ask. I'll see what she says on the drive back to her place." I dried my hands on my jeans and kicked the door open.

Tex followed me out, nodding.

Laughter floated from our table. Sera had moved seats to sit between Ginn and Harriot, and Rusty was handing out drinks to give her a proper Monster Squad welcome.

I leaned against the bar and gave Davy the barkeep the signal to quench my heavy lemonade craving. He nodded his acknowledgement. "Not too long ago if someone told me I'd be sitting in a bar with a vampire, werewolves and a snake-lady, I'd have called them a fuckin' nut job and told them to take a hike. Now look here, they're all my friends."

"Funny how quick your life can change, isn't it?" Tex said, before walking ahead to rejoin the group.

Davy set my pint of lemonade down on the bar next to me. I took it gratefully and slapped a ten down to cover the price, plus a heavy tip. "You're the god of all barkeeps, Davy," I said before taking a deep gulp of the nectar, "don't let anyone tell ya otherwise."

He gave me a wink and walked off to take care of other business.

I stood with my lemonade, pondering all the changes that had happened so far, and the possibility of what was to come.

# Breathe

I drove Sera—and her hoard of children—home later that evening, or at least, as close to home as I could get the car out in the wilds. We talked things over on the drive. I told her about our situation and asked if there was any way they could help us out. She agreed to 'speak to the council', whatever that meant. It was cryptic, but it was better than nothing. Tex had insisted on asking for their help, but I wasn't so sure. Could we use the help? Fuck yes. But I didn't want to drag anyone into our business that didn't need to be. I expressed my concerns to Sera after asking, but she dismissed them in an instant. She'd told me that while they are a peaceful species, an occasional violent purge helped to keep things healthy. They'd take a vote, and if it was unanimous they'd set aside a day for all out carnage, just to get it out of their systems. She had no doubt that the vote would be in my favour. It had been a while since they fought, and they were no friend to vampires, aside from Morgan. He could have charmed her pants off, if she'd been wearing any.

When I ran out of road, we said our goodbyes and Sera gave me a bone-crushing hug before slithering off into the night with her children. They moved faster than I could have ever expected and didn't make a damn sound. Within seconds, they had disappeared into the darkness leaving me standing alone in the glow of the car's headlights.

I met Ginn, Ali, Tex and Rusty in the hotel foyer the morning after and gave them the rundown of my conversation with Sera. Tex seemed pleased.

"So, what's the plan this morning?" I said to Rusty. "Anything been added to the to-do list?"

He shook his head. "I figure we've all earned a day off, wouldn't ya say? What's on the list can wait a little while longer."

I nodded along with the others. "Gotta say I wouldn't mind a day off from being covered in blood or something worse, I feel like I spend half my life doing laundry at the moment."

Rusty clapped his hands together. "That settles it then, I'm off to catch a movie. Feel free to join me, otherwise, you can find me in the Black Cat later this evening."

"Really? You'll be in the bar you're in every night without fail?" Ginn said, punching Rusty on the shoulder.

"Don't be a smart arse," he said.

If there'd been anything on at the movies I hadn't already seen, I would have joined him, but as it happened, I'd seen everything worth seeing. I fancied something a little more airy, maybe a little bit of beach. I settled on a wander around Santa Monica Pier.

"I think I'll head to the pier, maybe take a ride on the wheel and go for a stroll along the beach. How's the weather out there?"

Rusty took a glance back outside and shrugged. "Fine. Shirt and shorts kinda day if you ask me."

"I'll join you, Night," Ginn said.

Tex gave Rusty a pat on the shoulder. "I think I'll join you with that movie, ol' friend."

Ali scrunched his face in indecision; he clearly wanted to do both things. "Think I'll hit the beach too," he said.

"Sweet. I'm gonna go get changed. Meet back here in fifteen?"

Ginn nodded. "Sure thing."

Tex said, "Catch you later," as I turned to head back up to my room.

I threw on a fresh set of clothes, taking Rusty at his word:; shorts and a T-shirt. It was a nice change, wearing something light and breezy. A far cry from the heavy leather jacket and jeans I usually wore. I even left the Sisters behind for the first time in a long while. It made me feel like a different person.

I sat myself down on one of the lobby's sofas to wait for the others. I'd opted for some black linen shorts and an old, oversized Bowie tee. The one Suzie used to steal from me.

Ali strolled out of the elevator a few minutes later wearing the loudest Hawaiian shirt I'd ever laid eyes on, fully unbuttoned, with shorts and flip-flops to match. His hair was tied up in a tight bun and he had a set of shades propped on top of his head.

"You're looking colourful."

"Fancy, no?"

Ginn answered from behind, "Very fancy."

Ali stepped aside and gave her a long whistle. She was wearing a bikini with a sarong wrapped around her waist.

"Put your eyes back in your head big fella," she said.

"I guess we're all taking Rusty's word on it being a nice day huh?"

## [Track 29]

Thankfully, he was right. We hopped on the bus and were strolling along the beach in no time, ice creams in hand. It was a nice change of pace, but the lack of any weapons made me feel a little vulnerable. At that particular moment in time, if someone kicked up a ruckus, the best I could do would be to throw my ice cream at somebody's head. Not that I wanted to do that, I was enjoying the shit out of it, and so were Ali and Ginn from the looks on their faces.

We stepped off the sand and onto the boardwalk to take the steps up to the pier. Ginn and I wanted a ride on the wheel and God be damned, we were gonna get it. Ali chose to wait on the pier. He told us he didn't really fancy going on any rides and would just sit and wait for us on a bench down the way. Ginn reckoned he was just scared of heights and gave him a good jibing before we left him to take a ride.

It was one hell of a view up at the top, and being up there, away from everything, was the first time in a long time I felt safe. Sure, we were up in the air on

277

nothing but a bunch of rickety metal, but the knowledge that while I was up there, nothing was gonna jump out at me, was comforting. It was like I could finally breathe without a weight on my chest.

"You're looking thoughtful," Ginn said, making some strong eye contact.

"Yeah, I'm letting my single brain cell do some work for a change."

"What's it working on?"

I gave her a smile. "Enjoying the moment, I guess. It's tryin' to remind me that life can be nice when we slow down and take a minute. Like, in many ways I enjoy what I do now, but I can't help feeling there's a lot of anger and negativity in it, ya'know? I forget to take moments to look after myself. I try to put up the badass front to protect myself, but in the end, it isn't really me. I never wanted this kind of life. I wanted to settle down with Suzie, work an honest job, and live the quiet small-town life. I feel like that option was stolen from me, and from Suzie especially. I guess that's what drives me to do this kinda stuff. Even though I got my revenge, in the end, I'm still just pissed off and angry."

Ginn took a long breath, really pulling in that fresh air as her eyes moved past me and gazed out to sea. "You must have really loved her, huh?"

"You mean love? There's no past tense for me. I love her like I always have, it hasn't faded. I doubt it ever will, but the anger and the guilt over what happened is just as strong."

"You have every right to feel that way. We all do, don't we? Every single one of us in this little bunch of weirdos has had our lives irrecoverably changed by some monster or another. There's a life I can't go back to either. My family and friends think I'm dead, and when I think about what I am now, it's better off that way."

"You still haven't told us all of your tragic backstory. All we know is the 'kidnapped and immune to vampirism' bit."

"Another time," she said with a flap of the hand, "let's just let that brain cell of yours enjoy the moment, shall we?"

I sat back and took a deep breath as the wheel spun, bringing us up into the sky again, and I gave her a smile. "You're not getting off that easily. Come on, time to share."

She fiddled with her fingers for a moment before speaking. "I came over to the States to study. My family are quite well off, so it was an option for me."

"What'cha study?"

"Law, at Harvard. I wanted to make a difference, be the whole 'defender of the innocent' girl. I got about eight months in when I was attacked by the vampires. My roommate and I had been shopping for some snacks. We were on our way back to our room on campus. One of the vampires took a liking to me, so I guess I got off lightly."

"And your friend?" I asked, already knowing the answer.

Ginn hung her head. "They fucking butchered her. Ripped her to pieces and kidnapped me. They kept me chained to a basement radiator for months, tormenting me, taking turns biting me, trying to change me. They'd bring me newspapers just so I could read about my own disappearance. They ID'd my friend from what was left of her, but since they couldn't find me, they assumed I'd been abducted. And they were right."

I stayed silent, not wanting to interrupt.

"My parents offered money, lots of money, and I heard some of the vampires saying maybe they should take it and give me back, but the old one wanted to take me to Atrocitas so he could figure out why they couldn't turn me. It was six months before the authorities called off the search and considered me dead. I could have escaped at any point, I knew I was strong enough, but I kept it hidden, waiting for them to take me to Atrocitas."

"Don't you want to contact your family? I'm sure they'd love to know you're alive."

She gazed off into the sky as the wheel lowered us towards the ground. "I don't know what I'd do. They beat me. Tortured me any way they could."

"They didn't..." I hesitated to continue.

"Thankfully, no. The one who liked me tried one time, but the old one caught him and beat him senseless. Said I was to be saved, so Atrocitas could have me."

My face must have come with subtitles. One look and Ginn knew exactly how disgusted I was.

She sighed. "So yeah, that anger you feel, it's in me, too. I can't go back to my normal life now. I want Atrocitas dead. I want them all dead."

I looked her in the eyes and gave a small smile. "Stick around then; between the two of us and Ali and Tex, someday, we'll kill them all."

# Monster Maker

A bit of downtime at the beach had really done me some good. Chilling on the wheel with Ginn had left me feeling more wholesome than I had in a long time. It was a nice little bonding moment for sure, and the last I would have for a long time.

Later that evening, the three of us headed back to the hotel to change into something a little less beachy for our obligatory nighttime rendezvous at the Black Cat.

I had decided to take my time showering and getting changed, so I was the last of the group to walk through the bar's doors. As always, there was a drink waiting for me. Not whiskey this time, but some ice-cold lemonade courtesy of Ginn.

"Thanks," I said, picking it up and taking a long gulp as I sat down.

I was about to ask to be dealt in to the game of cards when the bar door flew open, and the Neon Nightmares strolled in.

"Well would you looky here," Tex said as they made their way over.

"Friends of yours?" Rusty inquired.

Leon answered, "We sure are, broski. Name's Leon, and this is Adrian."

They both gave out fist bumps to everyone at the table, with a nod to each of the Monster Squad. "Nice to meet you bros and bro-dette," Adrian said.

"To what do we owe this pleasure?" Tex asked.

"Just dropping by on a little business," Leon said, "word on the grapevine is there's been a werewolf spotted hanging around the movie studios over in Burbank. We couldn't pass up the opportunity to visit the studios, maybe sneak around a little, see what's being filmed. We're headed over there now. Wondered if any of you guys would wanna go check it out with us? Could be pretty sweet, my dudes."

The thought of getting into the movie studios set a fire in my brain, and I knew I could handle a werewolf no worries. I drained my lemonade and slammed my glass down.

"I'm in."

"Gnarly!" Adrian said, giving me yet another fist bump.

"One question though. How the fuck do you plan on us getting into the studios? Security's pretty tight."

Leon lowered his sunglasses and winked. "With a little movie magic."

"Anyone else joining me?"

Khearo and Morgan looked at each other and shrugged.

"Sure, we'll tag along," Khearo said.

Adrian smiled. "It's gonna be radical."

About an hour and thirty minutes later, Khearo, Morgan and I were hopping over a fence while Leon and Adrian were messing with a couple of security guards by tapping on their shoulders and disappearing before they could turn around. A few moments later, a scream rang out and the two guards ran away while one yelled, "I don't get paid enough to deal with no fuckin' ghosts!"

Leon poofed into existence in front of us. "That's that taken care of, Adrian's gonna chase them for a few minutes," he said.

"Nice," Morgan said.

Khearo sniffed the air. "So where's the werewolf supposed to be? I don't smell one around here."

"Last I heard is it hangs around studio two, this way," Leon said, strolling off while pointing ahead of him.

He took the lead, and we followed, hanging a good distance behind.

Khearo nudged me. "Something seems off, there's no werewolf around here. Not even a whiff of any but me. You trust this guy?"

I shrugged. "He's been a big help in the past and seems to be doing similar work to us."

"He's fuckin' weird," Morgan said, "they both are."

"Dunno what to tell yas, let's just see what happens huh?"

Khearo and Morgan exchanged a look but nodded anyway. I had no reason not to trust the Nightmares, and shit, I was just happy to be wandering around a movie studio; hoping to see how the sausage is made.

Adrian popped into view alongside Leon and whispered something to him that stopped him in his tracks.

He held a finger to his lips as we approached. "Werewolf's just around the corner," he said.

Khearo shot me a look that said, "No it's not".

I pulled one of the Sisters from my holster as we all tiptoed up to the corner of studio two. We all popped our heads around the corner like a bunch of cartoon characters, and sure enough, there it was: a werewolf. It stood about eight feet tall and was pacing back and forth outside of a big roller shutter door.

"That ain't no werewolf," Khearo said as we pulled back to hide around the corner.

Adrian tilted his head and said, "My dude, if that ain't a werewolf I'll eat my own ass cheeks for supper."

Morgan sniggered. "How would you like them served?"

"Watch this," Khearo said, pushing them aside as hair sprouted from his body and his clothes stretched.

He rounded the corner mid-transformation and walked towards the other werewolf, morphing from human to wolf as he approached it; all of his clothes aside from his big red boxer shorts fell to shreds around him. The other wolf stopped in its tracks, took a few steps back, then stumbled and fell back on its ass with a loud crashing noise.

Khearo strolled over and towered over it as it cowered on the ground, raising its arms in front of its face with a whine that sounded a lot like somebody saying, "Please don't hurt me."

We jumped out and rounded the corner as Khearo reached down and wrapped his hand around the other werewolf's muzzle before giving it a pull. The skin of the wolf's face stretched and slipped off its bones, bringing the fur from the neck and upper chest off with it to reveal

285

a man's head inside a metal frame shaped like a skull. He stared out at us in horror.

"Please," he spluttered, "please don't kill me."

Morgan turned to Adrian and smiled. "Prep yo' cheeks, boy, you're eating well tonight."

"It's just a dude?" I asked.

Leon stood with a look of awe on his face. "Not just a dude," he said, "a god…"

"Doesn't look like any kind of god to me," Khearo said as he shrank back down to human.

The guy on the grounds eyes darted from Khearo, to Leon, then to me. All the blood had drained from his face, and he looked on the verge of soiling his fancy wolf suit. I put out a hand to help him back to his feet.

He eyed it, hesitating.

"We're not gonna hurt you, what's your name, mister?"

"Jason fucking Carter, special effects extraordinaire," Leon said, batting my hand aside and holding his out instead.

"Hey, 'fucking' is my middle name too," Morgan said, giving me a playful nudge in the ribs.

Jason took Leon's hand, and both he and Adrian hauled him back up to his feet. He looked a little less shaken once he was off the ground and didn't have five strangers looking down at him.

"What the fuck is going on, who are you people?" he asked.

Leon stepped forward. "Please forgive us Mister Carter. We thought you were a real werewolf so we came to uhh… escort you off the premises."

"And straight to HELL," Morgan said, firing finger guns at him.

"You thought I was a real werewolf?" he asked.

"Yeah, sorry," Adrian said.

Jason cracked a smile. "No no no, this is good. This is great. And you, you're an actual werewolf? What did you think?" he asked, pointing to Khearo who was standing wearing nothing but his shorts.

He shrugged. "I knew you weren't by your scent, but you looked convincing enough, I'll say that much."

The look on Jason's face had done a total one-eighty. He'd gone from horrified to overjoyed in the space of a few moments. It seemed being told his costume looked authentic, by a real werewolf, was the highest of compliments. "Freddy, get out here you gotta see this," he yelled at the roller door.

A few moments later the door hummed then rattled upwards as it opened, spilling light out from inside and giving us a good look at the secrets it held. The door rose to reveal a paint-splattered floor, then crept higher to show eight long spindly legs. Up and up the shutter went, revealing tables covered in all manner of severed limbs, heads of monsters, knick-knacks and doodads. It came to a stop, showing off a gigantic rubber spider near the entrance, with a variety of full monster suits dotted around behind it. Another guy appeared at the side of the opening and stepped out. He ran a set of cold grey eyes over us as he stroked a long black beard.

"What's going on here?" he asked as he bent to pick the wolf mask up from the floor.

"Fred fucking Lopez," Leon said, walking over and extending a hand.

Fred shook it with a grunt and a look of confusion.

"Common middle name around here," I said to Morgan.

Jason turned to Khearo and said, "Can you do it again? Can you show Fred?"

"Show me what?" Fred asked, while taking a moment to process the sight of Khearo. "And where the fuck are your clothes, my guy?"

"Just watch," Khearo said before sprouting hair, claws and fangs, then shooting from six to eight feet tall in full wolf-man form.

Fred dropped the mask and slapped his hands to his head. "Ho-ho-hooooly fuck!" he yelled, "Are you fucking serious right now? A real fucking werewolf? Fuck!"

"Help me out of the suit, would you, Fred?"

Fred almost lost his shit in awe of Khearo before turning to unzip the back of Jason's suit. Jason stepped out with a little help and left the suit standing as he made his way over to observe the real-life monster.

"Let me get a good look at you, buddy," Fred said as he pulled a beaten old notebook out of his pocket and started making notes.

"I thought he was gonna kill me," Jason said to Fred, "they thought I was a real one too."

"This is amazing, we got the look down pretty well, didn't we?" Fred said. He pried his eyes off Khearo for a moment. "Who are you guys anyway?"

"I'm Night, this here's Morgan, Leon, Adrian, and that's Khearo," I said, gesturing to each person in turn. "We're... uh... monster hunters, for lack of a better term."

"And monsters, too," Morgan added.

"Well, you guys sure gave me a fright, Night. And say what? You're werewolves too?" Jason said.

Morgan winked and said, "Not quite. Get a load of this." He stepped forward into the light as his eyes flooded black, his jaw cracked and extended, and his fangs pushed their way out of his gums.

"Fuuuuuuck, that's gnarly," Fred said, flipping a page to take some notes on Morgan.

Jason leaned in for a closer look, giving Morgan a good inspection. "Damn, you're a... vampire?"

Morgan nodded.

Jason nudged Fred. "We may have got the wolf look down, but we've got vampires all wrong. Looks nothing like what we thought, huh? Nothing like Dracula at all, make sure you get this all noted."

Fred nodded, scribbling with the fury of the gods. "Way, WAY more fangs. And I'm getting it all, don't you worry."

Jason turned to Leon and Adrian. "What about you guys? Vampires too?"

"Nope," they said in unison. Leon lowered his sunglasses and flashed his eyes, nothing but purple swirling globes of mist with vapours drifting off of them. He clicked his fingers and disappeared with a bright purple flash, leaving a cloud of smoke.

Adrian followed suit but in green.

They reappeared a moment later, materialising behind Jason and tapping him on the shoulder.

"No fuckin' way," he said with a huge grin, "you see that, Freddy?"

"I saw," Fred said, making his way over, flipping to another page.

"What are you guys?" Jason asked, reaching out and touching Adrian's arm to see if his hand would pass through. It didn't.

"We're the Neon Nightmares," Leon said, "I guess we're kinda like ghosts? I prefer wraiths though, sounds more rad."

"Ghosts?" Fred said.

"Yeah, well, we died, and our souls got stuck on the neon light above our video store and we kinda came back, I guess, ya'know?"

Fred's pencil couldn't catch a break. "So you don't have a physical body, yet you can take corporeal form... this is... astounding."

Adrian chimed in, "Nah bro, our old bodies are buried back home in North Tarrytown."

"The place 'The Legend of Sleepy Hollow' is set?" Jason asked.

Adrian nodded. "Right on bro, you know your horror."

Fred smiled. "We're monster makers, horror is our bread and butter my friend."

They took a few minutes to observe Leon and Adrian then drifted my way, and Fred had his notebook ready.

"So, what do you have for us, Night?" Jason asked.

I shrugged. "I'm just a dude, sorry."

Khearo clapped a hand on my shoulder, back in his human form. "Not just a dude. This motherfucker may not look very mean and scary but he's as much a terror as the rest of us: superhuman speed, strength, all that Captain America shit once he gets riled up."

Fred raised an eyebrow. "Can we see?"

"Sure," I said.

I made my way over to the werewolf suit, wrapped an arm around the waist, carried it inside and set it down next to a small green animatronic creature with sharp teeth and big ears. Fred and Jason followed me in, with the others trailing behind.

"Doesn't that suit weigh, like, fivehundred pounds?" Fred muttered.

"Oh yeah, easily. I can barely move in it with the help of the hydraulics. He one-armed it and didn't break a sweat."

Fred made notes.

I pulled out the Sisters. "These guns are haunted if that's of any interest? Never miss a shot."

"Really? Let's see," Jason said, before rummaging around in a nearby box. He pulled out an old worn-out decapitated head with flaps of foam and latex hanging from it. "Reckon you can hit this if I throw it in the air?"

I turned my back to them. "On the count of three, toss it high."

"One," Fred said.

Jason continued, "Two."

"Three," I finished.

I couldn't see, but I heard Jason toss the head into the air with a little, "Hup."

I raised Sophia over my head, squeezed the trigger and blew the flying head into dust. Pieces of latex fell to the floor and a rubber eyeball bounced around the room as I spun and took a bow.

Jason gave me a round of applause as Fred's pencil almost set his notepad alight.

"Well, gentlemen," Jason said, glancing at his watch, "I think it's only fair to say that since you've shown us yours, we should show you ours. How'd you like to come back tomorrow afternoon, and we'll give you a tour of the place?"

Leon and Adrian fist-bumped each other and Leon said, "Fuckin' right on, man, let's do it."

Morgan and Khearo looked at the monster makers, then at me and nodded.

"Sounds good to me, can we bring some friends? We've got a whole squad."

Fred ripped out a piece of paper and handed it to Khearo. "A Monster Squad, eh? I like the sound of that.

You give that number a call in the morning and security will escort you here from the gate."

Adrian chuckled. "If they ever come back."

Jason picked up a rucksack that was sitting on the floor by a workbench. "I'd best get going, you okay to lock up, Fred?"

Fred nodded.

"Excellent," Jason said, "you guys didn't try to kill me, but if I'm not home soon, my wife sure will."

# Cock Fight

It was an easy morning. I woke up late, got myself dressed in shorts and a tee, then headed on out at a leisurely stroll. Once we'd left the monster makers' studios the previous night, we'd agreed to meet at Doughnut Shack, a little café on the corner of Santa Monica and Lincoln Boulevard, for around eleven thirty. It wasn't too far away, maybe a thirty-minute walk, so I took the shoelace express.

I was enjoying the relaxed mood the previous day had put me in; it was a nice change of pace. I mean, sure, I enjoyed the monster hunting but you've still gotta catch some downtime, ya'know?

I stepped out of the hotel's air-conditioned foyer and onto the sidewalk. The warmth swept over me like a warm blanket. I took a moment to have a nice stretch in the sun. The doors swung shut behind me then opened again a moment later. A familiar shape appeared by my side and took a big breath of the warm, dry air.

"Mornin'," I said to Ali.

"You had a lie in too, huh?" he said, looking at me over a pair of mirrored shades.

He had his hair tied up in a bun and was wearing shorts and a turquoise Hawaiian shirt open over a white vest.

"Yeah, figured why not," I said, squinting at him, "nice shirt."

"Thanks," he said, tugging the bottom of it, "I can't tell you how much I'm enjoying wearing something other than an orange jumpsuit."

"I can tell. Are the others already at the Shack?"

"Guess so, I heard Tex heading out earlier and Ginn left about a half hour ago."

"We best get steppin' then, eh?"

He gave me a light punch on the shoulder, and we set off down the street.

A few minutes passed by in silence until Ali said, "Here, put these on," as he whipped off his shades.

"It's cool, I'm good, thanks."

"My friend, you've been squinting like you're trying to read the small print, take the fucking sunglasses."

I let out a snort, gave in and took the shades from him and put them on. He was right; it was much easier to see. "Thanks."

Ali shook his head. "Typical northern gringo, can't handle a bit of sunlight."

I chuckled and flipped him the bird.

We strolled through the door of the Doughnut Shack half an hour later, greeted by the sight of the whole squad—Neon Nightmares included—gathered around a spot they'd monopolised by pulling together a couple of tables and a bunch of chairs. The place had a clean and simple décor, white furniture and light pink walls with a big, pink 'Doughnut Shack' neon sign on the wall behind the counter. A little light jazz sprinkled out of some hidden speakers and into our ears.

"Mornin'," Tex said, waving a frosted doughnut in the air.

Ali and I took our seats as Ginn lifted the lid on a huge tray of doughnuts.

"Get a couple of these 'nuts in you," she said with a smirk.

I picked out one with strawberry frosting and sprinkles as a young guy came over with a notepad.

"Can I get you fellas a drink?" he asked.

"Coffee for me please, hot, black and strong," Ali said.

Harriot nudged Ginn and mumbled, "Just the way I like my men."

"I'll take an iced tea please," I said.

"Coming right up," the kid said before disappearing.

Rusty reached over the table and plucked a chocolate frosted out of the box. "Ready for the Monster Squad's big day out, lads?" he said to me and Ali.

Ali nodded.

"Sure am, you guys are gonna love it. And if you monster-up the studio dudes will lose their minds."

We spent the next hour chatting away until the doughnut box was empty. When the last one was gone and drinks had been drunk, we cleared our mess, rearranged the tables to the way they usually were and headed out to catch the next bus to get us to the studios.

We got there for about two in the afternoon. One of the security guards ticked off a list of names and then escorted us all to the monster makers' spot.

The scent of paint and rubber rode the breeze, so we could smell the studio before we saw it. The roller shutter was up, giving us a good view of all the treasures inside. Fred and Jason came out and made their way around everyone, getting introductions and shaking all the hands. Once everybody had got themselves acquainted, Fred and Jason gave us the full tour of their workshop, giving us sneaky peeks at all the puppets, animatronics and costumes they were working on for upcoming movies. And I've gotta say, they were making some pretty cool shit. I'd tell you more, but they made us promise not to blab their secrets.

When the tour came to an end, Fred and Jason made it clear that they were quite keen to study the more monstrous sides of the supernatural folk in the group, purely in the interests of advancing their craft. With little to offer in that regard, Tex, Ginn, Ali and I gave our thanks, bid our farewells and left the Neon Nightmares and the actual monsters of the squad with the monster makers to be immortalised forevermore. The rest of us hit the nearest pizza joint to discuss the cool secrets we'd saw and ponder when we'd see them next in their respective movies.

* * *

I twisted the key and bumped the door to my hotel room with my hip, almost dropping the pizza box I had balancing in my other hand. I'd already eaten an entire pizza with the guys, but goddamn it I was still hungry, so I took one to go.

The others had headed on over to the Black Cat, but I was feeling a little in need of some alone time, so I told them I'd catch them in the morning and headed up to have a solitary evening of chilling with a couple of videotapes, beers and my pizza.

I put the big ol' pie on the foot of the bed, flicked the TV on and stuck a VHS into the player before grabbing a beer from the minibar, stripping off and getting into bed to watch my movie.

It was just after two in the morning when I woke with a snort and put a hand to my stomach, I had that old familiar twisting sensation: what I considered my psychic power to sense when something was about to go down. I put this one down to too much cheese before bed, though. I probably just needed to visit the john, I thought.

The pizza box was still sat open on my chest, with the half-eaten pie stone cold within. The TV bathed the room in a light glow and the sound of white noise hummed out of it. I couldn't see the remote control anywhere, so I shoved the pizza box to the other side of the bed and got up to turn the TV off by the button on the set. That's when I heard the voices outside my door. At first, I thought it might have been the guys getting in from a night of drinking, but, no, the voices weren't right.

I put my ear to the door just in time to hear someone whisper the word "Now." I jumped back as the door to my room came crashing open, almost tearing off the hinges. A huge foot followed the door and brought an iscarion vamp over the threshold with it. I could tell he was an iscarion on account of his size: the fuckers were almost always bigger than the others, and they always lead the attack. Out there in the hallway stood ten other vampires, fangs out and ready to fucking party.

I'll admit I was caught short. I'd just woken up from a pizza coma and I was balls naked. The Hot Sauce kicked in and sharpened my senses. Time seemed to slow as my heart threw itself into the highest gear and the sauce burned through my veins.

## [Track 31]

The big bastard in front of me tensed. The rest followed suit. I wished I'd put on some fucking shorts. And then... chaos.

The big fella flew at me and the others stampeded into the room. Eleven vampires in an enclosed space, all eager to get a piece of flesh, and there was plenty of flesh on display. I didn't like my odds.

While Big Boy was lunging forwards, I sprang back as far as I could to give myself a little breathing room. I landed by my nightstand, reached back and wrapped my hand around the neck of my beer bottle. Big Boy charged forward; I gave him a polite welcome in the form of a bottle across the noggin. It didn't even faze him, but I didn't expect it to. I just wanted to break the bottle.

I sidestepped Big Boy. He barrelled past me as I shattered the bottle on his skull and went head-first into the wall, over the top of my nightstand. His head crashed through the drywall and stopped at the shoulders. With him stuck for a moment, I set my sights on the nearest vamp: a female with some comically voluptuous boobs bouncing around as she came at me, mouth open wide and tongue lashing through the air. I jammed the broken bottle into her right eye socket and hammered it in with my palm. She went limp and flopped over on the edge of my bed. Blood spilled out of the bottleneck and splattered over the carpet.

Three vamps came at me at once. All three of them jumped into a tackle that smashed into my ribs and lifted me off my feet. The four of us flew over the bed and landed on the floor in a tangled heap. One of them had landed upside down with his legs up against the wall and struggled to correct himself. Another was at my side with his arms wrapped around my body, gnashing at me while I held his head back, and the other was awkwardly trapped under us, pinned to the floor with my balls resting on his ear. He flung his free fist and punched at whatever was convenient for him to reach, which happened to be my left ass cheek.

Thankfully, the iscarion still had his head stuck in the wall and the other six suckers had decided to watch the show from the other side of the bed, cheering on their buddies. One of them had even helped himself to the rest of my pizza. I shot the young pizza thief some heavy stink eye as he shovelled a slice into his face. He looked so fucking pleased with himself, standing there eating my goddamn Pepperoni Supreme.

The sucker who'd latched onto my side dug his claws into my skin, drawing blood. The one pounding at my ass cheek and listening to my ballsack writhed around, trying to escape and get a taste of me while his buddy snapped his fangs at my face.

As the one underneath me struggled to free himself, the one who'd landed upside down got himself right and started clambering to his feet. I couldn't fuck around; shit was about to go sideways for me. I was outnumbered and the Sisters were on the other side of the room, lying on top of my pile of clothes.

Taking the risk, I let the sucker stuck to my side get a little wiggle room so I could move too. He shot up closer to my face and manoeuvred so he was almost on top of me. I stuck my fingers between his lower fangs, planted my other hand on his forehead, pushed one way, pulled another and drove my knee into his nuts as the sides of his mouth ripped apart with a wet snapping sound.

Blood splattered across my neck and chest as I got a better grip on his jaw and gave it a good yank while hammering my other hand between his eyes. The claws ripping at my flesh loosened up as I tugged and snapped his jawbone from his skull, tearing the flesh right down his neck. It didn't kill him, but it got him off of me. He sprang up and stumbled backwards as I released my grip on his chin. He fell back into his formerly upside-down buddy. The jaw hung down to his chest like a gory necklace. He gathered it up and stumbled off into the bathroom, probably to find a Band-Aid.

I shimmied and planted a foot on the side of the head of the sucker pinned under me and used it to push myself up off the floor. His arms shot backwards, swiping at the air as I kept my foot on the side of his head, pinning it to the carpet. He'd gone from having my balls in his ear to having my big toe in there. I'd clearly hurt his dignity. Without three others on top of him, he'd freed up his arms and took the opportunity to stop punching my ass cheeks, and, instead, sink his claws into them. Both of them. Right into the fuckin' meat. I gritted my teeth and applied pressure to his head, pressing it into the carpet and wiggling my toe in his ear. Ass blood ran down my leg and onto his face, much to his pleasure.

Back on my feet, I was more of a threat, and the six suckers on the other side of the room knew it. Five of them were tensed up and ready to rumble, but the other was still tucking into my pizza. The iscarion had resorted to punching at the wall around his head, trying to free himself since nobody had stepped up to help him.

The sucker who had been upside down stood in front of me and held up a hand the way an animal tamer would to a lion. "Tell us where the girl is, and we'll let you live."

"What girl?" I said, poised and ready to continue the scrap.

"The one who belongs to Dominus Atrocitas, we know you've kept her. You were spotted with her."

"First of all, we haven't 'kept her'; she's not a stray fuckin' cat. And second, you see these?" I pointed to my dangling balls. "Tell your boss to fuckin' suck 'em, yeah?"

That pissed him off. He clenched his fists and snarled, "One more chance, where is she?"

I answered by lifting my foot from the carpet sucker's head, then smashing my heel into the side of his neck. It gave a loud crack, and his claws released my cheeks.

Time slowed again as the sucker in front of me lunged with his claws out in front of him. I leapt up onto the bed, giving the room a shower of ass blood as the iscarion yanked his head from the wall. Now, I'll admit I didn't have a plan here. I sprang onto the bed, used my momentum to bounce, and sent myself flying dong-first and sideways at the suckers on the other side. It was a dumb move. I'd left myself open and vulnerable. Big Boy, the iscarion, turned and watched me sail towards his buddies. I was about to crash into them like a bowling ball knocking down a bunch of pins when he intercepted me with a hard pounce and slammed into me.

My flight changed direction. I shot out through the open doorway and down the corridor, ass cheeks first. I hit the floor and skidded along the carpet on my back, giving me some serious rug burn on the ass, back and shoulders.

I came to a stop and gazed up at three familiar figures. "Oh, hi," I said, as Tex, Ginn and Ali looked down at me.

Tex pointed down at me and said, "Boy, where's ya strides?" before gently swaying and fixing his eyes on what was in my room. "An' who's that?"

Ginn let out a small hiccup, then followed Tex's gaze with a one-eyed squint. "Night's 'avin a party without us. Or... an orgy?"

Ali staggered forward and held out a hand to help me up.

"Wait jush oone second," Tex slurred, "ish that a vamp?"

"A room full of them," I said as I stood.

Ginn set off running down the corridor and threw herself through the open doorway yelling, "PARTAAAY!"

I ran back into the room after her and came to a stop just inside the doorway. The vampires were all standing looking around at each other in confusion as Ginn helped herself to the pizza thief's last slice.

"Is this her?" the Iscarion grunted.

"YES, FUCKING GRAB HER!" the sucker on the other side of the room yelled.

The iscarion sprang and made to grab Ginn, but she jumped backwards and up onto the bed with a laugh.

Ali and Tex pushed past me and into the room. Tex looked as though he was sobering up real quick, but Ali was still on another planet and could barely see straight. He threw his fists up and stepped towards the nearest sucker, who raised his own fists. Ali's brain may have been somewhere else, but his body was running on pure muscle memory, and it was ready for a brawl.

Tex whipped out his revolver and started waving it at the other vamps. "Now ya'll need to get gone before you taste lead," he said.

I was making no such offer, a taste of lead was their only option. I took the momentary distraction and threw myself at the pile of clothes on the floor. I wrapped a hand around the handle of one of the Sisters and the chaos kicked off again, all at once, as I aimed upwards and blew four rounds into Big Boy's crotch. He hit the floor, cradling his obliterated gonads.

Tex took that as a signal to get to the killin' and hammered a bullet through a sucker's forehead. Brain soup erupted out of the back of his head before he stumbled backward and fell. In hindsight, I should have moved from the floor because that sucker fell back onto me and a whole bunch of brains slopped out of his skull and onto my bare feet. And there's no worse sensation than having brains squelching between your toes.

While Tex turned his gun on another sucker and started filling him with lead, Ginn took the opportunity to jump from the bed—once she'd crammed the last of her pizza slice into her mouth—and rumble with the dude on the other side of the room.

She sprang at him while he was distracted, watching his buddies die, and latched onto his back like an angry backpack. She wrapped her legs around his waist and rained fists and elbows onto the back of his dome. He swung from side to side, trying to claw at her and fling her off, but she held on tight.

I hauled myself from the floor and took aim at a sucker making a run for it. He'd got past Tex and was halfway down the corridor. A squeeze of the trigger put a stop to that. He flew forward as his face exploded. He

305

skidded down the carpet on his front, leaving a streak of blood behind him. A stray eyeball rolled on ahead of him before coming to a stop, staring back at me.

Ali had beaten the living shit out of the sucker he'd been duking it out with. He'd received a few good punches himself but dealt way more damage. His vampire was a starfish on the floor, lying on his back with his arms—both snapped at the wrists—splayed out and limp. Ali was straddling him, and his fists and forearms were soaked in blood. He'd punched every last fang out of the sucker's head. They were broken and scattered around the floor. Ali kept on pummelling, but what was left was nothing more than a bloody mess of broken bone and tattered flesh.

After blowing the face off the corridor runner, I swung my gun around to face the only sucker left alive and unscathed. Pizza Snatcher. I was glad he was still alive; I wanted the pleasure of shooting him for munching all my 'ronis.

"What kind of asshole eats a man's pizza like that?" I asked, pointing the business end of the gun at his face.

He was a young guy, maybe in his early twenties, and looked a little too calm for somebody whose friends were being murdered around him. He shrugged. "Look man I didn't want to be here, but the boss said he'd kill me if I didn't do as I was told. And I'm sorry about the pizza, I'm trying to live blood-free, and I was starving."

I dropped the gun an inch. "What?"

The Snatcher stepped over Big Boy, who was still curled into a groaning ball, pushed the vamp with the bottle in her head to the floor then sat down on the edge of the bed. "I didn't want to be a fucking vampire, did I? Go ahead and kill me if you want to, living like this sucks. No pun intended."

Tex and Ali joined me, both standing by my side to see what the vampire had to say. Ginn was still busy with her sucker but was almost finished strangling him with her forearm.

"You're not gonna fight?" Ali said, somewhat more in control of his senses.

Tex chuckled. "Look at him, he couldn't even tear up my baby picture."

The Snatcher let out a long sigh before saying, "Nah. If I'm gonna die I'd rather make it quick and easy. It's pretty clear I wouldn't make it out of here alive anyway. Can I ask one thing though, before you kill me?"

"And what's that?"

He waved a hand at me. "Could you please put some fucking clothes on? I don't want my last sight to be some dude with his wang out."

Tex nodded. "That's fair, and you really should put some pants on, son. There's a lady present."

I looked from Tex, to Ginn. "I'm sorry I didn't have time to grab my shorts while I was fighting for my life. And she's already seen it anyway."

Tex grunted and blushed a little. "Well, uh, doesn't mean I want to."

Ali bent down to pluck my shorts from the pile of clothes and draped them over my shoulder.

"Anyway," I said, taking them and pulling them on with one hand while keeping my gun on the sucker with the other, "what do we do with him?"

Tex shrugged. "If he's lying, we kill him."

Ginn appeared beside Tex. The sucker she'd been using as a rodeo ride lay on the floor with his eyes bulging out of their sockets and long tongue dangling from his mouth. She'd pummelled him so hard, the top of his head had caved in. "Why not take him to Morgan?" she said.

I considered it for a moment then nodded. "That's a good idea. If he's telling the truth and is really trying to quit the blood, he could be useful."

Snatcher cut in, "Yeah, sure. I could help you."

Tex stepped up to him. "What's your name, kid?"

"Josh," Snatcher said.

"Okay, Josh, here's how it's gonna go. My friend Ali there is gonna take you down the road to meet our buddy, Morgan. He's a vampire too. Doesn't kill people, doesn't drink human blood. You're gonna have a chat with him. If you're telling the truth and you do choose to help us, Morgan will help you out; keep the other vampires off your back. Now, if you turn out to be bullshitting, he'll kill you. If you try to make a run for it, Ali will kill you," he pointed down at the vampire with the smashed head, "and there's your proof of his capability on the floor. Is that all crystal, boy?"

"Yes sir," Josh nodded.

Ali stepped forward and pulled Josh from the bed by the arm. "I'll go drop him off now," he said, and with that he steered Josh through the doorway and down the corridor.

Ginn looked down at Big Boy. "Is this one of the stronger ones?"

Tex nodded. "Sure is, an iscarion. Usually pretty hard to knock down, even with bullets, but it looks like Night hit the sweet spot."

"Can we please not refer to his balls as 'the sweet spot' and just kill him already?"

"Ooh, can I do it?" Ginn asked.

Tex stepped aside and sat himself down on the bed. "He's all yours."

I turned away as I caught sight of Ginn's boots heading for Big Boy's busted nuts. My room was wrecked. The carpet and most of the walls had turned red, the wall had a watermelon-sized hole in it, my TV had a cracked screen, and my pizza was gone.

What a goddamn mess.

I grabbed the edge of my bedsheet and tugged it off to wipe myself down, trying to get the worst of the blood off of me. I was covered in gouges and slashes, mostly on my ass, and I couldn't tell if the blood was mine or not. I'd just sat on the bottom of the bed and started scrubbing my face when I heard Ginn snort about something. I rubbed my eyes and dropped the sheet to see that she'd unplugged the TV and was waddling over to Big Boy with a smile on her face and the TV in her arms. With barely any effort, she hauled the big fuckin' machine over her head and held it up there as she frowned at something in the bathroom.

I turned to see one last sucker standing in the bathroom's open doorway. I had forgotten he was in there, and he'd raided the first aid kit. He'd tried to patch himself up by wrapping bandages around his neck and sticking his jaw back to his face with five or six strips of Band-Aid.

He made eye contact with Ginn, who was about to smash a TV on his buddy's head, just as the Band-Aids failed him and his jaw fell back down to his chest. I mean, who can blame him? It was a jaw-dropping sight, and it was the last he ever saw.

Tex didn't miss a beat. He whipped up his gun and cracked out two bullets, giving the bathroom a fresh lick of paint. With a spin around the finger, he holstered the gun as Ginn smashed the TV down on Big Boy's head. It burst like an old grape and sprayed mushed brains across the carpet.

I dropped the bedsheet down onto my lap and sighed. "Housekeeping's gonna fucking kill me."

# Spoiler Alert

After being moved into a new room, and paying a hefty charge for wrecking the old one, a couple of days passed by in a blur of VHS rentals, booze, pizza, chillin' and a little bit of vampire killin'. Oh, and can't forget the ass cheek healing. The cheeks were as good as new. My bruises were gone, my cuts all healed, and I could sit without wincing again.

Morgan had taken Josh, the young sucker, under his wing since Ali dropped him off. The kid seemed sincere enough, and he and Morgan seemed to have clicked quite well, what with him being on the straight and narrow himself.

Like almost every other night, we all sat in the Black Cat, drinking and playing cards. Mickey had returned without any news on Atrocitas, so we were all feeling a little deflated, especially after the attack. We were three rounds into a game of poker when his head drooped, signalling one of two things. Everyone at the table stopped to watch him for a moment, and Morgan whispered an explanation to Josh.

"Alright, ladies and gentlemen," Rusty said, "place your bets. Is he having a vision, or is he asleep? Five bucks a wager."

A storm of five-dollar bills hit the table as people babbled their guesses. I slapped mine down, betting Mickey had fallen asleep. The card game took a time out as we all held our breath, waiting for the inevitable awakening. Five minutes dragged by until Mickey's head finally bobbed up and down before he lifted it to see we were all watching, waiting.

"Well?" Rusty said.

Mickey's telepathic voice filled our heads, "Vision."

Harriot, Khearo and Tex cheered and fist-bumped each other as Rusty shared out the winnings with a disappointed grumble.

"Better luck next time," Tex said as he pocketed his share.

Rusty huffed and sat back in his chair with his arms crossed. "What's it this time then?"

Mickey's voice filled my brain again, "It was a vision of the fight with Dominus Atrocitas. We won the battle with no losses. Everyone survived."

That old familiar knot twisted up in my stomach, stronger than usual. Something was coming and it wasn't a trip to the shitter. Mickey's visions were always wrong, and frequently the opposite of what he'd seen, this one meant we were fucked. Man, we were fucked hard.

Ali sighed. "So... we're all going to die?"

Tex scratched his chin. "Couldn't be worse, could it?"

"Well, we've had a good run," Harriot said as she swirled her drink in her glass, "it was nice knowing everyone, I guess."

It wasn't often I heard such shit news, so I needed something to take the edge off, something special for just such an occasion. I reached into my jacket pocket and pulled out an emergency Baby Ruth candy bar. I tore through the wrapper and bit off a large chunk.

Ginn eyed the chocolate with a lustful look.

I pretended not to see and earned myself a punch on the shoulder. I wasn't happy about it, but I broke a piece off for her and handed it over. She inhaled it in a blink.

With some delicious sugary goodness coursing through my veins, my reasonable side reared its head. "Hold up," I said between chews, "we don't know for sure that it spells our doom. Maybe something happens and we don't have to fight? Maybe Atrocitas dies of old age in two days?"

Morgan snorted. "A vampire dying of old age? There's as much chance of him being BJ'd to death by Hulk Hogan."

"Good point, but you never really know with Mickey's visions, do ya?"

I looked around the table, trying to find a glimmer of hope in anyone's eyes. Even Ali, the eternal optimist, looked downtrodden. They were right though. There was no guarantee the naga would help us, and even with their help we still stood a good chance of getting our asses handed to us on silver platters. We had four humans, three werewolves, two ghosts, a vampire (maybe two), a murnock and perhaps a few snake-people. They had suckers by the hundreds. Shit, for all we knew, maybe even a couple thousand or more. The odds were not in our favour, no matter what angle we looked at it.

An idea popped into my head, and I held out a hand. "Wait, wait, wait, we might have a way to interpret the vision a little more accurately."

"How's that?" Khearo asked.

"You ever heard of Isabella the fortune teller?"

Ali slapped a hand down on the table. "Yes! Why didn't I think of that? She'll know. I'm sure of it."

Rusty held up a hand. "Woah now, who in the name of fuck is Isabella the fortune teller?"

Ali answered, "A fortune teller, genius. She lives in my hometown. She's a miserable old goat, but she's good. Real good."

"I can vouch for this. She didn't exactly read my fortune, but she knew things she shouldn't have been able to know. There's something about her. I bet she can help."

"Ah wey that solves it all, eh? An ol' witch who knows things is gonna save the day."

I could understand his scepticism, I'd be uncertain about Isabella myself if I hadn't met her, but the single interaction I'd had with her was enough to tell me she could actually shed some light on the situation.

"What else are we gonna do? We've spent the past week basically twiddling our fucking thumbs. We've done enough work together, we know each other's moves off by heart. We're as strong as we're gonna get. This is it. It's time to make a move before Atrocitas makes another one. If we're going to die, we're going to die fighting, and hopefully we'll take down a whole bunch of suckers with us. So, what now? Do we spend more time sitting here, playing cards every night and killing off the freak of the week while Atrocitas amasses even more of an army? Or do we go see a fucking old-ass fortune teller and get ready for a goddamn fight?"

The group sat in awe of my little speech. Tex had a big grin spread across his face.

Rusty sighed and sat forward. "Aye. I suppose you're right. It's about time we strap on our big boy balls and get ready to meet the Lord. Besides, I'll be alright. Everyone knows ye cannae kill the cripple anyway. You lot though? You're fucked."

Tex knocked back his glass and slammed it down on the table. "We leave at the crack of dawn, then." he said, reaching for the bottle of scotch in the middle to top it up again.

Ginn raised her glass to toast. "To us, and to the death."

Glasses clinked as the group toasted. "To the death."

We knocked back our drinks to the sound of Davy the bartender yelling, "Hey now you get the fuck on outta here."

I took a peek towards the entrance to see a real big motherfucker with a big purple mohawk standing in the doorway and a hoard of goons out in the parking lot behind him. His eyes flicked across the bar before landing on us and flooding black. He smiled and stepped forward as his jaw cracked and jagged fangs sprang out.

"To the death, eh?" he growled.

# Last Straw

So much for taking the fight to Atrocitas, eh? For the second time in one week, a hoard of vampires had shown up out of the blue. The message was clear: Atrocitas and his cronies knew Ginn's location, and they knew about us. They wanted her back and they wanted us dead.

**[Track 33]**

The big motherfucker—another iscarion, or of course—stepped further into the bar. I couldn't see exactly how many suckers he'd brought with him, but my guess was we were outnumbered.

Tex leaned back in his chair and said, "Fellas, if you so much as dream of messing with anyone in this bar, you better wake up and apologise."

"The Dominus sends his regards," Purple Mohawk said.

Davy the bartender levelled a shotgun at Mohawk's face and said, "Tell that old fuck he can suck our asses," before pulling the trigger and blowing away Mohawk's haircut.

The shot rang through the bar like thunder. The blast ripped through Mohawk's face and threw him off his feet. He flew off to the right and sprawled across the table of a man sitting on his lonesome. The fella was mid-way through a sip of his pint, and set his glass down on the edge of the table, barely seeming to register that a vampire was draped over it with blood leaking from his head.

Tex snorted. "Looks like he was all hat and no cowboy."

All of the suckers standing outside started pouring in through the door.

The squad and I all shot out of our seats… apart from Rusty. Everyone who was packing a piece whipped it out. Everyone who wasn't packing looked over to the bar. Davy was pulling all manner of weapons out from under it and spreading them across the top.

The Sisters were fully loaded, I was ready to dance. I popped a slug through the forehead of the first sucker to step through the door. He hit the deck with a wet plap as his flesh melted from his bones in a second. His buddies didn't stop to pay their respects. The next sucker charged through the doorway, splashing through the previous one's corpse juice. She was met with a hail of bullets courtesy of Tex, Ali and yours truly. Her convulsing body got shoved to the floor as two more suckers pushed their way in and trampled over her, with more following behind, all eager for a taste of lead.

While we were busy mowing down anyone who stepped over the threshold, creating a blockade of bodies at the entrance, Ginn and a few patrons had darted to the bar to grab something to fight with. Lucky for us, the Black Cat's regular patrons did not fuck about. They knew all about the Monster Squad and the risks of being in their vicinity, but they didn't care, real tough

317

motherfuckers, the lot of them. So, while that lonesome fella sat drinking his pint, totally unbothered, the rest of the clientele armed themselves to join us in a brawl.

I caught the eye of a heavily tattooed fella as he turned from the bar, swinging a spiked bat. He gave me 'the nod' and stepped to Ginn's side as she turned, holding a pair of mean-looking hatchets in each hand.

We served a main course of bullets until our guns ran dry, and in that moment when the triggers produced nothing but clicks, the vampires took the opportunity to flow in. They scrambled over the pile of decomposing bodies and streamed on through.

The dead vamps made the bar stink to high heaven.

One vamp set eyes on the lonesome fella and lunged at him as he took another sip of his beer. The man pulled a piece–a fucking huge stinking revolver, bigger than I'd ever seen–from under the table and burst three shots straight through the sucker's face without taking his lips from the glass.

Davy threw us a box of fresh bullets. It landed on the table with a clatter, knocking a few of our drinks to the floor. Ali, Tex and I made for it and got to reloading as quick as a blink. From behind us, something big whizzed past, a couple of big somethings, in fact. Khearo and Harriot had burst into wolf form and charged at the suckers. Morgan and Josh the new guy followed hot on their tails.

Mickey ran to the bar and picked up a large hunting knife for himself before throwing a shotgun over to Rusty. He caught it and checked it was loaded before sticking the stock between his legs and rolling himself forward into the fray.

All I could think was whenever he pulled that trigger with the gun there, it was gonna hurt if he had any feeling in his balls.

I stepped forward to really get in on the action, with Tex following at my side. A sucker with an especially upturned snout came at me with his tongue lashing the air. I held my shot, tightened the grip on Maria–the gun in my right hand–and rammed the barrel up into his left nostril. The noise that followed sounded like a scared pig. I shoved a little harder, and the noise turned into more of a grunting gurgle. The sucker grabbed hold of my arm and sank his claws into my flesh as he tried to pull the barrel out of his nasal cavity.

I wrestled with him as I steadied my left hand on his shoulder and rested Sophia's cylinder against his ear. I took aim and pulled the trigger, blowing a chunk from the back of another sucker's head. The fella on the end of my gun staggered sideways as the noise of the gunshot blew his eardrum to shit. In an act of kindness, I pulled Maria's trigger. The top of his head disappeared in an explosion of pink mist that left the barrel of the gun poking out through the ruin of his head.

He'd managed to scratch me up pretty bad, but it wasn't anything to get too worried about. I knew the bleeding would stop in a few minutes. I pointed the gun to the floor and gave it a shake as what was left of the dude's head slowly slid off the end. With a quick glance behind me, I found Ali standing on the table, popping off bullets with a big smile. He was looking highly entertained, and the Reapers were causing some serious damage.

The entire bar had descended into chaos. Davy kept on popping up from behind the bar to shoot something with his shotgun, Khearo and Harriot were shredding every sucker they laid eyes on, Ginn had buddied up with the tattooed guy and they were working on a vamp together. He had buried the spikes of his bat into a sucker's skull and Ginn was hacking at its neck with a hatchet.

And the fella on the table by himself just kept on sipping his pint, minding his damn business.

I decided to take a page from his book and stepped back to my table. Ali had vacated it, in favour of getting up close and personal with some devil spawn. My glass hadn't been knocked to the floor and still had a good measure of whiskey in it. I picked it up and took a slow sip, running my eyes over the carnage.

Rusty blew a gaping hole through a sucker's chest. The force of the shot sent his chair rolling backwards, bumping into Ginn.

One of the bar's patrons had a stroke of misfortune and ended up with one of the vampires crunching away at the back of his head. The sucker chomped his fangs into the guy's skull again and again. He looked dead to me, with his eyes all rolled back and mouth hanging open, but the repetition of fangs in the brain was making his body twitch and dance.

As the fella with the pint drained his glass, the iscarion on his table sat up straight with a jolt. The left-hand side of his head had been blown apart by Davy's shotgun blast. An eyeball hung from the socket and a clump of scalp flapped aside to reveal some exposed brain underneath the shattered skull. He was about to stand up from the table when an empty pint glass crashed down on his head.

The iscarion whipped around and set his one good eye on the fella sitting at his side. The guy looked him dead in the eye as he whipped his piece out from beneath the table and pressed it under the iscarion's chin. They spent a moment frozen, staring at each other before the fella ragged on the trigger and emptied the clip into the iscarion's head. Brains, bullets and bits of mohawk splattered across the ceiling.

Tex got caught in a shower of gore as he spun to face me, giving me a "did you see that" look. I nodded, looking from him then back to the guy, making a mental note to recruit him to the squad. He slouched back in his chair, pulled out a cigarette and lit it with a match before taking a long draw and exhaling a cloud towards the bloodstained ceiling.

It looked to me like everyone was occupied and handling themselves well enough. I took the moment's respite to close my eyes and take another sip of whiskey, savouring the taste. I swallowed and sighed, letting some of the stress melt away as the sounds of gunshots and smell of blood and dead vampires filled my senses. You'd think it'd be off-putting, but gunshots and dead vamp smell is a calming combo. It means you're getting the job done properly.

I opened my eyes to see a vampire standing in front of me, fangs and inky black eyes inches away from my face. He let out a roar and sprang forward like a fucking cheap jump-scare.

I dropped the glass and made a move to raise my gun, thinking, "have I just got myself killed over a sip of whiskey," as the vamp slumped forward, and his head rested on my shoulder. I stepped back and watched him drop to the floor with a hatchet buried deep in the back of his head.

Across the bar, Ginn yelled, "You're welcome."

Over near the door, Morgan was busy tearing the flesh from another vampire's back, trying to get them off of whomever they'd pinned to the floor. The other vampire didn't seem to be all that bothered about his skin being shredded. He was too busy pummelling his victim to pulp, and it seemed to be pissing Morgan off. With a roar of frustration, Morgan abandoned the tearing and grabbed the vamp's head from behind and gave a hard twist while pulling upwards. The sucker's face spun one-eighty and gave Morgan a look of surprise as he fell off to the side. Morgan threw the bubbling body out of the way to reveal Josh, the pizza snatcher. He was laid out on his back. His head was nothing but a hollowed-out bowl of mushed-up gore.

Morgan ran his claws through his hair and stepped back, mouthing, "fuck".

I couldn't count the number of dead lying around the bar. Thankfully it was almost all suckers, but a few of the patrons had drawn the short straw. Severed limbs were strewn around the place, chunks of flesh clung to the walls and every visible surface was covered in blood and other bodily fluids. Davy had his work cut out for him on the clean-up that's for damn sure. Only a few suckers remained. The situation was under control.

Tex made his way back over to the table, his boots sloshing through blood and guts. "Thanks," he said, taking a glass of whiskey I'd poured as he approached. "You hurt?"

I took a look at myself. My right arm had some pretty deep gauges that stung like a motherfucker, and a large splinter of wood had lodged itself into my thigh. In all the chaos, I hadn't noticed it. I reached down and gave the chunk a tug then threw it aside. Blood flowed down my leg from the wound, and the pain kicked in. "Seems so."

"Put some pressure on that," Tex said.

I nodded and pressed my palm over the wound with a hiss.

Harriot strode past us in wolf mode and caught a gym bag Davy threw at her, then disappeared into the ladies' bathroom.

Three suckers were left alive. One of them was dragging herself towards the door, leaving her legs behind. She'd placed a hand on the door and started pushing it open when a spiked bat cracked down onto the top of her head. The tattooed guy placed a foot on her shoulder and yanked the bat back with a squelchy crunch. He swung up behind his right shoulder and brought the bat back down, splitting the sucker's head.

Over by the bar, Khearo had hauled some poor fucker up in the air. He had one huge, clawed paw clamped over each shoulder. With a roar from Khearo and a scream from his vampire toy, he tugged each shoulder in different directions, ripping the sucker from the left clavicle, right down the middle. A torrent of blood gushed to the floor as his organs spilled out and splatted at Khearo's feet. Intestines, liver, kidneys, all of it spilled out into a pile.

Ali finished off the final one with a broken chair leg rammed under the chin. The pointy end stuck out of the sucker's forehead. His eyeballs melted in their sockets and dribbled down his face. The rest of his flesh followed a moment later. He fell to the floor in a puddle of bones and juice.

With the last sucker dead, everyone took a moment to breathe while looking around the bar. Most of the furniture had been smashed, and most of the bottles behind the bar had been caught in the crossfire.

"My bar..." Davy groaned.

The lonesome fella with the fuckin' big gun pushed his chair out from under the table, some of the only furniture still intact, and stood. He looked around at everyone, all drenched head to toe in blood. With a nod and a smile, he stepped over the iscarion's corpse and made his way over to the bar. He pulled out a crisp hundo and slapped it down on the bar top with a splash of blood and alcohol, saying, "Keep the change," before turning and strolling out the door.

"Who the fuck was that guy?" I asked Davy.

He shrugged. "Never seen him in here before."

The clientele left alive followed suit and paid their bills before heading out of the door. The tattooed guy handed Ginn a napkin with his phone number scrawled on it. He gave her a wink before setting his bat on the bar top and heading out. Ginn stuffed the napkin into her bra with a smile. She might have been blushing, but it was hard to tell with her being so covered in blood.

Khearo shrank back to human form and walked over to join me and Tex at the table. Harriot appeared wearing a fresh set of clothes. The rest of the crew gathered as Davy set to collecting stray weapons.

Tex looked around at everyone. "This is two big attacks in a couple of days. Atrocitas is sending a message and forcing our hand here. We've got to hit him, and we've got to do it soon. We can't let anyone else get caught in our fight. Innocent people have died here."

"And my bar is fucked!" Davy cut in.

Rusty turned to him. "We'll help out with the cost of repairs, my friend."

"We all will," Tex said as everyone nodded their agreement, "but this is the last straw. They're not going to stop until they get Ginn back."

"So, let's give them what they want," Ginn said.

Tex tapped a finger on his chin. "Indeed, indeed. Like Night said, it's now or never. Night, give the Neon

Nightmares a call and let them know the plan. We set off for Isabella's in the morning."

I gave him the thumbs up.

"Now, what was it the Nightmares said when we raided the motel a couple of weeks back?"

Ali grinned. "Let's fuck some Draculas."

Ginn let out a loud snort and the rest of the group cracked some smiles.

Tex nodded. "Let's fuck some Draculas."

Rusty clapped his hands together. "Davy, my good man, one last round of your finest surviving scotch, please."

Davy looked up, mid way through bending to pull a hatchet from a dead vampire's skull. "Get 'em your-fucking-selves, I've got your goddamn mess to clean up."

As the rest of the group helped Davy pile corpses and bits of corpses by the door, Rusty wheeled his way behind the bar to pour us all one last drink.

The last drink we'd all have together in the Black Cat.

# Exodus 22:18

We met at Mac's diner in Santa Monica for breakfast and got the day off to a good start with full bellies and a spark of hope that Mickey's vision would turn out to be a crock of shit. What Isabella had to say on the matter remained to be seen.

Everyone had scrubbed up well from the previous night. No more blood-soaked clothes or chunks of brain in our hair, but now that everyone was clean, the damage was clear. Ali had a serious black eye, Ginn was a patchwork of bruises, the squad were all covered in scratches, and my arm was bandaged up. Tex was fine, the lucky bastard.

The drive down to San Felipe passed by slowly. Ali, Ginn and I were in Tex's car. The Monster Squad were crammed uncomfortably in Harriot's. We pulled up in San Felipe in the early afternoon, following Ali's direction to stop outside of a crumbling old saloon I recognised: El Tirador. I'd stopped off there for a drink back when I was on the hunt for the Sisters. It hadn't been all that long ago, about eight months, but El Tirador looked as though it had aged ten years in that time. The whitewashed walls flaked and crumbled, and the wooden sign above the door was so sun bleached, I could barely read it. It didn't surprise me, though, the sun glared down with unrelenting force.

I stepped out of the car as Tex killed the engine and shimmied out of my jacket. It wasn't a day for leather. Nor pants, for that matter, but I assumed whipping them off wouldn't be best received, so I kept them on. Begrudgingly.

Ali and Ginn stepped out to join me as I watched Khearo place Rusty's wheelchair by his door. He slapped a hand up onto the roof and flung himself from one seat to the next with flawless form. I never tired of seeing Rusty defy his disability every chance he got.

"You guys wait here, I'll be a second," Ali said, back handing my chest before making his way inside the saloon. The sound of a roaracious greeting drifted through the door a moment later, followed by a lot of enthusiastic Spanish.

A few minutes later, Ali re-emerged carrying a case of frosty cold Cokes and handed them out as we set off in the direction of Isabella's. We cracked open the drinks in what felt like perfect synchronisation and guzzled the sweet black nectar. If there'd been a camera in front of me, I would have given it a wink after taking a long, refreshing sip. Cool Cola, available in all good grocery stores now.

## [Track 34]

The walk to Isabella's was quite a pleasant one, for most of us anyway. Rusty didn't seem too fond of it. The majority of the terrain was either cobbled streets or rough, pothole-ridden roads. His chair could handle anything, but he still breathed a sigh of relief for his ass when we finally rounded the corner and saw Isabella's mystic blue sign above her doorway. In contrast to El Tirador's sign, hers hadn't faded at all. I stepped up to rap on the door, but it opened before my hand fell. A blast of incense assaulted my nose. Isabella stood in the doorway, her small, wrinkled frame wrapped in a purple dress and shawl.

"I thought you'd be dead by now," she said, taking a long, hard look at me.

"I could say the same to you. Are you gonna let us in?"

She stood in the doorway, making no moves to let us over the threshold. Her beady little eyes scanned us and landed on Ali. "Alejandro Santos. It's good to see you're still getting yourself into trouble."

Ali smiled and nodded. "Isabella. May we come in?"

Her eyes scanned everyone, one at a time, searching our souls. Or most likely, trying to figure out who had the fattest wallet. "All but him," she said, pointing to Morgan.

His eyes narrowed. "And why the fuck not?" he sneered.

"I'll not let an affront to the Lord into my home. You are not welcome here, monster."

Rusty wheeled himself over and held up a hand. "Hey now, we're all monsters here. Morgan is as good a person as any one of us."

I didn't think it was possible, but the look of disgust on Isabella's face made her look fifty years older. The wrinkles wrinkled and creased her face up even more.

"The Lord says such creatures are an abomination. I'll not let him in."

Morgan took a moment to straighten his tie and said, "If we're bringing the Lord into the conversation, how about Exodus twenty-two eighteen?"

Isabella's face almost turned to stone.

"That's right: 'Thou shalt not suffer a witch to live.' Should I carry out the word of the Lord, witch?"

She stuck out a gnarled old finger and opened her mouth to respond, but the finger curled back and retreated as she realised Morgan had a good point. "Fine, you can come in. But know this," she said, reaching into the folds of her dress and pulling out a revolver almost as big as the Sisters, "if you move in any way I don't like, your friends will have to mop you up from my floor."

Morgan grinned, the slightest hint of a challenge flashed across his eyes. "She's got balls, this old hag."

I turned back to see Isabella's response, but she'd disappeared, leaving the door open for us to come inside. Ali stepped in first, and the rest of us followed. Morgan entered last and pulled the door closed behind him.

Isabella sat at her little round table with her crystal ball at the ready. Tex approached and took the chair opposite her. She held out her hand for Tex to cross her palm with silver. Tex's silver came in the form of a fistful of dollars, two hundred of them to be precise. Isabella snatched the cash away the moment it hit her hand, disappearing into her dress with expert speed.

She set her eyes on Mickey. "Now, I understand you have visions, but they're always wrong, yes?"

"Yes," Mickey thought for us all to hear.

Isabella snickered. "Useful."

"His most recent vision was of a battle to come," Tex said, "we win, and everyone survives."

"And you want to know if that means you're all going to fail?"

Tex nodded.

Everyone had gathered around the table and packed in tight, not wanting to miss a word of our fortunes. Ginn looked the most entertained, but Khearo and Morgan looked bored. Morgan was glancing around the room at all of Isabella's knick-knacks and curios.

Isabella waved her hands over the crystal ball, laying the theatrics on heavy for her audience. "Well, let us see what the future holds, shall we?"

All eyes hit the crystal ball. I watched as clouds swirled inside it as Isabella waved her hands back and forth and all around it. Caressing it, almost. She pulled a few faces that meant jack shit as far as I could see. The same kind of show the last time I'd seen her. I knew damn well she didn't need to be fondling a giant marble. The old witch just knew things. After a few minutes of humming and waving, her eyes flicked open.

"What did you see?" Tex asked.

"My vision is clouded. Your destiny is not yet set, the outcome of the fight, not yet decided."

Harriot tutted. "So what you're saying is, you don't know shit and I've wasted gas driving here?"

Isabella held up her hand for silence. "I can tell you this, not all of you will survive. Again, who lives and who dies is unclear. But no matter the result of the battle, death comes for some of you," she finished her sentence with a look towards Morgan.

Everyone exchanged nervous glances.

"And if some of us choose not to fight?" Tex asked.

"Then we're all fucked," Isabella said, as she leaned back in her chair and threw a black cloth over the crystal ball.

"How so?" Ginn asked.

Isabella heaved a long, rattling sigh. "Unless each and every one of you fights, Atrocitas will win. And if Atrocitas wins, we all lose. With the last of the slayers gone, there'll be nothing left to stop him from spreading his vile seed across the world."

Slayers. I liked the sound of that. Isaac the vampire slayer had a ring to it. Sounded like some badass they'd make a TV show about. Isaac Nightingale: Vampire Slayer, at your service.

Tex scratched at his stubble. "So you're saying there's a chance?"

"Of course there's a chance. Otherwise, all I'd see in the crystal ball would be chaos. Vampires and all sorts running rampant as humans lie dead in the streets. But that's only if you lose. No pressure."

"What do we do now?" Ginn asked, looking to Tex.

He spun in his chair to face everybody. "I guess we gather our things and get ready for a fuckin' real big fight."

Khearo and Morgan nodded their approval. Ali and Ginn looked a little more reluctant, and understandably so. They'd only just got their lives back on track. Shit, so had I. Everything had gone quite well in terms of learning how to fight and kill whatever supernatural creature I needed to, but I hadn't expected to be going toe-to-toe with the Vampire King so soon.

Isabella stood up from the table and shuffled her way around the room, deep in thought and looking at us each in turn. "If I may give you all a word of advice," she said, "I'd advise you all to get your affairs in order as soon as possible. You may not get another chance."

With that, the realisation hit. Some of us weren't gonna make it out of this alive.

# Well, Fuck

## [Track 35]

I found Isabella the next morning, dead; face down in a bowl of half-eaten spaghetti-os. I know right, what a fuckin' twist. Our last encounter left me feeling a little uneasy. Something felt off, and Isabella seemed to be acting weird. Weirder than usual, anyway. She'd been giving me the side-eye the entire time we were there, as if she had something on her mind she didn't want anyone else but me to know. Something she'd seen in the crystal ball, perhaps.

When it came to leaving, she pulled me to one side and said, "Don't take this off, whatever you do. You'll need it soon enough," while touching the broken key hanging around my neck, beneath my shirt. I hadn't taken it off since Spaghetti–o Jones gave it to me. To tell the truth, I'd forgotten I was even wearing it. Kind of like when you wear a ring for so long, you stop noticing it's on your finger. Her words lingered in my mind, and I wanted more answers. So, while everyone else slept soundly at Casa de Los Sueños, the local motel-slash-serial killer hotspot, I came out to speak to her before we headed off. And that's when I found her. Her door was ajar, but just enough so you'd only notice if you were about to knock on it. I pushed it open and made my way inside, calling out her name with the ripe smell of corpse filling my nostrils. She didn't answer, on account of being dead.

It took a moment for my eyes to adjust to the dingy room, and that's when I noticed an unusual lump hunched over the table behind the crystal ball. I felt around the wall for a light switch and clicked it on. The room filled with light, and the sight of blood splattered all over the wall to my right caught me off guard, even though I could smell blood and death from outside. The words 'SEE YOU IN HELL' had been smeared across the wall. I thought it was blood, but on closer inspection, it turned out to be sauce from her spaghetti-os.

I approached the figure slumped over the table. Sure enough, there she was. Isabella's shawl hung from her shoulders, caked in dried blood. Using my expert detective skills, I deduced the blood had come from the gaping hole in her skull. I took a walk around her corpse. She sat face down in her bowl with the side of her head blown off. A puddle of dark, sticky blood with floating chunks of brain had pooled around her head and dripped down onto her nice tiles. Her right hand hung down by her side, and a revolver lay on the floor below it. From every way I looked at it, it looked like Isabella had blown her brains out. But why? What could push a person like her to kill herself? Somebody so old and stubbornly dodging death. What had she seen in that crystal ball?

I picked up the phone and called the motel to get the squad over. Half an hour later, they were all crammed into Isabella's fortune-telling studio again.

"She's been dead a while," Rusty said, pointing out the obvious, "judging from the smell, I'd say she kicked the bucket not long after we left yesterday."

335

"What the fuck would make her do such a thing?" Harriot asked.

Tex strolled around the table, scratching his chin. "I've got the feeling she saw something in that there ball she didn't tell us. And if she's decided to take an early check-out, I don't think it bodes well for us."

Ali and Ginn moved in a little closer to my sides. Everyone took a moment to glance at each other, the room thick with tension. I could tell everyone was thinking it, but nobody wanted to say it: Isabella committing suicide looked a hell of a lot like she knew exactly how things were gonna play out, and she didn't wanna be around when it did.

All I could think was: if we were all gonna die soon, I wanted to go see my mom. I needed to say my goodbyes.

# The Last Good Chicken Sandwich

I'd decided to hightail it from San Felipe and go see my mom for what could have been the last time. I couldn't go out without one last goodbye. So, after a pit stop at Tex's place to stock up on as much firepower as we could fit in our cars, motorcycles, pockets and asses, we all drove up to my sleepy little hometown of Blackwater Lake. Yes, all of us: Tex, Ali, Ginn and the whole Monster Squad.

I figured the squad might have needed a little time to get their affairs in order before we left, and I said as much to Rusty, but his response was: "What the fuck would we do? Take the reserved sign off our table in the Black Cat? Lad, all we have is each other. We have no goodbyes to say, no stuff to take care of. Shit, all I need to do is miss a month's rent and my apartment will have someone else living in it before I know it. Same with the other guys. Besides, our stuff is already packed and in the trunk of Harriot's car. We didn't expect to be going back to LA."

Tex spent a bit of time babbling to Gabriel, and that was that.

I was the only one with any family left to say goodbye to. I figured we could all spend a couple of days up home. My mom could meet everyone, we could hit

Jackie's for one last drink, and I could say my last goodbye to Suzie.

We split ways as we entered Blackwater at five in the afternoon. Tex and I headed to my mom's. Ginn, Ali and the squad peeled off in the direction of the Hard-Nap Motel. We'd catch up with them later. I'd called ahead and let Mom know we'd be coming, and she had steaming mugs of hot chocolate waiting on the coffee table for us when we arrived. But of course, we couldn't get through the front door without paying the hug toll. And the price had risen.

"How you doing, sweetie?" Mom asked while squeezing the life out of me.

"Glad to be home."

"And good to see you, Tex. I assume you're both hungry?"

"Starving," I said, breaking off from the hug.

Tex nodded his agreement.

Mom shooed us through the door saying, "Good. Hot chocolate and sandwiches are on the coffee table. I made your favourite."

My mouth began to water immediately. Chicken smothered in barbeque sauce with red onions, heaven between bread. We dropped our bags down by the side of the sofa and then sat ourselves down on it. The sight of the food made my stomach rumble. It had been a while since I'd had my favourite sandwich. It brought back memories of prison, and how Ali had brought me one every day while I was in a coma, just in case I woke up, and how he'd eaten it himself when I didn't. Eight years of the same sandwich sounded like hell, but not for me. I could have eaten one every day 'till the day I died. So maybe another three days, if Mickey's visions and Isabella's suicide were anything to go by.

"How's the car hunting business going then?" Mom asked, sitting in the armchair opposite us.

"Well," Tex said, "we've been spending a lot of time in LA lately, but we're gonna head to Nebraska in a couple of days."

"Nebraska? Didn't you have to pass through to get here?"

I shook my head. "Nah, we came through Wyoming and North Dakota instead. Cut a little time off the trip. Only like, an hour, but it's something."

"That's still a lot of driving. I'm surprised that car of yours still has wheels, Tex. I could imagine them being worn down to nothing but nubs."

"It sure is a wonder they aren't, isn't it?" Tex chuckled.

Mom nodded, smiling, then continued, "Isn't your friend Ali with you?"

"He is, yeah. He's just off to check in at the Hard-Nap with Ginn."

Mom perked up a little extra, a spark flashed behind her eyes. "Ginn's here? So, when do I get to meet her?"

I knew that look. "Like I said, she's just a friend. Don't get too excited."

"Of course," she said, sipping her hot chocolate, "well why not call them over? We can't have them spending the evening in that boring old motel. I'll make us all a big dinner; I've got plenty of food in."

Tex looked at me to see what I thought of the idea.

"Sure, sounds good to me."

"I'll go call them in that case," Tex said. "Do you mind if I make another call while I'm at it?"

"Not at all, go for it."

Tex stood and made his way to the kitchen; I drained my mug and followed him under the guise of washing it.

"What's the plan?" I asked in hushed tones.

"I'll give Ali and Ginn a call, tell 'em to come over, then get the Neon Nightmares on the phone, tell 'em to meet us at Vidstar tomorrow."

"Cool cool cool," I said, giving my mug a rinse and setting it down on the rack to dry.

I made my way back into the living room to sit with my mom. She sat sipping her drink, smiling at me.

"So, tell me about Ginn," she said.

I knew this was coming and I'd planned ahead, just in case Mom and Ginn ever met. Ginn had been briefed on the story. We'd met through the car restoration community, struck up a good friendship, and now she helps with the business; specialises in finding buyers for the cars, all that kinda stuff. And that's exactly what I told Mom.

Tex came back through a few minutes later. "They said they'll be over in an hour or so. Would you like a hand with dinner, Mrs Nightingale?"

Mom stood and batted Tex on the shoulder as she passed on her way to the kitchen. "Oh you're forever the gentleman aren't you? Isaac can help me, darlin', you've done a lot of driving today, and you've earned a rest."

I followed Mom into the kitchen, leaving Tex to chill. He kicked off his boots and picked up the newspaper from the coffee table, then kicked back with a contented sigh.

* * *

It had almost ticked over to seven when we heard the rumble of Ali and Ginn's motorcycles pulling up out front. Mom left the kitchen to get the door, leaving me with the cooking. A risky move, but I managed to hold everything together until she'd greeted everybody and joined me again, with Ginn following close behind.

"Oh, now this is a sight I could get used to," Ginn said.

"Are you saying he doesn't cook often?" Mom asked.

Ginn snorted. "The Takeout King? This is maybe the second time I've witnessed it."

Mom batted me on the shoulder with an oven glove, saying, "Isaac Nightingale, you better not be living off nothing but pizza."

"I'm not, I promise," I said, shielding myself from the vicious attack, "I order chicken wings sometimes too."

The oven glove rose again, but just as a threat this time. "If you don't start eating better, I'll beat you senseless with this. Go on; get the table ready, if you still remember how."

I chuckled and took my leave of chef duties to set the table. Ginn drifted into helping, without asking whether or not I'd like the help. We set the table real proper and as the final touch, I pulled out the spare chair: an uncomfortable fold-out thing, about half the size of all the other chairs at the table. It was mine, of course.

When the smell of the food had reached its peak and our stomachs were screaming over it, Mom called out for Tex and Ali, telling them to come get it. We all sat as Mom loaded the table with all manner of food to make up a big, delicious dinner. And in that moment, seeing the smiles of the people I loved, I felt like a kid again. Memories of meals with Mom, Dad and Suzie flashed through my mind, bringing a dull ache to my chest. I'd never wanted those times to end, but they did, and I'd never get them back. The ache in my chest bloomed into a knot in my stomach; that old sixth-sense that something bad was about to happen. But this time it had a sense of finality about it. The sense of an ending.

# The Empire and the Conqueror

I slept like a baby that night, tucked up in my old bed. I'd enjoyed spending the evening with Mom and the guys. We'd stuffed ourselves with so much food we could barely move. But we managed to waddle to the sofa, and that's where we stayed the rest of the evening, just talking. Tex, Ginn and Ali had headed off to the Hard-Nap just before midnight, leaving Mom and me to hit the hay. And I hit it hard.

When morning came around, Mom had already left for work, so I threw on some clothes and inhaled the croissant she'd left me for breakfast before making my way outside to meet the guys at Vidstar. I was gonna be early, but it didn't matter. Just meant I'd have time to browse the tapes, see if there was anything interesting for the evening. According to Tex, the Neon Nightmares were gonna meet us there. We needed to give them the low-down on the situation. I had no doubt they'd keep to their word and join us; they seemed to enjoy a good fight. And when you're already a ghost, what do you gotta lose?

### [Track 37]

I hopped off the bus just before noon and made a beeline for Vidstar. More neon signs had crept into

343

Blackwater's main street. Vidstar Video and the Empire Arcade stood on opposite sides of the street, two neon giants facing each other down. Video store standees filled the window at Vidstar, advertising all manner of movies. I pushed through the doors, greeted by Blondie's "Call Me" and the unmistakable smell that all video stores seemed to have.

I made my way over to the horror section to see what was new. The cover of 'Zombie Punks from Mars' caught my eye, so I picked it up to have a read of the back.

"Awesome movie, that one bro," a voice to my right said.

I glanced up from the blurb to see Leon standing next to me, shades and purple Letterman jacket both in attendance. He lowered the shades enough for me to see his misty purple eyes before giving me a wink and pushing them back up.

"Good to see you. Anything else you'd recommend?"

Leon nodded. "Always, my dude."

I continued browsing as he pulled a selection of tapes off the shelves before handing me a bunch: The Fog, Maniac, and Hatchet Hands Harry: a trashy, low-budget-looking affair with an undead cowboy on the cover who had hatchets in place of hands. I took a moment to read the backs and heard the chatter of Ginn and Ali walking through the door. The conversation grew louder as they made their way over.

A heavy hand clapped me on the back. "Wha'cha got there buddy?" Ali asked.

I turned to show him the tapes and had to do a double-take. Ali stood in front of me, a big, macho mountain of muscle wearing a pair of short pink hot pants and a loose-fitting, bright green muscle vest.

I snorted, pointing at his shorts. "What the fuck are they?"

Ali gave a twirl. "You like them? Ginn took me shopping."

Ginn gave a squeak of delight.

"Looks like you're smuggling a butternut squash."

Leon abandoned all subtlety. "Nice cock, bro."

"Gracias," Ali said with a big ol' grin.

"We could be twins, couldn't we?" Ginn said, twirling to show her similar outfit.

"Sure, you know, if it wasn't for one of you being a big dicked Mexican."

Tex appeared behind Ali. "Are you ladies done checking each other out?"

"With Ali in those shorts? Never," Ginn said.

Tex's face was stone serious, not even cracking a smile, "Get your shit together, we have an important mission to do. Night, buy them tapes. Leon, find Adrian. Ali, Ginn, prepare for chaos. It's about to go down."

* * *

I watched as the undead monstrosity shambled towards me. Blood and gore spilled from its gaping mouth, it was all that was left of Ginn's corpse. We'd tried to save her but weren't quick enough. The hoard of zombies had overwhelmed us, and tore Ginn limb from limb, feasting on her flesh. There was nothing we could do. We had to keep going. The town depended on us, and it was only Tex and me left alive. Ali and Ginn were dead. The squad were nowhere to be seen, and we were trapped in an alleyway. Nowhere to run. Nowhere to hide.

Screams echoed around us as I stared down the barrel of my gun. My hand steady, my aim true. I squeezed the trigger and blew the head off a zombie right in front of me. Its head erupted and splattered red over the others. An eyeball fell to the floor with a wet plop. Two zombies came forwards, taking the dead one's place. I aimed and pulled the trigger. Zombie One's jaw left its face, leaving a tongue hanging beneath the rest of its head. Another shot sent a bullet boring a hole through the middle of its forehead. It dropped down dead, but more zombies just kept on coming.

Zombie Two had shambled closer, closing the gap between us. I put him in my sights and fired off three rounds, hammering them through his skull. It dropped to the floor, and more came forward.

"Shit, shit, shit," I heard Tex say, over the screams.

A couple of zombies had him, and he was out of bullets. I turned to shoot them, but I could tell I was already too late. They sunk their rotten teeth into his flesh as more piled onto him. Within seconds, they tore his head from his shoulders. I was alone. I pointed my gun at the zombie closest to me and pulled the trigger.

Nothing. Click after click, after click. Out of ammo and out of luck. There was no escape. I accepted my fate. The hoard sunk their teeth into me: into my arms, into my neck. Their filthy fingernails peeled the skin from my face, and with one final cry, I fell to the floor as two big, bright green words flashed in front of my eyes:

GAME OVER

"Goddamn, we were doing so well," Tex said, crashing a fist down into his palm.

I turned away from the machine, faced the squad and shrugged at the sight of grins all around.

"And here I thought ya were supposed to be good with a gun," Rusty said, "I coulda thrashed the lot of 'em with my eyes closed."

"Hey, I almost beat your high score."

Rusty snorted. "Nowhere near, laddie, dinnae fool ye'sel."

"Whatever you say, Hot Wheels," I said as I approached him.

That earned me a swift jab to the crotch. "Ya cheeky wee cunt," Rusty said.

I doubled over from the pain in my gonads while the group laughed before dispersing to play some games of their own. Mickey and Harriot marched off to stand behind some screaming teenagers playing a kung-fu fighting game, ready to take their turn. Khearo and Morgan had set their sights on another machine, and Tex, Ali and Ginn were making their way over to the snack area, where Leon and Adrian were already sitting, looking right at home under the blacklight.

"Come on, let's have a game of Space Invaders, you can wheel me over for being cheeky," Rusty said.

I took the handles of his chair and pushed him through the arcade. It took a lot more effort than I'd anticipated. For being such a small dude, he sure weighed a lot. "How the fuck are you so heavy?"

Rusty turned his head up to face me and winked. "It's all in the massive cock and balls lad."

I chuckled and parked Rusty up in front of the machine.

He pulled a fistful of quarters out of his pocket and fed them into the machine. "Let's make things interesting, eh? Lowest score buys the winner drinks tonight?" he said, sticking out a hand.

I shook it. "You're on."

I took hold of the joystick and rested my fingers on the buttons, ready to conquer the high scores. I gave the nod, hit the button and readied my cannons. It was time to blow up some alien scum.

# Another Whiskey, Please

We left the Empire Arcade with our wallets a hell of a lot lighter. Ultimate Zombie Slayer had ripped the flesh from my bones and the quarters from my pocket. Man, I fuckin' loved the eighties.

We'd played the day away, and after a hard day of shooting zombies, beating up ninjas, blowing up aliens and stacking blocks to the heavens, there was only one thing left to do: drink. So we made our way over to Jackie's to do just that. Ali took the lead. Being an ex-employee, he knew the bouncers, and he knew they were likely to take one look at us and tell us to take a hike then and there, but not if they saw him first. Lo and behold, he was correct. The bouncers let us all in, but not without a bunch of odd looks. Any other day, such looks would be fighting talk, but not this time. I'd made the conscious decision to do no fighting or hunting any time I visited home. Home time was downtime.

The bar was a little livelier than it was on my last visit. Groups of people sat around tables, chatting and laughing, giving the place a pleasant atmosphere. As with most drinking establishments we had a habit of visiting, this one had low lighting, dark corners and the ever-lingering smell of smoke.

We pounced on a free table in the corner as Rusty and Tex ordered drinks. Always best to take the corner table. The less normal people around us the better, especially where Rusty was concerned. The man had a tendency to lose control of his volume from time to time. The last thing I wanted was the Blackwater residents hearing of our antics. Talk travels fast in a small town.

We took our seats as Harriot made her way to the Jukebox with a handful of quarters. I always liked it when she chose the music, of all the Monster Squad, she had the best taste. Aside from myself, of course. Leon and Adrian sat to my left, gathering attention from the locals on account of their colourful outfits. Small drifts of coloured smoke floated out from behind their sunglasses, but you couldn't really see it unless you were up close.

"Can't you, like, turn that off?" I asked, waving a finger at my own eyes.

They both shrugged, but Leon spoke, "Nah, don't think so bro. Tried to make 'em look normal like they used to, but nothing seems to work."

Harriot took the seat to my right as the opening beats of 'You're the One That I Want' filled the bar. "It's always the eyes, remember," she said as her pupils narrowed to slits.

"Yeah, what's with that?" Ginn cut in. "I've noticed vampires and werewolves have some control over it, but no other monster. Sorry, monster feels weird to say."

Harriot smiled. "Windows to the soul, aren't they? The eyes always show someone's true nature."

Ali chipped in, "I've known it the whole time. One of the first things I said to Night was he has the eyes of a man who's seen the Devil, and I was right. Long before I knew about you spooky motherfuckers."

"Did someone mention spooky motherfuckers? Gotta be talking about these two fancy lads here," Rusty said as he appeared with the drinks. He handed them out then pulled himself close to the table, grinning at Leon and Adrian.

They smiled and fist-bumped each other, happy to be called 'fancy lads'.

"What's your story then, fellas?" Rusty asked.

Leon adjusted his sunglasses and then launched into a montage-worthy monologue, retelling their backstory and spilling all the secrets of the Neon Nightmares. The squad sat and listened in silence, hooked on the thrilling story of how two childhood friends from New York had grown up to become the country's biggest video store owners before being murdered and coming back as neon ghosts to exact their gruesome revenge on their one true nemesis: Killatron the Power Master, also known as Murder Nerd, and how they took his Power Gloves. All with the help of two badass dudes called Night and Tex.

"Well shit my pants," Rusty said. "And you say you still have those laser gloves? They'll come in quite fuckin' handy when we come to fight Atrocitas, I tell ya."

Leon and Adrian reached into their jackets and pulled out a glove each. "Feast your eyes bros and bro-dettes," Adrian said, displaying his glove, "A real-life Power Glove; powerful enough to vaporise an entire motherfucka in one single thrust of an arm. Murder Nerd may have been a punk bitch, but the kid was clever, it has to be said."

"It can end more than one motherfucka though, I reckon it could cut through at least a hundred people at once," Leon added.

"Impressive," Harriot said.

Khearo, Morgan and Mickey nodded their heads in agreement.

In the time it took them to tell their story, Ginn had started plaiting Ali's hair, and he had rolled with it. They seemed to have gotten quite close and comfortable with each other in a short amount of time. It was nice to see a side to Ali that would have been a death sentence in prison at worst or put him in line for a violent sexual assault at best. The squad and Nightmares chatted amongst themselves as I sat back and chilled in silence, floating in and out of various conversations going on around the table.

After tightening the final plait into Ali's hair, Ginn reached into her bag and pulled out a couple of small bottles. She put them down on the table for Ali to see. He rolled his eyes and chuckled at the sight of the nail polish as Ginn asked, "Which colour?" He pointed at the crimson one, and Ginn yanked his hand in her direction, dead set on making him look gorgeous.

Tex had taken to doing the same as me: he'd kicked back with his drink resting on his stomach, floating in and out of listening to conversations.

I caught his eye and gave him a smile. He returned it with a slow blink before downing his drink and standing. He clapped a hand down on Ali's shoulder and mumbled, "Back in a few minutes." I watched him make a swift exit out through the front door and decided to follow. Something felt off.

I pushed through the doors and took a glance around to see him sauntering down the street before stopping at the corner and lighting up a smoke.

"Since when do you smoke cigarettes?" I asked as I approached. "I thought it was cigars or nothing?"

Tex tipped his head back, looking to the stars as he exhaled a pungent cloud. "It's not a cigarette," he said.

"Yeah, I can smell that now," I said, wafting at the cloud. "What's the deal with the Devil's Lettuce then?"

Tex shrugged. "Just need a doobie to take the edge off now and again. Right now's one of those times. I ain't gonna lie to ya, kid; I'm scared of what's to come. My asshole's tighter than it's ever been right now."

"I'm sure I needed to know that. So, what's got your cheeks whistlin'?"

"Take a look around, son. This is a nice little town. You got your mom here, everyone's pleasant, and it's peaceful. Man, look at those stars. Rare I ever get to see 'em this bright. Beautiful, isn't it? What I'm saying is we've got all this to lose and more. It's just us. Our little rag-tag bunch of fools taking on a vampire army. And if we fail, all of this disappears. Can you imagine a world dominated by suckers? It'd be hell. It's all resting on our shoulders. If we fuck it up, we're fucked. Everyone and everything is fucked." He paused and took a long draw on his smoke. "So yeah, I could do with a hit of the ol' giggle bush right now. Wanna puff?" he said, holding out the doobie.

I took it and said, "Fuck it, why not," before taking a drag.

The smoke filled my lungs, stinging my throat. I almost coughed but held on and finally exhaled. Didn't really feel any different, but I figured it'd take a minute or two to kick in. And I was right. It was only then that I realised how tense I was. Muscles tight, jaw clenched, shoulders hunched up. For the first time in a long while, I took note and relaxed; let my shoulders drop, loosened my jaw and let out a long sigh while looking up at the stars.

"Hey," Tex said, nudging me, "if we save the world maybe they'll make a movie about us."

"Ha, yeah, maybe. You just know it'd be low budget as fuck though. Cheesy, trashy, straight-to-video B-movie shit."

"Nothing better," he said as he glanced at me with a half-smile before fixing his eyes on the sky.

"The stars really are beautiful, aren't they?" I said, as much to myself as to Tex.

"Sure are," he said.

A few peaceful moments went by. I turned my head to look down the street, through the bar's window, admiring my bunch of misfit friends: Rusty flailing his arms while Leon and Adrian laughed their asses off at whatever he was saying, Ali getting dolled up by Ginn...

"Ali and Ginn have really clicked, haven't they? Looks to me like someone's in love."

Tex's eyes searched my face for a moment. "Sure looks that way, but not with who you think."

"Wha'cha mean?"

He gave me a look that said, "Come on", before taking another puff on the doob.

"What, me? Naaah," I shook my head, then thought for a moment, "you think?"

Tex passed the smoke. "Son, he told me he brought you your favourite sandwich and sat by you every damn day you were in your coma, just in case you woke up. And when you didn't, he ate it himself. He sat by you and ate the same fuckin' sandwich almost three thousand times. If that's not an act of love, I don't know what is." He paused, added, "You better shape up, 'cos I need a man, and my heart is set on yooou," all out of tune.

I rolled my eyes so hard he could've heard it. I hadn't ever thought about it like that. Ali had told me this all himself soon after I came out of the coma, but I'd never really done the math to comprehend the commitment. A part of what Tex said made a lot of sense. But could it be true?

"Oh, and I've been meaning to ask, what's your plan for Rapey and Roids? You gonna put a bullet in their heads before we leave?"

I pondered for a moment. "Nah. The way I see it, killing them would be a mercy. They don't deserve it. If I die, they can stay right where they are and suffer 'till the end of time."

Tex gave a slow nod. We finished off the smoke in silence before returning to the bar.

Ali crossed our path as we entered. His makeover was complete, all crimson nails and plaited pigtails. It was a good look for him. For being a giant, muscled up murder machine, he suited a feminine touch. "Mi hermanos," he said, "I'm heading to the bar, what are you having?"

Both Tex and I gave him a look that said, "Do you really need to ask?"

Ali laughed and nodded. "Another whiskey it is."

# See You Soon

Morning came clear and crisp, sweetened by the rich scent of good coffee and some baked goods. I shuffled downstairs to the sight of Mom and Tex sitting at the dining table, sipping on cups of coffee and eating croissants.

"Morning sweetie, coffee's fresh in your mug," Mom said.

I thanked her, grabbed my mug and a croissant and joined them at the table.

"What's the plan for your last day at home then?" Mom asked.

"Last day?"

Tex answered, "Back on the road again tomorrow, remember?"

"Oh, yeah."

I had forgotten. Tex gave me a look that told me he knew.

"Reckon I'm gonna get dressed and go over to visit Suzie and Dad soon, might be a while 'till I get another chance."

Tex nodded. "I'll leave you to it if you don't mind? I have a little business of my own to take care of."

I took a long slurp of my coffee and then said, "I don't mind. Mom? Wha'cha up to?"

"I'm supposed to be meeting Joyce from work at the café. Want to get the bus into town together?"

"Sounds good."

"And how about a nice big dinner again tonight? Everyone's invited, of course."

Tex nodded. "I'd certainly not refuse, thank ya kindly. I can tell Ginn and Ali while you're visiting Suzie, Night."

"Sure thing, and thanks," I said to both Mom and Tex with a warm smile.

\* \* \*

The bus dropped Mom and me off on Barker Street. After a quick stop at the florists, we made our way down to the café. I figured I may as well walk her to it before heading to the cemetery. Spend as much time together as possible.

The windows had steamed up on the inside, and we couldn't see in, but Mom gave me a peck on the cheek at the door and said, "Meet you at Vidstar later? I fancy a look around."

"You've got a deal, see you later," I said, happy to have any excuse to visit what was essentially my church.

I was making my way down towards the cemetery, taking a slow stroll, when a familiar voice called out from behind me.

"Night!" the Scottish accent called.

I turned to see Rusty wheeling his way towards me. "Hey, Rusty."

"Where ya off to, laddie?" he asked.

I jiggled the flowers. "Just off to the cemetery to visit Suzie and my old man."

"Ah, I see. Prefer I leave you to it, or would ya like some company?"

"I wouldn't mind the company actually."

"Grand," Rusty said as he pushed himself forward.

I turned and walked alongside him. "What'cha up to anyway?" I asked. It was odd to see him alone. I couldn't recall a time I'd ever seen him without another one of the squad with him.

"I figured I'd take a roll, clear my head a little, you know?"

"I get'cha," I said, nodding as we made our way through the cemetery gates.

The wind blew through the trees as Rusty grew silent and let out a thoughtful sigh. I walked slightly ahead, guiding him through the headstones until I came to a stop by Dad's grave. I stood in silence for a while with Rusty sitting beside me.

"He never was much of a talker," I said after a few minutes.

Rusty chuckled. "Aye he's a quiet fella, isn't he?"

"I never got to say goodbye to him, never got to see him one last time. He died when I was in the coma. It's a different kind of pain, but it hurts just as much. What I wouldn't give for him to have been here just a little longer. He would have loved Vidstar. I've got him to thank for my movie obsession."

Rusty slapped me on the back. "Well he raised a good lad in the time he had, and I'm sure he knows it."

I smiled and said, "I'd leave him a flower, but he never cared for them."

Rusty looked thoughtful for a moment. "Did he enjoy a wee dram?" he asked while rustling about in his jacket pockets.

"He did. Like father like son, eh?"

"Here, leave him this instead," Rusty said, handing me a miniature bottle of whiskey.

I couldn't help but laugh. Of course he had miniature whiskeys in his pockets. "Thanks, don't know why I didn't think of this before. He'd love it," I said, placing it at the base of his headstone. "Let's go see Suzie."

"Aye," Rusty nodded, following as I stood and made my way through the graves over to the old willow tree that shaded Suzie's headstone.

About halfway there, another headstone caught my eye, and I did a double-take before coming to a stop to read the inscription.

David Flowers
1944 - 1973
A beloved son.
A wonderful brother.
A loyal friend.
A good man.

My breath caught in my chest. I didn't know David was buried here too and the surprise was a total sucker punch. His grave was well tended, though simple. A black headstone with a gold inscription and nothing more.

Rusty wheeled himself parallel to me. "Somebody else you know?"

I nodded, my eyes still on the stone. "He was my cellmate in prison and a goddamn good guy. He didn't deserve what happened to him. He didn't deserve any of it. Shouldn't have even been in prison. All he ever wanted to do was help the people he cared about," I ran my eyes over the last words, "he really was a good man."

Rusty nudged my arm, holding out another miniature whiskey. "I'd say he deserves one too then, eh?"

I smiled and took the bottle before splitting some flowers from the bouquet and placing them at the base of his headstone. I placed my hand on the grass and mumbled, "I miss you, buddy." I'd never known exactly when he died. Seeing that he had been gone almost the entire time I was in a coma was another kick to the gut.

## [Track 39]

A breeze caught the flowers and pulled a loose petal off into the sky, and I took that as David's response as I knelt for a few more moments before bidding him goodbye and heading off to see Suzie.

Her grave was as neat and tidy as it had been on my last visit. I assumed Mom had been looking after it like she did with Dad's. But as nice as it looked, it didn't help numb the pain. The old familiar ache bloomed through my chest, carving through my heart and leaving me feeling hollow as I read the words 'Dearly beloved, deeply missed' for what felt like the millionth time.

After a few minutes of silence, I crouched to place the flowers down but ended up falling down on my ass instead. I needed to stay a little longer.

Rusty placed a hand on my shoulder and gently squeezed. "I know how ya feel, lad. I lost my lass when we were young too. It's a hurt that never leaves, eh?"

"I didn't know," I said, fiddling with the bouquet, looking for the nicest way to leave them. "Mind if I ask what happened?"

Rusty heaved a big sigh and leaned back in his chair. "Well, it was a long time ago. Get comfy down there, yer in for a yarn now. Catriona was her name. Funny, that, isn't it? We used to call each other Cat and Dog. On account of me, ya'know, being a dog-man. We fell in love young, just like you and Suzie. Now, given the name Shacklejacker, you can assume I was a bit of a rascal back in the day. But I was a rascal for a good cause. See, me and my kin made it our goal to free any and every prisoner the English took. We'd break them free of their shackles, hence, the Shacklejackers."

I gave Rusty a suspicious look. "Just how old are you, exactly?"

"Well, I was born in twelve-seventy, so that'd make me... seven hundred and ten years old. Seven hundred and eleven when March comes around."

"Fuck me."

"Maybe later," Rusty said with a grin. "Anyway, aye, we'd free fellow Scots from the English. Cat lived in the next village over from mine; both of us were only a couple hours ride to Falkirk. Me da would take me over there when I was a wee bairn, whenever he'd go over to market."

"Bairn?"

"A young'un. I was thirteen when I first laid eyes on Cat, and I couldn't take them off her. We turned into fast friends, but we both fancied each other something fierce, and we both knew it. I courted her for years. We were finally wed in twelve-ninety, in a glen, by a waterfall. All in the proper old ways, of course; a true handfasting. None of this churchy shite you see nowadays. You've never seen romance like it, laddie. We led a good life, but there was always a need for the Shacklejackers. And when battle called, we answered. I fought alongside William Wallace, you know. Ya heard of him?"

I shook my head. "Can't say I have, sorry."

"Fierce warrior, he was. Aye, so in hopes of Scotland one day having her independence, and laying the Shacklejacker name to rest, I went off to fight. I first fought with Wallace at the Battle of Dunbar, where we got our arses kicked, then again at the Battle of Stirling Bridge, where we did all the arse kickin'. The last time we fought together was the Battle of Falkirk in twelve-ninety-eight. That one was bad, and a little too close to home. The English massacred us. Wallace and a few others, me included, managed to escape. So, I sculked off home with my tail between my legs, only to find my village, my home, burned to the ground by the English."

"Oh, shit."

"Aye, oh shit indeed. I found Cat's body among the ashes of my home, burnt to a crisp. She was with child at the time."

"Fuck, man, I'm so sorry," I said as I hauled myself up from the ground.

Rusty wiped the corner of his eye with his sleeve. "Dinnae have to be, lad. Wasn't you that did it. Besides, I found those that did, and I tore them into so many ribbons their own ma's couldnae recognised them. So when I say I know how it feels, I truly mean it."

"Thanks for telling me."

"It's a curse, this whole being a monster business. Over six hundred years, and I've never loved another like I loved Cat. 'Cos no matter how much good ya try to do, it's always the ones you love who get hurt in the end."

I pondered that statement for a moment, looking down at Suzie's grave. "You're not wrong. I lost Suzie, Tex lost his family, Ali lost his brother, you lost Cat. I can only assume something similar has happened to the others."

Rusty nodded. "Oh aye. That it has."

"I guess if our plan all goes to shit, one positive thing is that we might get to see them soon."

Rusty snorted and let out a chuckle. "Aye, I guess that's true. All this sadness has made me mighty hungry, care to grab a burger?"

I shrugged. "Yeah, sure, I can always eat. Speaking of, my mom's making a big dinner tonight. I'm sure she'd be happy to meet the squad if you guys wanna join."

Rusty set his wheels in motion, towards the cemetery gates. "Thanks for the offer, but I'll pass on behalf of all of us. I wouldn't want ya ma figuring out what we are and what you really do with ya time. We're not exactly inconspicuous. Besides, Jackie's joint suits us just fine for the evening. Feels like a home away from home."

"Suit yourself," I said, walking by his side, "you could be missing out on your last meal, though."

That earned me a punch on the leg. "Quit being such a fuckin' pessimist. We're gonna kick Atrocitas's ass."

I laughed. "Well, the rest of us are. I'm not so sure you'll be kicking anything."

Rusty looked down at his legs and gave me another punch. "You're a cheeky wee cunt, Isaac Nightingale."

I smiled at his remark while taking one last look back at Suzie's grave, resting peacefully beneath the willow. I couldn't help but think, "I'll see you soon".

# Throw the Dice

Forks clattered. Laughter and the smell of roast chicken filled the house. Mom had made a fantastic dinner, and everyone looked stuffed. But Mom took no prisoners, 'cos she was serving dessert. Fresh, warm chocolate cake appeared where our empty plates had been. Mom finished her assault by placing a jug of hot custard in the middle of the table before sitting back down between Tex and Ali.

The smell was intoxicating. The rich chocolate aroma, the warm vanilla scent of the custard. I was fit to burst, but I couldn't resist the temptation.

"Clean plates from everyone, or you'll get la chancla," Mom said with a smile.

Ali clapped a hand over his heart and laughed. "Yes. There's no escaping it."

He had taught her the ancient mystical art of 'La Chancla' over dinner and she loved every second of it. Shame she hadn't known about it when I was a child, or she could have been a master at throwing la chancla. Could have helped us fight Atrocitas, wielding her slipper like the hammer of Thor, striking fear into the hearts of our enemies.

"So, who's coming dancing with me after this?" Mom asked.

Ali nodded and gave the thumbs up, his mouth full of cake.

"I'd love to learn some new moves, I'm in," said Ginn.

Mom looked to Tex, then to me, but Tex shook his head. "Got a bit of urgent business I need to take care of. I'll need Night's assistance with it. I hope that's okay?"

"I suppose I'll allow it."

I looked to Tex for any indication as to what the urgent business consisted of, but he just carried on eating his cake and custard, not explaining a damn thing. I just hoped whatever it was, it was damn important. This was my last night with my mom before potentially going off to die in a hopeless battle, but for the time being, I put it out of my mind. Enjoying the time I had was the most important thing.

It passed by far too fast.

Fed, fat and feeling fine, I waddled to the door to see Mom, Ali and Ginn off for the evening. I could feel the excitement radiating from Mom. Ginn had offered her a ride on the back of her motorcycle and Mom had jumped on the offer like a rebellious teenager. She also offered Mom her helmet, so I wasn't too worried. I knew she was in good hands. She was safer on a motorcycle with Ginn than on the bus with Gordon the driver and his tendency to swerve and run red lights.

Tex and I waved them off until they disappeared around the corner. I closed the door and made my way over to the sofa. I sat down in it and slouched with a sigh as I undid the top button of my jeans.

Tex sat down next to me and took a moment to gather his thoughts.

"I'm sorry I've kept you from dancing, kid, but it's time."

"Time for what?"

"Lucifer," Tex said.

A loud crack and a blinding flash of light filled the room, like a bolt of lightning, leaving Lucifer standing by the fireplace, admiring the family photos.

"Oh for fuck's sake," I muttered.

"Good to see you too, Night," Lucifer said with a smirk.

I had been hoping to avoid seeing Lucifer again, but I knew it was coming, and I guess it was now or never. We were setting off on the warpath in the morning. What better time to take a deal for immortality?

"I've brought the contract for you to read through," Lucifer said, pulling a scroll from inside his suit jacket.

I took it and unfurled it, a huge thing written on parchment in an elegant script with red ink. Probably blood, but I didn't ask, didn't really want to know. I took my time reading it, making sure it all looked clear and straightforward. And it did. Pretty much everything Lucifer had already told me, but in fancy handwriting.

Whomsoever accepts the agreement gains immortality... twenty-five years minimum term... yearly basis after the initial term... immediate access to Heaven upon eventual death... agree to actively seek out and destroy evil... if the work isn't carried out by choice you lose all benefits after the initial term... agree to try my best to keep myself whole and intact... Lucifer is not liable for any disfigurement sustained... keep ya mouth shut... blah blah blah.

I finished reading and lay it down on the coffee table, still considering it all.

Lucifer snapped his fingers and produced a quill from nowhere. He held it out to me, and said, "Will you, Isaac Nightingale, bind your immortal soul to mine under oath? Will you, Isaac Nightingale, become my right hand? Do you, Isaac Nightingale, swear to rid this world of evil?"

I looked from the contract to the quill, to Lucifer, and finally, to Tex. If we were in a movie the music would have been swelling into a suspenseful crescendo. This was it: this was the moment to step up and become the hero of the story. To fulfil my destiny and become the ultimate monster hunter. The time had come. This was it. My moment.

And I said...

"No."

"No?" Lucifer and Tex said in unison.

I doubled down, "No."

"What the fuck, bro?" Lucifer said, losing his cool composure.

"Never thought I'd hear the original Devil call anyone 'bro'."

Tex sat in silence, looking baffled.

"Why the fuck not? This is the best thing anyone will ever offer you. You get to do what you're already doing. Something I know you enjoy. You get immortality. Eternal life if you want it. And a ticket to paradise on top, and you're telling me fucking no?"

"I guess that's not something you're used to hearing?"

The room grew visibly darker, and I felt the hairs on the back of my neck stand up.

Tex held up a hand to head off the incoming argument, and simply asked, "Why?"

I looked him in the eyes and said, "You, Tex. If it wasn't for you, I wouldn't have been given this choice. And as much as I appreciate it, as much as I would love it, I can't accept it. Not yet."

Tex sighed. "Night, we go to war tomorrow. This time tomorrow we'll be balls deep in vampires and fuck knows what else."

"That's exactly why I can't take the deal yet. If I take it now, you're vulnerable. Sure, you have years of experience, but I have the Hot Sauce. I'm not far off superhuman as it is. And as selfish as it is, I still need you around after this. There's still a lot I don't know. Who the fuck's gonna show me the best way to kill a ventripede if I take the deal and you die?"

There was a sadness in Tex's eyes, but he eventually nodded and stood. "I understand. Be back in a minute, I'm gonna go call the Neon Nightmares, make sure they're ready, see if they can get the message to the naga," he said as he turned and walked into the hallway.

"And what about you?" Lucifer said. "I should mention, if you're not under contract and get bitten by a vampire, you risk going to Hell. Anyone tainted by vampirism gets a one-way ticket."

I felt the Hot Sauce spike, burning through my veins and heightening my senses.

"You fucking what?"

Lucifer looked sheepish, like he'd said too much.

"There's a chance. Because of the origins of vampirism, all vampires go to Hell. You know all it takes is a bite for someone to turn."

"And if someone dies soon after a bite? What happens to them?"

"It's a coin toss. It depends on the person, everyone reacts differently. Vampirism takes hold of some quicker than others."

"Motherfucker!" I yelled.

"You seem pissed."

"I am pissed, get the fuck outta here, damn it."

Lucifer said no more. He bowed his head and disappeared with a crack and a flash.

The revelation brought fresh hatred, fresh fury and bloodlust. For all I knew, Suzie could have been in

Hell this entire fucking time all because of one filthy sucker. I didn't want to believe it, but Lucifer said it himself, there was a chance. The Hot Sauce raged through my body. I was ready to fight.

I needed to kill Atrocitas.

I needed to kill them all.

# End of the Road

We left early and we drove hard. It was about a nine-hour drive into Nebraska. No stops on this one. I was fuelled by a belly full of fire and had an appetite for nothing but murder.

I sat behind the wheel of my Firebird with the gas pedal pinned to the floor, Tex in the passenger seat and Rusty in the back. Ali and Ginn rode their motorcycles, and Harriot drove her Dodge Challenger with Mickey, Khearo and Morgan hitching a ride in it. We tore down the highway, all armed to the teeth and ready to kill every last sucker or die trying.

I took the lead up front, with Ginn and Ali riding side-by-side behind, and Harriot holding the back. Tex had the bright idea of picking up some walkie-talkies during one of his wanders around town, so we could communicate during the drive.

"We're coming up to Chadron Creek in a few minutes," Tex said into his walkie-talkie, looking down at the map, "strap on your biggest dicks, ladies and gentlemen, it's almost time."

I had my biggest dick fully loaded and ready to blow: good ol' Betsy the Gatling gun lay waiting, ready to unleash Hell.

Tex's walkie-talkie crackled to life and Ali's voice floated through, "Let's give these motherfuckers la chancla."

I let out a chuckle, thinking of Ali wielding nothing but a flip-flop and causing insane amounts of devastation. The thought led to the memory of the Power Gloves, once owned by Murder Nerd, now in the possession of the Neon Nightmares. "Hey," I said, side-eyeing Tex, "where are the Nightmares? You called them last night, right?"

Tex nodded. "They're gonna meet us there."

"Cool, cool, cool. For a moment I was worried they didn't know we're on the way."

"Oh, they know. Doncha worry. They know."

I nodded, pleased with the knowledge that with the Nightmares and their Power Gloves, we might not have been entirely fucked. Just a little fucked.

Tex pointed to a turning up ahead and fired up his walkie-talkie. "Next left, on to Buttermilk Road and drive 'till we can't no more."

"Roger that," a mix of voices responded.

I swung the wheel and flew around the corner, kicking up grit and dust before straightening up, stomping the pedal and taking off down the road. Next stop: copious bloodshed. And it was coming sooner than I expected. We were about two minutes down the road when I saw a line of vehicles way up ahead. Four cars drove side-by-side barricading the road, with a lot more behind the barricade.

"Shit," I muttered, "flick that walkie-talkie on for me, eh?"

Tex pushed the button and held it up to my face.

"Alright guys, looks like they've rolled out a welcome party up ahead. There's a barricade coming towards us and a whole convoy of assholes behind it. Harriot, in a sec, I'll put on the brakes. If you pass me and we keep Ali and Ginn in the middle, I'll cover the back. You plough through these motherfuckers, and I'll set Betsy on them. We clear?"

"Crystal," Harriot said.

"Alright then, on three," I said, nodding to Tex.

He took over. "One."

I pulled the Firebird to the left to give Harriot plenty of space to get by.

"Two."

Ginn and Ali revved their engines.

"Three," Tex yelled.

The sound of engines roaring filled my ears as I slammed the brakes. Harriot's Challenger flew past. I had enough time to see something I didn't think I'd ever see: two huge werewolves crammed into a muscle car, tearing down the asphalt. Both Harriot and Khearo had transformed into their werewolf suits. They shot past with the windows down and Khearo leaning out, gripping a sawn-off shotgun with his jowls flapping in the wind.

I stomped the gas as Ginn and Ali followed and closed the gap, keeping them in the middle. Ginn had had her blades strapped to her arms the entire ride. She took her hands off the handlebars for a moment and sent the swords shooting out in front of her. Ali pulled one of his Reaper revolvers from its holster and cocked the hammer.

Rusty threw a duffle bag full of guns over the seats for Tex to rummage through. He dropped it down between his feet and set a sawn-off shotgun and a bunch of grenades on his lap then pulled out an M16 assault rifle.

"You loaded?" he asked.

I nodded. I had the Sisters strapped on under my big coat, the one with an insane number of weapon-filled pockets. I was fuckin' packing.

"You ready, Rusty?" I asked, eyeing him in the rearview mirror.

"Aye," Rusty said as he pulled down the middle section of the back seat, "let's get tae fuckin' these cunts."

## [Track 41]

I smiled as I watched him throw himself into the hole and crawl through into the trunk.

The convoy drew closer. Tex turned up the radio, blasting the music. I pulled one of the Sisters out and cocked the hammer. The convoy was closing in. In a matter of seconds, we'd be balls-deep in carnage. A bullet pinged off Harriot's car, sending sparks flying. My eyes followed the sparks into the air, up, up, up until I saw a disembodied fist flying above the car with purple smoke billowing behind it. Tex nudged me and pointed to another one on the other side, trailing green smoke. The fists were gloved. Power Gloved.

"FUCK YES!" I yelled, rolling my window down to wave my gun in the air.

The fists flew ahead, over Ginn and Ali to the sides of Harriot's car. They held their position as the convoy closed in, then spun upside down and flipped the bird at the hoard before glowing blue. Khearo caught sight of them and swung his shotgun around his head. Lasers shot from either side of Harriot's car, right into the barricade they were seconds from smashing into.

All four cars exploded as the lasers cut through them like butter, the force wiped them clean off the road. The cars behind shot through the flames, past the wreckage and swerved to avoid a head-on collision with the Challenger.

With the barricade out of the way, I could see about twenty other vehicles shooting towards us, two by two. They split down the middle and flanked us. They were organised. But we were ready.

Khearo squeezed out a round as the first car passed him. The windscreen shattered and the head of the sucker driving painted the interior. The car swerved off the road and rolled into the field, flinging scraps of debris everywhere.

As Khearo lined up that first shot, Harriot focussed on her driving. Morgan crawled out of the window and onto the roof. He flung himself onto the car on the other side, landing on the roof. It sped past. Ali popped off a bullet and blew half the head off of the sucker shooting out of the passenger window. Morgan lay down, put a fist through the window and grabbed the driver's face, digging his claws in. He yanked and tore a hole out of the sucker's head. Morgan threw the handful of nose, teeth and an eyeball into the road and leapt as the car passed us, fishtailing out of control. He landed on my roof with a thud.

Ginn swerved and stuck her arm out as the second car on our side passed Harriot. She flew past the car, her motorcycle missing it by a hair's width. The blade sliced through the windscreen, the driver, the seat, the passenger in the back, and out the back window. Blood flecks splattered my windscreen as I watched the top half of the driver fold over, his face swinging down into his own crotch. I checked my rearview and saw the car slowing to a roll, veering into the middle of the road.

As Ginn was slicing up an entire car, Khearo was popping off another shell into the wheel of the second car on his side. The tire exploded and the car swerved. Ali lined up his gun and took two shots. One blew through the driver's eye, and the other pinged off his hand on the steering wheel. The combo of a bullet in the hand and face made him tug the steering wheel hard. The car swung around and sped off into the field, bouncing over the grass, and it just kept on going.

Tex leaned out the window and got a head start on shooting the third car approaching his side. A couple of bullets whizzed by his head as he pulled the trigger and volleyed a storm of bullets right back.

The third on my side whizzed past Harriot's car and escaped Ali's wrath with a few bullet holes. I let it pass, watching to see what it'd do. As I thought, it put on the brakes and swung around us to take us from behind. But fuck no, I wasn't gonna let any backwoods sucker take me from behind. And neither was Morgan.

379

The passenger of the car behind pinged off a few bullets, shattering my back window. Morgan leaped from the roof and through the windscreen of the car, landing right in the passenger's lap. I watched for long enough to see him tunnel a gaping hole right through the guy's chest before turning to the driver. The sound of an explosion up ahead tore my eyes from the mirror. I clapped eyes on the sight of the Neon Nightmares, now fully materialised, blowing the four cars at the rear end of the convoy off the road with their lasers.

Adrian held up his hands to signify there were ten cars left.

I picked the walkie-talkie up from the dash and said, "Just let them pass, guys, Betsy's thirsty, let's have some fun."

The message must have been heard loud and clear. The rest of the cars thundered past, bullets pinging and gunshots ringing heavy. A thud on the roof told me Morgan was Firebird surfing again. They all spun in an organised formation, two cars turning to tail me, the next to tail them and so on until they were all behind us.

Tex held his assault rifle in the air as he grabbed a grenade. I saw Morgan's hand reach down and grab the gun. Ginn and Ali pulled back to ride on either side of the car. Tex took the walkie-talkie, and I gave him the signal.

"Let's dance," he said.

The sound of gunfire erupted from above and either side of the car, mixed with a guttural roar, somehow still sounding Scottish.

380

The trunk flew open, and Rusty burst out in the form of a huge, dark orange werewolf. And he hauled Betsy up with him. He snarled, fixing his eyes on the two closest cars and cranked the handle with unrelenting fury. Bullets sprayed from Betsy's barrel, tearing the occupants of the cars to bloody shreds. The cars swerved inwards, hit each other, then fishtailed off the side of the road trailing steam, flames and red mist.

The Nightmares wiped out two more cars from the back, vaporising the occupants.

Rusty focused on one of the two cars closest and hammered fist-sized holes through the driver's chest. He dropped the gun he had been shooting out the window. It fired out another shot as it hit the ground and burst the front tire of the car next to it. The car swerved. The driver wrestled with the wheel, but Ginn pulled to the side and pulled her brakes. The car shot passed her and her blade raked right on through the side of it, sending it spinning off into the dirt.

One of the suckers from the car in the middle of what was left of the convoy popped out of the sunroof with a rifle and took aim at Rusty while he was turning his focus on the closest car. I was about to yell to warn him, but then Leon swept down towards the sunroof and turned to smoke. The entire cloud flew up the sucker's nostrils. He dropped the rifle onto the roof and flailed about, scratching at his face. He exploded, disappearing in a shower of vaporised flesh, and left Leon standing where he had been. He picked up the rifle, aimed down through the roof and blew the driver's face all over the windscreen.

"We're running low on road, let's finish this," Tex said into the walkie-talkie.

Rusty nodded, keeping his eyes fixed on the cars in front of him.

Another blast of blue tore through the roof of one of the remaining cars.

Three to go.

Rusty cranked Betsy's handle harder. Ali burst off rounds from his revolver. Morgan surfed the car and sprayed bullets everywhere, and Tex dropped a couple of grenades out of the window.

Bullets rained down on the remaining cars, punching holes in everyone inside. The grenades bounced right under one car and exploded, sending it flipping into the air and crashing into the side of the car next to it. They both slid off the road and into the dirt, upside down and trailing sparks from the roof.

One car left, and the driver had survived with nothing more than a bullet to the shoulder. All gunfire stopped as he put on the brakes and backed off, hoping to be left alive. A look of relief flashed across his face before his flesh disintegrated in a flash of blue.

The car slowed to a roll and stopped as we left it in our mirrors and put on our brakes. We were out of road. It was time to take the shoelace express and stamp those one-way tickets to Hell.

# Backwoods Rumble

Up ahead was nothing but land and trees as far as the eye could see. We knew Atrocitas's bunker was somewhere amongst the trees, and we wouldn't have to wait long to find it. We pulled up as the road turned into a dirt trail and stepped out of our cars. Everyone strapped themselves up, gathering as much firepower as we could carry. I reloaded the Sisters and tucked them away nice and snug as Ginn helped Ali get into the Plot Armour, with the longsword resting on the ground in front of him.

"Shoulda put that on before now," I said, noticing a blood stain on his side.

"Just a scratch," he said with a wave of his hand.

I took a glance at everyone else. Morgan was bleeding from the shoulder, Ginn was covered in scratches from flying shrapnel and Rusty had a chunk of his left ear missing, with blood dribbling down his neck. We were already taking damage, but there was no turning back.

And so, armed to the nuts, we left our vehicles behind and set ourselves to stepping towards the treeline. I took the lead, with Tex, Ali and Ginn behind me to the right and the Monster Squad to the left. Rusty wheeled himself over dirt and rocks with ease in wolf form. He had Betsy resting in his lap and belts of her bullets wrapped around his body. Harriot and Khearo walked either side of him. We walked for a total of five minutes before the floodgates opened and the suckers started pouring from between the trees.

Leon appeared beside me. "Looks like it's time to flex some muscle, brochacho."

Adrian materialised at my other side. "Let's fuck some more Draculas."

## [Track 42]

I held two gun-filled fists out to either side of me. The Neon Nightmares fist-bumped me with their Power Gloves before turning to smoke. I cocked the Sisters and took a look over my shoulder to see Tex and Ali prepping their guns. Ginn had her swords ready, still bloodstained from the car chase. To the left, behind the werewolves, Morgan and Mickey readied their weapons.

And the vampires came. Hundreds upon hundreds of them.

"Get in line for your ass kicking," Tex yelled.

I set out running to meet them, to send them to Hell or be sent there myself. I raised the Sisters to say hello, squeezed the triggers and shot out chaos. The sucker closest to me fell to the dirt, missing the majority of his head. I swung my guns side to side, up and down, aiming this way and that, conducting a symphony of slaughter as we tore through the wave of vampires in bloody glory. Harriot charged past me on the left, pushing Rusty's wheelchair as he roared and cranked Betsy's handle. Her bullets tore through scores of vampires, spilling guts, splitting skulls and staining the ground red.

Tex and Ali appeared to my right. Tex held up a combat shotgun, blasting holes through the chests of any unfortunate sucker he laid eyes on. Ali had his Reapers, as powerful as the Sisters, if not more so. He took aim and blew the head clean from a sucker's shoulders, leaving nothing but pink mist above a neck stump as bits of skull filled the air.

Suckers fell in droves. Some of them decomposed instantly, some stayed as trip hazards. The land between us and the treeline filled with corpses in all stages of decomposition, and the air grew thick with blood and the stench of death. Up ahead, the Neon Nightmares stood back-to-back, sweeping blue lasers through the crowd of the undead. We raced through the carnage to meet them, murdering as we approached. Harriot and Rusty got there first, followed by Ginn, who was soaked in blood from head to toe. The rest of us gathered, and as one group we pushed our way into the tree line.

Khearo, being the tallest, spotted the entrance to the bunker and pointed it out with a howl. More vampires flooded towards us from all angles, even from above as some dropped down from the trees.

I emptied the Sisters as I blew the jaw from one sucker in front of me, and relieved another of the top half of her head as she jumped from a tree. I pointed the barrel of Maria at an asshole running at me, and pulled the trigger, hoping I had one last bullet left. Nothing.

"Shit," I said, as I crammed the Sisters back into their holsters and plunged my hand into a hidden pocket.

A spray of blood shot out of the side of the head of the vampire running at me, and his legs crumpled under him, sending him rolling through the dirt. I looked to my left and caught Tex giving me a wink and holstering his pistol before focusing his attention on a set of vampires approaching him, and raising his shotgun to meet them.

In that moment of distraction, I found myself surrounded. Suckers had dropped down from the trees and circled me. I was caught short, and they all pounced at once.

A barrage of flesh and claws slammed me from all angles. Bodies piled on top of me, slashing at any bit they could. I went down under the weight of the dogpile. Claws raked my flesh, and a storm of fists battered me into the dirt; thankfully, it was too many fists for a sucker to stick their face in and bite me. They were gonna pummel me to death, but at least I wouldn't be their dinner. I struggled and writhed as punch after punch rained down on my body. My hand wrapped around the handle of a gun, and I tugged, pulling my sawn-off out of its hiding place. I pulled it upwards. I couldn't see where I was pointing it, but I pulled the trigger anyway.

Buckshot ripped through flesh, blowing bits of multiple vampires into the sky, giving me a glimpse of the treetops. The fists stopped as the suckers stumbled backwards a little, stunned by the blast. Blood splattered down on my face. I stayed on my back and pumped off another shot. A couple of vamps hit the dirt. The others regained their senses and were about to pile back on top of me when a wall of fur flew over me with a roar and sent them scattering in every direction.

I stood and nodded my thanks to Harriot before she bounded off back to Rusty. A vampire flew over my head, to end up skewered on Ginn's blades. I reloaded the shotgun and blew a hole through the back of a sucker that was trying to blindside Ali. Blood and chunks of the vamp's internal organs splattered all over his armour and face. He didn't so much as bat an eyelid, nor miss a beat as he swung his sword into the face of the closest vampire, hitting a homerun.

Rusty let out a roar as Betsy used up her last bullet. He stuffed the Gatling gun between his legs and gave Harriot a nod. She stopped pushing his chair and ran off with a vicious snarl on her face. She grabbed the nearest vampire, sunk her claws into his chest and ripped him in half, right down the middle. I made a mental note never to piss her off.

Mickey's gun lay on the floor a few feet behind him. For once, he'd removed his sunglasses as well as his eyes from their sockets. Two glowing orbs swayed on long stalks protruding from the eyeholes of his face, and a writhing mass of tentacles spilled from his mouth. They whipped and snapped through the air, sending yellow arcs of electricity between them as they searched for a soul to feast on.

Electrified screams ran out behind me as I turned to see Khearo and Morgan double-team a big vampire. Morgan thrust a fist into the vampire's mouth as Khearo palmed the top half of his head like a basketball. Morgan pulled down, Khearo pulled up. The vampire's jaw, throat and rib cage hit the floor as his skull ripped from the rest of him, bringing half of his spine with it.

Closer to the bunker entrance, Leon and Adrian had decided on a bit of deforestation. Beams of blue light blasted through vampires and trees, cutting down multiples of both. Trees fell with deafening crashes, crushing any vampire in their way. As much as the Nightmares made a mess, they sure were good for crowd control.

But it wasn't enough.

Betsy was dry, and the hail of gunshots was growing less frequent by the second.

I blew the tits off a sucker running at me and searched my pocket for more shells as I saw five of them jump on top of Ginn, dragging her to the ground with claws sinking into her flesh. They didn't last long. Within seconds, Ginn had carved them up, spilling blood and guts all over herself.

The Nightmares appeared by my side. "Shit's fucked, bro," Leon said, holding up his power-gloved fist. Trails of smoke rose from the glove, peppered with the occasional spark.

"Outta juice, huh? Yours too, Adrian?"

Adrian held up his glove and nodded.

Tex eyed us from a few feet away. "Form up on me!" he yelled as he ran over to us.

"Wha'cha thinking boss, time for operation Deus Ex Machina?" Leon asked Tex.

Tex nodded. "Do it."

388

The Nightmares disappeared in a puff of smoke as the others gathered around us, bursting off shots at any straggling suckers we hadn't already put the boot to. The few that were left retreated into the distance, disappearing into the entrance of the bunker. I had no doubt in my mind that what we'd killed was nothing but the vanguard. They may as well have been the doormen sent out to take our hats and coats, and we were all already beaten and bloody.

Tex hustled everyone around him. "Reload what you can and do it sharp. We've got maybe a minute before the real fight starts."

I thumbed some bullets into the Sisters' chambers for a moment then stopped to see if anyone else could feel what I was feeling. Everyone looked around with looks that said "what the fuck" louder than any words ever could.

"You all feel the ground shaking, right?"

Ginn nodded, wiping blood from her face. "Feels like time's up."

# Hail to the King

The earth trembled below us, and the vampire hoard spilled from the bunker. I ran the numbers in my head. We were down to nine since the Neon Nightmares had disappeared. The vampires were in the high hundreds, way more than the welcome party. And they'd be on top of us in seconds. Looked to me like this was it. Nine of us against a tsunami of vampires? We were fucked, no other way of looking at it. We were lucky to fend off the first wave, mainly thanks to the Power Gloves. And now they were gone. This was suicide.

We faced the oncoming wave, readying our weapons and ourselves. This was it. War cries filled the air as the vampires charged towards us, and somewhere within the cries, I heard the words: "Deus Ex Machina, motherfuckers!" And in that moment, I realised the war cries were coming from behind us as Leon rode past on a gigantic snake, swinging a sword through the air.

I didn't have time to wonder how he'd found a snake the size of a bus. I turned to see a huge army of reptilian faces hurtling towards us, with a familiar face leading the charge: Seraphina. She wore a warrior's headdress, chest armour, and a face full of war paint.

I had time for neither thought nor greeting as she thundered forwards and grabbed me by the arm and threw me onto her back. The rest of the naga followed suit, grabbing whoever they could offer a ride to. Only

Khearo and Harriot were left to run alongside, as one of the naga grabbed the handles of Rusty's wheelchair and thrust him forward at high speed.

Arrows whizzed past our heads and found their homes in the hearts and heads of suckers. I held on to the back of Seraphina's armour with one hand and levelled one of the Sisters with the other, putting bullets through skulls.

Seraphina pulled a sword from a scabbard at her hip and raised it high. Two giant snakes thrashed past us, sending dirt flying as they lunged into the crowd of suckers. Vampires fell and burst open under the crushing weight of the snake's bodies, spilling mushed gore. Those who avoided being flattened flew through the air, whipped up by the snakes' writhing tails.

Blood soaked the dirt as the naga flew through the suckers, cutting them down like blades of grass. It was a massacre, and I was glad to be a part of it. With the Naga on our side, we closed the distance to the entrance of the bunker in a matter of minutes. And yet, the vampires kept on comin'.

Seraphina charged through the large entrance, slicing vampires in half and severing heads with nothing but a flick of her wrist. The inside of the bunker had one huge entrance room branching off into smaller corridors, leading deeper into the facility. I hopped off her back as we came to a stop in the large room and got to shootin'. Shrill screams rang out and bounced off the walls as a group of suckers took down one of the naga, ripping through his scales and into the flesh underneath. I aimed the Sisters and shattered some heads, but the naga warrior was already dead.

The giant snakes pushed down the corridors, smearing members of Atrocitas's hoard across the walls and floors. Everyone gathered in the room and hopped off their rides before huddling up as some of the naga formed a barrier around us, butchering any vamp that tried to get through while others shot down corridors with their swords raised high.

"What do we do?"

"I say we split up," Morgan said.

Ginn gave him a 'pfft'. "Have you not seen any horror movies? If you split up, you die."

Mickey cut in, "Rusty says if we all cram down one corridor, we're sitting ducks. It's best to split into groups to take the corridors."

Rusty growled and nodded to show Mickey's translation was right.

Blood rained over us and a severed arm sailed down over Ali's shoulder. It landed on the floor between everyone.

Tex sighed, looking at the arm. "Afraid to say he's right. We take a corridor in threes and leave the Nightmares to do their own thing. The naga should thin out the numbers for us. Sound good?"

Leon and Adrian nodded then exploded into clouds of smoke and disappeared.

Tex continued, "Ginn and Harriot, you're with me."

"Knew you were a ladies' man," Ginn said.

"Rusty says: me and Morgan with him," Mickey said.

"And that leaves us, my brothers," Ali said, looking from me to Khearo.

Seraphina squeezed through her troops. "I've already sssent people down the corridorsss after the Titanboasss, they ssshould clear out the majority of the vampiresss for you."

"Thank you, Sera, you've saved all of our asses today."

"Then my debt to you isss paid, my friend," Sera said, offering her hand.

I shook it. "Tenfold."

She gave me one last smile before thrusting her sword into the air screaming a shrill war cry.

Our barricade of half-snake, half-human warriors dispersed and scattered, forcing the majority of vampires back down the corridors.

"This is it, ladies and gents," Tex said, "make sure to keep your ears open and on the walkie-talkies. First one to find Atrocitas, scream like the goddamn Devil."

"See you on the other side," Morgan said as he took the handles of Rusty's chair and ran down a corridor on the left. Mickey followed, his tentacles flailing.

"Chainsaws for arms, kid," Tex said to me, "stay sharp."

Harriot lunged off down a corridor at the back of the room. Ginn skipped behind her, swinging her blades all carefree-like.

"Chainsaws for arms," I muttered to myself as I turned to face one of the corridors to the right. I took a look over my shoulders to see Khearo at my left and Ali at my right. With the Hot Sauce raging through my veins, I took the first step into the tunnel with my buddies close behind. The scent of blood mingled with the cold damp smell of the neglected building.

Even with the naga helping, I couldn't get rid of the twisting in my stomach. The others were putting on their brave faces, but I could tell everyone was scared. Everyone was hurt, and we had walked right into the biggest of all traps. We were at a huge disadvantage, and as much as the Hot Sauce and the rage kept me going, I wasn't sure I could make it out of this.

The tube lights overhead flickered, weak and ready to blow out, but they gave off enough light to see where we were going, and that every surface had been smeared with blood and gore. Bits of flesh hung from the exposed pipework running alongside the wall. Every now and then, the corridor produced another path to the left or right. The place was a fucking maze, so we stayed on the straight.

True to what Sera had said, the naga had wiped out a fucking shitload of suckers. We had walked for almost two minutes before the first sucker jumped out at us like a scare actor in a haunted house. Ali wasted no time in bringing his sword down on the centre of the sucker's head, splitting it in two. His eyes rolled back and watched his brains slop out of his skull before he hit the floor with them.

"Nice one, thanks."

"De nada," Ali smiled.

Wet footsteps slapped on the ground, coming towards us from the path to the left where the sucker had jumped from. It sounded like there were at least six of them, and they were getting quicker. I raised the Sisters as a face full of jagged fangs sprang from around the corner. I squeezed Sophia's trigger and had myself a shower of bone and wet meat.

Khearo tore past and disappeared around the corner just as I heard the sounds of more running behind us. I turned to see six more suckers running towards us. I glanced around the corner in time to see Khearo chasing two vamps around another turn, with two more chasing behind him. Another lay on the floor with her head and ribcage stomped to mush.

"Shit," I said, moving around the corner and stepping over the stomped corpse, "you think they're trying to pick us off?"

"Looks like it," Ali said. He sheathed his sword and pulled out the Reapers.

He lined up his shot and blew the knees off the first vamp to turn the corner. She crumpled to the floor with a screech, and the five others tumbled over her.

"Motherfucker," one of them growled, "get them."

"Or don't," I said, moving to stand next to Ali.

We gave them all an eyeful of revolver and blew them to chunks, emptying our chambers. I sunk a hand into a pocket and pulled out more bullets. My pockets were getting light. It wouldn't be long 'till the Sisters were out of action and I'd have to really flex some muscle. I didn't mind the prospect. I was packing a real big knife and I was happy to get all up in smoochin' distance if need be.

With the Sisters freshly loaded, I swung around the corner that Khearo had disappeared around a moment ago. Nothing but decomposing corpses scattered the tunnel. The light overhead blinked on and off. I'd have said I could smell an ambush, but all I could really smell now was shit, blood and rotting flesh. But I could hear something, and it sounded like a struggle up ahead, through a door to the left. Maria and Sophia took the lead, guiding me to the door. I gave Ali the eye then put my boot to the door, flinging it open. I was greeted with the business end of a sword to the neck, lightly pressing into my skin. The naga warrior on the other end let out a sigh of relief and lowered the blade. In the room behind him, I counted maybe nine diced-up suckers all draped and splattered over office furniture. The poor guy looked exhausted, and a bit battered too.

"Take a breath, my friend," Ali said, "the way out should be clear if you need to leave."

The naga propped an elbow on a cubicle partition and took a moment before saying, "Thanksss. Your wolf friend went that way, if you're sssearching for him," he waved his sword to the right, pointing down the corridor and deeper into the bunker.

"Thanks," I said with a nod before continuing on, leaving the warrior to rest a little longer.

We'd got about a minute in and came to a crossroads when a deafening alarm filled the bunker. Pain seared through my head. I clapped my hands over my ears and looked at Ali, trying to see which way he thought we should go, but he just shrugged, covering his own ears. I took a look down each passageway. The one to the right had a door close by that I thought we could investigate. The path to the left trailed off into darkness, and I thought I saw movement down the passage straight ahead. I took a couple of steps towards the movement, still covering my ears, then a couple more. There was something on the floor up ahead that didn't look like a vampire corpse.

I turned in time to see Ali swept from the crossroads by a tidal wave of vampires smashing into him, carrying him off down the left-hand passage. They had managed to get under him and pick him up. Twelve of the dirty fuckers crowd-surfed him away into the darkness. He swung his sword and managed to slice some flesh, but the armour made it awkward for him to move, leaving him stuck like a tortoise on its back. I gave chase as they turned a corner, sprinting all out to catch them. I flung myself around the turn, ready to start shooting, but they were gone, and I had three more passages in front of me.

I tried Ali on the walkie-talkie but got no answer. I was alone.

Fuck.

The blinking light of a CCTV camera caught my attention. I stepped side to side and watched it follow me before raising a gun and blowing it to pieces. The alarm stopped a split second before the camera exploded. The tinkling of glass replaced the ringing in my ears. A moment later, I heard the faint sound of something struggling back the way I'd come.

Not wanting to get even more lost without investigating, I turned around and headed in the direction of whatever was making the noise. I retraced my steps until the thing on the floor came into view. It wasn't what was making the noise, but a few steps closer and I recognised a mass of tentacles lying limp on the floor. I hurried over and dropped down, running my eyes over the creature. He'd been ripped out of his skin suit. Severed tentacles lay scattered around a wet mass of flesh connected to two dull grey orbs. All of the yellow light had drained from his eyes.

"He's gone lad," I heard a voice say up ahead.

I pushed myself back to my feet and squinted into the darkness at another heap on the floor.

"Fuck, Rusty?" I said, hurrying over.

Rusty lay on the floor, all human and naked. He'd been flung from his chair and lay in a crumpled mess. "Save that for later, laddie," he said with a chuckle before coughing up blood.

"Shit, you're bleeding."

He lifted his hand from his stomach, a torrent of blood pulsed from a ragged hole across his waist. "Ever the perceptive one ain't ya?"

I put my hands on his stomach and applied pressure. "We're gonna get you outta here, you'll be alright."

Rusty snorted and grimaced in pain. "Half those tentacles over there are my guts, lad. There's no coming back from this one."

I didn't know what to do. Rusty was right, the wound was bad, but I didn't want to leave him to die. I thought if I could just get back to the entrance, the naga could help him out somehow. But we were way out in the wilderness. What could we do?

Rusty could see my mind racing. "Just stay with me, aye?" he asked.

I nodded and took hold of the hand he'd held out for me. My cheeks burned and I felt my eyes filling up. I wasn't ready for this. I wasn't foolish enough to think we'd all survive, but no amount of metal prep will help when your friend is dying beside you.

"Nee bubbling now, ya'hear? I'll not have you going soft when you need ta stay sharp."

I nodded again, not knowing what to say.

"Promise me something, aye?"

"Sure thing," I said, squeezing his hand.

"Kick all their arses for an old dog with no legs, eh? And when you're done, and I'm gone, don't leave us in here, would ya not? I dinnae wanna rot with the filth down here. Put me somewhere nice. Mickey too, aye?"

"I promise. I'm gonna put my foot so far up Atrocitas's ass he'll taste the colour of my socks."

Rusty chuckled then heaved a long, ragged sigh. "I can hear her voice, lad," he said, "I can hear her callin' to me, my Catriona."

I looked him in the eyes, but he looked right through me as if I was no longer there.

"I'm on me way, lass. I'm on me…" he trailed off.

A tear escaped from the corner of my eye and landed on his hand as it went limp.

At least two of my friends were dead, and I'd been separated from all the others. As far as I knew, they could all be dead, and I could end up wandering around a giant fucking maze until I dropped dead myself.

I wiped my face with my sleeve, still kneeling, when I had an idea. And I didn't wait long to put it into action. I stood and pulled the knife out from its hiding place and slashed it across my forearm. Blood dripped to the floor, forming a pool with a faint orange glow. Within a minute, the smell of my Hot Sauce blood brought a couple of curious vampires snooping.

I held up the knife and tucked it back inside my coat as they watched the blood trail down my arm. With my hands held out in front of me, I edged closer to the pair of suckers that would take me directly to Dominus Atrocitas. It was time to end this, one way or another.

"I'm yours, I give up, take me to the boss."

* * *

The pair of fuckheads led me down winding passageways until we came to a stop outside of a pair of heavy metal doors. As one of them bashed a fist against the door in a rhythmic pattern, I pulled out my walkie-talkie and said, "Found him."

It wasn't all that far of a walk. I hoped whoever else was left alive would find me sharpish. My pockets were feeling a hell of a lot lighter, too. I must have had a hole in one 'cos it felt like I'd dropped some bullets.

"Fuck you just say?" the other sucker said, whipping his head around a moment too late to see me stuffing the device back into my pocket.

"I said 'thank you'. You know, for bringing me here."

The sucker chuckled. "The boss is going to love this. He'll make that blood of yours last, just you wait and see."

"I'm honoured to know he's gonna enjoy sucking me off."

The goon's head snapped back, and he was about to say something when the doors swung open.

They took me by the shoulders and led me into the room. The last thing I expected to see was a gigantic nuclear missile chamber turned into a throne room, but there it was. The big fuckin' nuke stood tall and proud in the middle of the chamber, and Dominus Atrocitas sat at the base, on a throne of bones. 'Cos of course he had a goddamn throne of bones.

"Bow before your king," one of the goons growled as he pushed me to my knees.

I knelt before the crusty old fuck sitting on his edgy death pile. Dominus Atrocitas, the great King of

Vampires, sat reclining on his throne. Around the room, he had cronies dotted here and there, with humans chained up in various states of life and death, hanging upside down by their feet with tubes sticking out of their bodies. My eyes followed the blood-filled tubes down to a modified gas mask stuck over Atrocitas's face, pumping him with fresh blood.

Man, I was pissed. We'd fought so hard to find the Vampire King and he turned out to be some old gimp on fucking life support. This was the big bad guy we were all supposed to be afraid of; a skinny little bitch.

"Night!" a familiar voice yelled.

I found the source of the voice trapped in a cage to the left of the throne. "Ginn? What the fuck happened to you?"

She pointed to an absolute tank of a vampire standing to the side of the room, in front of another door. "This cunt took my sword!"

"Yeah, and your fucking arm along with it, huh?"

She looked down at the ragged stump of her left arm, missing beneath the elbow. "Yeah that too."

She was the only person I recognised. All the other people chained up or in cages were strangers, but that offered no comfort.

Atrocitas held up his hand.

"SILENCE!" the tank bellowed. "The King speaks."

Atrocitas reached up and pulled the blood mask from his face. The old fuck was all teeth, everywhere. Fangs stuck out in all directions and his eyes were so shrunken and beady, I could barely see them. Blood was stained all around the car crash he called a mouth, like he'd been at the Kool-Aid for a little too long.

"Isaac Nightingale," he rasped, "I must thank you for returning my property to me," he gestured towards Ginn. "And I thank you for coming to your senses and ending your foolish crusade before that oh-so-interesting blood of yours was wasted on the ground. I would say I'd grant you a swift death, but I'm going to savour you for a long time, Mister Nightingale. Oh yes, a long time indeed. I shall feast on that which gives you life."

Classic villain monologue, they just can't help themselves. "Oh shut the fuck up," I muttered.

"But first," Atrocitas continued, "a bit of seasoning, yes? A little terror-induced adrenaline in the blood. Bring out the other one."

The tank vamp hammered a fist on the door behind him, then stepped aside. The door swung open, and four vampires tugged on chains, dragging Ali out into the room, stripped of his armour, tied up and badly beaten. They pushed him to his knees between me and Atrocitas.

"Vladimir, if you would do the honours," Atrocitas said as he pulled his mask back over his face.

Ali looked me in the eyes, as best he could. His face was all puffy and bloody, his eyes were swollen to small slits.

The tank stepped forward and squeezed a mechanism in his hand. Ginn's stolen blade shot out in front of him, and he brought it to rest on Ali's neck.

"No!" I yelled, struggling to my feet.

The suckers at my side took hold of my arms and tried to force me back to my knees. I was having none of it. The Hot Sauce spiked, and it spiked hard. Time slowed down as the tank goon began to raise the blade. The goons holding me had their arms wrapped around mine. I pulled them in close and yanked my arms across my body with all the force I could muster. Blood splattered my face as the flesh of their shoulders tore and the bones popped from the sockets. I spun, swinging the severed arms and beat them both across the face with their own limbs. They fell to the floor, howling.

The tank goon held the blade high above his head as Dominus Atrocitas bellowed, "STOOOP HIIIM!"

I watched as the blade started to fall, and I sprung, flying over Ali. I caught the tank's arm and used his momentum against him, twisting his arm at such an angle that the tip of the blade pushed down through his stomach and out through his crotch. The tank squealed as something soft flopped out of the bottom of his pant leg. While he was busy trying to see if it was his cock, balls, or both, I reached into my jacket, pulled out the big knife and jammed it up under his jaw, right up there, deep into his brain.

His body shuddered and hands clenched, retracting Ginn's blade from his crotch as I pulled the knife out of his brain. He fell to the floor in a convulsing heap.

The eight vampires dotted around the room surrounded me.

"Night!" a voice at the big doors yelled.

I looked through the little swarm to see Tex, Morgan and Harriot charging into the room.

Harriot lunged into the crowd, knocking four suckers down, sending them sprawling as she focussed her attention on one and clamped her jaws over his head.

Morgan sprang at another vampire. The two of them turned into a flurry of flying claws and gnashing teeth.

Tex ran in swinging Lucifer's sword and cleaved it through the nearest vampire, from the shoulder down. "Found this on the floor then followed your trail of bullets," he said.

"I hoped someone would figure that out," I said, then pointed to Ali, "protect him. I'm ending this." I punctuated my sentence by stomping the skulls of the armless vamps on the floor, one after another.

Tex nodded. He knew the plan.

With the Hot Sauce raging through me, I launched myself into the air, up to Atrocitas's throne. I raised my knife and brought it down hard, but Atrocitas was fast. He shot a hand up to protect himself. The knife plunged down through his palm, and he wrestled to push me away. I tore his blood mask off with my free hand. He choked and gasped like a fish out of water, desperate for his blood. Even with his mask off and a knife in his palm, he was surprisingly strong.

We locked ourselves into a struggle: me trying to plunge the knife into his face, him trying to get me off of him. He tore his hand off the knife, bisecting his palm between the two middle fingers and used both hands to push me away from him.

I fell backwards, tumbling down the throne's steps. Atrocitas lunged after me. I landed on my back at the bottom, cracking the back of my head off the floor. It sent my vision spinning. The dead tank goon lay beside me. His clouded eyes stared into mine.

I glanced around the room. Ali lay on his side not far from me with a pool of blood slowly growing around him. Ginn had slumped over in the cage and turned a grim shade of grey. Morgan and the vamp he was fighting slashed at each other, sending shredded skin flying around them, both losing a lot of blood. Harriot swung around with a vampire clinging to her neck, then fell back through the doorway they'd come from, disappearing into the darkness. And over in a corner, with his back against the wall and all out of guns, Tex was duking it out bare-knuckle style with the last of the vampires, but he was flagging, his punches not hitting as hard, his dodges not as quick.

Atrocitas landed on top of me and wasted no time in trying to relieve me of my face. His teeth gnashed and snapped shut an ass hair's width in front of my nose. I used one arm under his neck to prop him as far away from me as I could, while I used the knife to stab him as many times as I could, wherever I could.

Thick black blood oozed out of his wounds. He gasped for breath, rasping and rattling as I jammed the knife into the side of his ribs again and again. The vigorous shanking didn't sap his strength though, the

406

fucker. He dug his claws deep into my chest and raked away flesh. Sharp, burning pain spread over my body as he tore his claws through my skin.

I stabbed relentlessly then pulled my knife from Atrocitas's ribs and smashed my fist into the soft, tattered flesh, over and over, as he clawed at my chest, ripping my flesh and spilling my blood. It was a race for the heart. I put all of my strength into tipping him off me and pushed him over onto his side. Before he had the chance to get up, I straddled him, took the knife into my left hand and plunged it deep into his sternum as I held on to the handle and hammered my free fist into his torn-up ribs. His jaw snapped at me and his claws sunk through the flesh of my chest, tearing fresh chunks of skin away. I didn't know how much more I could take. The pain was all-consuming, and darkness was creeping into my vision. I knew I had a matter of seconds before I succumbed to the pain and blood loss. My body was telling me to give up. I'd done my best. Time to let go.

With one last fist raised to the gods, I summoned all my might and brought it smashing down into his ribs, shattering his bones, sinking through flesh and breaking through to the cavity of his chest. I felt his dirty black heart beating against my knuckles. I sunk my hand in deeper and wrapped my fingers around the hammering lump of flesh, and I squeezed.

And squeezed.

And squeezed.

And squeezed, until flesh and blood oozed between my fingers.

I yanked my fist from the Vampire King's chest and with the pulverised heart held high I breathed a sigh of relief as he went limp. It was over. I fell to my side, pulling Atrocitas with me, his face inches from mine. We landed with his big goon at my back.

I was soaked in blood. Both mine and Atrocitas's. I didn't know whose blood was whose, and it didn't matter. With the last of the life left in him, Atrocitas reached over me, passing a hand over my torn and tattered shoulder and around my back, as if for one last embrace before he faded away to oblivion. My senses faded too as the Hot Sauce wore off. Somewhere in the room, as if underwater, I heard someone shout, "NO!" moments before I heard a mechanical click from behind my back, and Ginn's stolen blade burst out of the front of my chest.

The pain was like nothing I'd ever felt. Worse than anything that had happened before. White hot fire spread over me. I faded in and out of consciousness, looking down at the blade protruding from my sternum at an angle. The tip had lodged in Atrocitas' throat, and what was left of his blood bubbled out of the wound as he took his last breath.

My vision grew dark. I had a feeling all the vampires were dead because there were no more fighting noises. No more screams. No more shouts. Just peace.

The pain slowly left me. All I could feel was cold and the slowing of my heart as each waning beat dragged the little lump of dying muscle across the blade, filling my chest with blood.

Tex yelled something and a thunderous crack filled the room, but I couldn't focus on what he was trying to say to me. A bunch of blurred faces hung over me, trying to tell me something, but all I could see was a white light, way up above me.

I caught onto some words.

Dying...

Shake...

Hurry...

With the last of my strength, as the life seeped out of me and my vision faded to black, I held out my hand.

# 'Till Death

## [Track 44]

Warmth and the feeling of peace poured over me as a bright light welcomed me. I opened my eyes to nothing but white, as far as the eye could see. I didn't know where I was, or what was going on, but it felt like... home.

"Strange, isn't it?" A familiar voice said from behind me.

I turned to see who'd spoken.

"Dad?"

The man in front of me smiled and stepped forward with his arms outstretched. He looked exactly the way I remembered him. I stepped forward and fell into a tight hug, my breath catching in my chest.

"Where am I? Am I dead?"

Dad broke off the hug and looked me over, his hands still on my shoulders. "That's entirely up to you, son. This is a crossroads. You can carry on forward, or you can go back," he nodded towards something over my shoulder, "but it looks like I'm not the only one here to see you."

Another voice spoke from behind, "Didn't expect to see you so soon."

I turned and was met with more than one familiar face.

"David?"

He smiled and nodded.

410

"Mickey? Rusty?"

Mickey winked. Rusty broke into a big grin and stepped forward, holding hands with an unfamiliar face. He threw an arm around me and slapped my back.

I spluttered. "Where's your chair? And who's this?"

Rusty snorted and stepped back. "Turns out wheelchairs don't follow you to the afterlife, lad. Thankfully, I can use my legs again," he laughed, "and this... this is Cat. After all this time, we're together at last."

Cat let go of Rusty's hand and hugged me tight. "Thank you for being such a fierce friend to this old dog," she said, "I wish we could have met under different circumstances."

I broke down and held my arms open for everyone else to get in on the hug. The warmth enveloped me as the spirits of those I loved gathered around me. After what could have been an eternity, I let go and looked at them all standing in front of me.

"What does this mean? Is Suzie here?"

I wiped my face with the back of my hand. The atmosphere grew colder. My dad put an arm around my shoulder, sharing his warmth.

"When I passed on, I was greeted by loved ones. The same goes for your friends. The people we love always find us. For those of us already here, it's like a pull, right here," he placed a hand over my heart, "I knew where you were and how to find you."

I put my hand over his and looked him in the eyes as the feeling of falling filled my stomach. My vision grew blurry and darkness crept in.

"So that means..."

He nodded. "It means she's not here. But we will be, when you get back."

David added, "A long, long time from now."

The feeling of something pulling me backwards filled my chest, and everything faded back to black.

# Hell Hath No Fury

Three days passed before I woke in my bed back at Tex's place. Like a mummy rising from the sarcophagus, I sat up with a groan and took a look at my body. I'd say I was in nothing but a pair of shorts, but I was bandaged from the waist to the neck. Everything hurt, but I felt strong. It felt like coming out of the coma with the Hot Sauce fuelling me all over again.

I swung my feet over the side of the bed and stood, stretching as I walked over to the mirror to take a look at myself. The bandages were clean, so I unwound them and dropped them to the floor. The sight of my bare chest surprised me. It was whole. Covered in thick, red scars, sure, but whole. I'd half expected to take off the bandages to see a gaping hole in my chest and my cold, dead heart on show through the torn-up flesh.

I ran my palm across the scars and felt my heart, warm and beating right where it was supposed to be. A jagged line above my heart stood out from all the other scars, a reminder of the blade that would have killed me if I hadn't taken the deal at the last moment. So this was it. This is what immortality looked like: a lifetime of scars, but a lifetime that wasn't gonna end any time soon.

My eyes fell from the scars to the reflection of the nightstand and fixed on the necklace Spaghetti-o Jones had given to me: the broken key.

A knock at the door pulled my eyes from the key, "Yeah?" I called through the door.

"Can I come in? Thought I heard movement," Ginn said.

I walked over and pulled the door open to the sight of Ginn smiling at me. We stood in silence for a moment. Ginn ran her eyes over my body, across the map of scars. She'd earned a few more of her own too, and lost an arm while she was at it. Her left arm ended just below her elbow. Like my injuries, hers had healed fast. The scarring was fresh and red, but the wound was gone.

"How you feeling?" she asked.

"Honestly, pretty good. You?"

She shrugged. "I'm all right," she said, then stared at me for a moment. "GET IT? All right. 'Cos I've lost my left."

I shook my head with a smile. "For fuck's sake, Ginn."

"What? It's just an 'armless joke."

I turned and left the doorway, still shaking my head as I opened the wardrobe to pull out a T-shirt.

"ARMLESS, Night," Ginn said, following me into the room. "I'd give you a hand finding a shirt, but I'm pretty short on them at the moment."

"Nothing kills your sense of humour huh?"

"Fuck no. We slaughtered the Vampire King and his whole fucking army. Not a single one of us expected to survive, but we did. I'd say that calls for a bit of happiness."

"You've got a point," I said, pulling a shirt and pair of sweatpants on, "not all of us made it out though."

Ginn dropped her head. "No, I guess not."

I picked up the broken key from the nightstand, put it around my neck and tucked it down into my shirt. "Did you get Rusty and Mickey out of there? I was with Rusty when he died. He didn't wanna be left there."

"We got them," she nodded, "we found a place called Burford Lake in the Wichita Mountains and buried them there. Lovely place. They'd love it, I'm sure."

"Thank you."

Ginn waved her hand. "Come on, people want to see you."

I followed her out and into Tex's living room to the sight of all my friends crammed in, watching a movie on the VCR. A wave of relief washed over me to see Khearo sitting amongst them, on the sofa between Harriot and Tex. I hadn't seen him since he tore past me in the bunker's corridors. It was good to see he'd survived. Morgan sat on the floor, his back up against the arm of the sofa. He gave me a nod. The Neon Nightmares were sat on the floor too, directly in front of the TV, as close as they could get. Ali turned to see me and cracked a gigantic smile while pushing himself up from the armchair with a groan. Most of his face was a mottled mix of purples and browns, but all the swelling had left his eyes. Being a regular ol' human didn't come with great healing benefits, and he was clearly still in a lot of pain.

He pulled me into a tight hug, saying, "It's good to see you awake, my brother."

We broke apart and I took a moment to look over his face. "Good to see you alive."

"Pretty close call for both of us, huh?" he said.

"Sure was."

Tex unfolded a camping chair and set it down next to another one Ginn had sat down in. He looked older. His hair had turned full grey. "Welcome back to the land of the living," he said.

I smiled. "Thanks for keeping me here."

He smiled back. "Couldn't let you leave without paying the bill, could I?"

"I have no idea what that means," I said, shaking my head.

He shrugged then continued, "So how do you feel now that you can live forever?"

I took a seat. "I feel like doing something stupid."

Morgan snorted. "More stupid than eleven people deciding to take on an army?"

I scanned the faces of my friends. In my time asleep, I'd had plenty of time to dream, plenty of time to imagine what I could do with my life, and I could only think of one thing. "Much more stupid."

"Care to elaborate?" Harriot asked.

Khearo added, "What's left to do? Atrocitas is dead. We've killed the big bad guy, saved the world. The story's finished, right? We can just go back to our regular monster hunting."

I took a breath. "Killing Atrocitas was never gonna be my ending. Rapey and Roids were my own big villains, the Nightmares had Murder Nerd, and Atrocitas was everyone else's. They may all be gone, or as good as gone, but I can't stop here. I need to do something none of you are gonna like. But I need to do it, and I need to do it alone. Look, back in the bunker when I was dying, I got a taste of Heaven. Saw the light and everything. It was beautiful, but Suzie wasn't there, so…"

Tex held a hand up to stop me while he reached into his pocket and pulled something out. He threw what he was holding over to me. I caught it and smiled as I opened my fist, showing a large key with the words "Clavis Inferni" etched on the shaft.

"So go to Hell," he said.

"How did you know?"

Tex smirked. "After Lucifer told you there's a fifty-fifty chance of her being in Heaven, I knew if you took the deal you'd want to try to find her if she wasn't up there. And you talk a lot in your sleep, kid. Heard all about your plans to find her while you were playing Sleeping Beauty and I was changing your bandages."

Ginn exchanged looks with Ali and what was left of the squad. "Wait, are you actually serious?" she asked. "You're voluntarily going to Hell to find your dead girlfriend?"

I wiggled the key. "Always said I'd go to Hell and back for her. Now I can."

Everyone sat silent for a long moment.

"That's the dumbest fucking shit I've ever heard," Ginn said.

I shrugged.

Ginn continued, "How do you expect to survive? Sure, we fight monsters, but the things down there have got to be a lot worse. A lot worse and a lot more of them, surely? And fucking demons, actual physical fucking demons, Night. And you want to do it alone? How do you expect to get back, if you even can, you dumbass—"

Tex held up a hand to stop her tirade. "He'll be just fine, I'm sure. He killed the Vampire King, and now he's an immortal with the original Devil on his side. Besides, you forgot what he has to help get him through it all."

Ginn threw her hand into the air, dumbstruck. "What, Tex, what the fuck does Night have that can get him through fucking Hell and back?"

# CHAINSAWS FOR ARMS

**[Track 45]**

# NEON NIGHTMARES

**Writer**
Isaac Nightingale
(But really, Liam Blaney)

**Tea provider**
Liam Blaney
Hannah (Sometimes)

**Director of music**
Liam Blaney

With a big, juicy **thank you** to the following:

**Tali Wilson**
For editing the absolute tits off of this thing with the eyes
of an eagle and the patience of a saint.

## Hannah
For all the everlasting support and for dealing with me while rambling what would have seemed like an absolute nonsense bunch of thoughts and ideas.


## Tanya, Kiki, T.M Lunn, Kirsty & Kayley
For reading the early drafts and providing all the valuable feedback. You're all awesome!

## All of my friends, some of my family
For all the support and encouragement, even if some of you still haven't read the first damn book ;)

## The horror community
For giving an unknown author a chance, and for so many of you being enthusiastic with the lovin' for my work so far. I've met a lot of wonderful people, both writers and readers, and made a lot of lovely friends. Thank you to each and every one of you.

And finally,
Thank you to anyone who's bought, read, recommended, enjoyed, hated, reviewed, sniffed, donated or borrowed any of my work.
But especially those who've bought it. Thank you for the money.

## Reviews!

Please don't forget to leave a review on the likes of Goodreads, Amazon, or any other bookseller's sites you can.

Each and every review is greatly appreciated and is a huge help towards any success my books may have in the future. Even if you think my work is shit, let me know.


You can close the book now, there's no end credits scene to tease **the third book...**

Curious fucker, aren't you?

Printed in Great Britain
by Amazon